The Code Within

S. L. Jones

Published by Huston & Sumair Global
PO Box 7626
Silver Spring, MD 20907

Formatting by Polgarus Studio
Copy Edited by Marcus Trower
Cover Art by Hristo Kovatliev

ISBN: 978-0-9916662-1-8

**Dedicated to the memory of Ivor Reginald Jones,
Company HQ, 2nd Ranger Battalion.**

He was welcomed to Pointe du Hoc, France by way of a mortar round on June 6, 1944. Although wounded from the blast, he bravely scaled the 100-foot cliffs as a part of those bold first steps to help his country liberate German-occupied Western Europe. Decades later, Ivor traveled to Normandy for the 60th anniversary of D-Day. He suffered a stroke while he was there, and when the French hospital ran into complications when trying to secure the medical payments from Blue Cross, the hospital's Board of Directors informed his son that there would be no bill. They had said it was the least they could do for his service to their country. The board's gesture personified the man, and the contrast in events from his first visit so many years ago underscored the purpose served by those original Rangers. In between that time, Ivor Jones helped to make his nephew George's son the man he is today. He did so by believing in him and instilling words of wisdom that can only come from a man who was fortunate enough to survive the journey to hell and back. Thank you Uncle Ivor, for being the incredible man you were, a true hero among heros, and for leaving an indelible mark on my life. This one's for you.

"We knew about Osama bin Laden in the early '90s. After 9/11, it was a worldwide name. I believe that type of thing can and will happen in the cyber environment. And I think after it does, people will start to pay attention."

—Shawn Henry, the FBI's former head of cyber crime
Black Hat Conference opening keynote 2012

Chapter 1

Friday evening, Maryland – Washington, DC border

ETZY MILLAR INSTINCTIVELY ducked down into his seat.

"Max, what the hell's going on?" he yelled.

More gunshots rang out from behind and left a series of cracks in the windshield above him. He nervously looked over at Max, who appeared to be fading in and out of consciousness at the wheel. The blinding lights from the sedan bearing down on the BMW Roadster helped him slip further into a state of confusion.

"I…I don't…know," Max said. Blood flowed down the side of his face and he struggled to speak. "I think I'm…going to…"

The car began to drift toward oncoming traffic on Wisconsin Avenue, just south of Bethesda, Maryland. Millar's eyes widened when he saw his friend's were closed. He watched Max's head bounce like a Bobblehead toy and sensed the car taking the path of least resistance over the uneven pavement.

"What the fuck!" he screamed. "Max, are you okay? Max!"

Millar felt the BMW begin to accelerate and could see that the weight of Max's leg was bearing down on the pedal. He pushed his blood-soaked companion against the driver's-side door and peered over the dashboard into the oncoming headlights.

"Shit!" he shouted, and jerked the wheel to the right, narrowly missing a head-on collision.

A cacophony of horns erupted, followed by more gunshots, which peppered the windshield with holes.

1

The vehicle continued to accelerate. Millar's floppy brown hair whipped into his eyes, making it all the more difficult to see in the chaos of the night. He tried in vain to release the accelerator, but there wasn't enough room to maneuver in the confines of the compact two-seater. He was forced to steer through traffic recklessly and cower as low as he could in the speeding death trap.

More gunshots spat out from behind. Millar's heart pounded in his chest, and his breath quickened. If he slowed the car down, he was a dead man, but if he didn't, the outcome would be no different.

Why the hell is this happening to me?

He saw a large Neiman Marcus sign come into view on the side of a building above and made a split-second decision. A sharp pull on the stick shift put the car in neutral and sent the engine into a deafening whine. He strained to reach the brake pedal with his left hand and quickly jerked the steering wheel to the right. The Roadster answered back and headed toward a gap in the line of parked cars along the street. Millar sideswiped a station wagon before leveling a patch of bushes and slamming into an entrance of the upscale shopping mall.

What panes of glass hadn't already been broken by the car's impact were shattered in a hail of bullets. There were screams. Dazed, Millar looked over at the driver's seat and saw Maximillian Soller motionless, covered with blood. If he jumped over the door, he could make a quick exit, but he thought better of exposing his tall, lanky body to the gunman. Instead, he fumbled to find the handle to open the car door, pulled it, and kicked the door open with his foot.

Silence.

I'd better go now.

He darted toward the gap in a shattered glass door, severe pain shooting through his ribs. He steadied himself on the frame and negotiated the shards of broken glass littering the floor. A jagged edge sliced deep into the palm of his hand, but a combination of fear and panic masked the pain. If he wanted to stay alive, Millar needed to find somewhere to hide.

Chapter 2

THE BLACK CHRYSLER 300 came to a screeching halt outside the entrance to the shopping mall. Its passenger quickly emptied the remaining rounds in his Sig Sauer P226R from the bouncing car.

"Shit. One of them is still alive," he said to the driver. The assassin opened his car door and motioned for the driver to leave.

If the target got away, the operation would be at risk, and he would be a dead man. "I'll get the hacker. Don't talk to the boss. I'll tell him how it went down," he said before he slammed the door shut and headed toward the mangled sports car.

The gunman peered inside the vehicle and saw a man crumpled against the door. He seated a fresh magazine into his pistol and squeezed the trigger. Two rounds hammered into the driver's head. He noticed the devices on the floorboard of the car, but there was no time to take them with him. The target was in motion, and he needed to close the gap.

He moved quickly through the remnants of the mall entrance and stopped to survey the area for a sign of his next victim. "Shit, shit, shit," he muttered, noting the Muzak playing in the background. The shoppers had already scrambled into the stores to take cover, and there were so many places where the skinny bastard could hide. He checked behind him and knew it wouldn't be long before the police would be on the scene.

The glass on the floor crackled as he stepped, drawing his attention downward. He peered over his shoulder and noted blood dripping down the doorframe. He looked back down to the marble floor.

Perfect.

Blood had dribbled from the target's wounded hand. It left the assassin with the biological equivalent of breadcrumbs. He quickly followed the trail of blood.

Chapter 3

ETZY MILLAR'S HEART raced, his breathing painful from the damage to his ribs. The shot of adrenaline that had gotten him this far had worn off enough for him to notice the injury to his hand. He was crouched behind a clothing display when his eyes turned to the drops of blood he had left behind. A feeling of helplessness started to overcome him as he weighed his options.

He was still in shock from seeing his friend murdered and suddenly realized he was being hunted because of the job they'd taken. Millar's survival instincts kicked in and helped to clear his mind. He grabbed a red shirt off a shelf and wrapped it around the seeping wound on his hand. He looked up and saw his attacker approach, and immediately dropped down, unsure if he had been seen. The crazed look in the killer's eyes told him the chase would be relentless. He stayed down as low as he could and scurried through the narrow aisles to put some distance between him and his trail of blood. A wall stopped his progress.

He listened intently and recognized the chorus of squeaking clothes hangers. The sound grew louder. The assassin was navigating his way through rows of clothing toward him. Millar looked up at his only option.

If I can't hear him, he can't hear me.

The shrieking sound of the fire alarm was much louder than he had expected. Etzy Millar spied a look through the displays and saw the gunman surveying the whole of the store. Millar took his chance and sprinted through an army of mannequins and out the door. He ran across the street pushing his way through the pedestrians in the crosswalk.

He quickly glanced over his shoulder and saw the assassin closing in. The heavy breathing caused his broken ribs to scream out in pain, but there was no stopping if he wanted to live. Another shot of adrenaline kicked in when he saw a tall, brown column with a capital M emblazoned on the top. He knew the killer wouldn't have a SmarTrip card, and the fact that he didn't shoot at him in public gave him a little confidence.

He sprinted toward the Friendship Heights Metro station, putting every ounce of energy into the effort. There was no time to check for oncoming traffic, but luck proved to be on his side as he narrowly skirted in front of an oncoming SUV.

Millar fumbled his way down the escalator and into the depths of the underground world. The Metrorail system meant familiar stomping grounds for the carless college student. As he reached the bottom of the escalator, he slowed to a brisk walk and quickly pulled out his wallet. He slid it over the turnstile machine's sensor. The second the plastic flaps took to open seemed like an eternity. He looked back and didn't see any sign of the killer yet.

His relief from gaining entry was quickly wiped away by the 1980s-style digital readout hanging above the entrance to the platforms. The next train was forty-five seconds away—a Red Line train toward Shady Grove. Factoring in the time it would take for the doors to open and close, it would be more than a minute before the train left.

Etzy Millar pressed on. He found himself in a new kind of war, one that took place covertly, and that he had only heard whispers about. He and his friend were involved in a computer hacker group called The Collective, and it was clear to him now that they had been used.

Chapter 4

Interstate 95 south

THE DRIVE DOWN the New Jersey Turnpike seemed like an eternity. Trent Turner wore a pained expression on his face, oblivious to the incessant squeaking of the windshield wipers as they cleared away the last hints of rain. Today his eyes held a threatening gaze that mirrored the storm clouds he was leaving behind. Normally that meant something completely different. Today, he was the one in pain.

It had been nearly seven years since he had made his decision. He chose a self-imposed exile from the ones he loved. The remnants of his previous life consisted of calling his mother on her birthday and late in the evening on Christmas, and even that was frowned upon by his employer.

His father had been insufferably stubborn in previous conversations, and learned not to pick up the phone when Trent was expected to call. He understood any attempt to talk his son into coming home would only result in the droning sound of a dial tone. At least when Trent spoke to his mother, Cathy, his father would gain some comfort in knowing he was doing all right.

This afternoon was the first time his mother had used the emergency contact number he had given her. As he drove south, he knew when she saw him in person she would try once again to bring him back into their lives, but it was too late for him. That sort of change wasn't possible.

Turner viewed his line of work as a necessary evil. It was complicated at best. His activities were scarcely known to the world but delivered high impact. Anyone who knew about his work either employed him, or could expect to have a short lifespan. What he did wasn't about thank you cards or recognition. Trent Turner was the kind of man who was content working in the shadows. He had his own motivations.

He had felt the impact from September 11, 2001.

Nancy had worked for the financial services firm Cantor Fitzgerald at its headquarters in One World Trade Center. He met her halfway around the world on the Spanish island of Mallorca, just months before the terrorist attack on the buildings would take her life.

He replayed the sunny afternoon in his head as he continued south. It was something he did often. It helped him to rationalize his decision to live this way, to sacrifice a normal life in order to perform a crucial service for his country. They were visiting the city of Palma de Mallorca, and it was a day full of memorable conversations that shined a light onto her kindness and potential. He and his brother were just teenagers looking forward to college at the time, and he had hoped to one day see her again. Even at his age, he knew the world needed more people like Nancy.

Fate would soon see her promise extinguished by a dark reality. Her loss, and the deaths of thousands more, opened his eyes to a world that many refused to see or chose to ignore. The tragedy served as motivation for his chosen career path. A lot of people hated his country. Whether ideologues or religious fundamentalists, they sought to take advantage of the freedom America provided and what its constitution stood for. He considered himself part of the last line of defense, and, unlike that fateful day in September, he was the hunter and would make them suffer.

Brake lights snapped him to the present, and he reached to turn off the groaning windshield wipers.

Turner had felt it. He didn't know what it was at the time, but something had happened. It woke him up on Wednesday night, his first night at home in over a month. A sick feeling deep inside left the hair standing up on the back of his neck. He couldn't fall back to sleep. He was always keenly aware of what was happening around him, especially when it came to his brother. Having a sixth sense was essential in his line of work if you wanted to stay alive.

He was trying to put the pieces together, attempting to make sense out of the situation from what little he knew. The conversation with his mother was as short as it was brutal. His brother was in intensive care, likely brain-dead, with a gunshot wound to his head. Every possible scenario he ran through pointed right back at him, a case of mistaken identity. They were, after all, identical twins.

Chapter 5

Inova Fairfax Hospital, Fairfax, Virginia

RYAN TURNER'S MOTHER had been sitting in the chair next to his bed for nearly two days. Rest became secondary as she tried to extract what information she could from the steady stream of doctors that shuffled in and out of the room. She had taken notes diligently and used her iPad to scour the Internet with the hope of uncovering some morsel of information that could help save her son. She knew it was a long shot with the severity of his brain injuries, but the research, and classical music she played for him, helped to occupy her mind.

Cathy Turner was a fighter. Harvard educated and a competitive long-distance runner in her youth, she was forced away from her partnership at one of Washington, DC's premier law firms to battle cancer. The disease had been in remission for more than three years now, and rather than step back into the world of criminal justice, she decided to focus on what was most important to her: spending time with her grandchildren, son, and loving husband, Joe.

Just as exhaustion wrestled her to sleep, she was jolted to consciousness by a man entering the private hospital room. He pushed aside the book still locked in her hand so he could gain access to Ryan's IV.

"Someone was just here to give him medication a few minutes ago," she said in a scratchy, fading voice. She was a bit disoriented from exhaustion, but concern for her children was ingrained like a reflex.

"Just one more shot of vitamins to help build up his immune system, ma'am," the male nurse explained.

She rubbed her eyes and noticed his slicked-back hair and ill-fitting hospital scrubs.

"I suppose they don't have many nurses your size, now do they?" she joked.

The striations of muscle in his arms tested the limits of the seams. It was a moment of self-amusement for the concerned mother and brought the first hint of a smile to her face since she had arrived at the hospital.

"Not too many, ma'am," the nurse replied as he pushed the syringe into Ryan's IV and jammed down the plunger.

He nodded a half-smile and walked purposefully out of the room.

She tried to place his accent. It had a touch of a British wrapped around a gruff Eastern Bloc twang. The effort helped her fall back to sleep.

Chapter 6

Friendship Heights Metro, Washington, DC

THE GUNMAN FOLLOWED his target across the street toward the Metro station. He moved as fast as he could without drawing attention from the police gathering en masse fifty meters to his right. He knew it would take the cops a few minutes to piece everything together, so he still had some time. He was still in the game.

He angled his head away from the cameras as he scanned the area and headed down the escalator. Despite the nondescript clothing, his physical presence betrayed him. It was impossible for a man of his size to blend in. His assignments normally took that into consideration, but this was a fuckup. The two hackers had gotten lucky. He knew pursuing his mark in public was an enormous risk, but the personal risk of being identified was outweighed by the damage the hacker would cause should he survive long enough to reach a computer. He looked to the digital signs hanging above the platforms and judged he would have enough time to get a fare card and make it to the platform before the next train arrived.

The plan had been successful thus far. They had been recruiting members of The Collective to systematically infect computers with their malware. Using experienced hackers was a way to reduce the possibility of exposure for his employer. A talented cyberpunk would easily stay under the radar of the commercial antivirus companies.

There could be no connection between the hackers, the malware, and their organization, so phase two of the plan was carried out by an assassin to sever the final tie. If word got out that they eliminated the hackers they contracted, The Collective would turn its ire on them and retaliate, and if they were successful, everything would be lost.

The assassin peeled a fifty-dollar bill off the top of his money clip and fed it into the fare card machine. He watched the bill disappear into the horizontal slit before he noticed the graphic that indicated the highest denomination the machine would accept was a ten. The precious seconds it would take for his money to spit back out were too expensive to waste, so he quickly sidestepped to the next machine and fumbled for a smaller bill. He inserted the money and printed out his fare card. Within seconds he was headed through the turnstile toward the platform for the next incoming train. Its destination was Shady Grove. A slight smile formed on his face when he saw the platforms were almost empty. He had eleven seconds to spare.

Two women were on the platform when the train screeched to a halt. Both boarded through the sliding doors, and nobody stepped off. The gunman surveyed the area and waited for any sudden movements. He kept a door within range as he continued to stalk his prey.

The rank smell of hot trash invaded his nose with each controlled breath. The minimalist design of the Metro station made it easy for him to clear the space. It was a skill that had been deeply ingrained in the assassin after his years of military service. He cut his teeth in special operations but was dishonorably discharged after killing a man in a bar fight. His temper had gotten the best of him then, and it was the same anger that boiled within him now. He hated "the system" in America for what it had done to him, and took great pleasure in doing his part to help unravel it.

A chime sounded as he walked toward the far end of the platform. The doors to the train slid shut as he zeroed in on the concrete trash can. It was the only hiding place that remained. The train pulled away, its sound fading into the background.

The station appeared to be empty, but the assassin knew there was at least one more person present. A rush of hot air passed through the station's massive expanse and signaled an arrival on the opposite platform. He moved his gun closer to the opening in his jacket and approached his objective. He looked forward to another deadly encounter.

Chapter 7

Inova Fairfax Hospital, Fairfax, Virginia

SHE AWOKE SUDDENLY to commotion.

"Get Dr. Marks!" someone yelled.

The once-steady beeps of the heart monitor had been replaced by a pandemonium of noise. Ryan Turner's mother was overwhelmed with dread as she watched helplessly. Time seemed to stand still. Seconds felt like minutes and minutes hours.

Cathy Turner secretly hoped Ryan's tragic injury would somehow bring her broken family back together. She had played it over and over in her head, willing it to happen. Trent could transfer from his government job in New York and move back down to the Washington, DC area. The emptiness she had felt for so long would become a distant memory.

"We've lost him," the doctor said, his voice trailing off.

Turner was stunned. Nobody was supposed to bury their child, she thought bitterly.

"I'm sorry, Mrs. Turner. Would you like me to have one of my staff stay here with you until your husband arrives?" the doctor asked in a somber tone.

The silence was excruciating. Her mouth moved as she tried to answer, but no words came out. She collapsed in tears, her head coming to rest on Ryan.

"This is something we weren't expecting," the doctor said of her son's sudden death. He shook his head. "His condition had stabilized."

Cathy Turner was a realist. Deep inside she knew that, barring a miracle, even if he had woken up, he would have never been able to care for himself. These last moments had been a gift. Most people don't survive a gunshot wound to the head. She found herself alone, hollow inside, without the strength to call her husband to deliver the painful news. Seeing her son Trent would be even more difficult now. Ryan's death would taint any joy it may have brought her.

Raw emotion was punctuated by the gentle motion Dr. Marks used to close her son's eyes. Tears streaked down her face as she wished there was some way she could have taken his place. He had so much life left to live.

It had been almost two weeks since Ryan had won the Boston Marathon. After a long period of uncertainty, her son was finally motivated again. For a while it looked like the death of Ryan's second son would destroy him. He had let himself go, losing the competitive drive that had kept him and his brother so popular during their youth.

With his pedigree, he was expected to be successful in sports. Being in the headlines again had felt good. He told her it reminded him of the old days when he and his brother performed head and shoulders above the rest without much effort. It gave her son something he desperately needed: a sense of pride.

Sports had been a healthy distraction, something to help fill the void left by the loss of his son. He donated the two hundred and fifty thousand dollars in prize money to charity. Specifically, to the pediatric hospital that tried so desperately to solve his young son's heart problem. His generosity was championed by all of the major newspapers and sports magazines. Ryan Turner was branded the amateur sensation whose heart was even bigger than his lungs. His race-winning image had been heralded by the press.

She saw how Ryan's wife, April, was so proud of her husband. The young mother admitted to reporters that the biggest source of his motivation had come from a friend at work. The turn of events was something that brought Cathy Turner a great sense of relief. The couple had their challenges, one of them being the scarce details when it came to what Ryan did for his father's multibillion-dollar technology company. April knew his work was highly classified, but the late nights and inability to explain wore on the couple. It seemed they had finally developed a mutual understanding, and the feelings of animosity about his job had begun to evaporate.

She knew this because April had told her that even though it wasn't possible for her to meet the person who had changed Ryan's life, she was thankful that someone was able to make such a positive impact on their family.

Chapter 8

Friendship Heights Metro, Washington, DC

ETZY MILLAR WAITED anxiously behind the trash can for the right moment. He needed to time his break for the train's doors perfectly. The Metro station's cavernous tunnels with their futuristic patterns were surreal to him. The artificial light and the shadows it cast throughout the massive space brought on a childlike fear and a sense of vulnerability.

He was at the farthest end of the platform, so he had a clear view of the train headed in the opposite direction across the tracks. The blinking lights on the floor in front of him signaled an arrival. His heart pounded as noise from the approaching train continued to build. He could see the killer was cautiously nearing the last section of the platform. He knew it was a gamble to take the train to Silver Spring, but with less than a minute separating the arrival times of his two choices, he liked the odds with making the unconventional choice.

He was just a few steps away from freedom. Once he heard the chime that signaled the train's departure, he bolted from behind his cover and through the closing doors. He made eye contact with the assassin on the platform across from him as the train pulled away. The assassin shot him an icy stare that was paralyzing.

Pain came to him in waves as he sat back and contemplated what had just happened. He replayed the events leading up to this night in his head and was certain he had covered his tracks. Even the payments would have been untraceable.

He made twenty-five bucks for each successful installation of the bot malware from his mystery employer. The college scholarship he had been awarded only went so far, so the new gig had provided Etzy Millar with some financial hope for a change. His friend Max had made the initial contact about the job, so he figured that's where something must have gone wrong. He knew it only took one slipup for a good hacker to trace the way back to you.

Millar had a lot of experience with botnets and knew how powerful they could be. That was something The Collective had consistently demonstrated with their various operations. He thought it was funny how tech jargon came to life. The word "bot" was simply shorthand for "robot," and it was a form of malware, a term that combined the words "malicious" and "software." Simple enough, but most people, he thought, were so intimidated by technology they chose to remain clueless.

As he pondered naming conventions on the train, he thought about how things could have gone so horribly wrong. The Collective, a hacktivist group he and Max had both been involved with, was known for using its technology skills to combat censorship and unjust oppression around the globe—at least that was its mantra. Millar had heard rumors about members of the group being sought out by hard-core criminals. Most members of their ranks brushed the warning off as a scare tactic the Feds put out there to get them to stop. Now he knew the rumors were true.

The more he thought about it, the more obvious it became—brute force and cyberwar would prove to be a potent and profitable combination, a new kind of weapon. The world had become a target-rich environment now that technology had woven its way deep into the fabric of society.

The hum from the train was hypnotic as he traveled farther into the city. Millar thought about how the train was controlled by a central system that was programmed to avoid collisions and keep people safe. He guessed it was only a matter of time before someone figured out how to use the trains as weapons, just like botnets.

Etzy Millar had grown up in the midst of the Internet revolution, his interest piqued by those first bots, the ones that would combine computer resources to perform massive scientific calculations. Working together they had the processing power to rival that of supercomputers.

He knew the bots he had deployed were different. They wouldn't be used for something as simple as a distributed denial-of-service attack, which in his world was called a DDoS. He contemplated the value of directing thousands of infected computers to flood a website and make it inoperable. If the people who hired him planned to carry out a DDoS, it would only be done as a distraction for technology teams, while the real threat slipped in the back door. They wouldn't use the bots he had deployed. The malware he had been installing was much too sophisticated to expose for something as trivial as that. He knew those systems would be a part of their end game.

His mind drifted, and he smiled to himself when he considered the fact that it was porn that saved him from the violence. Porn was the reason his father always paid their Internet bill on time. The connection to cyberspace was what freed Millar from his hell in West Virginia and gave him a new world to learn and explore. The Internet was a place to escape from an abusive alcoholic.

His mood darkened when he considered how fast things had changed. Botnets were once a tool for nonprofits, operated with the computer owner's consent, but now their application was being exploited. The power and capability of botnets had evolved into something worth killing for.

He was disgusted with himself. He had been distancing himself from The Collective in recent months. The growing number of random actions being carried out in the group's name was bullshit, and now this. Millar hadn't really considered the gravity of what he was doing before. For him, hijacking a computer was like borrowing a car when someone was on vacation. As long as you didn't crash it, nobody was going to notice the extra miles.

It all seemed harmless until now. What if they used the botnet to do something where someone got killed? He felt a weight come down on him like a ton of bricks. Someone had died. Max was dead. He shook his head and thought about how it would be poetic justice if the people who hired him used the bots to crash this train right now. From what he'd seen, they were clearly good enough.

He questioned whether it was possible for things to get better. There was no way to explain away what had just happened. The police would find his laptop and the rest of his stuff in the car. The information on his laptop was safe. He had made sure of that. What really scared him was the realization that the walls had only just begun to close in.

Soller's father was an extremely powerful man. He would put resources into play with capabilities well beyond that of the local police. On top of that, Millar had never seen a bot as sophisticated as the one he had been paid to deploy. His fascination with how it worked had become an obsession. Its design had piqued his interest. The way it was coded to proactively cover its tracks was nothing short of genius.

Until now he hadn't considered what the requirement for surgical installation of the malware had meant. The people who hired him wanted its existence to be kept secret. It was now painfully obvious that he and Max were as good as dead the second they took the job. Killing them was a requirement. Nobody outside their organization could know the bots had been put in place. Whatever he had gotten himself into was big-time. He should have known. Whoever hired them had to have some serious cash. It would have taken a monumental effort to pull off what he had uncovered so far.

The only bright spot in the situation was that his curiosity had gotten the better of him. He had written his own piece of software to deploy alongside the malware and report back details about how it worked.

Millar was fortunate to have a card to play, and with what he was up against he could only see one way of playing it. He realized figuring out what they were doing with those bots was his only chance.

Chapter 9

Island Industries, Brooklyn, New York

IT WAS RAINING. The musty smell in the alley was challenged by wafts of cigarette smoke as he stamped his butt out in the pedestal ashtray. Visually, this was the most depressing area of an otherwise modern complex.

Retired admiral John Simpson stood under the awning, his thoughts accompanied by the hypnotic sound of rain splattering rhythmically on the concrete. Cigarettes were a guilty pleasure but also a nasty habit, so he only smoked them sparingly. His eyes narrowed as he turned toward the metal door opening behind him. The looming conversation wasn't something he was looking forward to.

"With all due respect, Addy, I think we have to step in here." Reed let the door close behind him and took a step forward. "You've got an operative who's been compromised," Dr. Charles Reed argued.

The doctor was second-in-command at Island Industries, a clandestine organization set up by Simpson with the help of some powerful friends. It was funded by the spoils of war from his days as the CIA's Director of Central Intelligence. The company was a security consulting firm on the surface, but the real extent of its power remained hidden below, like the illusion from an iceberg.

Reed, a tall, thin man with a light complexion, pushed his round glasses up from the edge of his nose and persisted. "You have to do something, you know I'm right." Reed was animated. "You saw him. He had that look in his eyes...he won't listen to reason here." The psychologist shook his head back and forth and looked to the ground intently before he continued. "If I've told you once, I've told you a thousand times: their connection is too deep, and there's no way he'll let it rest."

"Not here, Charles," Simpson replied in a measured tone. "I know you're upset, but this is not the place to discuss the matter."

He was annoyed with the break in protocol. Speaking in the relative open about company business could have serious consequences. You never knew when someone might be listening.

There was no denying Simpson saw the rage in Trent Turner's eyes. His top operative's state was soon confirmed when he disobeyed the admiral's direct order to stay in New York. He knew this would require action, but the course of that action was something he needed more time to consider. There was too much at stake.

Simpson had been running Island Industries for the past nine years and, although he would never admit it, his relationship with Trent Turner had developed to a point where he represented the son he never had. Emotion couldn't be allowed to affect decision making in the world of black ops, and he knew he needed to tread carefully.

It wasn't only the situation with Trent Turner that had thrown Addy Simpson for a loop. Reed had been working with The Island, as the insiders called it, since its inception, and his unexpected resignation a week ago had put a strain on their relationship. As one of America's foremost psychologists, he had been an integral part of both the company's selection process and the ongoing evaluation of its covert operatives.

This wasn't a typical nine-to-five job. There were always concerns when someone wanted out, since the work that was done by The Island involved secrets that needed to be taken to one's grave.

Chapter 10

HIS ATTENTION WAS elsewhere when the car horn jolted him to attention. Aliaksandr Petrov was a perfectionist, borderline obsessive-compulsive. The trait served an assassin well. It helped ensure every move was calculated and efficient.

Something was off. Petrov didn't feel the satisfaction he normally would after completing a job. It was something that bothered the typically unflappable Russian.

He wasn't expecting to pump a 20 cc blast of air into his victim with the syringe, but he was confident the improvisation would serve its purpose and eliminate the man he knew as The American. A long list of powerful individuals would soon be celebrating this outcome.

If he were honest, Petrov was a little disappointed with how easy it was to complete his crowning achievement, and it had nothing to do with botching his first attempt. He had seen The American's work at a distance and envied the way the man who had lived a double life as Ryan Turner had operated. For the first time in his career, he was apprehensive about taking on a job, but the contract's five-million-euro price tag had all but sealed the deal. It was a payday that would allow him to retire from the game for good.

Petrov was hired because of his reputation, and the indirect way with which the offer presented itself only served to reinforce his standard operating procedure. The assassin took every precaution to distance himself from his client. With the target's high value, it was almost expected that he might be next on their list, so he was even suspicious of his middleman. It was an occupational hazard, if you will, but the Russian knew just the man to sniff out the transactions. Knowing the banker his middleman had used gave him a money trail to follow. Knowledge was a form of insurance in his line of business, and he already had a lead nearby to check up on.

Petrov never expected there to be such a letdown. Rather than take a full week to learn the target's routine, he was remarkably comfortable with cutting his surveillance short. He realized the value of killing The American sooner rather than later. Expediency could help keep his own head out of the cross hairs.

The assassin found a steep, tall hill in the adjacent park that dumped into the woods meters from the man's home. His client informed him he wouldn't have a problem getting in close, but for a trained sniper like the Russian, keeping your distance held a significant advantage. He took it as a good sign that nature had provided the perfect perch from which to take his shot.

For two and a half days he watched in awe as The American went about his double life without there being so much as a hint of his darker side. Sure, he carried himself with a certain graceful power, something that was easy for a man in Petrov's position to recognize, but the operative was unbelievably careless, considering the impressive list of people who would like to see him dead.

His cover was working for a company called the IntelliShield Corporation that built high-end software to secure computer systems, headquartered in Arlington, Virginia. Security for the company's building was too advanced to chance doing the job there. The risk of getting in over his head would have been too great, but it didn't matter: the Russian was content with taking the target out at his home.

From the details provided by his client, he saw this as the perfect opportunity to use his Lobaev SVL. He had the rifle made to his specifications by Tsar-Cannon Ltd, a small company that afforded him the opportunity to keep his dealings in firearms discreet. The barrel was cut shorter than a typical sniper's weapon, making the rifle easier to conceal and handle. Its shorter length was sufficient for a shot like this one, in the sub two-hundred-meter range. The stock was made of carbon fiber to keep the weight down, and it delivered its deadly payload from a magazine that held five 5.56 x 45 mm NATO rounds.

The low caliber of the rifle would turn away most snipers, but for Petrov it was a way to level the playing field, albeit slightly. Using a rifle with less power left no room for error. He thought of it as giving the target a chance. For him, it was a way to add some thrill to taking down an unsuspecting victim.

With this particular marksman behind the scope, making a mistake was never expected to enter into the equation. Everything would have been perfect if it wasn't for that damn dog.

Petrov prided himself on his shooting ability, but when he lined up the sight and squeezed the weapon's trigger, something unusual happened. The massive Great Dane owned by his target affectionately nudged its head under the man's arm. The resulting movement caused the shot to hit low.

The barking started immediately. The deep sound of the canine's voice reverberated through the broken kitchen window and overwhelmed the once-still neighborhood. The Russian had never heard an animal project so loudly. Its cries of desperation punched through the night air as it stood guard over its master's body.

Petrov was forced to retreat through the wooded park to his rental car and head back to his hotel in Tysons Corner. It was sloppy, but he managed to finish the job in the end.

Chapter 11

Inova Fairfax Hospital, Fairfax, Virginia

TRENT TURNER PULLED into the Inova Fairfax visitors' parking lot and blasted his horn. "What an idiot," he said under his breath. The car that had just pulled out nearly clipped his rental car. He scowled at the driver noting he had squeezed himself into a hospital-issue scrub top that was too small.

"Here's a tip: check the mirror first, pal. Your lack of fashion sense is cutting off the circulation to your brain," he grumbled with a shake of his head. Bad drivers, poor dressers, and hospitals were all things annoying on different levels.

Emotions he had suppressed for many years hit him all at once. Being anxious was uncharacteristic for the experienced operative, but seeing his family under these circumstances would be difficult for anyone. He scanned the area and didn't see signs of a welcoming committee from The Island waiting to bring him in. He knew blowing off Addy Simpson's order to stay in New York would be cause for some serious tension back home. The operative was unsettled by the fact that he hadn't heard from his handler yet. It was normal to expect a delay, since he wasn't on an operation, but this time it was different. Trent had sent the code to put himself into stealth mode more than three hours ago. It was something he'd never done before, and his handler knew it would cause some major waves.

The code meant Turner had disabled the ability for The Island to track his movements. He would use aliases that only he knew, and his devices would be masked. Trent Turner would disappear from the radar. His handler, Tak, was the only person who could contact him when he went dark.

He and Tak had hit it off from the second they exchanged call signs, and over the years they had become extremely close. Turner had chosen Goldfinger for his handle. It was an inside joke that reminded him of the drawn-out arguments he had with his father and brother. He liked Sean Connery as James Bond, and they preferred Roger Moore. The instant his handler replied that his call sign would be AVtaK, he knew they would get along just fine. *A View to a Kill* was one of the Bond flicks that starred Moore. It was like a small taste of home.

Trent's alias morphed into several nicknames that his handler used to lighten up tense situations. Solid Gold, Goldilocks, Golden Boy, Stinky Finger, but as they gained more experience and grew closer together, he finally settled on calling him Finger. Trent ended up shortening his handler's name to Tak.

They never met in person—protocol wouldn't allow it—but in a world of evolving communication, the absence of physical contact seemed increasingly normal. For security reasons both men—at least Turner believed Tak was a man—had their voices altered by computer software when they spoke. The program was designed to catalog speech patterns and develop a profile for each individual. The software provided a consistent, normal flow and experience during conversation.

Turner decided the security measures were to protect his handler. Since there was no traceable connection between them, Tak could lead a relatively normal life. He wouldn't have the threat of a rogue operative hunting him down, or the risk of his identity being revealed under extreme torture.

BOMBTRACK. That was the code that switched Turner into stealth mode. The twist was that nobody at Island Industries or The Shop, the nickname for the company where Tak worked, had any idea the two would still be in contact. Turner knew going underground would be the biggest test yet for their trust.

A trip to the hospital was a risk, but Turner decided there wouldn't be any alarm bells ringing unless The Island had tried to contact him in the past four hours. Going to visit his brother was too important; it was something he couldn't pass on.

The operative didn't know how long it would take to track down the person who executed the hit on his brother, but he knew The Island wouldn't tolerate a personal operation like this. That was something he'd have to worry about later. He would have to figure out a way to repair the damage when this was over. He knew what he signed up for, what this meant, and realized, if he was accepted back into the fold, there wouldn't be a welcome mat.

Chapter 12

Island Industries, Brooklyn, New York

"HEY, ADDY. ANY word on Trent yet?" Gordon Peterson asked as his boss entered the training facility.

Addy Simpson shook his head and said, "No, not yet. Word sure gets around fast in this place."

Peterson flashed him a knowing smile. "We're fast. That's why you pay us the big bucks," he said.

Simpson shrugged his shoulders and laughed. "Good point, Gordo."

His friend had the typical résumé of an Islander: a former Special Forces soldier handpicked by Simpson who specialized in covert operations. The two sailors met when Simpson was a team leader on SEAL Team 6, which had since changed its name to the United States Naval Special Warfare Development Group, or DEVGRU for short.

Simpson went on to earn the rank of vice admiral after his time with the SEALs. He played an integral role with the SEAL team's move under the United States Naval Special Warfare Command, and became the original commander of the Joint Special Operations Command. He was then appointed to run the CIA, until an incident with an old adversary forced him from his post. It turned out to be an opportunity in disguise, and the resignation saw him start up his private firm, Island Industries.

"You can't beat yourself up about this," Peterson said. He could see the concern hanging on Simpson's face and knew about the death of Turner's brother. "We all know the risks. Trent knew the risks. I feel like shit about it too," he admitted, "but it's not our first tragedy, and it sure as hell won't be our last."

Simpson looked his good friend in the eye and said, "I just—"

"Look," Peterson interrupted. "Beating yourself up about it isn't going to help anyone. It's not like you could have pulled him off the operation. We couldn't have known he was compromised and someone put a hit out there. We did everything we could on our end, Addy."

They exchanged frustrated looks.

"We did," Peterson insisted.

Simpson's thoughts drifted as Peterson worked the console in front of him. The sound of motors echoed through the warehouse-sized space as he reconfigured the three-story kill room for a training exercise. He had a network of contacts that would help him find individuals like Trent Turner. Potential recruits who had a combination of wit, physical talent, and what he referred to as honorable detachment.

The Island sought out young men and women who withdrew or were forced from an otherwise promising life for reasons out of their control. He gave them a unique opportunity, a second chance to realize their full potential. The Island represented a new family structure that the operatives could grow with and trust.

Simpson found Trent Turner in a place that was practically local to The Island. He was nearly finished with his senior year at Yale University. The Event, as Simpson referred to it, needed to be significant enough to detach a person from their family. He would step in and offer new recruits a chance at something that would help them redefine their purpose. They would perform an invaluable service for their country. Connections to people on the outside were severed when Island Industries entered the picture. Trent Turner had become the one exception to that rule.

Before the "event", he and his brother, Ryan, had been virtually inseparable. There had been some unspoken tension between the two for several weeks, and it was something Trent hadn't felt in their twenty-two years together. He feared the worst and thought his brother may have gotten into some trouble and was keeping quiet about it to protect him.

The situation had turned out to be much simpler than that. Ryan had kept his relationship with a new girl on campus a secret from his brother. Trent had always been the charmer of the two, and Ryan had wanted the relationship to mature before making an introduction.

April Pearson had been seeing Ryan for a little over a month. She had no idea the love she was falling into was about to take a heart-wrenching turn. It would have been the first time Ryan and April had made love. Her girlfriends had dropped her off at the apartment just after ten-thirty that evening. She had a few Cosmos at a local bar, and the effect of the alcohol had been amplified by constant urging from friends visiting for the weekend. Pearson only knew a few people on campus, so Ryan had become the center of her new universe. She thought it would be fun to surprise him and take the next step, a move that would bring more intimacy into their relationship.

When Trent opened the door to the dorm, he was surprised by the beautiful girl who tackled him onto the couch and had started to unbutton his pants.

"Did Ryan send you here?" Trent asked with a laugh, assuming his brother knew he had been worried.

"You bet he did. He's the only reason you're about to get laid on a school night," she joked. "Now, let's not waste any time. We wouldn't want to disappoint Mr. Ryan!"

It wouldn't have been the first time one of the brothers had sent a sorority girl after the other, but it would be the last. The couple of beers Trent had put down before she arrived had laid any usual questions to rest. When the apartment door swung open unexpectedly a few minutes later, the time that Trent and April had spent together changed everything. Ryan and April shared a look of horror before Ryan's gaze panned up to Trent. His grin quickly turned to a look of confusion as Ryan sprinted toward him, his fists flying through the air.

Pearson didn't appreciate being kept in the dark about her new boyfriend's identical twin. She had no idea Ryan had kept such an incredible secret from her. Life would have turned out much different for all of them had he not.

Initially, the romance between April and Ryan had been shattered, but an unexpected twist of fate brought them back together. In time the couple were able to resume the passion they had left behind that fateful night, but there would always be a scar.

By the time Trent was released from Yale–New Haven Hospital, he had already been tagged by one of Simpson's men. The doctor had taken his share of late-night calls to put Addy's operatives back together again, and he had made sure Turner was assigned to him. Trent's broken jaw from the one-sided brawl with Ryan didn't do them any favors when it came to the brothers trying to reconcile their differences. Their relationship quickly deteriorated, and Trent ultimately decided he wanted nothing more to do with him. His parents tried to get their sons past something neither of them knew any details about, and it only served to put more distance between the family and Trent.

Simpson knew from their first meeting that something about Trent was different. Physical abilities aside, he was a man who listened with the intent to understand rather than to respond, and it was a trait that was incredibly valuable and rare. Keen senses and intuition were what Simpson had built his reputation on, and he wasn't a man to doubt his instincts. Choosing someone like Trent for the program was something he knew could come back to bite him someday, but he decided he'd take his chances, and now he was paying the price.

Peterson had finished configuring the room and noticed Simpson had completely spaced out. "Addy, you okay?" he asked.

Simpson's thoughts evaporated and he came back to the present. "Yeah, I'm fine thanks."

Chapter 13

Inova Fairfax Hospital, Fairfax, Virginia

TRENT TURNER TOOK a deep breath as he waited for the elevator to arrive. The familiar hospital smell threatened to stir up bad memories, but he managed to fight them off. He'd seen too many good people die, and when they made it as far as a hospital, in many cases it brought more pain and suffering for everyone involved. If he could have his way, he'd want to go quickly.

The operative pulled up his brother's room number from his smartphone to avoid contact with the information desk. At first glance the device looked like a top-of-the-line model purchased from a high-end mobile store, but in reality it was an XHD3, which stood for Xtreme Handheld Device 3. This was the third generation of the top-secret piece of hardware, and it was capable of delivering a stream of intelligence to an operative's fingertips.

Trent used an application called Cannibal to pull up the room number. He and his handler had developed the program together. Both were talented software developers, which was half the battle when it came to their encounters with the dark art of hacking. They initially created Cannibal for doing the legwork needed in the field quickly and accurately, but it had since evolved. With the advances in its hardware platform, the device was now capable of accomplishing much more.

The application connected to several top-secret systems inside the CIA, FBI, NSA, and NRO over secure connections in data centers managed by The Shop. Turner knew better than to pry for details, but The Shop seemed to have legitimate contracts with the intelligence community to replicate, mine, and secure its most sensitive data. The agencies were aware of most of the connections they had made, but when pockets of guarded information were discovered, they would tap into those systems with ingenuity rather than approval.

Cannibal's job was simple. It would take a question and spit out the answer. It was simple enough in theory, but the logic involved was based on a series of complex algorithms developed by Tak and Turner. It was the Google Search of black ops, and an invaluable tool in the field.

As he counted down the numbers to his brother's room, he became increasingly nervous. Each step down the bland hospital hallway seemed less sure. After years of being solid as a rock, the unwelcome sensations were a dangerous distraction.

"Excuse me, sir," the nurse said as she wheeled a covered gurney out of the room.

When her eyes connected with Trent's, she looked shocked. *Seeing a dead man's twin must be like seeing a ghost,* Trent thought.

"I'm so sorry for your loss," she said.

"Is this Ryan?" Trent asked. There was a hint of fear in his voice.

"Yes. I'm afraid it is."

Trent said nothing, but the expression on his face screamed agony. He channeled the grief into anger and carefully pulled back the sheet that was covering his brother. A tear streaked from the corner of his eye as he kissed his brother on the forehead.

"I'm sorry, Ryan," he said softly. His eyes hardened as he searched for words. "It's my fault…I can't make this right, but I'll try to make you proud." He gently pulled the cover back over his head. "I love you," he said, his voice trailing off.

The sound of sobbing brought Trent's attention to his mother's inconsolable form. She had been watching from inside the hospital room in tears. She'd just lost the son she had, and now she was faced with the one she'd lost. Trent knew his mother was strong, but this was too much even for a woman as strong as Cathy Turner. He shut his eyes to fight back tears and thought about what he had done to her.

"Hi, Mom," were the only words he could say.

He gave her a loving hug as they watched the nurse push Ryan's gurney down the hallway. Trent was stunned, but he slowly began to snap out of it. This would be difficult. He knew he needed to craft his next words carefully.

"I've missed you so much," his mother said as she clung to him tightly. "I know he wanted to hang on until you got here. He loved you so much," she said, her voice shaky. She hugged Trent tighter. "He almost made it...so you could say good-bye. He fought so hard."

The pain in her voice ripped through his soul.

"I was sure he'd hang on," she said. "I told him you'd come."

The sadness and anger he felt was sharp. His limits were being tested like never before. After a couple of deep breaths, he regained his composure.

"It's my fault, Mom."

"Listen to me, Trent. You and your brother had your problems, but you can't try to put this on—"

"No, Mom, you don't understand," Trent insisted in a measured tone. "It's my fault. I can't really explain it, and I know that's not fair, but I promise you, this was about me, not Ryan."

He thought intently about how much he could share with his family. Things were complicated, and he knew they could also be in danger. The fact that his brother had been compromised meant the killing could continue, unless he worked fast. He wasn't sure who the next target might be, but he needed to find some answers.

"My job isn't exactly a government job up north," Trent admitted. "We work with the government, but..." He considered his next words carefully. "We fix things that are difficult to fix."

He realized this wouldn't make much sense to her, but it wasn't like he had a choice. He needed to say enough to make sure they would stay safe until he could take care of any threats.

"What I'm trying to say is there are a lot of shady people who don't like what the company I work for does. I'm so sorry, Mom. I never meant for anyone to get—"

"Enough, Trent, enough," she snapped. "Between your father and your uncle, there are plenty of people in this world who would like to do us harm."

"Yes, but—"

"No buts." Her eyes burned with intensity and sadness. She wiped the tears from her face. "Your brother just died, and dammit, I won't hear any more of this nonsense."

They stood in silence. Trent tried his best to comfort her while he worked this out in his head. He needed to ask some questions. There would never be a good time for this conversation, and time was something he didn't have.

"Mom, I need your help," he said gently.

"Sure, anything," she said. His worried tone calmed her down and filled the grieving mother with concern. "What is it? Are you in trouble?"

"No, it's nothing like that. I need to ask you some questions about what happened to Ryan. It's not something that can wait. I'm sorry, Mom. Are you okay with that?"

"This isn't a good time, honey," she said. "I need to…" She saw an intensity in her son's eyes she'd never seen before.

"I know," he said, "but if I'm going to find the people who did this to Ryan, I need answers now." He knew he'd better keep going so she couldn't interrupt. "You sounded surprised that Ryan didn't hang on longer. Did you think he wasn't in danger of dying?"

"He was in really bad shape," she said. Her voice was shaking again, so she composed herself before continuing. "But the doctors said his condition was stable. We were expecting him to hang on for a little while longer. They didn't give him much of a chance for recovery." She wiped her tears away with a tissue and said, "I just wasn't ready to say good-bye to him yet."

Trent found it difficult to concentrate as emotions invaded his thoughts. His gut was telling him the botched assassination attempt would have drawn the killer out to finish the job. If there was any chance for recovery, he knew it would be too dangerous to leave a man like him alive.

"Mom, have you noticed anything out of the ordinary? Something strange?"

She looked at him as if she wasn't quite sure how to answer.

"Maybe it's a person you had seen several times in a day, or someone that just didn't fit in. Just something that's off. Something that doesn't add up or seem normal." He knew it was a long shot, but his only hope was that the killer had been sloppy and made a mistake.

She let Trent's questions sink in. She framed his cheeks with her palms and took in the sight of her son.

The emotions hammered him. He needed something to have any chance of finding Ryan's killer.

"Especially in the hours leading up to his death. Mom? Anything, even if it seems silly."

"Silly?" The word seemed to jar her memory and send a chill down her spine.

Chapter 14

Georgetown, Washington, DC

HE STOOD IN his contemporary studio apartment with a look of complete satisfaction on his face. Its dark walnut floors contrasted with the white walls, and floor-to-ceiling windows bathed the space in sunlight. Nevin Perlman knew Eugène Ysaÿe's Sonata No. 3 in D Minor, Op. 27—"Ballade"—had never been performed with such perfection. Perlman adored the Belgian's intricate and demanding composition. It was a work created for the solo violinist, and a piece that only the very best could aspire to master. There was only one other person he had heard perform this particular sonata with the combination of precision and emotion that now held him captive. That man was the late, great violin master Valentino D'Angelo, his former pupil and dear friend.

With her long legs and toned figure, Victoria Eden D'Angelo wouldn't be out of place sauntering down the catwalk in a high-fashion show in Milan. Her fingers floated up and down the instrument effortlessly as she played awe-inspiring double and triple stops. Her thoughtful green eyes echoed the emotion that sang from her instrument, punctuation marks for the strikingly beautiful features of her thin face, framed by long jet-black hair. She performed commandingly in the center of the room, her body moving in step with the grace of royalty and the confidence of a matador. Her elegance complemented the display of aural perfection.

She was a child prodigy who was pushed too hard by a well-intending father. After all, he was one of the world's most renowned violinists, and his only child clearly had the talent to do what was once unimaginable—take his own playing to the next level.

"Well, what do you think?" she asked.

Perlman broke out into applause and said, "Exquisite. Absolutely exquisite. Bra-vo."

If he hadn't seen it himself, he wouldn't have believed it. It was impossible. Her natural ability was far beyond that of her father's. He had no idea his goddaughter had started playing again after she had graduated from university. He had been immensely proud of her valedictorian speech and, until now, hadn't thought she could have made him any prouder than he was that day.

"Your father was right, Victoria," he said as he looked out the window at the hustle and bustle on M Street. "You have a gift that transcends the instrument." He met her eyes. "You are the instrument. The violin is merely a vehicle for your passion to be heard." He smiled at his words and kissed her on the cheek.

"I know it must be hard for you with my father being gone, but you mustn't overreact—"

"Victoria. Never in my life have I heard anything as beautiful," he demanded. "It's not because I love you like a daughter." He shook his head. "No, no, no. What I'm telling you is true. Can't you see the tears in my eyes when I tell you this?"

Tears of joy streaked down the wrinkles on his face, and her eyes began to well up.

"Do you think they would be proud?" she asked softly, thinking of her parents.

"Do not put those tragedies on your shoulders, my dear," he said. He put his hand on her shoulder. "Your father was a very difficult man. I loved him like a son, but he…well, he had a certain way about him that could be very abrasive. You had every right to choose to do what made you happy. It hurt him, yes, but everything that happened was because of the choices he made. It was of his own doing."

She had rebelled rather than follow in her father's footsteps, and turned herself into a tomboy. Anything to get away.

"I always loved playing the violin, but he made it very difficult to enjoy," she admitted.

"I know. Pushing you too hard was your father's biggest regret. He was a perfectionist, and early on in his career he was ripped apart by the critics in the press. It was part of what drove him to excel, but it is also something he didn't want to happen to you." He put his arm around her shoulder. "Especially given his—shall we say—attitude. There would be no punches pulled for the daughter of Valentino D'Angelo—that you could count on."

She had always wondered how different life would have been if her mother had been around. Even after all these years, her death still left unanswered questions that she wasn't sure she wanted answered.

"How about Victoria Eden?" she asked with raised eyebrows. "Will the world accept her?"

"Victoria Eden's talent cannot be denied," he said emphatically. "You will take the music world by storm, and they won't know what hit them." He gave her an adoring smile. "Truly, Victoria, I am at a loss for words. Your father tried to tell me how special you were, but I dismissed it as the ramblings of someone who had consumed one too many bottles of Cabernet. For the life of me, I cannot see how you were able to advance your playing on your own."

"Don't forget, Uncle Nevin, from the time I was a child I listened to my father play every day. I have every warm-up, practice routine, and piece he played permanently etched in my memory. It was a simple matter of practicing," she said as if the answer should have been obvious.

She began to play her father's favorite warm-up sequence, and Perlman beamed with recognition.

"My dear, it is more than just practice to play the way you do, but that would certainly explain a lot. I cannot wait for you to tell me about your first audition."

She gave him a hug and said, "Thank you so much for setting it up."

Chapter 15

Inova Fairfax Hospital, Fairfax, Virginia

CATHY TURNER CONSIDERED her son's last question, trying to connect the dots as the memory began to surface. *Silly*, she thought.

"Well, there was a nurse who came in and woke me," she said. "He looked ridiculous. His clothes were really tight, and he certainly wasn't from around here. He had a strange accent."

Trent Turner's expression was tense. "What sort of accent was it?"

"It sounded—I don't know—kind of Eastern Bloc, but it was strange."

"Go on."

"His words took on a British enunciation."

"Excuse me, nurse," Trent called out, and waved his hand.

The nurse walked over.

"Could you please tell me if there are any foreign nurses working this evening?" Trent asked her. "Someone with an accent."

She creased her brow and replied, "Sure, we have two on duty right now."

"See, honey, it's okay," his mother said. "We're both having trouble thinking straight."

"Would you mind giving me their names?" Trent asked the nurse.

"It's okay, honey. I'll call your father, and we can go to the chapel to say a prayer. It will make us both feel better," his mother insisted.

The nurse turned to Trent. His expression demanded an answer. "Sure, it's no problem at all. Sam and Chris are on duty now." She gestured toward the nurse's station. "If it's any help, they're both standing over there."

They turned their heads in unison to see a pair of nurses discussing a patient's chart.

"They're women?" Trent's mother said with complete surprise.

"Yes," she said, laughing. "They certainly are. We don't have any male nurses on this floor."

Cathy Turner's heart began to race. Anger churned inside as she considered the evil that would possess someone to murder a defenseless man under his mother's nose. "Oh my God," was all she could say as the nurse walked off.

"Mom. Mom. It's okay," Trent said. He held her hands tightly in his. "There's no way you could have known. Now, Mom, I really need you to focus." He dipped down to make eye contact and snap her out of the shock. "What did you see him do? I need you to replay every detail back to me. I'll find him, don't you worry. I promise you I'll find him."

"No, honey," she fired back, and shook her head. "I've already lost one son, and I won't lose the only one I have left."

"You don't understand, Mom. He was coming for me," Trent said flatly. "Right now I have an advantage. He thinks I'm dead. If he realizes I'm alive, then he'll just come after me to finish the job. It's what he does. Concentrate, Mom. I need you to concentrate."

She looked down, overwhelmed with emotion. After a long moment she met his eyes and he continued.

"Now what did he do while he was in the room? Did he open the door?"

"I don't know. I was sleeping when he came in. He moved my arm to give Ryan some medication."

"So he touched your arm?"

"No. He never touched me."

"Then how did he move your arm?"

"I was holding my book. He pushed my arm aside using my book."

"Was he wearing gloves?"

"No. I don't know." She struggled to remember. "I don't think so."

"What did he do next?"

"He gave Ryan a shot through the port in his IV. Then he said good-bye and left."

"Did he touch the IV?"

"No. I'm pretty sure he didn't. Only my book."

He pulled out his XHD3 and said, "Point to the part of the book he touched, Mom. Let's hope he was sloppy since you were in here alone."

"Right there," she said, pointing to a spot on the book.

"Hold up your hands, Mom."

She let him scan her fingerprints and palm prints into the device, and he told her it was so he could remove them from the equation. He then showed her how to activate the XHD3's thermal-imaging system and held the device steady over the book. He explained that it worked on the premise that materials absorb and release heat in a specific manner. If there was a slight alteration to the material—in this case the amino acids from human contact—it would produce a noticeable change in the book's thermal signature.

"Mom, I've got something here, but I need to go now—there isn't much time. Could you draw the man you saw?"

She shrugged her shoulders, and he pulled up the EtchMe application on the screen and handed the device to her.

"You and your brother were two peas in a pod," she said with a smile. "He loved his tech gadgets too, you know. I'm surprised you're not wearing the same shoes."

She was amazed with how quickly she was able to assemble the features of the assassin. What started off as a crude outline was quickly transformed into a detailed visage through a series of questions, where she would select shapes and trace lines on the display with her finger. Within a couple of minutes, the heartbroken mother was staring at a likeness of the man she despised most in this world.

"That's him," she said.

"Okay, listen. You and Dad need to be very careful. You need to get in touch with Uncle Jack, okay?"

"We'll be fine—"

"You need to tell Dad to get in touch with Uncle Jack." He put his hands on her shoulders, and the severity in his eyes filled her with fear. "Tell him that the same people who got Ryan may come looking for you." Even though his mother was still alive after having made contact with the assassin, he wasn't about to take any chances. "Ryan's family too."

"But—"

"Do it, Mom. Please. Promise me it will be the first thing you do."

She looked at her son and the man he'd grown into. He was tall, fit, and handsome. His piercing blue eyes were still able to disarm her after all these years.

"Okay, honey. Okay."
"I love you, Mom. And please be careful."
"I love you too, honey."

Chapter 16

TRENT TURNER STUDIED the image of his brother's assassin on the screen of his XHD3 and headed back to his car. He knew there was something familiar about the man but couldn't quite place him. A vibration from the device broke his train of thought. An envelope flashed in the corner of the screen. He opened up the secure-messaging application and began to read.

> *Heckler: Tak is off the grid. Message loud and clear. BOMBTRACK received, stealth confirmed. You're clear on this end. Let me know what you need.*

The message took him by surprise. He knew the delayed response meant something had been going on with his handler. The fact Tak had shared their secret with someone else meant one of two things. Either Tak was passing him over to The Island so they could bring him in, or he had been put on another operation, and Heckler was someone he could trust for help. He wondered if he was just being paranoid. It wasn't out of the question that the handlers at The Shop were a tight-knit group and could trust one another implicitly.

The icon on his screen showed Heckler was online. They had worked together on several operations in the past, but Trent still had doubts about his intention. He launched the chat interface and responded.

> *Finger: Hi, Heckler, I was expecting Tak, considering the situation.*
> *Heckler: I know. He would be here if it was an option. I'm sure you understand that. Tak left me clear instructions on this. We're very close. You can trust me.*

Turner had no way to confirm whether Heckler was on his side. He struggled as he mulled over the options and decided he couldn't take a chance with trusting him.

Finger: Sorry, but I think I'm going to have to fly solo on this one. I appreciate the offer.

Heckler: Tak told me to expect this. His instructions were to tell you to "feed Cannibal himself and your flick." I have no idea what that means, but he said you would understand.

Trent cracked a smile and realized Tak would have already thought every possible outcome out. This was as funny as it was brilliant. Nobody at The Shop would understand what that meant. Energized, he opened up the Cannibal application and typed in three words—"Eddy Merckx Goldfinger"—and submitted the search. The double entendre in the application's name was something they had kept to themselves. Cycling was another thing the pair had in common, and Cannibal was the nickname of legendary cyclist Eddy Merckx. Less than a second later, a note from Tak popped up on his screen.

Finger,

If you're reading this, there's no doubt you're working with Heckler on something and he's followed my instructions. I obfuscated this note within Cannibal's code in case of a rainy day. It will only show on your device, so don't sweat it being discovered. Good thing you don't suck at trivia or you'd be up shit's creek right about now!

Listen, you can trust Heckler as if he were me. This note is meant to be a failsafe in case something critical is in the works preventing me from giving you the news myself. No worries here on my end. I've probably just won the lottery and bugged out to paradise! Seriously, though, take care of yourself, and keep Heckler online. Knowing the kind of situations you get yourself into, you'll probably need him!

Catch you on the flip side,

Tak

He shook his head and laughed. The note was vintage Tak and quickly erased any doubts he had about Heckler being on the level. He needed some good news right about now, and this had been a welcome relief.

Finger: Heckler, we're good. Thanks for the support. Could you check to see if Cannibal has any intel on the image I'm about to send you?

Heckler: Sure thing. Just pass it along.

Finger: Check your contacts with MI6. He may be Czech or Russian, and he's likely been around the Brits.

Heckler: Got it.

Finger: I'll also need you to check the Washington, DC area for possible connections to the death of Ryan Turner. I'll need everything you have on that. I'll send you a fingerprint to go with the photo if my device manages to pull one up.

Heckler: Anything else?

Finger: There's one other thing. Cannibal's proximity search reported a homicide in DC. There were some interesting details about it in the FBI's system. Some sort of wireless hacking device and a laptop were found at the scene.

Heckler: Sounds like it's right up your alley.

Finger: It's probably nothing, but it wouldn't hurt to run the correlation algorithm to see if anything pops up. It sounds like there could be more to it, based on the collective freak-out they're having at the bureau. The dead guy is the son of a man who will be of particular interest to Addy.

Heckler: Should I pass the info along then?

Finger: If there's anything to it, I'll work on it while I'm taking care of my current situation. If I can find anything interesting on this, it might help me get a warmer reception when I come back online. After pulling this move, I'll need all of the help I can get.

Heckler: Roger that. I'll analyze the results and get them to you directly.

Finger: Tx.

Chapter 17

Safe house, Twinbrook, Maryland

BRUCE CAMPBELL CONTEMPLATED being on Pavel Kozlov's shit list. He was absolutely furious with himself for letting the skinny bastard outsmart him at the Metro station. The morning's six-mile run was meant help him to blow off some steam, but it did his temperamental mind little good.

Going back to working as a bodyguard would be like a kick in the teeth. He felt he was entitled to a bit of slack—after all, if it wasn't for him the high-profile Russian would either be in jail or dead. It was simple: Kozlov couldn't be convicted without any witnesses, so snuffing out a couple of FBI agents had been a small price to pay for job security.

He was working in the cinder block detached garage of the safe house, taking care of business that needed to be done in private. The walls were off-white, and the building was empty aside from a makeshift plywood table piled with dirty rags and a random collection of power tools. He used a solvent to scrub down the black Chrysler 300 and strip away its temporary coat of paint. The car was slowly turning back to its original color of metallic gray.

Campbell anxiously waited for a call from Kozlov. He wasn't on edge because one of the targets had gotten away—that detail had become the least of his worries. His real concern was how his boss would react when he found out he had killed the son of such a powerful man.

His cell phone started to play the opening for "Back in Black" by AC/DC. He picked it up off the table, looked at the display and confirmed it was the Russian.

"Yeah," he answered.

"It seems that it's raining fuckups in Washington," Pavel Kozlov said. His thick Russian accent dripping with sarcasm.

"It wasn't one of my better days," Campbell admitted.

"You are lucky. Today I feel like being generous."

Campbell winced. He knew there was always a catch.

"I have something to keep you occupied while Dimitri locates our missing friend," Kozlov continued. "Log on to your computer to get the information. I want you to get started immediately. If you can take care of this minor detail for me, you will have earned yourself another chance."

The line went dead.

Campbell headed into the house, went into the study and pulled out his laptop. He hated computers, and the shit the organization made him do to log on kept getting more complicated. The soldier used a bookmark saved on his desktop to connect to their server. He spoke the predetermined code words into the laptop's built-in camera, and when the screen told him to, he blinked three times and turned his head to the right and then to the left.

Footsteps in the background signaled his driver walking into the room. He could sense the man was reading over his shoulder, but Campbell ignored him. It only took a couple of clicks and the laptop displayed a surveillance photo. The man looked like he was a professional. Campbell scrolled down the page to read the details:

Subject: Aliaksandr Petrov
Nationality: Russian
Known languages: Russian (native), English (British), Spanish (Castellano), French (Canadian)
Age: Late thirties
Height: 6' 2"
Profession: Assassin
Proficiencies: Expert marksman, trained sniper, hand-to-hand combat, explosives
Details: Approach with caution. Hired to eliminate the operative known as The American. Operation completed.

*Last Known Location (11 hours ago): Suite 129, Hilton Garden
Inn, 8301 Boone Boulevard, Tysons Corner, VA 22182*

*If you can take care of this minor detail for me, you will have
earned yourself another chance.*

Kozlov's words were telling. Bruce Campbell wasn't familiar with the
individual on the screen, but he had heard of The American. The man had
recently crippled their European operation. Those who were lucky enough
to survive said the operative worked with devastating effect, like a one-man
army. It was obvious to Campbell that any person capable of eliminating
The American would be a difficult man to kill.

He couldn't resist clicking on the hyperlink to pull up The American's
profile. There were some blurry images that were obviously taken from
video surveillance cameras, but as he scrolled through the photos he came
to a few professional shots where The American, whose alias was listed as
Ryan Turner, wore a numbered bib across his chest that read "Boston
Marathon." His employer was listed as a computer company, but that
didn't make much sense. Now that he was dead it didn't really matter.

"The American? He doesn't look like much," the driver said
dismissively.

Campbell shook his head. "You'd better stick to driving."

Chapter 18

Marriot Hotel, Woodley Park, Washington, DC

ETZY MILLAR WOKE to the sound of the latest CNN headlines. Pain from his ribs shot through his body as he eased himself up into a sitting position. He gathered up the makeshift bandage that had fallen off his hand during the night and looked down at the patches of dried blood his wound had left on the sheets.

Forty-eight hours ago he would have been worried about the stains on the sheets, but today they were the least of his concerns. He shivered involuntarily as the events from the previous night rushed through his head. He shook them away and turned to the television. He was still in a state of denial. The newscaster launched into a story about the abduction of a journalist in Gaza City.

She detailed the abductee's exposé of a DEVGRU operative last year. An image of the soldier flashed on the screen, his face mostly obscured by a bushy beard typical of those worn by American soldiers serving in the Middle East. This was a story Millar knew well. He remembered the media frenzy when the operative's identity had been revealed. The soldier had been part of a mission that had taken out several key figures of a radical Islamist terrorist organization.

The newscaster reminded Millar that the SEAL's name was Brendan Manion. The classified details that the captured journalist published, which included the soldier's name, provided the terrorists with enough motivation and information to exact revenge. Within a week a US-based terror cell had hunted down and murdered Manion's wife and unborn child. Soon after

49

the soldier had buried his family, he was killed in a Black Hawk helicopter crash in Afghanistan.

Images of the candlelight vigils that had been held around the nation for his family flashed on the screen. Millar supposed the journalist's kidnapping was karma coming back around.

His thoughts returned to the previous evening. He caught his first break when he made it to the hotel room on Capitol Hill. It was the place where he and his friend Max launched their DC hacking exploits from. The room was paid for by Max's father's office to accommodate out-of-towners heading into the District to meet with him. The room was normally empty, and the staff at the Hotel George's front desk knew Millar well. Getting a key to the suite was easy, especially since nobody wanted to feel the wrath of the man who paid the bill.

Working up the courage to open the door to the room had been daunting. The hacker stood there for five agonizing minutes before he made a move. First he slid the card key through the lock and ran down the hall. The fact that the beep didn't spark off gunshots had been encouraging, but Etzy Millar still had a hard time mustering up the courage to go inside. His fear that the assassin was on the other side of the door gave way to the reality that the killer could possibly show up in the hallway. The possibility that he could have been followed provided enough motivation for him to do the deed.

When he whipped the door open, Millar was momentarily relieved that the lights had been left on by the hotel's turndown service. He let out an awkward scream and froze when he saw a flurry of movement from the curtains. It only took a second to resign himself to defeat and hope that his death would be quick. By the time he realized it was the vent from the air conditioner blowing on the curtains, his mental state was frayed. It took a minute for him to get his heart rate down and recover.

Millar was relieved to see his laptop sitting on the desk where he had left it. It was the reason he'd risked returning to the hotel. The computer contained the only copy of the bot software he had, and it was also where he kept the source code for the shadow program he had deployed. He pilfered a dark blue backpack from the dresser, an obvious souvenir meant for the suite's next occupant, and stuffed his laptop inside.

An envelope in the nightstand labeled "Petty Cash" had nine hundred and fifty-six dollars inside. It was more than enough for him to score a hotel room while he considered his next move. He stuffed his laptop into the backpack and quickly headed down the stairs and out the door to E Street.

The local portion of the morning newscast snapped him back to the present. It opened up with what Millar feared most.

"And now we turn it over to our Washington, DC local correspondent, Layne Stewart," the newscaster said as the screen displayed a dramatic graphic titled "Maryland Senator's Son Murdered."

"Thank you, Kate," Stewart said in a solemn tone. "There are no new developments in the fatal shooting that occurred last night in Northwest, Washington, DC outside the upscale Mazza Gallerie shopping mall. The victim was Maximillian Soller II, the son of Maryland senator and majority leader Maximillian Soller." Stewart paused and ruffled his brow for dramatic effect. "The twenty-one-year-old was shot to death following what witnesses have called a dramatic car chase southbound on Wisconsin Avenue."

The screen flashed to an image of the crumpled car with yellow police tape blocking off the perimeter. The footage showed forensic investigators examining the crime scene.

"His BMW sports car," Stewart continued, "crashed at high speed into an entrance of the shopping mall, where a man fled the scene and was chased by a gunman. A police spokesman confirmed to CNN that both the gunman and the individual who fled the scene are still at large."

The newscaster looked down to reference his notes and looked back into the camera.

"At this early stage of the investigation, neither man has been identified. Investigators say that the gunman arrived in a black, late-model Chrysler 300 with Maryland tag EST 5-4-4. Anyone with information on this crime should call the tip hotline that has been set up for this case at 2-0-2-5-5-5-5-5-5-5. There is a hundred-fifty-thousand-dollar reward being offered for information leading to the arrest of the suspects."

The gravity of the situation started to sink in, and his hands began to shake. Life as Etzy Millar knew it was over. Max was dead, and it was only a matter of time before his fingerprints were identified from handling the equipment he'd left at the scene. The images broadcasted from the crime scene confirmed his fears. The three yellow letters on the back of the navy-blue jackets—FBI—meant the investigation had already been escalated, and he only had one option left.

Chapter 19

HE PUT ON his turn signal and slowed down to pull into the gas station. His mind had been tortured all night, and he had found it difficult to sleep. He was distracted by emotion and knew his lack of focus was dangerous. Ryan's death haunted his every thought.

Trent Turner considered the pain his brother's wife and kids must be feeling right now. He wished with all his being that there was some way he could turn back the clock and take his brother's place.

He considered the stroke of luck he had last night with his mother's book. The reagent he had treated the cover with did its job, and the nanoparticles illuminated the faint traces of the assassin's fingerprint. The new technology impressed him.

Heckler had sent him what they were able to learn from the fingerprint and composite image he had gotten from his mother in less than an hour. The information that came back was no surprise. It turned out that the man who had killed his brother was a Russian called Aliaksandr Petrov. He was a freelance assassin who was once a top agent for Russia's counterpart to the CIA, the Sluzhba Vneshney Razvedki, or SVR for short. The Shop's contacts at MI6 confirmed that Petrov was an extremely capable individual and had spent a lot of time in Britain.

Now he was waiting for Heckler to get back to him on the assassin's possible whereabouts. Turner pulled the car next to the gas pump and headed inside to pay. He tried to remember the last time he'd been in

Tysons Corner. He wasn't sure whether it was the gas station bringing back old memories, or there was something else that was pinging his radar.

"Thirty dollars on pump three please," he said to the cashier inside.

"Sure thing, hon," she replied.

She cracked her chewing gum as she worked the register.

Turner laughed. "You're pretty good at that."

She looked up thoughtfully and offered a playful smile. He guessed she was in her late fifties, and she had kept herself in great shape.

"That's not all I'm good at, cutie," she said, adding a few more cracks of her gum for effect.

He nodded toward the wedding picture on top of the cash register and said, "I'll bet. Too bad he beat me to it."

"He sure did, and I wouldn't have it any other way," she replied with a wink.

"My advice…" her husband chimed in from behind the counter. He pursed his lips as if to consider something of significance. "Stay single."

His wife tossed a bag of chips at him, and they both laughed.

Trent smiled and handed over the cash. A bell sounded as he pushed the glass door open. He had to admit he envied the couple inside. It was clear they were in love. They had made a nice, simple life for themselves in suburbia, a luxury he knew he would never have.

Something was still gnawing at him as he pressed the button on the fuel pump and began to fill the tank. His eyes were transfixed on the digital readout showing the dollars and gallons tick by. He shifted his weight and felt uneasy. When his glance drifted across the island of gas pumps, he recognized the barrel of a pistol being leveled at his head.

He recognized the outline of Aliaksandr Petrov's face behind the weapon before an ingrained reflex pulled him down and to the left simultaneously. The loud report of the weapon was followed by an arc of sparks on the roof of his car.

He carefully peered around the gas pump as Petrov slammed his door shut and threw the car into gear. Turner quickly squeezed off a round from his HK45 Compact Tactical pistol, splintering the driver's side of the rear window. The grimace on Turner's face showed his frustration. He didn't have the angle to deliver a kill shot.

He jumped into his rental car, fired up the engine and jammed the black Ford Focus into gear. A loud popping sound signaled that the gas nozzle had reached the end of its length. He saw the rubber hose snap back toward the pump in his rearview mirror and shook his head. He pointed the car at the median strip that separated the two directions on Route 7 and swerved through the traffic after the Russian.

The Focus sped through the grass divider, and Turner made a beeline for the on-ramp that led to Interstate 495. His frustration grew as the blue Chevy Impala continued to pull away from view. He shook his head and wished he'd chosen a car with a set of balls.

Chapter 20

HIS FOOT WAS pinned to the accelerator when the XHD3 rang out. Trent Turner cursed under his breath, annoyed with his current automotive disaster. He didn't have to look at the display to know the call was from Heckler. He was the only person with his number.

"Finger here," he answered.

"I've got some good news and some bad news," Heckler said. "What do you want first?"

He was losing ground quickly in the pursuit.

"Might as well start with the bad news to help get my spirits up," Turner said sarcastically.

"All right then. There wasn't much on Ryan Turner. He won the Boston Marathon recently and donated the prize money to a foundation. There's nothing that ties the win to his death. The only other intel was that he was a software developer and worked for his father's company."

Turner wished his brother's death and the marathon win weren't related, but he knew better. It would have taken time for The Shop to modify the images of his brother used in the news reports. Even with the infrastructure they had in place for damage control, it would have been impossible to catch everything. He was sure major news publications posting pictures of his identical twin from the marathon was what led to his death. Someone had seen the images and thought it was him. It was a deadly case of mistaken identity.

"Okay, what else do you have for me?" Trent asked.

"The incident with the senator's son. It doesn't look like a one-time thing."

"What? People are killing politicians' sons?"

"No, no. Cannibal has been working overtime. It ran the comparison algorithm through our copy of the National Crime Information Center database and was able to correlate five—wait, hold on a sec…"

Turner exhaled in frustration as the assassin's car vanished from view. It would have been a different story had he been driving his Tesla.

"Six cities," Heckler confirmed. "It tied them together with intelligence from the NSA's database on hackers known to be associated with The Collective."

"You can't be serious? The senator's son was a member of The Collective?"

"Serious as a heart attack. It says the kid was a low-level hack," Heckler said in a less-than-confident tone that hinted it would mean something to Finger. "It says he'd help out with distributed denial-of-service attacks. He used something called a Low Orbit—"

"Ion Cannon, yeah, yeah. The open-source app that the script kiddies play with so they can call themselves hackers. Go on."

"Well, he went by mil1Ion2 in the hacker forums, and based on his posts, the analysts said he was actively working to develop his skills. He made a lot of posts, and they could tell he was new to the game, but they pointed out one thread in particular that stood out."

"How so?"

"It was for some sort of job posting, but the posts in between the Soller kid's responses were wiped clean."

"So you only saw posts by him?"

"Yeah, like half the conversation was gone. Our guys hacked into the server that hosts the forum and couldn't find any trace of what was said in the missing posts, or any clues that would tell us who might have removed them."

"That was fast."

"They're on top of things. For now we're replicating the forums that he had an account on to our servers so we can try to catch any new recruiting going on."

"Good call," Trent agreed. "Hopefully they'll be stupid enough to try it again."

"That's only part of the story," Heckler continued. "The other hackers who were killed were all involved in a job-posting thread, and every one of them had missing entries. Most of them were college pukes."

"Really? So whoever these guys are, they won't shy away from pulling the trigger. It looks like the cleaner who came in behind was sloppy," Trent pointed out.

"How's that?"

"When they hacked into the database to cover their tracks, they screwed up. Instead of thinking it through and running a delete query to remove the entire thread from the database, they wrote one that only deleted the posts made by their user name."

"So they could have wiped everything clean?"

"Absolutely. Normally you wouldn't give something like that much thought. The easy route would be to remove everything done by the account they used." Turner paused to let that sink in, knowing Heckler excelled in tactics rather than technology, which was the opposite of his handler, Tak. "You see, doing it quick and dirty like that left us with a way to tie all of the killings together. That's huge."

He had turned the car around and was heading back toward his hotel in Tysons Corner. The news was welcome after his anticlimactic car chase.

"The lab said something about a screw-up. I still don't really get it, so I'll leave that hacker mojo shit to you smart kids. I've got my own computer right here."

Turner imagined Heckler pointing to his head and smiled.

"And I'll tell you something else," Heckler continued with a laugh. "It won't ask for a damn reboot at the most inconvenient time possible either."

"You give Tak a run for his money as far as entertainment value goes, that's for sure."

"Wait till you get the bill."

Turner laughed. "By the way you throw around words like 'kid' and 'college puke,' I take it you're well seasoned."

"Don't start—"

"No, no," he joked. "I'm sure I'll be thankful for that soon enough!"

"Damn skippy, kiddo. Damn skippy."

"So the forum entries—that was the good news?"

"No, it gets better. According to the analysts, this case is about to blow wide open."

Chapter 21

Island Industries, Brooklyn, New York

HE LOOKED UP from his desk to see who had just barged into his office. "It's personal with you two, isn't it?" Addy Simpson asked.

"No," Dr. Charles Reed replied in a less-than-convincing tone. He closed the door behind him and turned toward the admiral.

Simpson laughed. "It's a scary thing when someone can see right through you."

Reed looked at him nervously. He was trying to judge whether or not he'd been exposed. If Simpson knew the real reason for his retirement, it would be a serious problem. The doctor shook his head in an effort to wipe away his guilty look.

"Not me, Trent," Simpson added.

He sat down in one of the two chairs in front of the large maple desk and leaned back. His eyes drifted ponderously around the office and settled on the room's only window. He watched a raindrop connect the dots down the window's surface, then let out a sigh.

"It's unnerving, Addy," he said flatly.

Reed had worked with Trent Turner extensively and knew what made him tick better than most. He never felt like the sessions he had with their top operative were under his control. Instead, it felt like a jousting tournament, and he was left with the short stick. He might have been the one calling for the session, but it was as if Trent Turner only showed up for his personal amusement.

"I'll bet," Simpson said. "I'm sure most doctors would prefer not to be psychoanalyzed by their patients."

The doctor couldn't hide the annoyed look on his face, even though he knew Simpson's comment wasn't meant to criticize. "He figures out the layers I'm trying to peel back and then..." He shrugged his shoulders. "Trying to get in his head is like cutting into a goddamn onion. The first cut is easy enough, but if you want to slice it wide open, where you have a chance for some real insight, the stinging worsens with each cut. It makes you question the effort in the first place."

"At least he doesn't make you cry, does he?" Simpson laughed, and was met with an angry glare.

"Funny. Look, Trent is unique. The killing, it's something he takes in stride. It doesn't faze him, even when it's up close and personal."

Simpson nodded.

Both men had seen their share of soldiers come unraveled by the brutal reality of violence. If you dwell on what you've done or see too much death, the long-term effects can prove fatal. Reed's work had taught him that people die hard, and it became increasingly personal and gruesome as the distance from which the deed was done decreased.

"Look, Charles, it's not an easy job. Everyone has their own way of switching off, detaching the emotion from what needs to be done. If an operative can't do that, they don't stand a chance in this business. That's not news to you."

"I can understand that in the field, but—"

"He's the best I've ever seen. Maybe that's what makes the difference for him. Being able to shut it out completely."

"Sure, and a mechanism for doing so includes getting a rise out of his shrink? The guy who's trying to help him? Smart move," Reed said sarcastically.

Turner's rivalry with the doctor had been obvious from the start, but it wasn't personal for Trent, and both men knew that.

"Maybe he doesn't need any help," Simpson suggested, as if Reed was past the point of being able to be objective when it came to Turner. "It's not like he has a tough time sleeping or he's having flashbacks."

"Perhaps," Reed said. His failure to make any significant progress in getting through Trent's mental barriers after all of these years had become a bit of an obsession for the doctor. The circumstances behind the death of his twin brother had the potential to change all of that. Leaving at a time when there could be a breakthrough would be difficult, but he didn't have a choice. "That could change after what's happened. How are you going to get this under control? If he hasn't already started hunting down his brother's killer, he will soon."

Simpson started to say something and stopped himself before saying, "I'm heading to Virginia to meet with Jack."

Reed was taken aback. "Really?" He knew Jack Turner was head and shoulders above any operative Simpson had ever worked with during his time as a SEAL, and he was also Trent's uncle.

"He's the best chance we have to turn this around."

Reed squinted in disbelief and said, "So you're expecting a happy ending?"

"Are you having doubts about your assessment?"

"No," Reed said. "He won't fly off the handle, but he's not someone you, his uncle, or anyone else for that matter can control."

Trent Turner's move to Island Industries sealed the deal that finally brought his old friend and former commanding officer of the Navy's Basic Underwater Demolition/SEAL (BUD/S) training program over to his new team. The job and the California lifestyle had suited Jack Turner well, but family was family.

"It's never about control," Simpson said evenly. "It's about respect."

"Jack..." Reed shook his head and considered the number of times the man had refused to come to work for The Island.

The doctor had always thought the fact that Simpson was the one who recommended taking him out of the field had something to do with his previous refusals. It was never easy for an operator of his caliber to accept defeat at the hands of injury. The tough old cuss would have rather been shot and killed on an operation than sent out to pasture.

"He'll do whatever he can to salvage this," Reed agreed. "He feels obligated to look after his nephew for his younger brother."

Working with Trent was something Jack had been doing under the radar. No one in the family knew of their new relationship. Mentor and prodigy.

Simpson rubbed his chin and said, "That's the reason we were finally able to bring him on board, sure, but he believes in what we're doing. He understands the big picture."

"That's not the problem, Addy. The problem is how you'll go about finding a person who had a major hand in developing the very systems we use to track people down."

Simpson hated it when people pointed out the obvious. "That's not something you'll have to worry about," he said, alluding to his resignation.

Chapter 22

Hilton Hotel, Tysons Corner, Virginia

BRUCE CAMPBELL ENTERED the Hilton Garden Inn on edge. He looked at the small child throwing a temper tantrum at the front desk and was happy for the distraction. His target, Aliaksandr Petrov, had been reported as being on the first floor. The first floor wouldn't have been Campbell's preference, so he began to wonder whether the assassin was expecting an uninvited guest. Perhaps the room was just a decoy. He knew his employer had incredible resources and would have provided the information if there were any indication of a trap, but his target was a top-notch professional, so he couldn't discount the idea.

Doubts began to creep into his mind as he casually surveyed the hotel. An inflated ego made coming to the hotel alone an easy choice. He reasoned that he could catch the Russian off guard and score the kill, so bringing his driver along for an extra set of eyes wasn't necessary. He hoped taking care of Petrov would get him back on good terms with his employer. Pressure from Pavel Kozlov about the previous fuckup had unsettled his nerves and chipped away at his confidence. Kozlov wasn't a man who tolerated failure.

After exploring the layout of the building, Campbell decided to make a casual pass by the target's room. Lobby signs directed him down a hallway to the left of the reception desk. The long corridor had a bend, presumably to help keep the noise down for the hotel's first-floor guests. His level of anticipation remained high. Petrov's room was still out of view because of the curvature.

He carefully rounded the bend and was presented with the cleaning crew's rolling station. The cart was situated in the middle of the hallway, with a guest room door propped open on either side for quick access to the cleaning supplies. Campbell counted the rooms and knew the open door on the right led to the Russian's. He readied his weapon as he crept to within earshot and steadied his breathing.

A quick check behind confirmed nobody else was in the hallway, but a flash of movement as he turned back to the room was enough for him to brandish his Sig Sauer P226R. The adrenaline shot spiked his heart rate as his laser-like focus switched to the object in motion. He took a deep breath as a white towel lazily slinked its way down the side of the cleaning cart and fell to the floor. Campbell quickly stuffed the weapon back into his sport coat and checked his six, annoyed with his edginess, knowing the assassin wouldn't be expecting him. He approached the door slowly and peered around its frame.

The maid gasped in surprise when he appeared, and raised her hand to her heart. She quickly resumed smoothing out the sheets.

He took quick stock of the room and asked, "Will you be much longer?"

"Yes, sir…I mean, no, sir. I'm just about finished."

He entered the room as she rushed nervously to complete the job. Campbell was an imposing figure, and the sport jacket didn't do much to soften his look. After making the bed, she walked to the window and began to open the shades.

"That won't be necessary," he said firmly.

She took the hint and scurried out of the room with her head bowed.

Once she closed the door, Campbell began his search. First he checked the night tables, and then he moved to the dresser under the window. He heard the telltale beep and click from the lock on the door and, without turning to expose his face, waited for the maid to address him. He stood there and looked down at the laptop that sat on the dresser. Once she left the room again, he decided the laptop would be his next move.

Cold steel pressed against his right temple and startled him. His heart rate doubled when he considered the fact that the hotel staff would have knocked first.

"What are you doing here?" a voice barked in a harsh accent.

Campbell knew the man connected to the barrel nestled into his skin played for keeps. His encounter with the cleaning staff had made him careless. It wasn't until now that he truly appreciated his decision to rush the housekeeper out of the room. He slowly reached for the bottle of Windex the woman had left on the dresser, and knew he needed to make this count. Otherwise, it would end up being his farewell performance.

"I...I...I'm the manager for hotel housekeeping," Campbell said, doing his best to sound nervous. "She did a good job in the bathroom...and...and with making up the bed. Five points on both."

He was impressed with himself. He'd never made his voice crack like that before, and he thought the bullshit he'd come up with was pretty convincing. He paused for effect before adding some icing to the cake.

"It's our top score," he added. "I...I just needed to check that the windows were cleaned. We only do that once a week. On Saturdays."

The Russian stopped applying pressure with his gun, but Campbell could tell he was still being sized up. He knew his physical presence would be tough for the assassin to write off. He could sense the doubt, so he needed to add credibility to his story.

He made his hand shake just enough to disrupt the blue liquid in the bottle he was holding and said, "M-my staff should still be just outside. In the hallway. With their cart."

"Turn around very slowly. Keep your hands where I can see them," Petrov said.

He followed the Russian's direction and slowly turned counterclockwise toward the assassin. Campbell wore a twisted facial expression, like he'd just bitten into a sour grape. His awkward appearance served its purpose. He noticed a change in the Russian's eyes. Some of the intensity had faded, and he looked somewhat amused. He knew this would be his only chance.

He timed squirting a stream of Windex into the assassin's face perfectly. As the liquid made contact with Petrov's eyes, he landed a well-placed blow to dislodge his weapon. Campbell immediately followed it up with a leg sweep and strike to the head that sent the assassin face first to the ground. He looked down at the Russian, who was sprawled out on the ground. He had landed next to his MP-443 Grach pistol. Campbell quickly delivered a brutal stomp to the back of Petrov's neck that stopped his motion toward the gun.

Campbell looked down with satisfaction as blood began to stain the carpet below the Russian's face. He drew his weapon from its holster and surveyed the room. It was protocol to deliver an insurance bullet to the back of the head, but before he could squeeze off a round, his attention was drawn to the pair of bloodshot eyes staring back at him from the base of the room's full-length mirror.

Petrov flipped over like a displaced fish and sprung to life, wildly pumping rounds in the direction of his attacker. The Russian struggled to get to his feet and jumped backwards as Campbell unloaded several rounds into his chest. The assassin slammed violently into the wall behind him, and blood from the back of his head painted a trail as he slid against it clumsily to the floor.

Campbell's chest was pounding, his ears ringing, when he registered the vacant look in the Russian's eyes. He stashed his weapon and bolted out of the room. He quickly made his way through the chaos that had ensued in the lobby from the gunfight. The concierge tried to stop him to see if he was okay, and he answered with a sharp elbow, the man unconscious before he hit the tiled floor. He headed to his car and sped out of the parking lot to the rising sound of sirens.

Chapter 23

HE WAS HEADING back to his hotel when his handler dropped the bomb.

"Okay, Heckler, let's hear the good news," Trent Turner said.

"Sure. The kid who was with Soller when he was killed, Francis Millar, he reached out to our s4feT account in one of the hacker forums online."

Turner's brow creased. Once The Shop realized organized crime had begun using strong-arm recruiting practices on hackers, it had created the account so they would have a way to contact them for help. Technology had become a lucrative business, and the safety account represented a lifeline for those who found themselves in over their heads. The Shop offered them protection, a way out, and the hackers provided them with a treasure trove of information in return.

"Really? Has the FBI released his name yet?" Turner asked. "Or is he still labeled as the unidentified passenger?"

"No, they haven't put it out there. As far as I can tell, besides the bureau, we're the only ones who know his identity at this point."

"So how did it go down?"

"He's scared to death," Heckler said. "They dug up what they could on him. Apparently he's from a poor family and earned himself a scholarship to the University of Maryland. He met the Soller kid there. The university's database has them listed in the same class. He's like you—a computer freakin' genius."

Turner laughed. "So based on what the analysts said, the job was beyond Soller's capabilities. Are you thinking he brought in Millar to help?"

"Exactly. He wanted to learn," Heckler reasoned. "The analysts were thinking along those lines. It makes sense to me, but I'm operational. I try to stay out of that technology crap."

Turner laughed, knowing that would be the case, and asked, "Were the two of them friends before the job?" He wasn't sure whether to be concerned about the fact that the FBI hadn't released Francis Millar's name as someone they were looking to question. The bureau had to know they were friends at this point, so the skeptic in him thought it could mean something significant.

"I don't know when they became friends. I'll have them check into that."

"Okay, great."

"I'm not sure how valuable this is, but the Millar kid's hacker name is 'Slash Etc.,' whatever that's supposed to mean. It brought a pretty big reaction from the analysts."

Turner's raised his brow. "Heckler, did you say Slash Echo Tango Charlie?"

"Yeah, that's right," he confirmed.

"You would pronounce it Etzy," he said. "It's an inside thing only us computer geeks would understand." Heckler laughed, and Trent's tone turned serious. "Wow, this guy is incredibly smart. I know quite a bit about him, at least as far as his online persona goes. I'm not sure if he's still a part of The Collective after the bullshit operations it's done as of late." Turner was referring to several actions that had been carried out in the name of the group where an attack had been leveled on a target based on false information. "He's been on the scene for five, maybe six years, and he's always been a white-hat guy. The Collective has stepped into some serious gray areas over the past year, and he wanted no part of that."

"So he's one of the good kids then?"

"Yeah, you could say that," Turner said. He was impressed that Heckler knew the difference between white- and black-hat hackers. "He's done some impressive work on botnets, zero-day vulnerabilities. Shit, he should have a scholarship to MIT," he said frankly. This was the sort of break they needed. "So when can I pick him up?"

"He hasn't gotten back to me with any details on an RV yet. I gave him a number where he can reach me. All he said, aside from wanting to come in, was that there is something big going on. He stressed that it was really big, and it was going down soon. He needed help and stated the obvious: people are trying to kill him."

"Welcome to the club," Trent joked. "If he's saying it's big, you need to have the guys at The Shop work on this around the clock."

The development was a welcome distraction from his internal chaos, and he knew it was something that would help him get his head on straight.

"They're already on it," Heckler said. "Everyone's been called in, and nobody's leaving until this is all sorted."

Something else was bothering Turner, so he decided it was best to just throw it out there. "Has anyone from The Island been poking around asking about me?"

There was a short pause. He could sense Heckler was uncomfortable.

"Simpson sent notice that you went dark," he admitted. "But he hasn't been asking around."

"Shit!" Turner yelled.

"What's going on?"

Turner shook his head and said, "Some asshole just tagged the side of my car and took off. I've got to go. Ping me the minute you hear from Etzy."

Trent Turner was again ruing his choice in automobiles. He quickly turned the Ford Focus around, but the gray Chrysler 300 had already disappeared from view. This was getting old, but then he realized it would have been stupid to expose himself in a scene like that anyway. He was being way too sloppy. When he turned around and pulled into the Hilton Garden Inn's parking lot, police cars with sirens wailing had started to funnel in.

The hotel was a swarm of activity, so he carefully eased his way past the panic and found a place to park. The operative was stuck in a holding pattern while he waited for news on Etzy Millar. Turner's thoughts turned to his family. He did his best to shake them off, knowing his Uncle Jack would keep his family safe. Distractions had almost gotten him killed once, so he needed to concentrate on the job at hand.

He opened the car door, got out and winced at the freshly minted gray streak across the driver's-side quarter panel. It was much worse than the gash in the roof the assassin's bullet had left at the gas station. Something didn't feel right. The commotion near the hotel's lobby held his attention, so it took him a moment to process the blue Impala parked in the spot catty-corner to him. His eyes intensified as he dropped down to a crouch.

Turner worked his way toward the back of the Chevy and scanned the parking lot for threats. The bullet hole in the driver's side of the rear window confirmed what his instincts had already told him. He pulled out his XHD3 and quickly headed toward the building's side entrance. He took in a deep breath as he considered another lapse in focus that could have gotten him killed.

Chapter 24

FBI Headquarters, Washington, DC

"WHAT DO YOU mean you lost it?" FBI Director Frank Culder said. "We're not talking about a set of fucking car keys!"

There was a long pause. His twisted expression showed his disgust with the person squirming on the other end of the line.

"Erased? Erased! By whom?"

There was an awkward pause, and his responses went up in volume and ferocity with each word.

"It's complicated?" he yelled. "Complicated! Try me. I'm a smart guy."

He listened intently for a minute and ran his hand through the Brillo Pad of gray on his head before speaking again. "Why the hell not? Christ, you've got to be fucking kidding me."

Culder's cell phone rang and drew his attention. He read the display and immediately slammed the receiver he was holding down into its cradle on his desk. His face reddened with anger. The director exhaled as he tried to compose himself. He closed his eyes and touched the display to answer the call. He didn't have a chance to speak before the caller started.

"What do you have for me?" Senator Maximillian Soller asked.

"We haven't been able to find him," Culder said. "Nobody's seen Francis Millar since Friday afternoon. We've kept his name out of the news for now." He knew the politician wouldn't be happy with the progress, so he searched for something positive to say. "Everyone we have is on this, Senator. We recovered a laptop and some sort of electronic device from the car."

He began to sweat as soon as he blurted the words out. He knew the senator's next question wouldn't have a satisfactory answer. There was no reasonable explanation for the colossal screw up his team had made. The technology lab had just informed him that when they powered on Millar's laptop, the hard drive had wiped itself clean. It was some sort of booby trap that was set to protect the data. The technician who had been tasked with the job was fairly new and hadn't taken the extra precaution to make a copy of the data on the hard disk before turning the device on. Someone's head was about to roll.

"So what have they found out?" the senator asked.

"My technology lab expects to have some information this evening," Culder lied.

"You don't sound too sure about that, Frank," he said, picking up on the FBI man's lack of confidence. "Don't bullshit me. If you screw this up, don't expect to survive in this town. I think you know how the story will end. Do I make myself clear, Director?"

"Crystal," Culder replied. It was Soller's influence that brought him from his position as the US attorney for the Southern District of New York to the top spot at the FBI. Throwing the head of the CIA under the bus was the director's stepping stone to the bureau and cemented his role as a full-fledged political puppet.

"If I had known the MPD could do a better job, I wouldn't have bothered to bring you into this, Culder," the senator quipped, referring to DC's Metropolitan Police Department.

Culder knew he could always expect to be treated like a dog by Soller, and it had gotten old over the years.

"Are you finished?" Culder said curtly. The veins protruded from his temple as he struggled to stay calm.

"It's not your place to question when I'm finished, Culder, and don't you forget it. It's time to make use of our special arrangement," he barked and then the line went dead.

Culder knew the senator was right, and he had already set that ball into motion. Francis Millar was the key to breaking this investigation wide open, and he needed his best people on the case. The "special arrangement" he had set up with the senator was perfect for such an occasion, and they would do whatever was necessary to get the job done.

An agent had already paid a visit to Millar's father, but the man wasn't sober enough to answer her questions coherently. From the visit, two things had become immediately clear: Millar and his father didn't see eye to eye on much of anything, and they had very little contact.

The house Millar's father lived in had been described as run-down and littered with trash in the report he had displayed on his computer. There were two small bedrooms and a single bathroom. Remnants of cartoon stickers on the walls and furniture in the smaller of the two rooms displayed evidence that the home had once been occupied by Millar and his younger sister. Both children had apparently left for what were obvious reasons to the agent—to get away from an alcoholic father.

Culder was still steaming from his conversation with the senator. He managed to clear his mind and called a number from his cell phone's recent call list. He needed some more details before he could bring his special arrangement with the senator into full gear.

"Special Agent Moynihan," she answered after the first ring.

"It's Culder. What do you have for me?"

"Well, sir, his father is a drunk, and he hasn't seen his son or daughter since Millar went off to college."

"I can read," Culder said impatiently, referring to the report she'd filed. "Have you found his sister?"

"No, sir. Not yet. He thinks she's living with a friend somewhere near Gaithersburg. She's…Melody is only seventeen years old, and by the looks of it, both of them have had a tough life."

"It's not your job to throw a pity party for them, Agent Moynihan," Culder said in a condescending tone. "I've read the report. Your job is to find Francis Millar at any cost, and his sister is our best bet right now. Do I make myself clear?"

"Absolutely, sir."

"Were you able to dig up any recent photos?"

"Yes, he had one of the girl. I made a copy, and we found a recent shot of Millar on Soller's mobile phone. Both were added to our facial-recognition systems about an hour ago."

"Good, Agent Moynihan, good. It sounds like you're moving in the right direction. If you manage to find him first, it would be in your career's best interest," he lied in an attempt to increase her motivation.

"Yes, sir. I'll do everything within my power to make that happen."

Her voice sounded skeptical, and Culder decided being called in by the FBI director might have been unsettling. Then he thought better of his initial assessment. There was something more he sensed in her voice, and he didn't like it one bit.

"This is very important to me personally, Agent Moynihan," he said, trying to smooth out her nerves. "If you need something beyond your power to make it happen, don't hesitate to give me a call."

"Will do, but there's something else..." she said, before she realized Culder had already ended the call.

Chapter 25

Dulles Airport, Virginia

THE FLIGHT FROM New York to Dulles International Airport took the Island Industries' Gulfstream G650 just over thirty minutes. It gave Jack Turner enough time to make it to the company's private hangar. He pulled up in his bright yellow RAM 1500 extended-cab pickup truck. Hemis and Harleys represented his hard-ass nature and material pleasures in life simultaneously. His toys were always impeccably clean and kept in perfect running order. The hangar was large enough for Jack to drive his truck inside.

The admiral walked briskly to his truck.

"Good to see you, Jack," Simpson said with his hand extended.

"Likewise, Addy. It's been a rough week all around, that's for sure," he admitted as they shook hands.

Both men were over six feet tall and atypically fit for their age. They stood eye to eye, two old friends not concerned with softening the edges on what needed to be said.

"I'm really sorry about your nephew," Simpson said. "How are your brother and his wife holding up?"

"Cathy's a complete mess." Turner's face hardened. "Trent stopped by to see Ryan, and they had a conversation that wasn't what she expected."

Simpson nodded.

"He told her Ryan's death was his fault." Turner shrugged his shoulders.

"How much did he clue her in on?"

"Not much. He was vague, as you would expect. He's a loyal kid, though, and I think he felt obligated to open up to her. You know, try to come clean the best he could under the circumstances."

"Understood." Simpson drew in a deep breath. "That's a lot of weight to carry on your shoulders," he said, referring to Ryan's death. "Keeping your head clear is your biggest asset. It's impossible to stay alive in this business if you don't. Hopefully this won't throw him off."

Simpson knew Jack would be loyal to him. The concept of family was something that their world completely redefined. Absolute trust was implicit.

"She said he was having a hard time with Ryan's death," Turner said. "He got there as they were rolling him out of the room." Jack Turner massaged his temples with his forefinger and thumb before elaborating. "Trent just missed his chance to say good-bye." He shook his head, his face reflecting raw emotion. "That had to hurt."

Simpson closed his eyes and rubbed them before looking back to his friend.

"The short of it," Turner continued, "is that there was someone in the room who finished him off a couple minutes before he got there. Trent pulled any details his mother could give him out of her and took off to hunt the guy down. She hasn't heard from him since."

Simpson contemplated the situation. He owed a lot to Trent Turner, so there was no way he was going to jump to conclusions about him going off the deep end. He needed to find out everything he could. His thoughts were muddied with concerns about whether the situation would escalate to the point of no return. If Trent had lost control, it would be a complete disaster. Not only for him personally but the company as well. He needed to be direct. Jack understood what was at stake, and if Trent Turner had gone rogue he'd have to be eliminated.

Simpson's eyes narrowed. "So has Trent had anything to do with the killings going on in the area? He went dark. I need your help, or this could get really ugly."

Jack Turner let out a long exhale. "Hop in. I'll fill you in on the way to the office. You're not going to like it."

The two men got in his truck, and Jack turned to his friend and said, "This is going to be a tough one for me."

Chapter 26

Hilton Hotel, Tysons Corner, Virginia

TRENT TURNER CONTEMPLATED whether he might have some sort of death wish. He let the thought hang in the air as he avoided contact with the emergency personnel congregating at the hotel. His brother's murder had hit him hard. The incredible guilt had played its part and managed to overwhelm him with emotion. He found it lucky that he hadn't already gotten himself killed. There were some things in life where no amount of training could help to soften the blow.

He headed down the long first-floor hallway toward the room Cannibal had indicated was the most likely to belong to the assassin. The police were getting organized. His XHD3 knew his physical location, and it had automatically sent the information that had been provided to the police about the incident. They would soon start their room-to-room searches for a possible gunman, so there wasn't much time for him to make his move.

As he approached the hotel room, he noticed the door was cracked open. The telltale smell from a discharged firearm grew stronger with each step. He could see the casing from a 9 mm round had prevented the door from closing. He noted the positions of the doors for the neighboring suites and tried to predict the layout of the room. He checked the hallway as he drew his HK45CT and married it to its suppressor. He reached for the doorknob and prepared for an aggressive entry.

The door opened silently, and he swung his eyes and weapon from left to right. There was no sign of Aliaksandr Petrov in the main room. The streaks of blood that ran down the wall and dark stains on the floor told part of the story, but the sound of running water coming from the bathroom was about to tell the rest.

"We've got some unfinished business," Turner said.

The Russian moved the towel from his bloodshot eyes and looked at the operative through the haze of fog that had begun to work its way up the mirror. His expression suddenly turned to one of disbelief. Before he could speak, Turner delivered a heavy blow to the back of his head, knocking him unconscious.

Turner put his weapon away, heaved the large frame of Petrov over his right shoulder, bounced his limp body into a stable position, and grabbed the assassin's laptop from the dresser before leaving the room. The trip out the door and up the stairwell to his third-floor suite was as short as it was strenuous. He used plastic flex-cuffs to secure the massive Russian to the desk chair and sent his handler a message.

Smelling salts snapped Petrov back to consciousness. His eyes were still blood red, and he was confused. He was in bad shape physically. He had been shot a couple of times but was lucky that no vital organs had been hit. The assassin was still bleeding but had done a good job of staunching the blood flow before Turner had arrived. He would need medical treatment soon to stay alive.

"We both know there isn't much time for a chat," Turner said curtly. His eyes were full of anger.

"You are a hard man to kill. Mr. Turner, is it?" Petrov responded.

"Who sent you?"

"Now that is a difficult question indeed." His tone was mocking, and it only served to piss Turner off. "What if I told you I don't know?"

"I'll kill you," he said.

"Ahhh." He paused for a moment to consider the operative's answer. "And if I tell you who it was, then what?"

Turner's eyes were hard, but there was no emotion in his voice. "I'll kill you quickly."

"You know, Mr. Turner, it is nothing personal." He spit some blood onto the floor and looked back up at him. "Like you, I am just doing my job." The assassin was in pain, but the words were said with a clinical detachment.

"Who sent you?"

"I cannot tell you that. I would if I could, but I cannot."

Trent looked toward the laptop sitting on the bed and then back to the Russian. He had already assumed he wouldn't know who his employer was, but he needed to be sure.

"So, all the information you have is on that computer?" he asked.

The operative didn't expect an answer without applying some pressure, but it never hurt to ask. He stood up and walked into the bathroom to turn on the shower. He grabbed a hand towel and came back out, before turning on the clock's radio. The DJ had just cackled his familiar laugh. Turner remembered Elliot Segal from when he was much younger, and the talk show DJ put on a song that made him crack half a smile. It was a remake of "Man of Constant Sorrow" recorded by the Charm City Devils. He turned up the volume and thought about how apropos the soundtrack was.

Petrov watched him appraisingly as he approached. "Are you feeling a little dirty, Mr. Turner?" he asked, now eyeing the towel. His tone was mocking.

Turner glowered at him and picked up a pen that was on the desk. A smug look replaced the pained expression on Petrov's face. Turner shoved the pen into the wound above his collarbone, ready to mask his screams of pain with the towel. The assassin only let out an angry grunt.

"Who hired you?" Turner asked calmly as he slowly withdrew the pen.

Petrov would know this wasn't the first interrogation this man had conducted. He braced himself for the pain. The Russian had been in this type of situation before.

Turner tilted his head sideways and studied the Russian. Petrov smiled. His bloodshot eyes reflected the look of a madman, and he let out a maniacal laugh.

"I told you. I cannot give you the answer."

The operative jammed the pen back into the wound and twisted it around. The Russian grunted again and looked down at the object that was digging into his skin. Turner had to admit he was impressed with the man's tolerance for pain.

"I've been a big fan of your work," Petrov said. He was now sweating profusely, and his breathing seemed more pained. "Until now, of course," he added. He squinted his eyes like he had something to say that would be of interest.

"Spit it out," Turner said.

"You should be more careful. That man I killed—Ryan—he didn't know what you had gotten him into, did he?"

Turner twisted the pen around a few more times in anger, but this time the Russian didn't make a sound.

"Aren't you concerned someone might hear me scream?"

Turner walked behind the Russian and said, "Dead people don't make noise."

He put his hands under the assassin's chin and snapped his neck with a swift counterclockwise motion. He looked down at the man who had killed his brother and took a deep breath to regain control. He searched Petrov and emptied his pocket litter onto the desk.

The vibration from his XHD3 drew his attention. He pulled the device out of his pocket and read the response from Heckler.

Finger,

> I'll have a cleaner take care of the room within the hour.
>
> Etzy wants you to pick him up tonight. I'm trying to secure some assets to cover your back. You need to stand down and wait for help. We can't afford to lose this kid. Wait to hear back from me before moving in. I'll send you the details in another message with some photos we downloaded from the FBI's servers.

Heckler

The operative's eyes were drawn to a folded-up piece of paper he had pulled out of Petrov's pocket. He unfolded it carefully and read the two words the Russian had scribbled in pencil. "Soller." "Potomac." His heart raced as he looked to the dead man. This man was somehow connected to the senator's son and Etzy Millar. He hoped the assassin's laptop would yield some answers.

Turner decided he would get some dinner while he considered his next move. By the time he finished eating, it would be dusk. Losing Millar wasn't an option, and regardless of what Heckler had said, he knew he didn't have the luxury of waiting around for help. The hacker was their only chance of figuring out what was going on, and they weren't the only ones looking for him. His motivation grew as he contemplated finding the Russian's employer and finishing the job.

Chapter 27

THE DRONING SOUND of computer fans filled the subterranean den the men referred to as The Dungeon. The area was bathed in a surreal, high-tech glow from the dual-monitor computer workstations strewn about the long, rectangular room. Columns of smoke rose from several ashtrays, sucked away by vents at regular intervals. The room had a door at each of its short walls, and its main entrance was guarded by attentive Russian ex-military, each armed with an AK-74 assault rifle and a sidearm.

The inhabitants of the work space had formed cliques. Several Russians faced across from one another on the right as you first entered the room from the hallway, with three other distinct groupings staggered to either side as you approached the door at the other end. These individuals represented the Kozlov Bratva's hacker brain trust in the United States, the technology arm of the Russian mafia's largest faction. They were all seasoned computer hackers. Some were brought over from the motherland and Eastern Bloc countries, while others had been recruited in America.

The door at the far end of the room served as the gateway to the operation's primary Command-and-Control servers, or C&C servers as they were known in tech circles. They were the computers that commanded the Bratva's various botnets, providing instructions to the compromised machines. C&C servers were the Internet's version of a mafia boss: they directed their cyber assets with absolute authority.

There had been some complications in Switzerland six weeks ago, but Pavel Kozlov felt everything was back on track. He was now confident that the primary objective of their operation hadn't been compromised. Some assets were lost, but the man responsible, an operative known as The American, had paid the ultimate price for his interference. There had been a new development, however, and the Bratva leader was under pressure as they readied for the final stage of execution.

Dimitri Sokov, who reigned supreme over the hacking division, was in the server room when the Bratva leader called.

"I want the hacker dead," Kozlov barked in Russian.

Sokov winced. "It will take time before I can find the one who did this."

"Make an example of him. Do you understand?"

"Yes." He bit his lip and looked over at the man standing next to him. "I will have the guards take care of the matter here, in The Dungeon, in front of the others. Mikhail is in the server room with me. I will inform him of the problem."

"Good," Kozlov said, before he ended the call.

Sokov knew the old-timer hated computers and thought little of what he referred to as his "socially inept degenerates" that he kept in The Dungeon. The one thing the Bratva leader couldn't ignore about his new recruits was the bottom line. The Russian was amazed at just how lucrative his army of hackers had become in just a few short years.

Operation Berlin had been in process for the past eighteen months. It was the most sophisticated and audacious operation the Bratva leader and his *siloviki* backers had ever attempted, and the powerful group of Russians expected it to yield the biggest payday in history.

The name of the operation was symbolic. The hatred and anger that burned deep inside him and his comrades was no less than the day the Wall came down. If he were asked, he would probably say their hatred of the United States of America was even stronger.

In their enemies' eyes, the collapse of the Berlin Wall was the beginning of the end for the Soviet Union, and the event had served as bitter motivation over the years that had passed. There had been some close calls along the way, but this was the operation that would put balance back into the world and finally swing the pendulum in their favor.

These men loathed the United States and had sworn to transform their motherland into what it once was: powerful, feared, and communist. They had planned the modern-day version of a coup d'état, one where they would use technology to cause enough chaos for the American people to revolt.

Chapter 28

DENNIS ZANDER LOOKED over at the door to the server room when it opened. A wiry man whom he knew as Mikhail appeared, his frame backlit by the bright lights from inside. A loud voice could be heard barking out in Russian, before the door sealed shut behind him. The tone of the voice was angry. The hacker had been working hard to learn the language, and his work had finally paid off. He knew they were talking about the death of a US senator's son.

Zander shrunk nervously in his chair as Mikhail approached the group he was sitting with.

"Some shit is going down," Mikhail said with a thick Russian accent. His voice was deeper than it should have been.

"Good thing I won't be here to catch any grief," Zander said nervously. "I need to head out for my dentist appointment." He shrugged his shoulders and forced a smile. He always talked too much when he got nervous, and this time was no different. "Now that I think about it, I'm not sure which would be worse. Maybe I should just stay here." He laughed, and it sounded more contrived than he would have liked.

Mikhail wasn't amused. "Very funny," he said. "I suggest you not act like such a fool."

"What's the big deal?" Zander asked, unable to shut himself up.

The Russian shook his head and changed the subject. His tone was gravely serious. "When will your work be completed?"

"I've got data for the past three months from the locations you requested. It's already loaded on the servers. The script is inserting the records into the database as we speak. It should be finished in a couple of hours. The script will fire off the rest of the jobs once that's done." He was uncomfortable but tried to act normal. "I'd say it'll be done by the time I get back from my appointment."

From the conversation he had just overheard, Zander knew coming back wouldn't be an option if he wanted to stay alive. He hoped his bullshit sounded convincing.

"Good," Mikhail said with a raised eyebrow, and walked away.

Since the unexpected death of his mother a month ago, Zander had been hell-bent on figuring out a way to get back at the Bratva. The bastards had threatened to kill her if he didn't come to work for them, and the fact that the mafia had robbed him of being there to support her during the final days of her life was something he wouldn't let go.

He imagined her fear and sense of loneliness and would never forgive himself, even though it wasn't his fault. Now he had nothing to lose. In his mind, he represented the only chance for his fellow hackers to make it out of this miserable situation. The trick was finding a way to get back at them without getting his head blown off. He needed to make sure there was no way they could figure out what he'd done.

Running into Maximillian Soller in the hacker forums was serendipitous. His username, mi11Ion2, made it a fairly simple task for someone with Zander's unique skill set to confirm his identity after tracing the communications back to his college dorm. It was the break he'd been waiting for. He knew it was a long shot. It would take some serious luck for his selection of the senator's son to materialize into a problem for the mafia, but it was an opportunity he couldn't pass up.

For the time being, he had the advantage. Nobody knew his mother was dead. The hackers all lived in fear knowing the Bratva might be tracking their every move. As far as he could tell, the Bratva only tracked their movements by their cell phones and the video surveillance in and around the apartment building where they all stayed. The complex was owned by Kozlov, so he never felt comfortable there.

"What's going on?" Zander heard one of the guards ask Mikhail.

"Dimitri is sifting through the logs trying to figure out who put the senator's son in the queue," Mikhail said.

The queue was what they called the list of hackers who were good enough to install their bots without getting caught. Zander knew Soller wasn't a skilled hacker, and that was one of the main reasons he chose him. Maximillian Soller II was a time bomb he hoped would eventually go off. Zander was purposely sloppy when deleting the communications between him and Soller. He was equally as careless with the messages between the other hacker recruits. The more opportunities he left for the authorities to uncover something untoward, the more chances of the Bratva being exposed.

He was concerned about the length of time it would take Sokov to work through the logs to figure out who had done the deed. He decided he only had a couple of hours before they would come after him. The hackers had been put on lock-down before, so he needed to move fast to make sure he wasn't trapped in The Dungeon.

Zander had never been so thankful for a dentist appointment in his life. He walked over to the guard and submitted himself to the routine search. When they were finished, he rushed through the dank catacombs of the building and out to the street. He took the bus straight to his apartment, knowing he wouldn't need a dentist if he didn't hurry.

Chapter 29

Woodley Park, Washington, DC

THE BENIGN CLOUDS above had delivered night early. Smells swirled through the air of the nation's capital and propelled summer into full swing. Plants were in bloom, and a light breeze delivered hints of culinary creations from a line of restaurants up ahead.

Trent Turner cautiously walked down Connecticut Avenue toward the Marriott Wardman Park. Out of habit, he would take a detour into a store, this time a Starbucks, to make sure he wasn't being followed. He decided it would be a good idea to double back through a neighborhood before making his final approach to the hotel.

Turner hailed a taxi outside the coffee shop and directed the driver to take Cathedral Avenue and then head down Woodley Road toward the Marriott. A cab was his best option to go in unnoticed. Just before turning into the hotel driveway, he noted the gray Chrysler 300 parked on the street. There was a black scrape down the front driver's-side quarter panel. He sized up the damage with his rental car in mind and knew the car's owner was somehow connected to his brother's death. He wasn't a man that believed in coincidences, so he began to run the possible scenarios for Millar's pickup through his head. It was an extremely busy hotel, and he would never risk involving innocent people.

As the cab approached the lobby entrance, the operative instructed the driver to slow down. He wanted to make sure the bellhop was busy with another arrival when he exited the vehicle. He paid the cabbie as he scanned the area. A small family was exiting the sliding glass doors from the lobby, the concierge was going over a map with a tourist, and a thin man with a Washington Nationals baseball cap was leaning against the building. He used reflections to confirm no cars had followed him and headed inside.

The hotel lobby was posh and bustling with Friday-night activity. He made his way to the bank of elevators and walked toward the ding that signaled one had just arrived. The doors slid open.

"What's wrong, mister?" a little boy asked as he exited the lift.

It had been a long time since Turner had spent time around children. He marveled at how astute their observations were. A child's earnest concern and innocent, sometimes brutal honesty represented hope. In another life he would have enjoyed being a father, but he had made his choice, and fatherhood wasn't in the cards. Any relationship he entered was bound to end in disaster; Ryan's death had only underscored that point. He could live with his decision. What he did, the big picture of things, provided plenty of motivation for his work.

He made a mental note. The young boy had picked up an air of concern about him, which was significant. It confirmed he wasn't on top of his game.

Turner put on a big smile and said, "Nothing that a young man like yourself can't fix when you grow up."

"I like fixing things," the boy said as he held up his toy car with pride. "My name is Liam."

Turner watched Liam's embarrassed parents briskly escort him away.

"Nice to meet you, Liam," Turner said quietly as the elevator door shut.

He wore an amused smirk as he rose to the sixth floor. When the door opened, he stepped out and listened intently. The corridor was filled with sounds of people gearing up for a night on the town. He pulled a card key from his pocket and tested it on a room next to some of the louder occupants on the floor. The swipe emitted a beep as the LED on the lock flashed green. He turned the handle to gauge the effort and noise involved. He repeated the task two more times and realized there would be no surprise entrance. He quickly headed down the hall toward Millar's room.

Turner made a quick check to confirm none of the hotel's occupants were in the hallway. He drew his pistol and screwed on the suppressor as he considered the reaction the beeping sound from the door might bring. There was no doubt the man who drove the Chrysler 300 would have made it to the room first. He didn't know what the intentions of Petrov's assassin were toward Millar, so he needed to take care of business fast. If the assassin was there to kill the hacker, this could already be over.

With one swift motion, he unlocked the door and swung it open. He quickly scanned the room for threats and sprinted to the other side to clear the bathroom. He spun back around to the door and checked the space behind the bed. The only thing left inside the hotel room was a dark blue backpack that sat on the bed. It had the words "United States Senate" embroidered on it, along with the Maryland state seal. There were no signs of a major struggle. That was a good thing. The cigarette smoke streaming out of the ashtray was also a good sign.

He ran down the hallway and through a door that led to the stairs and began his descent. He navigated his way down, taking several steps at a time. When he reached the first floor, he slowed to a brisk walk and made his way through the lobby. His eyes worked double-time, taking in everything as he strained for a glimpse of Etzy Millar. He could just make out the hacker's lanky form though the glass doors. He was being guided firmly into a cab by an assassin. Several cabs were waiting at the curb, so Turner jumped into the first one in line.

"Follow that cab," he directed the driver. "But don't get too close."

Chapter 30

Soller Residence, Potomac, Maryland

SHE WAS ANXIOUSLY awaiting a message from her boyfriend. The couple had been secretly dating for almost a year, and her mother was the only other person who knew about their relationship.

Maria Soller was confused, lovesick, and mourning her brother's death all at once. She had overheard one of her father's conversations about her brother's investigation, and it weighed heavily on her conscience. She wasn't used to being an emotional wreck and could normally keep her act together no matter the circumstances, like her parents. Her phone hadn't left her hand since she'd heard the news.

The text message arrived with the simultaneous beep and vibration of her iPhone. She looked down at the device and saw the message was from a number she didn't recognize. Her pulse quickened. She slid her thumb across the display and unlocked the device with trepidation. Her iPhone launched into the message, and she began reading. Tears streamed down her face, and her hands started to tremble.

"Mom...oh my God. Mom. Mom!" she yelled with increasing urgency. She ran up the stairs to the kitchen.

"What's the matter, honey?"

"It's him! He just sent me a text. He's in trouble," she blurted out.

She handed the phone to her mother so she could read the message for herself.

m, i'm so sorry about max—i hope to explain later in person, but i had nothing to do with it, you have to know that. the guy who killed him is outside my door right now and says he has melody. he said he'll kill her if i don't go with him. pls check on her and make sure she's ok. i'm going with him…i have no choice. pls text me back as soon as u find out if she's safe. i love u! / etc

Matilde Soller's eyes narrowed after reading the text. "Dear God."

"Dad said Etzy was with Max when he was killed," Maria said in a fearful voice. "He was talking on the phone with someone. I don't know who, but…I don't know. I was too scared to tell you."

"Don't worry, honey. I know it wasn't Etzy's fault. You can't put this on your shoulders. Look what it's doing to you. We'll find out what happened to your brother."

"He'd still be here if it wasn't for me," she said, her sobs breaking up the words. Now that her mother knew, some of the weight had been lifted, but this was complicated, and the emotion was still smothering her. It was she who had asked Etzy to help her brother out with school. Max had trouble making friends, and their chance meeting on campus had changed everything.

She was looking for her brother's classroom, and Etzy happened to be in the same class. Their first conversation took them both by surprise and provided the first spark between the unlikely couple. The guilt was overwhelming as she wondered whether Max would still be alive if she hadn't tried looking out for him.

"Do you know where his sister is?" her mother asked.

"Yeah, I know where she's staying. She's staying in an apartment complex." Her hands were still shaking, and her face was streaked with tears. "In Gaithersburg. I have the address saved on my phone."

"Okay, calm down, honey. Calm down," her mother said. It was a soothing, confident voice. Her words carried the sort of comfort that can only come from a mother ready to do anything for her child. "Does she trust you?" she continued.

"Yes, she's super nice."

"Good. We'll go check on her now. I'm sure she's okay. We can find out if she knows anything about what Etzy and Max were up to."

"Mom, did you read that message? Have you heard some of the things Dad has been saying?"

It was impossible not to hear the senator's booming voice echo through the house. "Relax, honey," she said, taking charge of the situation. "You need to relax. We'll get through this, okay? First things first."

Maria squeezed her mother tight.

Matilde Soller rubbed a caring hand up and down her daughter's back and said, "Let's make sure Melody is okay and find out if she knows anything that can help Etzy. If someone does have his sister, they won't stay in her apartment. We'll have a look from a distance first. If something isn't right, we'll go with plan B."

The ability to reason was something that came easily to Matilde Soller. Being the wife of a high-profile senator put her in the spotlight more than she liked, but it was nothing the former Fortune 500 executive couldn't handle.

"I love you, Mom," Maria said with another squeeze.

"I love you too, honey."

"I should have told Max that we were dating," she said, her voice shaking.

"It wouldn't have mattered, Maria." She shook her head. "It wouldn't have mattered."

"How do you know?"

"I know," she said, invoking the definitive authority of a parent.

Maria was the one who had broken the quiet soul out of his shell and that increased her feeling of guilt. "But—"

"Let's try to help Etzy through this," her mother said in a gentle yet firm tone. "We could both use a distraction right about now. I have someone we can trust. Someone who can help. I'll give him a call after we check on Melody."

Chapter 31

Kozlov Bratva compound, Chicago, Illinois

"YES, MY OLD friend, there is nothing to be concerned about," Pavel Kozlov said. "Everything is under control. The only change may be with the schedule. We may have to move things up." The Bratva boss anxiously clenched his fist as he considered the silence on the other end of the line. Kozlov looked at the steel door to his office, and then down at the calendar pad on his desk. He picked up a pen and traced a circle over and over before he started talking again. "It is not a problem if we do. We have already planned for such a circumstance."

There was another long pause before Yuri Khrushchev spoke. "We only have one chance at this, Pavel."

Khrushchev was an old-school spy, once the head of Russia's Sixteenth Directorate, responsible for the KGB's signals intelligence and communications interception, or SIGINT for those who ran in his circles. Kozlov's mentor was a deliberate man and would respond only after careful consideration.

"This operation has cost us far too much," he continued. "The organization has risked everything to make this happen. Failure is not an option."

Kozlov shifted in his chair and said, "Yes, I understand. We will not fail. The operation will be our greatest success, and we will soon rise to power once again."

Khrushchev didn't respond immediately. "What about our loose end?"

"I just received word that it will be taken care of within the hour."

"That is something I have heard before, Pavel," Khrushchev said.

Kozlov knew the hardline communist on the other end of the line wasn't a man who gave second chances, but the Bratva leader was still confident their underground organization hadn't been compromised. Before he could respond, Khrushchev continued.

"This Turner. The American. Whatever you call him. This is a matter that we cannot afford to leave unresolved."

"Yes, I agree."

"Now that he knows we're after him, the job will be considerably more difficult. Nobody can know we are in control before the operation is complete."

"He will be dealt with. I have men putting the squeeze on him in Washington, DC as we speak. He won't know what hit him." There was another lengthy pause, so he continued. "I have another angle," he said simply, not wanting to elaborate.

"Keep me informed. And what of the senator's son?"

"The matter is being taken care of."

"He's dead. Don't you think it's a little late to take care of it?"

"No," he said, shaking his head. "What I meant is that we will make an example of the one who chose him. It will keep the hackers quiet until this is over. Then we will get rid of them all."

"I want results, not promises," Khrushchev replied, far from satisfied. "I need to know when we will be moving forward with the operation so I can make sure everything is ready here. The Group is meeting on Sunday. Let me know if Andrei should move forward."

"Of course."

"I will need to know as soon as possible. Our man cannot be in the United States when this happens."

Kozlov knew exactly whom he was talking about. It would be a complicated situation if the Russian President was trapped in America at the G8 summit when all hell broke loose. He recognized the displeasure in Khrushchev's voice before he heard the line disconnect.

He headed out of his office and down the dank hallway of the compound to The Dungeon. The Russian pounded his already-clenched fist on the metal door and glared at the camera above until the door opened. He stomped into the room.

"Mikhail, where is Dimitri?" Kozlov said in an angry tone.

Fear filled the room as the hackers diverted their eyes from his direction.

Mikhail stood quickly. "Please follow me this way. He is inside the server room."

Mikhail led him across to the server room door and affixed his eye to the retinal scanning device until he heard the lock disengage. He opened the door to the sound of a swooshing noise as the server room depressurized. Dimitri Sokov stood over a workstation built into one of the large computer racks.

"What have you found, Dimitri?" Kozlov asked.

Sokov was visibly frustrated. "Nothing yet, but I'm getting close."

"Are all of your hackers present?"

"No, not all of them," Mikhail said.

Kozlov's face began to redden as he digested the news. "What did you say?"

"There are two that are not present right now. Sofia has returned to Russia to help work on the operation there, and Dennis, one of the Americans, had a dentist's visit."

Kozlov's eyes flashed with anger.

"It's something he had planned several days ago," Mikhail added. "He has a problem with his tooth."

Kozlov looked to Sokov and said, "Is this Dennis capable of clearing his tracks, Dimitri?"

"They are all capable of such a thing," he said intensely. "We only bring highly skilled people into an operation such as this."

"Then find him," Kozlov barked, his head cocked angrily to the side. "Yuri thinks very highly of you, Dimitri, but a problem with this operation will not be tolerated, no matter how long you have been friends."

"I have already sent our best man to bring him back. His computer skills will be of no use in this situation."

Chapter 32

Apartment complex, Gaithersburg, Maryland

THEY HAD BEEN driving for less than fifteen minutes when they reached Melody Millar's apartment complex. Maria Soller was considering the trouble her brother and boyfriend had gotten themselves into when she snapped, "No, no, turn right here, Mom."

Her mother jumped at the sudden sound of her voice.

"Are you sure, honey?" Matilde Soller asked.

"Yeah, it's one of those crazy apartment complexes," she said, not wanting her mother to follow the instructions given by the car's built-in GPS. "It's like a maze. We can go this way and won't have to hunt for a parking spot. It's the way Etzy and I went there."

Mentioning his name increased the sense of urgency. Maria directed her mother through a few short zigzags until they came to a dead end flanked by two empty parking spots.

"See." Maria pointed across a short grassy field. "That's where she's staying. Their parking lot is always full. This way is much easier."

The narrow clearing offered a perfect view of the bottom-floor apartment. Its sliding glass door opened up into the connecting field.

"Is that her sitting on the couch?" Matilde asked.

A sense of relief began to run through Maria as she exhaled. "Yeah, I think so."

"Honey, it looks like she's fine. Let me go and check on her to make sure. She should come with us until we get this all sorted out."

"Are you crazy?" Maria said nervously. "She'll freak out if some random old lady comes knocking on her door. I'll go. Just keep a lookout, okay? It's really dark and this is kind of creepy."

Matilde Soller shook her head as if to wipe away the comment. "Maybe we should both—"

"No, Mom," Maria said. "I don't want you to scare her."

"Okay, honey, whatever you say." Matilde raised an insistent eyebrow and said, "But I want you to turn around immediately if anything doesn't look right. Okay?"

"Sure thing, Mom."

Maria made her way out the door and jogged across the field. She wrapped her knuckle softly on the glass door, but the television was on too loud for Melody Millar to hear her. The second time was louder, and the young woman looked up in surprise before hopping to her feet and walking to the door.

Melody slid the door open, the regret in her eyes apparent. "Hey, I'm sorry about Max," she said.

Maria fought back tears, and the two embraced for a moment.

"What are you doing here? I mean, with all that's going on..."

She pulled out her iPhone and showed her the message from Etzy without saying a word.

Melody looked up at Maria with tears welling in her eyes.

"I'm fine, but..." Maria started, and then breathed in deep. "Come with me, Melody. My mom is waiting for us in the car." She pointed to the other side of the field.

"I can't," she said starting to panic. "What if he tries to call me? I don't have a cell phone."

Bright lights from the parking lot forced Maria to shade her eyes with her hand. She wasn't sure what she should do. "Let me go talk to my mom. I'll be right back."

She turned and ran out into the dark field. Her eyes hadn't yet adjusted from the bright lights when she found herself sprawled out on the ground.

"Shh," she heard as she tried to see through the remnant spots of light to get her bearings.

"What are you doing, Mom?" Maria said, realizing they had just run into each other.

"Shh. Turn around and look," she said quietly.

Maria was scared. She'd never seen her mother like this. She turned around and saw five men exit three black SUVs and converge on Melody's apartment. "Holy shit..."

Maria got up and remained crouched down next to her mother watching in disbelief. The men quickly slid the glass door open and flashed some sort of identification as they surrounded the teenager. Two men had entered through the front door and were searching the rest of the apartment. They watched in horror as the men directed the young woman out the glass door and marched her to the waiting SUVs.

"That was too close, honey," her mother said. "Why didn't you bring her with you?"

"She didn't want to leave, in case Etzy tried to call. She doesn't have a cell phone, so..." she said with a disappointed look on her face.

"Poor thing."

"Oh my God, what do we do now, Mom? We've got to do something."

Chapter 33

Adams Morgan, Washington, DC

ETZY MILLAR WAS still reeling as he sat in the cab next to the assassin who had killed his friend. His mood had descended to beyond grim. His sister was the most important person in his life, although his girlfriend, Maria Soller, was becoming a close second. He couldn't believe the online account he used to try to get help was some sort of a setup. He couldn't think of any other way the man would have been able to find him. These were desperate times for the hacker.

Millar flinched when the killer's arm moved. He watched closely as the man wrapped his knuckles on the Plexiglas that separated them from the driver's compartment and said, "Take a right up here on Columbia and let us out in front of the park. It's three blocks up on the right."

The cabbie followed his instruction and pulled over. Millar read the sign: "Kalorama Recreational Center." There was a small building with a driveway.

The cabdriver turned his head toward the back of the cab and said, "That'll be eight dollars and ninety-three cents."

The killer flipped a ten-dollar bill through the hole in the divider. He glanced out the back window and clamped his hand firmly around Millar's arm. The hacker opened the passenger door and felt himself being ushered out.

"Remember, if you do anything stupid, your sister is dead," the killer scoffed as he guided him slowly down the narrow driveway.

Millar was scared and confused. The physical threat bearing down on him was minimized by the concern he had for his sister. He could feel a weapon violating the small of his back and had already resigned himself to expect the worst. He'd soon be joining his friend.

He could sense that the assassin was on edge. The cab had stopped three times on the short drive to this place, and he was certain something was about to happen. He felt like he was walking the plank in the dark trying to anticipate the moment he would fall.

His only consolation was that the killer hadn't searched him. His cell phone was still tucked into his back pocket, and it gave him a tiny glimmer of hope. He guessed he had sent the text message to Maria about fifteen minutes ago, thirty at the most, and he had no idea how she would react. He forced himself to consider the reality of what was happening. How Maria took the news didn't really matter. This was the man who killed Max, which to him meant he'd never see her again.

Their pace slowed as a small building appeared on the right. He noticed the killer's steps forward seemed more deliberate. He struggled to see into the dark of night, knowing they had reached their destination.

Chapter 34

HE WAS ON full alert. Trent Turner now knew the man who had hit his car was somehow connected to his brother's death, but the thing he couldn't work out was why the man had taken a cab. The vehicle moved slowly and had stopped a couple of times along the way. He was certain there was something more to this as he watched the cab pull over once again, this time to let the two passengers out. He had the feeling he had been invited to an impromptu meeting that he wasn't expected to leave.

Turner exited the cab and silently darted through a playground toward Etzy Millar and the man who had grabbed him as they entered the park. The operative zeroed in on the man who was manhandling the hacker. Despite his doubts about the situation, Turner knew this was his only chance to pick up Etzy Millar alive. He thought about why the suspect might leave himself so vulnerable and understood the killer's thinking. The assassin knew Turner would want to extract information.

The operative hopped a low fence and landed onto the narrow road. He changed gears to a full sprint and, as he approached his target, he could see the assassin holding a weapon against the hacker's waist. It was dark, and things were moving too fast to get a clear view, so he'd have to take a chance and go for it.

Turner lined up his shots, first knocking the weapon loose and then delivering a stabbing blow to the captor's rib cage. The assassin crumpled to the ground.

Etzy Millar clutched his laptop and ran toward the small building. The hacker fumbled with the doorknob, and when he found it was locked, his face turned to a mask of fear.

Turner looked down at the man on the ground as he struggled to straighten himself from the ball of pain he'd curled into. The operative smiled. This would be his first chance to use a new toy.

He took a step toward Millar and then saw someone emerge from the shadows of the building. He immediately recognized the man with the thin frame and Washington Nationals cap cocked to the side. It confirmed what he already knew. This was a setup.

The newcomer leveled his Beretta at Turner's head and said, "You're a fuckin' dead man now."

Turner knew instantly the man wasn't a pro. A professional would have taken him out from the shadows and skipped the Hollywood theatrics. The man looked scared and seemed to be waiting for further instructions.

The silence was broken by an agonizing groan from his friend on the ground. Turner had no doubt he was a man who would have already pulled the trigger.

"What the fuck are you waiting for? Kill him," Millar's captor coughed as he slowly regained his feet.

Trent Turner's eyes darted over to the assassin and then back to the gunman. He knew this was about to get ugly. He noticed a telltale squint followed by a slight lift of the gun's barrel.

Chapter 35

ETZY MILLAR'S HEART was pounding as the events unfolded in front of him. The pain from his ribs was washed away by the adrenaline coursing through his veins. He'd only seen one person killed before, and that was just yesterday. Millar was paralyzed by a potent combination of fear and confusion. He had no idea what was going on. He was having trouble wrapping his mind around this, but from the looks of it, things would soon turn deadly.

He had tunnel vision, and the constant throbbing of his heart intensified as the blood pulsed through his veins. He saw the killer bark out a command to the man in the baseball cap and then turn his attention back to the man who had come from out of nowhere.

A few moments went by before the assassin began to walk toward the spot where his weapon had landed. It was the loud groan the assassin let loose that brought Millar out of his trance. He watched the killer fall flat on his face and start to convulse. The next thing that invaded his senses was the sound of metal skidding across the ground. He looked down and saw the pistol in front of him at his feet. His sensory overload leveled off, and he instinctively traded his laptop for the gun. He looked over at the killer. He had stopped convulsing.

"Sizzle, sizzle," the stranger said with a smile.

The killer had a pissed-off look on his face. Millar was still confused, but the situation was becoming clear. He already liked the new guy.

"Okay," Millar said in a shaky voice. "Nobody move, or I'm just going to start shooting."

His hands were trembling, his eyes full of a crazed fear of what might happen if he blinked. He cycled the gun from one person to the next as he tried to figure out what to do next.

"Be careful, or your sister is dead," the killer coughed as he stood back up.

"Don't move," Millar said. He was visibly more nervous.

"Calm down, calm down. I'm just getting my phone. I'll move slowly. Just take it easy." The killer spat a mix of blood and saliva onto the ground and slowly took out his cell phone. "I have to make a call." He punched a number into his phone and raised the device to his ear.

"Who are you calling?" Millar asked, shifting his weight nervously.

He shot a cold stare at Millar. "If this conversation ends without me, kill the girl," he said into the phone.

A new wave of fear washed over Etzy Millar. It started at the back of his head and worked its way forward. "What are you doing?" he insisted.

The assassin pointed out the stranger. "Kill that man now, or your sister is dead," he said.

Millar's hands went from a tremble to a shake as he redirected the weapon, aiming at the man.

"You don't want to do that," the man said. "I'm here to help. He doesn't have your sister."

His voice was confident, and the expression on Millar's face turned to a deeper shade of confusion.

"Come see. You can speak with her," the killer said as he held out his phone.

He started to move toward Millar, and the stranger sent him a quick jolt that stopped him in his tracks, almost dropping the phone.

"Sizzle, sizzle," the stranger repeated.

Millar gave the stranger a questioning look.

"nsEP," he said with a wink. "A Nano-Second Electrical Pulse. Not something you'd want to attach to your balls." He looked to the killer as though he had a second thought. "Well, at least for most of us."

The killer tried to reach for the Taser leads in his back, but he zapped him again.

"Ah ah ah," the stranger said as he shook an angry finger back and forth. He turned to Millar and said, "Don't let him get near you. He'll take that gun away and snap your neck before you can blink."

The hacker turned the gun on the assassin and slowly reached into his back pocket to pull out his cell phone. "Stay there," he said nervously, and then rattled off a number for them to call.

The assassin shook his head in disgust and then spoke quietly into the phone as he stared down the hacker.

"I can't hear you. What are you saying?" Millar said, his voice panicked.

"Ease up. I gave him the number," the killer barked.

A few seconds later Millar's phone began to vibrate. He angled it toward his face to view the caller's number. It was bogus, all sixes.

"You'd better answer that, or they'll kill her," the killer said.

Millar fumbled to answer the phone. "Hello? Melody?"

"Kill him or she's dead," the caller said.

The words caused Millar's stomach to crawl.

"Do it now, or it's all over," the assassin ordered in a dark tone.

"I want to talk to my sister," Millar said, sounding desperate.

"You don't make the demands here," the caller told him.

The man's tone was patronizing, and his foreign accent made him sound even more sinister. He clamped the phone between his shoulder and ear and turned the gun toward the stranger with both hands. He squinted as he tried to squeeze the trigger.

"I heard that Etzy was looking for some help on the boards," the stranger said coolly. "It'll be tough to help you out if you put a bullet in my head."

Millar released the pressure on the trigger, unsure of what to do next.

"Kill him or she dies," the voice on the phone barked with a sense of finality.

It had been a long time since Etzy Millar's father had taken him to the range to shoot a gun like this. That was in happier times, before his father had turned into an alcoholic.

Nothing had happened the last time he tried to squeeze the trigger. He nervously turned the side of the weapon toward him and flicked off the safety. Millar would do anything to save his little sister. He took a deep breath as he prepared himself to go through with the deed.

Chapter 36

"LOOK OUT, MOM!" Maria Soller yelled.

Her mother swerved, narrowly missing a group of men in dark clothing. The two women sped out of the apartment complex, trying to make it to the exit in time to link up with the vehicles that had taken Melody Millar. They had barely made it.

Maria pointed to the right and said, "Look, they're over there."

"I see them, I see them," Matilde Soller confirmed. She stepped on the gas to close the distance.

Nerves augmented the frantic twists and turns in the road as they tried to keep pace with the SUVs at a distance. It wasn't long before they reached the Washington, DC suburb of Germantown and then the lightly traveled roads in the small community of Poolesville, Maryland. Both of them had been mostly silent as they concentrated on the trio of vehicles.

"Mom, turn off your headlights," Maria said. "You know, like they do in the movies."

Matilde glanced at her daughter and then back to the road. The farther they got from the city, the more deserted and rural the roads became. She doused the headlights, and a few turns later the three SUVs pulled into a long driveway.

"Pull over, Mom, or they'll see us," Maria said.

Matilde carefully pulled the car onto the grass on the side of the road and turned off the engine.

"Don't do that, Mom," Maria said nervously.

Matilde shot her daughter a quizzical look. "What?"

"Turn off the engine." Her voice was a panicked whisper.

"Why not, honey?"

"What if it won't start? Please turn it back on before they get out and can hear it start."

"Okay, honey. Don't worry, everything will be fine."

Matilde turned the key, and the engine came quietly to life.

Maria breathed a sigh of relief. "I'm not so sure, Mom. Did you see what just happened?"

"It's okay," she said firmly. "Calm down. I'll go have a look."

"Are you crazy?" Maria locked her fearful eyes with her mother's. She had sensed the doubt in her mother. "You're not fast enough to get out of there if they see you. I'll go. Just keep the car running, okay?"

Matilde's expression left no room for negotiation. "Absolutely not."

"Look, Mom, I'll call you and keep my cell phone on speaker. That way you can hear what's going on. Just don't say anything, or they'll hear you."

"No. Honey, we need to call my friend. This is already out of control. We can tell him where Etzy's sister is and let him work out how to get her out of there."

Maria shook her head no and said, "Mom, I'll just take a quick peek. I'll leave the phone on. Don't worry. I won't get too close."

A beam of light burned through the trees and killed their conversation. They both ducked down in a panic.

"Oh my God, it was one of those trucks." Maria was shaking with fear, and her pulse had quickened. "Do you think they saw us?"

"No. Just stay low." Matilde pushed her daughter's shoulder down.

The Mercedes's engine was practically silent, so they heard the sound of gravel crackling as the heavy SUV made its way down the driveway. The sound evaporated into the rev of an engine that then faded off into the distance.

Maria slowly began to peer over the dashboard, her eyes wide with fear. "Holy shit, that was close."

"You're not going near that house," she decided. "I need to make a call."

"I'll just be a minute," Maria insisted. "You need to stay here in case something happens. If we both go, nobody can get help."

In a single motion she dialed her mother's number, opened the door and dashed toward the line of trees surrounding the perimeter of the house. Slowly, she crept her way down the property line along the trees. Soller stayed perfectly still for a couple of minutes, straining to see or hear anything inside. She was about to run across the lawn into some bushes when she heard car doors slam shut. She froze in her tracks.

"Mom," she whispered into her phone. "Get down. I think another car is coming."

Chapter 37

Adams Morgan, Washington, DC

SWEAT POURED DOWN his face, and his hands continued to shake. The gun he gripped tightly was getting heavier by the second as the irony of the situation weighed on his mind. Etzy Millar now knew the man he saw down the length of the gun's barrel was there to help him. Every avenue leading away from killing a man in cold blood, especially this one, was blocked by the cruel realization that his sister's life was on the line. His mind raced as he considered what he believed to be inevitable. He was about to kill his only hope.

His trancelike state was broken by the vibration from his phone. There was only one other person who knew this number. He nervously removed a hand from the gun and took the device from his ear. He looked down at the display, and it confirmed what he had already been told. It was a text message from his girlfriend, Maria. The message was a single digit. He began to breathe again and swung the weapon toward the man with the baseball cap.

"Freeze, police!"

The words jolted Millar. He looked over to his left and saw an officer with his service revolver aimed directly at him, and froze.

"It's okay, Etzy, just relax. Everything's going to be fine," the stranger said. His voice was only loud enough for Millar to hear.

"I said, put the gun down!" the officer yelled again.

This time there was more urgency. Sirens echoed through the city in the background.

"I'm only going to—shit!" the officer yelled.

Millar watched the killer and his sidekick take off and then disappear around the side of the building. He tossed the weapon to the ground, and the police officer cautiously approached. The sirens grew louder, and the officer seemed to have more confidence, until the screeching sound of tires followed by the sound of scraping metal took center stage.

"Motherfucker!" the officer barked.

The cop watched the double-parked gray Chrysler 300 ram into his squad car several times. It was what had raised his suspicions enough to check out the park. With a final surge, the vehicle slammed his black-and-white into a line of parked cars on the other side of the street and sped off.

Before the officer could turn back to the two men, he found himself flex-cuffed to a railing.

"Sorry about this," the stranger said as he emptied the rounds from the policeman's gun. "Be safe out there."

Millar watched curiously as the stranger wiped everything clean and handed the weapon back to the officer. He then pocketed the weapon Millar had tossed to the ground.

"Grab your laptop," he said. "We need to get out of here."

He followed the stranger across the street, and within two minutes they had reached the hustle and bustle of Adams Morgan. They quickly ducked into a basement bar called Club Asylum. The place was small and dark, with exposed redbrick walls and a couple of pool tables crammed before its single bar at the far end of the room. He followed the stranger to one of the small tables that provided some privacy from the line of patrons situated along the bar. Millar was glad to be sitting again. He was getting used to the pain in his ribs, but it hurt like hell when he ran.

"Who are you?" Millar asked, noticing the stranger had positioned himself to keep an eye on the club's entrance.

"Trent."

He offered his hand, and Millar shook it nervously.

"Nice to meet you." Millar knew the man sitting across from him had everything under control, and it helped to calm him down. "So, what happens now?"

"That depends on you, Etzy."

Millar's voice was uneasy. "Look, I don't know what's going on. One minute we're driving down the road, and the next thing I know, Max is dead and…" His voice trailed off as he tried to regain his composure. "Max, he got shot, and then this guy comes after me, and I'm, like, holy shit, you know, what the hell is going on?" He thought about it some more and made sure nobody in the bar was listening. He wasn't sure what he should share but shook his head, knowing he had nothing to lose. "The same guy shows up at the hotel after I ask for help on the boards, and he says he's going to kill my little sister. I don't know what to do, you know? She's all I've got now." Millar stopped speaking for a long time. He was startled by the sound of a cue ball assaulting freshly racked balls.

"What happened?" Trent asked, his voice clinical like a doctor's. "What were you and Max Soller up to when he was killed?"

Millar looked down at the dirty floor and back up at Turner. His eyes were heavy. "That's the thing. You see it was just supposed to be some easy money. Max found someone on the boards online who wanted us to hack into computers and install this bot they'd developed." He turned his head to the side and stared at the wood-paneled wall while he got his thoughts together. "We had been doing it for the past couple weeks," he admitted, and turned back to the operative. "Max let me have the money so I could help support Melody. She's my little sister. He didn't need it. His family is set, you know, when it comes to money." He turned back toward the wall to think some more before he continued. "At first I was just happy that it would help me make ends meet, but, you know, if it seems too good to be true—"

"It usually is. Yeah, I hear you."

Trent's eyes moved to the entrance as a group of people came into the bar.

"After the first night of wardriving was done, I got a bit curious—you know, about what we were doing. You know, what the code did. What it was up to."

"Go on."

Millar got the sense this Trent guy would understand and said, "Well, luck isn't exactly something that follows me around, if you know what I mean?" He cleared his throat. "So I began to reverse engineer the code in order to figure out how it worked. It was the most sophisticated bot I'd ever seen, and I've seen a lot of—"

"I know," Trent said. "I'm a big fan."

They both smiled, and Millar kept going. "Well, at first I didn't know much about it. The easiest way to learn more was to build a new install package that would also deploy some code of my own—you know, in order to keep an eye on things while I tried to work out what they were up to."

"So you developed something that would spy on their bot?"

"Exactly!" Millar said. "But it was more than that," he continued enthusiastically. "I'm getting close to where I can extend their bot and inject my own code in order to take control of the computer if I need to." He looked over at the exit and back to Turner. "These people, whoever developed it, were hard-core paranoid."

"How so?"

"Before the malware would install on a system, it would check for software that an advanced user might use. If it saw anything that signaled the person might know a little something about technology, it prevented itself from being installed."

Turner furrowed his brow. "Interesting."

"Part of the deal was that we were supposed to make sure that certain stuff wasn't loaded on a computer before we did our install." He looked around again to make sure nobody was listening in. "For the past couple of days, I've been working with a virtual environment here," he said as he patted his laptop. "I'm trying to develop a way to propagate my code out to the rest of their botnet. The thing accepts new modules so they can extend its capabilities. Once I figure that out, I'll be able to see what they're up to and engineer a way to shut it down."

Trent creased his brow and asked, "How far along are you with that?"

"It'll take some work, but I've made a lot of progress. In the process I've figured out a lot of details about how the bot software works." Millar paused for a moment. "The bot is programmed to proactively cover its tracks in predefined scenarios."

"So it's a new breed of intelligent bot?"

"For sure," Millar said with a slow nod.

"Anything else?"

"Yeah. Last night one of the bots we installed scared the shit out of me."

"I'm going to need more detail than that."

"Look, I don't even know who you are. People have been trying to kill me. Before we go any further with this, I need to know that I can trust you."

The operative smiled expectantly.

"The way I see it," Millar continued, "I'm pretty sure I'll end up dead in a ditch at some point. The truth is I don't care, as long as my sister is okay."

The desperation came through in the hacker's voice.

"I'll see what I can do about that," Trent said.

Chapter 38

FBI black site, Poolesville, MD

HEADLIGHTS PIERCED THE darkness of the long gravel driveway. Special Agent Cathy Moynihan squinted as she observed the imposing convoy of SUVs approach. She was looking through what was once the kitchen window of a rural residence. The FBI had converted the home into a secure location—a place where they could conduct special business away from prying eyes. What happened at the black site stayed at the black site. At least that's what the agent she had spoken to said in so many words. He had instructed her to meet him here during their brief call.

She had just hung up her cell phone. It was her third attempt at calling FBI Director Frank Culder since he'd cut their last conversation short. It was annoying to say the least, but she wanted to pass along some new information about their murder suspect and discuss the safe house meeting. It turned out that Senator Soller's daughter may have been dating Francis Millar. It seemed an insignificant sliver of information at this point in the investigation, but it was her job to keep the director informed, and it was something she took very seriously.

"Okay, go ahead and get out," she heard one of the agents say.

She opened the side door to let them inside as one of the black SUVs turned around and made its way back down the driveway. Four men filed into the house with a frightened Melody Millar sandwiched in between them. They headed down the narrow staircase that led to the basement without so much as acknowledging her presence.

She noticed the young girl was in a state of shock. Her makeup had streaked down the side of her face, and she was already past the point of crying. Moynihan followed them down to the basement. It was split into three rooms. There was a large space with a table that led to a room that was for interrogation, and another that was for observation. The observation room had a bank of monitors connected to cameras that covered the interrogation room and the grounds outside. Two of the men ushered the teenager into the soundproof room, then stepped out and locked the door behind them.

"We'll let her sweat it out in there for a while," the team leader said.

She clenched her teeth at the base of the stairs, unable to take it anymore.

"Special Agent Moynihan," she said firmly, and held her hand out. "And you gentlemen are?"

All four of them gave her indifferent looks. After an awkward few seconds, the leader forced a smile.

"We could use some coffee. What do you say?" he said.

She recognized the voice. It was the man who had called earlier to give her the address.

"I'd say you're shit out of luck." She exaggerated a glance to the man on his right and then the two on his left, and said, "It doesn't look like your mother works here." She shrugged her shoulders. "Unless, of course, you keep her locked up in that room too." Moynihan twisted her lips and shook her head before adding, "Probably not. It looks like you just keep unruly prisoners in there." She locked eyes with the leader as the other three started to laugh.

He cracked a big smile. "Jake, Jake Sanders," he said. "You win. I'll get the coffee. I think you'll fit in with this bunch of monkeys just fine."

"I wouldn't go that far," she said, obviously disgusted.

Sanders shrugged his shoulders. "Sorry. You can't blame a guy for wanting a good cup of Joe. It always tastes like shit when I make it. Best to experience that on your own, I suppose." He pounded the front of his shirt with his fists. "It'll put a little hair on your chest."

"I might have to pass on that. I hear it can get expensive if you want to get that waxed, but I'll bet it saves you on your heating bills in the winter."

Sanders let out a big laugh. "Stay here, boys, while I get Special Agent Moynihan and me a brew."

The men laughed as Moynihan and Sanders headed up to the kitchen. One of them chimed in and said, "Word has it that Jakester's chest carpet is legendary."

They walked into the worn galley kitchen, and he turned to face her.

Moynihan looked Sanders in the eye and said, "So how long are you going to let that poor girl sit in there?"

He frowned and said, "She'll be ready in an hour or so. That would be my guess."

Moynihan was weary of this latest move by the FBI's leadership. She kept telling herself she needed to follow orders and trust Director Culder. She decided the director had to have clearance with other top brass before making moves like this. Telling herself that was a way of getting past this without placing the phone call she had been avoiding. "What if she doesn't talk?" she asked.

"Oh, she'll talk. Believe me, she'll talk."

Moynihan didn't like the sound of that. "You can't be planning to break a seventeen-year-old. She's just a kid."

Sanders rummaged through the cupboards and said, "We're not planning to, but Culder said this case has to do with national security. We have to find out what she knows." Sanders stopped his search momentarily to look her in the eye. "There's no choice, I'm afraid."

She could sense it wasn't something he was looking forward to. The fact that this case had to do with national security had taken her by surprise. She decided the less she said, the better.

"Understood."

"God damn it," Sanders barked suddenly.

Moynihan jumped. She was glad he didn't see her.

"It's fuckin' common courtesy in my book. Why can't people replace shit when they finish it off? Jesus." Sanders walked toward the staircase and yelled down, "Gotta pick up some Joe. Be back in twenty."

A group laugh roared back from the basement.

"Go fuck yourselves," Sanders blasted back.

"I'll drive," Moynihan said. "My car won't be as conspicuous."

Sanders smiled as the two made their way out the door to her blue Toyota Camry.

"Don't they give you a company car?"

"Not on the weekends. I'm not that important."

He laughed. "Hold on a sec."

He went to the nearest SUV, grabbed a folder from inside and hopped into her car. She turned her car around, drove down the driveway and made a right.

Sanders turned on the reading light and began to flip through the contents of the folder. "You know where the 7-Eleven is, right?" he said without looking up.

"I know how to get there." She noticed a Mercedes parked twenty meters from the end of the driveway and asked, "Are there many residents out here?"

His eyes remained glued to the papers. "Nah, not too many. It's a good place for this setup."

As they rounded a curve in the road, she saw another parked car. It was black with tinted windows. Two of its doors were open, and she noticed the dome light hadn't come on to illuminate the interior of the car.

"Did you see the two cars we just passed?"

"What?" Sanders looked up, but they'd already made it past the cars. "Ah, don't sweat it. We only bought one house, not the whole neighborhood."

She decided to drop the conversation. She didn't want to sound like an amateur.

Chapter 39

Club Asylum, Adams Morgan, Washington, DC

THEY STAYED AT Club Asylum long enough for their untouched beers to turn lukewarm. Trent Turner offered them up to a couple of scruffy bicycle couriers playing pool on the way out.

The two men headed northwest on Eighteenth Street toward Calvert Street and made their way to Connecticut Avenue, using the neighborhood when possible. The police would be on the lookout for two men, so Turner followed twenty meters behind the hacker. Appearing to walk alone, they would be less likely to raise any suspicions. Once they reached Connecticut Avenue, it was a short cab ride to the parking lot where Turner had parked his rental car.

Turner pulled the keys out and unlocked the door. When he glanced over at Etzy Millar, the hacker wore a look of disbelief.

Turner offered him a wry smile and said, "The Aston Martin is in the shop." He casually opened the door to the Ford Focus as Millar let out a nervous laugh.

"Sure, okay."

Turner turned to the hacker with a thoughtful glance and started the car. "So tell me. What did the message on your phone say?"

"Nothing."

"No, really. Something changed your mind about taking the shot back at the park."

"It was nothing. Literally." Millar smiled. "A zero. My girlfriend…" He paused for a long moment before he continued. "Well, I'm not so sure she's my girlfriend anymore, but she sent me a message to let me know my sister was okay." He looked over at Turner. "You know, it's binary. One means yes and—"

"I take it she sent a zero."

"Yeah, a 'no'. I taught her that, you know. It's at least fifty percent more efficient when you chat online or send text messages."

The operative smiled. Good programmers were always looking for ways to minimize the code.

"Well, I owe her one," Turner said. "It's been a rough couple of days. I'm glad I didn't have to test my reflexes."

"At least they don't have my sister."

Turner nodded. "That's good news."

"How did you know that they didn't have her?"

"It's just one of those things that come with the job. You're either good at it, or you don't last long."

"And what job is that?"

Turner smiled and ignored the question. "We need to call a friend of mine." He thought about how to approach explaining the protocol for the conversation and looked to Millar. "He calls me Finger. It's my call sign. We don't use real names around here."

"Seriously? What are you? Some kind of secret agent?"

"I wouldn't go that far."

Millar raised his eyebrows as if he knew he'd hit the nail on the head. "You say you don't use real names around here. Can you define here?"

Turner laughed. "Do you really want to know?"

"I'm not so sure, but I imagine it's probably a good idea."

"I was going to give you a little time to recover and adjust, but I'll fill you in if you think you're ready."

"Ready as I'll ever be."

The operative thought about it for a few seconds and said, "You can think of it this way. You're familiar with two worlds. You have the good old US of A. We've got a democratic government, laws, a culture, expectations. It operates around a mature system that keeps things stable and makes it a nice place to live."

"Sure, okay."

"The other world you know is virtual. Like the US, you've got both good and bad, but there's a lot more of the Wild West out there. You've got a whole community of hackers and the like who couldn't care less about laws, local or international. They're not worried about how they behave or the systems they destroy. Collateral damage means nothing to them." He stopped at a red light and again turned to Millar. "It's easier to wreak unfettered havoc on that which is not real."

Millar squinted questioningly.

"Let me explain," Turner said. "Did you ever think about the bots you were deploying? What the consequences could be for the owner of the computer you installed them on?"

"Not really. Well, at least not until all of this happened."

"Right. It wasn't real to you. It was an extension of your gamer mentality, and you think it's only the online world."

"Yeah, I suppose."

"I get it. It's much easier to detach yourself from the reality of what's going on when it's not physical. It's not something happening right there in front of you."

Millar thought for a moment and said, "I'm not sure what you mean."

"Think about it this way, Etzy. If you were forced to watch someone die every time you installed a bot, you'd have a lot more at stake emotionally."

Millar's expression showed surprise. "I'll say."

"It's easier to ignore the damage you're doing when you don't have to see the results. It's not too difficult to justify the act. Part of human nature is justifying your actions. Whether it's rational or not, a human will find a way to justify the things that bring them some sort of gratification." He kept checking his mirrors to make sure they weren't being followed. "This society is all about instant gratification. Think about professional athletes who cheat. How they deflect and attempt to minimize what they have done when they're caught. The common defense is to say everyone else is doping, so it doesn't meet their personal definition, or whatever their criteria is, for cheating."

"That's deep."

Millar thought about how he had justified installing the bots. It was easy for him to go along with Max. He was helping him learn about hacking, after all. Another upside was that he would pick up some extra cash and have the opportunity to learn more about the botnet. He told himself that was the only way to improve your skills at his level. You needed real-world experience, something that a classroom can't give you. There was some truth buried in there that made it easy.

Turner continued. "If you're forced in some way to experience the pain you cause, it's harder to keep on going with the lie."

"Yeah, I see what you're saying," Etzy admitted.

"There are a lot of people out there who don't think the way we do, like the typical American. For them, killing someone is only a means to an end. They don't think much about the act. Death, killing are a big part of life in some parts of the world. Making more dead people out of those who don't agree with you is simply getting terrorists one step closer to their objective."

"That's messed up."

"That's the way it is. They're motivated by the objective. Whether it's religion, power, revenge, the target is just something that's in the way. They don't think of people emotionally, as a person or people with lives, kids, parents."

Millar thought about the last twenty-four hours and said, "Shit."

"It's reality, Etzy, and you've landed smack in the middle of it." He had the hacker's undivided attention.

"I feel like I'm in a *Twilight Zone* episode, you know. It just doesn't seem like things could really be…people could really think that way."

Turner nodded with a laugh that had no humor. "The general public is insulated from what you've experienced." There was a slight pause before he said, "At least for the most part. When something slips through the cracks, things can get ugly."

The traffic light turned green, and they continued south down Connecticut Avenue.

"Once people get a taste of it, the unfiltered violence, or even a leak that exposes some of the things that are done in attempts to prevent it, they spit it back out. There's no appetite for doing what needs to be done." Turner shook his head, and his tone turned sharp. "There is this illusion that the world will simply listen when they say stop, and the greater good will prevail. That attitude develops because of their belief system, or from the reality they know. People only trust what they've been exposed to and what people they confide in tell them. It's human nature."

"So is that what you do? Provide insulation?"

"I guess you could say that."

Millar wasn't completely convinced. "It can't be that cut-and-dry."

"Tell that to your friend back at the park."

His eyes widened as he considered the killer's relentless nature.

"Do you think he gave a shit about your right to free speech? Your right to privacy?"

Millar shifted in his seat but didn't respond.

Chapter 40

TRENT TURNER PULLED the car over to the side of the road and turned to face Etzy Millar. He sensed he was losing him, and it was imperative that he understand exactly what he'd gotten himself into.

"I'll try to help you out with this, Etzy," he said flatly. "The only right that guy back there cared about was the right time to put a bullet through Max Soller's head without getting caught." He cocked his head to one side before he continued. "He wanted you dead too, but this time around he needed to keep you alive. At least long enough to find out what damage you might have done to their operation. After that, you were as good as dead."

The blood drained from Millar's face.

Turner checked for traffic, pulled back onto Connecticut Avenue and continued driving south. He sensed he had finally gotten through.

He glanced over at Etzy and said, "If it makes you feel any better, he wanted to kill me too."

"Super," Millar said unenthusiastically. "At least I'm not alone."

"Look, I have to tell you like it is. Assuming someone gives a shit about things they don't is the fastest way to get yourself killed. Keep that in mind. It will come in handy as we navigate through this together."

He turned to the hacker and saw that including him in future plans seemed to have had the intended effect. Millar's eyes now held a glimmer of hope.

Turner was done teaching Reality 101 and pulled out his XHD3. "By the way, if you tell the guy we're about to call my real name, I'm going to have to kill you." He shot Millar a wink and placed the call.

The phone rang once before Heckler answered. Trent turned on the speaker.

"Yeah, it's me."

"Hey, Heck. I'm here with Etzy. He's got some information for you."

"Good to hear. I've got some news on the dead guy you left in the hotel room."

Millar looked over at Turner. The hacker fidgeted in his seat.

"It's okay, Etzy. He was one of the bad guys," Turner said with a slight smile.

"Tell me what you know, Etzy," Heckler said.

Millar explained how he and Max Soller were paid to install the bots and had started to go into the technical details when Turner interrupted. He explained to the hacker that technology wasn't Heckler's strong suit, so Millar did his best to offer a low-tech version. Turner liked his handler's replacement but was starting to get frustrated.

"Heckler, we really need Tak to be the lead on this with Etzy. Is he back yet?"

There was an awkward pause before he answered. "No, Finger, he's not. The Shop's got it covered."

That wasn't news Turner wanted to hear. Tak was the obvious best choice for the job, and his absence raised serious questions.

"The guy in the hotel was a Russian called Aliaksandr Petrov," Heckler said over the uncomfortable silence. "Probably no shock to you that he was an assassin."

"Not really," Turner said.

"Well, he was a damn good one. You're lucky you're still alive."

Turner thought of his brother. "It depends on how you look at it," he said bitterly.

"The laptop had some good intel," Heckler continued. "Petrov didn't know who hired him. The guy he had looking into it sent him back a few accounts. We were able to find the remnants of an email message in the cache on his computer, and our new friends in Switzerland were happy to help us do a trace."

It was good to hear his new relationships overseas had already started to pan out.

"Great, what could they tell us?"

"The money originated from a Russian crime family in Chicago. The Kozlov Bratva. It's run by Pavel Kozlov. He was an up-and-comer in the former Soviet Union, has a lot of ties with the *siloviki*—the politicians from the KGB, GRU, SVR...the guys with the guns and intel."

Millar chimed in. "You know, the core framework for the bot was written by someone—well, more than one person—but a Cyrillic keyboard was used for a lot of it."

"Are you sure it was more than one person?" Turner asked.

"Yep. You can tell by the way they wrote their code."

Turner understood all too well. It was no different than comparing two handwriting styles.

"Off the top of my head, I'd say there were at least six, seven...maybe a couple more," Millar continued.

"They've got money," Turner said. "The guy in the park was no hacker, and he knew who I was. If they can hire a top assassin and then kill him, that tells us something."

"The one at the park was definitely the guy who killed Max," Millar said. "I'll never forget him for as long as I live." His tone seemed more relaxed. "Some data was passed through one of the bots we installed last night. The botnet looks like it's talking to the mother of all banks. The Federal Reserve."

Heckler laughed, but it was half-hearted. "What, are they going to destroy Wall Street? Madoff and the real-estate collapse already took care of that one."

Millar shrugged and said, "I don't know, but they're up to something."

"This recession has people scared," Turner added, realizing the importance of what Millar had said. "Unemployment is at an all-time high. Retirement accounts were demolished. It wouldn't take much to disrupt things, cause panic, have people lose what little confidence they might have left."

"True," Heckler considered. "By the sound of it, I'll need to send this all the way up the chain."

Turner knew that could mean problems with The Island, but for the first time since this ordeal began, things looked like they were lining up in his favor. His brother's killer was dead, and the people who hired him had something big brewing. He would like nothing more than to serve them up a heaping plate of fuck you and have his revenge.

"Like I told you, I've never seen anything this advanced," Millar said.

Turner nodded and said, "Yeah, run it all the way to the top, Heck."

"Hold on a sec," Heckler said.

Turner and Millar could hear a phone ringing in the background.

"Okay…yeah…I'll be there as soon as I can," he told the caller. "Something's come up. I have to go now," Heckler explained.

"Well, it looks like we're going on a road trip to Chicago," Turner said to Millar. "They know I'm involved now, and I'm sure they have no idea who I work for. Heckler, I'll catch up with you later. Let your bagman know I'm going to need him tonight."

"Sure thing," he said, and then disconnected the call.

"Bagman?" Etzy questioned.

"Don't worry about it."

Chapter 41

THE THREE FBI agents jumped up from their card game when the alarm sounded. The surveillance equipment had detected an intruder on the grounds. The older systems had given off false alarms in the past, but technology had advanced to a point with the various sensors—microwave, thermal, active and passive infrared—where it was rare. This was the real deal.

The men gathered around the bank of monitors and read the flashing message that indicated a pressure plate on the perimeter had been triggered. An infrared feed was automatically displayed on the center monitor and locked onto the suspect. The monitor displayed the image of a female slowly making her way toward the house.

"She doesn't look armed," Scott Richardson said. "You want to handle this one, Joe?"

"Fuck off."

"Come on, I think you can take her. She doesn't look like the type who'd kick a man where it counts," Richardson said with the grin of a true smartass. He was the senior man there.

Joe shot him a pissed off look. "I'll never live that down, will I?"

"Nope. And don't forget your cup."

The agent headed out the back door, up the stairs and bolted along the side of the house, putting a copse of shrubs between him and the intruder. His eyes had almost adjusted to the darkness by the time she had made her way past his location.

She approached the front window on the left side of the house. He waited patiently to make sure she didn't have a weapon. Satisfied that she was unarmed, the former football player quickly made his move.

Maria Soller let out a muted scream as she was lifted off the ground and carried toward the house. She started kicking her legs as they headed down the narrow stairwell that led to the basement.

"Put me the fuck down!" she yelled, banging her fists on his back.

The other two agents had formed a welcoming committee at the bottom of the stairs. Both men were already laughing.

"Mom, get out of here!" she yelled as they quickly pulled her into the house.

Joe put her down, and she looked as if she was sizing them up.

"Mom, huh," Richardson said in a mocking tone. "Ken, go see if Mom's out there too, will ya?"

"Fuck you!" Maria drilled her knee into Richardson's crotch.

The other two men laughed heartily as he crumbled into a chair with a groan. His face turned beet red.

"Put that bitch in the room with the other one," he barked.

Ken nodded toward the alarm that just popped up on the monitors. "I'll go ahead and check outside for Mommy," he said with a raised eyebrow.

He stopped at the base of the steps for effect and turned to Richardson. "Don't worry. I'll make sure I keep the jewels safe. I hear abuse is something that runs in the family."

He shot up the steps, leaving the door cracked open so it would be easier to bring their new guest inside.

Chapter 42

Safe house, Rosslyn, VA

TRENT TURNER TOOK a straight shot south through Washington, DC into Georgetown and crossed over the Key Bridge. He parked the Ford Focus in a quiet neighborhood less than five minutes from the bridge. He approached the townhouse on foot. Etzy Millar was told to wait at a bus stop half a block away while the operative made sure there wasn't unwelcome company inside. He was fairly confident the place hadn't been burned, but under the circumstances he wasn't taking any chances.

A few minutes later Turner returned for the hacker, and they headed to the safe house.

"We can get kitted up here for the trip," Turner said as Millar scoped out the place.

"I take it you're a minimalist," the hacker said, his eyes taking in the sleek decor. "Is this where you live?"

"Not exactly. Think of it more as a place I can go if I want to live." He smiled. "Come on downstairs."

Turner led them down a flight of stairs and into a sitting room. The entertainment center had a television flanked by bookshelves. He worked a couple of latches until one of the bookcases pulled out on a hinge to reveal a small armory.

Millar's eyes widened. "Holy shit! That's rad!"

Turner grabbed one of the blue duffel bags hanging inside and began to fill it up with gear.

"I'm going to have to head out for a couple of minutes," he said as he handed Millar a network cable and a device with an RJ45 connector on the side. He started packing again and said, "You can get online securely with this. Just plug in, and the device will find you a connection and hide your IP address using proxy servers, amongst other things."

Millar gave him a look of disgust.

"I know you're a pro, Etzy, but this saves a little bit of time and leaves you with no doubt about whether you're being traced. Trust me, it's worth it."

"I guess you're right. I'm still not sure how they found me at the hotel." He examined the device approvingly and then looked to the operative. "So what now?"

"We head to Chicago, and we dig deeper. Try to figure out what they're up to."

"How did you get into this? I mean, how does someone decide to become a techno spy or whatever it is you are?"

Turner laughed. "It's a long story. Maybe one day we can talk about it over beers." He looked up and smiled. "This time we'll actually drink them."

"Yeah, that would be cool. I could use one." Millar sat down on the couch before continuing. "So these people you told me about, The Shop. Do you really think they can help?"

Turner nodded confidently. "Absolutely. Tak is brilliant."

"Yeah, but Heckler said he wasn't working on this. You sounded pretty sure that he should be running things, especially with the bot traffic, you know, confirmed as going to the Federal Reserve. It seemed like you didn't think you got a straight answer on that."

Turner noted that Etzy could read him pretty well. "They're no doubt the best team out there. Even without Tak."

"If you say so."

"Look, I have to go meet someone so I can get our ride to Chicago taken care of."

"What's that?" Millar asked. He pointed at the toy-like object Turner was shoving into the bag.

Turner looked at the hacker. "This, my friend, is a PMD."

"A PMD?"

"Don't worry about it," Turner said, laughing. "You'll find out soon enough."

Chapter 43

"I CAN'T MAKE it," Senator Maximillian Soller said reluctantly.

The two men were cut from the same cloth, so he knew the caller wasn't about to give in.

"There's a lot on the line," Federal Reserve chairman Bart Stapleton said. "I think we'll need you to drum up support for this."

"How would it look after what's happened? Would that really be a good idea come campaign time? Think about it."

"Fly straight there and back. Nobody will even know you left. Sorry about your son, by the way. I know it's been a struggle for you. Not everyone can be molded into a politician, especially one of your caliber."

The senator shook his head in disgust. "He was starting to come around, spending a lot of time downtown." The politician had recently become hell-bent on making his son the heir apparent to his political empire. This made his recent death even more significant. "I let him use the room I reserve on Capitol Hill. That was what broke the ice. The hotel staff would keep track of his comings and goings for me, and it seemed he was finally showing some interest."

He stopped talking when he realized he'd said too much. Politics was a world where you had to keep your thoughts, and especially your emotions, on a short leash, even when it came to old friends. It was important to never show weakness or dwell on failure.

"I don't think anyone will ever be able to fill your shoes, Max. I've never met a man who could put people in their place as effectively as you."

Soller laughed at the compliment. How he loved to browbeat people. "I'd consider it a personal favor if you handle this. You'll have the others there to back you up. This thing in Iraq has dragged on longer than expected, and if we don't do something now, we stand to lose everything we've invested and gain some enemies if we don't deliver." He reflected for a moment on what he had left in life, and realized it was only his career. "They will know you have my proxy," he said, referring to The Group.

As innocuous as the name was, they seldom mentioned it in context. For anyone on the outside, The Group simply didn't exist.

"Your proxy will only be good if we can get the support we need. Sure, there will be a couple of us to work the room, but we already know there's no way the Russians will go for this. They'll want the situation to fall apart so they can sweep in and take over from where they left off. We'll need to swing everyone we can onto our side."

"Since when are the decisions made there democratic?" Soller was never shy about throwing the weight of the US contingent he controlled behind The Group's cloak-and-dagger decisions. Collectively, the men who represented his country there had more power over major corporations in the world than a sane man would find comfortable. "Please, Bart, do tell me you can handle this," he said with a hint of annoyance.

"There's a lot at stake here," Stapleton said flatly.

"I have full confidence you will come through. They will respect you as they do me. If not, we'll work out how to make up our losses in other ways. I can't do it this time."

Soller knew this deal with The Group meant much more to Stapleton than it did to him. Power was money, and taking care of their would-be friends in the oil industry was something he knew the chairman had hoped would set him up for life.

"Then I'll fill you in when I return," Stapleton said, and then paused thoughtfully for a moment. "You do realize this will be the first time a Soller hasn't been present in more than half a century."

The senator cringed at the thought. He was starting to feel the magnitude of what that meant. He would be the final Soller to be a part of a group conspiracy theorists had been trying to expose for decades. He lamented the fact that his daughter, Maria, wasn't an option, based on long-standing tradition. The Group would never allow a woman representative, not even if she was a Soller. In his eyes, his wife had failed him by giving birth to a male who was uninterested in politics. Bitter didn't even begin to describe his feelings toward the bitch.

He drew in a deep breath and said, "Yes, I do."

Soller ended the call and considered the conversation. His thoughts immediately drifted to his son. Anger began to pool inside as he thought about the importance of what would now be lost. Power, tradition, the very foundation that his life had been built upon. Somebody would pay for what had happened.

His mood escalated from ruthless to evil as his phone began to ring. He recognized the caller and answered the phone by saying, "Speak."

"We've got something on him now," FBI Director Frank Culder said.

Soller tightened his grip on the phone. "Who?"

"Max's *friend.*"

"Really, and what would that be?"

"His sister. Our special arrangement has just escorted her off the radar," Culder confirmed.

"Will that bring him to you?"

"I think so. I had someone who wasn't on the team checking things out. I couldn't risk sending one of the men. We need to keep a low profile. She said the two of them were very close."

"She...who?"

"It doesn't matter. No one important. I'll take care of it. I'll make sure nobody comes sniffing around."

"What has she told you about her brother?" Soller's tone was dark. "I want you to find him. Do you understand me, Culder?"

"We'll get Millar, don't you worry about that."

"Good. I'll make sure it's worth your while," the senator said, knowing his lapdog had been waiting for an opportunity like this to move up the food chain.

"We're on it," he said with a smile coming through in his voice. "It won't be long."

"Do it privately, Frank," he said, his use of the director's first name underscoring the importance. "I want him to feel maximum pain. Maximum suffering."

"We won't let the press know about Millar. You'll have what you want soon enough."

Chapter 44

THE FBI AGENT took the stairs two at a time as he went to investigate the alarm. There was a hint of laughter in the air, which served to lighten what would otherwise have been a serious mood. He smiled as he thought about Scott Richardson being kneed in the balls. The FBI agent's guard was down, and a part of him almost looked forward to the pending confrontation with the girl's mother.

Ken didn't have a chance to register the shot the suppressed pistol spat out. It signaled the start of the 9 x 18 mm Parabellum round's deadly journey into his forehead. The man used a Makarov, a nostalgic choice, yet a capable weapon. A thud marked the FBI agent's body hitting the ground.

The four soldiers had anticipated that an alarm would be triggered. They had seen the convoy of SUVs emerge from the apartment complex when their first attempt to collect the girl they had been following failed. The sudden presence of the vehicles meant something these particular individuals were all too familiar with: the FBI was involved. The men were collectively confused, almost entertained, by the carelessness of the man they had just snuffed out. The last thing they had expected was to be shooting fish in a barrel.

The recent development meant the two women inside the house were connected in some way. The looming question was whether or not it was by a common thread they should be concerned about. It was made

131

abundantly clear by the man who sent them that no mistakes would be tolerated. The girl was to be taken alive.

For the past week they had worked in pairs to keep track of her movements. They knew her as the girlfriend of a person of considerable interest. She would be used as leverage if it was needed. Earlier in the day, they were told to bring her to a location nearby. Something had gone wrong, and now they needed that leverage.

The former Spetsnaz soldiers were ordered to be discreet, but this was an occasion where they were required to improvise. Extreme violence was necessary, and the accompanying adrenaline rush provided a familiar high. The men had been on high alert, having nearly been run over by their target's companion when she had sped out of the apartment complex. It was a nervous few minutes for the Russians. They quickly determined the action wasn't caused by their presence but rather the FBI's abduction of the other female.

They split into pairs and circled the home. There was no sound as the first man descended into the stairwell that led to the basement. He noted the door was propped open and signaled for his partner to follow him down. He pushed the door open and went in low. The Russian drilled rounds from his Makarov into the FBI agents before they could react. It was over in an instant.

The flurry of carnage gave way to screams of horror from the two young women huddled together. An angry look from one of the Russians commanded their silence. The blood-spattered walls wept as the bodies on the floor leaked their last remnants of life.

"I love you, Mom..." Maria said.

It was almost a whisper, but one of the soldiers heard her words. "Both of you, quiet!" he barked.

The heavy Russian accent amplified Maria Soller's fear. She could sense these men were different than the others and prayed that her mother had gotten away. One of them quickly confirmed her assessment by shoving his weapon into Melody's temple.

"Do you have something else to say?" he asked, with a menacing look in his eyes.

Soller quickly shook her head back and forth. She had fallen into a state of shock.

The killer motioned toward the stairs and said, "Come."

One of the assassins led them past the bodies and up the stairs. They headed toward the road, and Soller nearly tripped over the dead agent on the lawn.

Her fear increased as they approached the road. She secretly checked her iPhone and saw that the battery was dead. Her heart raced as they approached the line of trees that separated the property from the road. Each step brought her closer to knowing her mother's fate and whether she should have any hope.

Chapter 45

Englewood neighborhood, Chicago, IL

TIME WAS A funny thing, Dennis Zander thought. When you're enjoying yourself, it goes by so fast, but the opposite is true when all you want is for something to end. The hacker was coming to the realization that time passed at a relentless pace when people were trying to kill you.

He had left the Bratva's Chicago base late this afternoon, and the hours since had felt like seconds. The hacker had been watching his apartment building for the past thirty minutes, and he didn't see anything that looked suspicious.

The bar he'd taken refuge in was dark and dingy, and the stench from stale beer and ammonia was uncomfortable. Reruns of outdated TV shows played on a battered television perched atop a makeshift stand on the right side of the room. Zander was sitting at one of three small tables in the front, next to the windows that looked out onto the road. There were three additional large tables set up on each side, and the bar stretched across the far end of the room opposite him, ending at a single door that led to the dingy bar's solitary bathroom.

He calculated how long it would take to run up the three flights of stairs to the apartment he shared with another member of The Collective, and figured it would take just over a minute to make it inside from the bar. He and his roommate had both been strong-armed into working for the Kozlov Bratva, and sharing a room was one of the few bright spots in a situation that had become progressively worse. He couldn't believe he had grabbed the wrong laptop when he took off this afternoon. He wasn't sure what he was waiting for. If Dimitri Sokov wasn't onto him already, he knew he would be soon.

The hacker felt the waitress's presence behind him. She started cracking her chewing gum again. This would be the third time she had invaded his personal space since he'd sat down at the table near the front window.

"What'll it be?" the waitress asked. Her tone was insistent.

He turned to look at her this time. "Uh, nothing. I'm fine." He turned back to the window so he could keep an eye on the apartment building.

"Aw, well isn't that just terrific," she said. "You're fine. Just fine."

From the time he'd arrived, Zander could sense that he wasn't welcome in New Generations Lounge. He figured the sentiment was par for the course in the armpit of Chicago's Englewood neighborhood.

He let out a muted laugh as he considered making a remark about her clientele's collective IQ, but decided being a smartass wouldn't be the brightest move. Instead he said, "Really, I don't need anything."

"This is my table," she yapped, placing her hands on her waist. "How am I supposed to earn a living with an inconsiderate prick like yourself taking my space, ergo my tips?"

Zander looked around the room. She was the only employee there, and the place was practically empty. There were three hard-looking locals sitting on stools at the bar, and each shot him a gaze that oozed violence.

He shifted nervously in his seat and said, "Look, lady, there's nobody here. I don't see the prob—"

"Dwayne, do you hear how he's talkin' to your woman?"

Zander watched a hulking man with a pockmarked face push himself away from the bar and take three long strides toward him.

"You disrespectin' my woman, boy?" Dwayne said with a scowl.

He reached for the hacker with violence in his eyes.

The grip he had on Zander's shoulder was painful enough for him to break a sweat. "No, no…it's cool," he said.

"It's not cool," Dwayne shot back, and lifted Zander up off of the chair.

He needed to think fast, or he'd end up with a first-class beating. He jammed his foot into the ringer's slot of a wheeled yellow mopping station next to him and wrapped his legs around the man.

"What are you doing, punk?" Dwayne barked as the yellow bucket rolled behind him.

Zander thrust both hands into the man's face. His flailing motion caught the man by surprise, and the squeezing motion from his legs wedged the metal handle for the mop ringer between the brute's legs.

The meathead began to lose his balance.

"You little fucker," he yelled as they both started to tumble backward over the rolling yellow bucket. He released his grip on the hacker and tried to catch his fall.

Zander managed to stay on his feet and latched on to the table to regain his balance. He watched the beast crash to the ground, then grabbed his backpack so he could make a break for the door. He threw the door open and sprinted across the street to his apartment building, pushed through the entrance and ran up the stairs to his apartment. He fumbled for his key and entered as quickly as he could, before locking the door behind him.

"Dennis."

It was a deep voice, definitely Russian.

"Where have you been?"

He was still out of breath and realized he had jumped from one fire into another.

"Man, you scared the shit out of me," was the only thing he could think to say.

The Russian pushed his chair back so it was on two legs. "Do you have something to hide? Is that why you're scared?"

"No," Zander said. He turned the light on so he could get a better look. "It's a rough neighborhood."

Zander recognized the man's face. He was one of the soldiers who normally guarded the server room. He didn't have his gun out, but given the fierce look in his eyes, he didn't need one. The hacker focused on trying to act normal.

"We need to take a ride. Dimitri would like to speak to you."

The potent combination of pressure and fear challenged his concentration. "Sure thing," he said as he switched the laptops. "I was just heading back there anyway." He forced a smile. "I realized I grabbed the wrong computer on my way out." He decided he'd try to sound excited. "I've got some great news. I finally fixed that bug I've been working on. Can you believe it?"

The Russian wasn't affected by his words and motioned Zander toward the door. "Let's go."

They headed down the stairs and then outside.

"This way to the car," the Russian said with a shove to the left.

Zander knew once he got to his car there would be no way out.

Chapter 46

Island Industries satellite office, Reston, VA

"CALM DOWN, MATILDE, I can't understand a word you're saying," Addy Simpson said in a calm but deliberate voice. He had spoken to Matilde Soller infrequently after she'd married his old college rival, but each time she reached out to him it was for something significant. He tapped his index finger on his desk. His other hand held his cell phone to his ear.

"They took my baby, Addy," she said, sobbing uncontrollably. "They took my baby. She's all I have left!"

"Who, Matilde? Who?"

"I don't know. I just don't know."

He had never heard her so terrified.

"People are dead. She was screaming. They tried to get me, but I got away."

"Who's dead?"

Matilde's voice was desperate. "I...I don't know. God, they better not hurt my baby."

The news filled him with anger. "Who tried to grab you?"

"I don't know, Addy. They came at my car while Maria was checking the house. She wanted to see if she could find out who they were."

"Hold on a second, wait," he said. He needed to calm her down. "Bella, you're losing me. Where are you?"

"I'm driving," she said.

"Okay. Take some deep breaths and start over from the beginning."

Simpson hadn't called her Bella since they had been dating in college. He hoped doing so would slow down her panicked thoughts and help to ground her.

He told her to pull the car over to the side of the road to collect herself, and then she gave him the details about everything she could remember. She explained how the phone had cut out, and that it had happened just after she had driven away. She said it sounded like they were leaving the house at the time.

"Does your car have a GPS?"

"Yes."

"Good. Tell me about the house. I'll have an analyst examine the waypoints from your car."

"It was offset from the road, surrounded by trees in a very quiet area. It had a long gravel driveway. Someone left in a car just before Maria went to take a closer look. It wasn't one of the SUVs. I'm not sure what kind of car it was."

"Do you know how many people were in there?"

"No. I heard several different voices. The men that went inside after they grabbed Maria sounded Russian."

"Russian? Are you sure?" He could sense she was reliving the event in her mind, and winced.

"I don't know for sure. Their accents were pretty thick, but the phone cut out and…" She paused, and he could hear her try to reel in her sobs before she continued. "And they said they wouldn't kill them if they cooperated." Despair had crept into her voice by the time she added, "She said she loved me, Addy."

There was an uncomfortable silence.

"It was the last thing she said to me. I was too scared to tell her I love her too."

He heard her sobbing and then try to regain control.

"I didn't want them to know I was listening," she said.

"Don't worry, Bella. I'll find her. You did the right thing. Does Max know you've called me?"

"No."

Simpson knew how to handle her husband. He'd been doing it for years. First he got the best of him on the field, and then, despite the man's attempts to bring him down, in Washington. It was a jealous rivalry that ran deep. The senator had gotten the woman in the end, but he was never able to steal her heart.

He used the phone on his desk to confirm the Poolesville location with an analyst at The Shop. It pained him to hear her crying in the background, and just before he relayed the news, she spoke.

"I'm sorry, Addy." There was a deep sadness in her voice. "For everything."

Leaving him when he had finally achieved his goal of becoming a Navy SEAL, she had once told him, was her biggest regret in life, and marrying Max Soller two years later was a close second. Her husband had cost Simpson his post at the CIA, and when she found out about what the senator had done, it was the beginning of the end of their marriage. Maximillian Soller was a powerful politician, and the couple had stayed together, first for the children, and then for appearance's sake. That, she confided in him, had been another mistake.

Simpson closed his eyes and took a deep breath before finally saying, "There's no need to apologize, Bella." He needed to compartmentalize and treat this like any other operation. "Maria needs you to be strong and keep your head clear. Let me know if you think of anything else. Anything," he insisted.

Chapter 47

Dulles Airport, Northern Virginia

THE AIRPORT WAS light on travelers for a Saturday evening, which would make it easier for Trent Turner to spot anything out of the ordinary. Heckler put Etzy Millar in contact with technology assets at The Shop before they headed to the airport, and under the circumstances, the fact that someone else knew their itinerary made the operative a bit uneasy. He used a kit at the townhouse to create a new driver's license for Millar, and the hacker was now Jerry Rask, someone with the same birth date and age to make things easier. The Shop had made sure everything would check out when his ID was scanned into the airport's computer systems.

"Okay, Etzy, are you ready for this?"

"Yeah, I think so."

"Do you remember the signals for the cameras?"

"Yeah, you'll be like a third-base coach."

Turner laughed. "I'll try to be a little more discreet than that. We don't want the cameras to scan our faces, or we might end up having some company."

"Are you sure they have facial recognition?"

"These days they can recognize people by their walk."

"So let me get this straight," he said, pulling his baseball cap down. "I go first, and if I get searched at the checkpoint, you'll be behind me or mess with your stuff until I'm clear, and if you get searched I should keep going toward the gate but find a place to wait for you so you can point out the cameras."

"That's right. If I'm searched, remember to keep your head down until we link up." Turner put a firm hand on Millar's shoulder to calm him. "Just take it easy. It'll be fine. Remember what I told you about being anonymous. It works. You can become invisible."

"What about the bag?"

Turner winked. The hacker's smile told him he'd finally put it together.

"Bagman. I get it."

Turner dropped Millar off at the departures area and drove to short-term parking. Less than five minutes had passed when Turner casually strolled past him and led them to the ticket kiosks. He made sure the machine spit out the hacker's plane ticket after he scanned in his new driver's license.

They headed toward the security checkpoint. The operative used the reflections in the massive windows to make sure they were in the clear and that Etzy recognized his signals. He stopped to adjust his bag so the hacker could go through the security-checkpoint line first, as planned. Both men emptied their bags and placed their electronic devices, jackets, belts, and shoes into plastic containers. Turner was concerned with the amount of cameras that canvased the checkpoint area and hoped Millar would do a good job of keeping his head down.

The fact that Francis "Etzy" Millar's name had been kept out of the headlines made their trip through the airport easier, but there was a bigger problem brewing, based on Cannibal's latest report. It had revealed that the top man at the FBI had been purposely holding back information about his presence at the murder scene. Millar was already nervous enough, so the development wasn't something that Turner wanted to share just yet.

He overtook Millar on their way to the gate so he could identify the cameras. He took the seat with the best vantage point when they arrived at the gate, and Millar sat across from him without making eye contact. The slog through the cameras was over. Now it was time for the nerve-racking part. Turner stood and placed a newspaper on his seat.

"Excuse me," he said to the elderly woman sitting next to him.

"Yes?"

He gave her a warm smile and said, "I'll be right back. Could you please make sure the plane doesn't leave without me?"

"Of course." She laughed, before her expression changed to one of concern. "Don't you fly much?"

"No, ma'am. I try to keep my feet on the ground."

She smiled. "They don't wait for anyone these days, so it's best for you to hurry back."

Turner bowed his head in thanks and grabbed his bag before heading down the corridor to take care of business.

Chapter 48

Englewood neighborhood, Chicago, IL

EVERY COUPLE OF steps he felt a push to hurry him along. Dennis Zander was walking as slowly as he could, and his Russian chaperone was clearly getting annoyed. They were headed toward South Halsted Street, where he assumed the Bratva soldier's car was parked, when he had an idea. It was crazy, desperate even, but he wasn't exactly drowning in options.

Zander looked up at the Russian and said, "Hey, can we take care of my car really quick? I don't want it to get towed." He didn't even own a car, but he hoped the Bratva man wouldn't know that.

The Russian ignored him.

"Look, man, if it gets towed, I'll be up shit's creek. I've got a bunch of unpaid parking tickets, and I don't want this to turn into a mess. The cops might put me on the radar and start asking around, you know. They're real assholes at the place I park it, so things could get ugly."

He watched the Bratva soldier's face as he considered the request. Zander knew that back in Russia the police had no problem making life miserable for less, so he hoped the soldier would want to stay clear of any kind of police involvement.

"Okay, but I will go with you," he said.

"Sure, you can help smooth things over." He couldn't help but smile. "It's this way."

Zander directed them across the street and headed for the building on the corner.

"It's parked out back," he said. "Hopefully they won't be too pissed off. They can get a little testy in this place."

Not much had changed at the New Generations Lounge since his unceremonious exit. There were now two men sitting at the bar instead of three. The third, Dwayne, was being attended to by his waitress girlfriend behind the bar. Nobody turned around at the sound of the door chime, so Zander walked straight to the bar.

The Bratva soldier had stopped a few feet short and quickly became engrossed in the *Miami Vice* episode that was on the television. Zander made it all the way to the bar and still no one had bothered to acknowledge his presence. He knew Dwayne's fuse would burn fast, and he planned to take advantage of it. A chase scene was blaring on the television, so the hacker kept his volume low enough so the Russian wouldn't be able to hear.

"Hey. Hey, Dwaynie boy," he goaded. His smart-assed tone drew scowls from the couple behind the bar, and he motioned his thumb back indicating the Russian. "My buddy here has no problem taking care of your pussy ass for me." He looked over at the two men sitting on stools with half-full pint glasses in front of them. He could feel the tension rise the moment he engaged them, and decided the more the merrier. "He said he'll take out your asshole friends too. You might want to let him finish watching his TV program, though, or you'll really piss him off."

"Your ass is fucking dead!" Dwayne yelled.

Zander backed up enough to position the Russian between them and feigned a look of surprise. He looked to the soldier and said, "I think they're a little upset about the car."

Dwayne's face reddened as he began to charge from behind the bar. The other men jumped up from their stools and waited for their friend to take the first shot. Dwayne didn't have a chance. The Russian was lightning quick and landed a blow that shattered his nose and sent him straight to the ground.

His friends began to charge the former Spetsnaz soldier, and Zander took the opportunity to make a break for the door. His forward progress stopped suddenly. He felt the straps of his backpack pulling him backward and tried to shake loose, but the soldier was too strong. He was ripped back violently, but the Russian's sudden change in attention provided the opportunity the other men needed. The two who had been sitting at the bar tackled the soldier to the ground, and the trio landed with a sickening thud.

Zander shook himself loose and turned to see the waitress standing behind the bar with her hands on her head. Cracking sounds and grunts erupted from the violent mass on the floor, and then the motion stopped.

The hacker was frozen as the Russian stood up. His face was bloody, and his clothes were torn. Zander trembled violently, and his heart thumped. His legs felt like they were glued to the floor. The soldier took his first step toward him, when a shrill scream demanded their attention.

The waitress launched herself through the air like a wild cat and sank her teeth into the Russian's face. The hacker felt like he had been transported into some kind of zombie flick and quickly scrambled out the door and took off into the night.

Chapter 49

SENATOR SOLLER HAD been in his office for most of the day and through the evening. The Director of the FBI had just filled him in on a new development in the case concerning an incident at a Dulles Airport TSA security checkpoint. His anger had risen to a boiling rage as he paced back and forth. His cell phone broke the silence, and when he saw the number on the display, he was ready to unleash his fury.

"What do you want?" he said coldly.

"Someone has taken Maria," Matilde Soller said with a hint of panic.

The senator fumed as he processed the information. There was no compassion left in the man.

"What the hell are you talking about?"

"Her boyfriend was with Max when he was killed. Nobody knows that."

"She was dating Francis Millar?" the senator said angrily.

"Yes. You know?" she asked, sounding confused.

He gritted his teeth and said, "I do now."

"He asked us to check on his sister. When we went to see if she was okay, some men took her away." There was desperation in her voice. "I had to call Addy. He's going to help."

"You stupid bitch!" Maximillian Soller yelled. "Do you even know that man anymore?" His face turned to a scowl. "I'll tell you the answer. You don't!"

He put this information together with the news the FBI director had just given him, and he was sure his lifelong enemy was involved. The thought of the man targeting his children and then pulling the wool over his dipshit wife's eyes enraged him.

She breathed in audibly. "You don't understand—"

"No, *you* don't understand." He clenched his fist, and his face reddened. "If you knew half of what I do about your would-be boyfriend, especially with what I was just told, you'd slit his throat yourself!"

"Did you hear me?" she said loudly so he couldn't interrupt. "Some bastards took our daughter! All you can think about is your poor, jealous, deflated ego. You're pathetic!"

"You wouldn't know pathetic if it smacked you in the face, woman," he yelled. His temper was beyond the point of no return. All he cared about now was getting in the last word. "Gullible as you are, you shouldn't find it hard to believe that your Mr. Perfect has his hands in all of this. And I'll tell you another thing, I'm going to take him down if it's the last goddamn thing I do. Don't you worry those sagging cheeks of yours: I'll make sure the FBI knows what's going on and acts accordingly." He shook his head defiantly and spitefully ended the call by saying, "You two deserve each other."

His breathing was heavy as he fought the urge to smash his phone against the wall, but he stopped short, knowing he would need it for his next call. He barely interacted with his children, but they were his, so the fact that Addy Simpson was using them to get back at him wasn't terribly surprising. He resolved to make this their final battle, and he planned on winning. He punched the screen on his phone, and the man picked up on the first ring.

"Yeah," FBI Director Culder answered.

"I want you to take him and his organization down." His voice was seething with hate. "I don't care what you have to do, but make sure you get it done."

"I know, I'm working on it," Culder said.

"Simpson and his goons have taken my daughter," he said, the paranoia creeping into his voice, even more so than during their previous call.

"What are you talking about?"

"My bitch wife called, and our daughter's been taken," Soller spat. "The fucking bitch called him for help."

"Any details on what happened?"

"No, but you can damn well be sure you'll find her when you find Millar. No question about it. She told me my daughter was dating that bastard, and now that we know he's on Simpson's payroll..." There was a long pause as he considered the implications of the sighting at Dulles airport. "It's not rocket science," he said confidently. "He's fucking with my life, and he'll damn sure regret it."

Soller decided Culder wouldn't be too surprised about Simpson targeting his kids. He knew the director had seen crazier things when it came to the actions of politicians and spooks, and this went beyond that—the hatred between the two men was personal.

"Understood," the FBI director said. "I have the goods for just such an occasion." He couldn't help but smile at the timing of it all. "You've always said this day would come."

"Can our special friends make it to the airport in time?"

"If he's not there already, he should be any minute."

"Don't call me unless it's good news."

Chapter 50

Dulles Airport, Northern Virginia

LESS THAN FIFTEEN patrons were scattered throughout Moe's Grill & Bar. Trent Turner looked them over carefully from a distance, feigning interest in the posters on display and the flat-screen TVs bolted to the wall. He didn't see anything out of the ordinary. The man sitting alone at the table in the back had everything set up as expected. It was a go. This would be the big test for Heckler. Trent knew it would be easy to set him up here, if that had been his intention.

Turner placed his bag on the ground and pretended to send a text message. In the corner of his eye, he saw the man casually pull out enough cash to cover his bill and pick up his large earth-tone carry-on. Turner headed to the men's bathroom in search of a pair of empty stalls. Once he decided on the location, he entered the stall on the left and latched the door behind. He placed two squares of toilet paper on the floor just inside his stall as someone approached. The footsteps stopped before they reached him. He heard a loud cough, and the operative cleared his throat in response. The man entered the adjacent stall.

Two other stalls in the long row were occupied, which gave Turner some cause for concern. He'd have to play it by ear. Another cough erupted from the stall next to him. Turner tapped his foot just before sending his bag under the divider. It was quickly pulled in by the man on the other side. He heard footsteps as new patrons filed in the restroom. Turner waited, somewhat amused by the gurgling soundtrack of a bad meal playing a few stalls down. He had to question whether it could be a distraction, but if it was real, at least the smell of bleach was strong.

A toilet flushed as footsteps approached. The man stopped in front of Turner's stall, seemed to survey the place and headed back to the other end of the bathroom. Turner waited anxiously as he listened to the rustling sounds from the stall next door. He smiled as the expression "Getting caught with your pants down" came to mind. He heard another cough and responded by tapping his foot. He grabbed the blue bag on offer. It was identical to his but weighed significantly more. He made a quick check of the contents as the bagman left the bathroom, then quickly followed suit.

Turner walked through the terminal toward his gate, and a sense of relief rushed through him now that Heckler had come through. He still had plenty of time to kill before his flight left, so he sized up the Starbucks in front of him. Lack of sleep had started to dull his mind, so caffeine seemed like a good option. He stood in line and turned around when he sensed someone close behind him.

Their eyes met and he felt a jolt of electricity. She was tall, beautiful, with long black hair, but her bright green eyes were what threw him off.

"Hi," he heard her say.

He had already averted his eyes, knowing they had given away too much. Curiosity pulled with the force of a black hole as he casually glanced in her direction. He had hoped she was talking to someone else, but she wasn't.

"Hi," he replied with a forced smile, and then turned to the menu on the wall behind the counter.

He exhaled slowly and tried to erase the image of the striking beauty from his mind. A half smile formed when he considered the crazy thoughts going through his head. It was like he was in the fourth grade again, having a crush at first sight. There was no way she had felt what he did, although it felt good to imagine she might have, if only for a moment. Sleep deprivation could do funny things, and he banked on his pending conversation with the barista to bail him out of any potential for small talk.

"A venti iced mocha. No whip, please," he said.

"A man after my own heart," the green-eyed beauty said.

She looked at him appraisingly.

Trent Turner was an attractive man, fit, his hair dark, like hers. He dressed stylishly, but his look was equal parts restraint and refinement.

Turner exhaled. He couldn't believe she was still talking to him after the obvious blow off. He wasn't sure which was worse: being uncomfortable with her persistence or being intoxicated by her beauty. He turned toward the young woman and noticed the violin case slung over her shoulder. Their eyes locked, and he felt it again. The hairs on his neck began to tingle, and he considered for a moment that his thumping heart meant the connection might be real.

His eyes drifted back to the violin case and then met hers. "The heart is the only broken instrument that works," he said, before heading to the pickup counter.

He could sense she was alone. Perhaps a kindred spirit. His goal was to get her off his mind by the time his drink hit the counter. Turner felt his XHD3 vibrate, signaling a new development, but before he could have a look it happened again.

"Victoria. Victoria Eden. And you are?" she said.

He turned around and there she was. Her hand was extended, awaiting his. He felt like an ABC book, an easy read, something incredibly uncomfortable for a man in his profession. She had obviously felt the connection too. Maybe it was about wanting what you couldn't have, but he could tell she enjoyed making him squirm.

"Tony, Tony E. Kalem," he said. He decided it would only be a half truth if he associated his name with the quote he'd used.

"What does the *E* stand for?"

He flashed a friendly smile to the barista, who was headed for the counter with his drink and turned back to Victoria. "Everything," he said. "Have a safe flight."

He scooped up his drink and headed for the gate, trying to work out what had just happened.

Chapter 51

JAKE SANDERS HAD a shit-eating grin on his face.

"Can you believe that gas station sold good coffee? Here, in the boondocks?"

He had to admit Special Agent Cathy Moynihan had managed to break him out of his shell. It was unusual to find a woman who could dish out attitude with her aptitude for precision and wit.

"It's the strong stuff too. Café Verona. Mmm mmm good," she said. "Are you sure there's a coffee grinder there?"

He liked her skeptical nature. "Absolutely. We don't mess around."

"If you didn't mess around, we'd be drinking coffee, not picking it up."

"Touché!" All he could do was smile. For a second he considered that he may well have met the perfect woman, but then her next question smacked him with reality.

"So what division are you in?"

Sanders spat out the canned response. "We work out of Baltimore. You?" He already knew the answer to the question, but this was about changing the subject to her.

"DC. I'm hoping to make the Hawaii beat one day." There was an awkward silence, like she knew he didn't want her to ask any more prying questions. "So…" Her tone was serious. "What are a bunch of guys out of Baltimore doing grabbing teenagers and driving them around in kit like that? I mean, come on. Three decked-out Tahoes? Pretty impressive considering how stingy the bureau has been about every request I've ever made."

He needed to shut this down fast.

"Jealousy will get you nowhere in this business." He flashed her his shit-eating grin again.

She shook her head as she turned onto the gravel driveway that led to the black site. Sanders knew she wasn't buying his bullshit, and he respected her for it. This was one of those times where being intelligent wasn't in one's best interest. He wasn't sure how his boss would want him to handle this one.

Over the past decade the scope of his job had increased significantly. He was getting used to working in the gray area after being moved out of TacOps. When he was with the FBI Tactical Operations team, he was responsible for the bureau's black-bag operations, but when he and his crew of trusted men were promoted to create a new unit, that new assignment had morphed into something well beyond illegal entry-and-search missions and surveillance. They had added terrorist hit squad to their list of duties.

The HVT Squad, short for High-Value Target Squad, was put in place for matters of national security. One-off missions like the one they were currently on muddied the waters between right and wrong, but the squad had become desensitized to the work over the years. Its team filled the gap that the CIA, unable to run black operations on US soil, was legally bound to leave. The squad had lost a few good men in the fight, but it was still five-strong and extremely capable.

Moynihan and Sanders got out of the car. Sanders caught a quick glimpse of her in the moonlight and noticed she was the complete package. He was beginning to imagine the possibilities when she spoke.

"Do you smell that?" she asked.

He snapped out of his daydream and said, "Huh?"

"It smells like someone discharged a weapon." She tilted her head slightly as if it would catch more air and took a couple more whiffs.

"Don't be..." He lowered his voice to a whisper. "Yeah, I smell it now."

"It's probably nothing," she said. "We'd already be dead if there was a problem."

He realized she was probably right. The fact that she picked up on both points first annoyed him.

"Tell my ex that," he said.

She turned to him and squinted. "What?"

He smiled and said, "I'm dead to her."

They shared a laugh, and it helped to lighten the mood as they approached the house. He slid his thumb across the reader and unlocked the door. The smells released by the open door caused them both to instinctively draw their weapons. Someone had definitely fired a gun.

"Ken? Scott?" Sanders's voice was a little tentative. "Glen... Guys?" He strained to see inside. "No fucking around. Are you in there?"

He led them through the door. Their training was evident from their cadence and actions. He signaled Moynihan to check the upper floors with a nod of his head.

The smell of violence grew stronger as he silently made his way down the stairs. His weapon was leveled, and his heart pounded as he took in the scene. Both Scott and Glen were dead. They had been shot execution-style, each with a dime-sized bullet hole in the center of his forehead. He continued to clear the basement and checked the outside stairwell. The situation hit him like a ton of bricks.

"Holy shit," he said under his breath. He backtracked and shouted up the stairs. "Moynihan, you okay?"

"Yeah, nothing up here," she said.

He heard her staccato footsteps navigate down the stairs to the basement. He hadn't had a chance to warn her. When he turned in her direction, she was frozen, with her hand held to her mouth.

"Oh my God..." she said, followed by an audible swallow.

Sanders had already gone into the control room to check the surveillance equipment. The system still showed that an alarm had been triggered and the time that had lapsed. He pushed the button to reset the sensors and checked the monitor bank to verify they were alone. He fumbled with the controls in an attempt to pull up the recording of his men being taken down.

Working the surveillance gear had always been Scott Richardson's job, and he was lying in a pool of his own blood just outside the door. Sanders had only managed to make the computer screen a jumble of windows. He shook his head in frustration.

"We'll have to get someone out here to examine the video feed. These systems are cut off from the rest of the world."

Sanders noticed she had taken the shock well and was impressed that she hadn't tossed her cookies.

"Whoever did this already took off," he said.

Moynihan pointed out the bright side. "I guess that's not such a bad thing."

They shared a look, knowing the carnage could have just as easily included them.

His eyes narrowed. "Yeah," he said, "it sure could have."

He walked into the room with his dead men, and now that he had calmed down, the overpowering metallic smell of blood overpowered his senses.

Moynihan motioned toward the basement door and dashed up the stairs. Her footsteps gave way to muted heaving sounds.

"Take your time," Sanders yelled out the doorway. "I need to make a call."

Her puking would have been funny for him if the situation wasn't so fucked up.

Sanders took out his phone and called Director Culder.

"What do you have for me?" he answered.

Sanders closed his eyes and said, "I've got two men dead, one missing."

"It had to be Simpson."

Jake Sanders knew they had worked together long enough for Culder to trust him.

"I'll deal with it. I'll figure out what's going on."

He turned toward the door when he heard Moynihan coming down the stairs and cupped his hand over the mouthpiece.

"Your other agent is in the yard. Single bullet to the head like the others. I'll call this in," she said.

"No," Sanders blurted out a little louder than he would have liked. He covered the receiver with his hand more tightly before continuing. "No," he told her, this time more composed. "I've got the director on the line now. I'll take care of this. Turn off your cell phone as a precaution. I've got a spare in the truck we can use. Mine's off after this call."

Sanders could tell she wasn't crazy about the order but knew she would also be concerned about whom they might be dealing with. He whisked her back up the stairs with his hand.

"She's there then?" Culder said.

"Yeah, and make it three dead." He looked down at his men. The team was now down to two.

"This is not good. She knows too much," the director said. "Are we going to have a problem?"

"No. No problem with her." Sanders knew he wouldn't like the director's plan for resolution. "Our problem is with the team. It's just me and Pagano, so we'll be extremely limited until we do some recruiting."

"That's something we can figure out later. We can't have any loose ends, not with what's going on."

Sanders took a deep breath, annoyed at the lack of immediate commitment with bringing the team back up to full strength. He was already used to the absence of condolences.

"We can still use her. No loose ends. If I sense there's a problem, I'll deal with it."

"Good. Keep me informed," Culder said.

Chapter 52

Lucky Stone Quarry, Ashburn, VA

IMAGES OF THE dead men were still ruling her thoughts when she felt the car come to a stop. This time the driver turned the engine off. Maria Soller estimated they had been driving for forty-five minutes, maybe an hour. She had no idea where they had been taken, but she was thankful they were both still alive. Every time she felt panic beginning to set in, she'd will herself to stay strong, like her mother would. She hung on to the hope that it would only be a matter of time before her mother's friend swooped in and rescued them from this mess. She didn't even know who the man was, but he was the glue that was keeping her together. His invisible presence helped her focus on doing her part and staying alive.

The nervous moment of silence was broken by the sound of the door opening, immediately followed by a harsh voice.

"Get out," it said.

Both of the girls rose from a fetal position in the backseat and eased their way out of the car. They had rank-smelling hoods over their heads, and their hands had been zip-tied behind their backs.

"Faster," he barked.

Her legs were unsteady from being cramped up in the car for so long. He prodded her along every nervous step as the smell of rotting trash joined the assault the filthy hood had already launched against her senses. She could hear Melody Millar starting to sob again, and she feared for both of them. When Melody had cried loudly in the car, they had been relentless. The men spoke freely in Russian amongst themselves, and not knowing what they were saying caused a panicked feeling to surface. Her foot kicked into something solid, and it made a metallic sound.

He stopped her progress and said, "Step up."

She brought her foot up and he barked, "Two more."

She heard a door open and sensed she was entering some kind of building. Her mind had transformed the cover over her head into a hiding place, so she hoped they wouldn't take it off. His powerful hand pressed down on her shoulder.

"Sit!" he said.

The chair was cold and ripped her mind from its hiding place. She could hear Melody starting to cry again and realized the sudden chill from the chair had frightened her too. She needed to calm her down.

"It's okay, Melody," she said. "We're going to be okay."

"Silence," he yelled.

His voice made her jump and managed to set the teenager off. This time her crying was much worse. She knew trying to help her would end badly, so she silently prayed that she would be okay. Melody's sobs became muffled, and Soller heard ruffling sounds from her direction. She shut her eyes tight and tried to block out the sounds. The rustling stopped, and she clenched her fists, gripped by fear.

"I said silence," he demanded, this time in a more sinister tone.

The room was now quiet, and Soller's hands began to shake. There was a massive heave as Melody gasped for air. Soller was relieved to hear her breathing but was afraid she would go into hysterics. She listened as Melody started to catch her breath. There was only one convulsive sob before she quieted down.

She could hear traffic in the distance, and she wished it were closer— close enough for someone to hear her scream. Maria Soller was too scared to speak. She didn't know if they were alone, and all she wanted to do was help the poor girl.

She concentrated on the sound from the cars. Every time a vehicle passed, she imagined its make and model as a way to occupy her mind and cope with the fear. She listened intently and tried to discover anything new that might help take her away from this hell.

Soller noticed her iPhone was pressing hard against her body, and fear crept into her mind as she worried that its outline could be seen through her pocket.

Chapter 53

ADDY SIMPSON LOOKED up from his desk and said, "Thanks for getting here so fast, Jack."

"No problem. What's up?" Jack Turner asked.

Simpson's office was one of three in the single-floor building, and was furnished with the bare minimum. It had plain white walls with gray thin-pile carpet covering the floor, and a desk with two chairs opposite to where he was seated. There was a dark brown leather couch along one of the walls, and one in the reception area, that would accommodate the occasional all-nighter. The two men had always been straight with one another, and the admiral understood the difficult position his friend was in.

"Do you have any news you can share about Trent?" Simpson asked, phrasing the question in a way that left Jack Turner with a little wiggle room. He wouldn't necessarily have to lie if he had spoken to Trent and wasn't ready to pass it along.

"No, nothing for you yet," Turner said, easing himself into one of the chairs.

Simpson acknowledged. "Have you heard about what's going on at The Shop?"

"Sure, I figured that's what this was about."

"The latest news has everyone taking this threat very seriously. I'm going to have to let POTUS know what they've found. We're getting some solid help from the hacker who was targeted along with Soller's son."

"All the way to the top sounds about right." Turner's eyes narrowed. "Look, Addy, what's going on?"

Simpson's eyes reflected his inner turmoil, and Turner had picked up on it, likely concerned that it was bad news about his nephew.

"Matilde called," Simpson said.

"Jesus. About her son?"

"No." His eyes now burned with a familiar intensity and he said, "Someone's taken her daughter."

Turner's eyebrows rose. "You've got to be shitting me."

Simpson shook his head. "Afraid not."

"What does she want you to do about it?"

"Find her."

"For fuck's sake, Addy! We can't let personal problems get in the way of our work." He threw up his hands. "You're already on Trent's case. You don't even know how you're going to handle the situation with him. You can't go helping out some old flame." He shook his head. "No way. No fucking way. It's not even an option."

They shared an intense moment. The former admiral wasn't about to back down.

"You don't care, do you?" Turner said.

"I wouldn't say that. I see your point, and you're right. This isn't something I should be considering." Simpson drew in a deep breath and said, "But I have to help her out. I wouldn't be able to look in the mirror if I didn't."

"You've lost it, haven't you?"

"No, I'm being serious."

"Love can do some crazy things to a man"—Turner's eyes narrowed—"like diluting his judgment. No question about it." Simpson didn't respond. "What? Do you want my permission to do something stupid?" Jack Turner paused for a long moment. "I want you to think about this, Addy. I mean, really think about it." Turner stood and began to pace back and forth. "Some days it seems like Senator Soller's sole purpose in life is finding ways to throw you under the bus." He shook his head. "It's only a matter of time before he finds the right bus."

Simpson laughed. "Come on, Jack. Like it's possible to make things worse with him."

Turner shook his head again. "Sticking our noses into his daughter's boyfriend problems? That's just asking for trouble."

Simpson smiled as he stood and walked to the weapon safe. "Oh, come on. Stop being so melodramatic."

"So I take it you're going to cut Trent some slack. You know, for what's going on with Ryan?"

He opened the safe, and his tone turned serious. "We'll cross that bridge when we come to it, but for now I need you to check something out with me."

"And what's that?"

"A house in Poolesville."

He watched as Simpson collected some gear. "I guess you're expecting company?"

"You only live once, so I'd rather go over prepared." Simpson smiled. "We'll need your truck. I'll give POTUS a call on the way there."

Chapter 54

PRESIDENT VINCENT CROSS fixed his gaze on a painting across the room as he waited for the man on the other end of the phone to respond. His eyes had drifted down to the wooden trim on the *Resolute* desk before there was an answer.

"Mr. President, this is quite a surprise," Federal Reserve Chairman Bart Stapleton finally said.

"Bart, call me Vincent please," President Cross said. "Sorry to interrupt your Saturday evening. Something's come up and I need your help."

"Of course. What can I do for you?"

"Please keep this conversation between the two of us. It's of an extremely sensitive nature."

"Absolutely. What is it that you need?" Stapleton responded without any real conviction.

This was a sticky subject, so Cross figured it would be best just to lay it all out there. "I need you to work out how to get someone on my team access to the Federal Reserve computer systems."

"Why on earth would I want to do that?"

"We've discovered a computer threat in the wild, and there's a chance the Fed might be a target. They'll need to check every system that deals with money. Rates, transfers, domestic and foreign accounts."

There was an uncomfortable silence as the chairman considered the request. "Our computer systems?"

"Yes. It's a matter of national security."

162

"I'll need a little more information than that to consider something like this."

"Unfortunately, at this point in the investigation we're short on details, but we won't be at liberty to share them until there's more clarity on the situation. Suffice it to say, this is a highly advanced threat, and this is now our number-one priority. It's imperative that the investigation be centralized to minimize the risk of setting off alarm bells."

"That's convenient, Vincent, now isn't it?" Stapleton's tone had quickly changed to one of a skeptic. "Giving your people the keys to the kingdom under the auspices of national security without offering a shred of detail."

Stapleton was a man with enough power to do battle with the president. His position at the Federal Reserve gave him the power to use interest rates as a tool to stabilize the economy as much as he could a weapon to destroy the current administration's economic policies. Cross knew the man had no qualms about doing whatever it would take to suit his needs.

"I appreciate your concern," Stapleton barked in a belittling tone, "but I think you knew the answer to this question before you made the call."

President Cross quickly realized his mistake. The United States Code restricted what information the Government Accountability Office could access about the country's central bank. Congress had tried repeatedly to have the records showing its dealings with foreign governments and entities made available, but had had little success. Many had fallen in the fight, but the Federal Reserve's financial records abroad remained shrouded in secrecy. Cross's request had been interpreted as a back door to gain information, and he knew changing Stapleton's attitude at this point would be practically impossible.

He took a deep breath as he considered the long odds, and gave it his best shot. "Bart, this is real," he said. "There's something going on right now, and the scope of the problem isn't completely known, but it will be in your..." He thought better of putting it directly on him and changed his approach. "It will be in our best interest to work together here."

"In our best interest," Stapleton repeated in a scathing tone. "I see. Unfortunately, politics provides for many interpretations of what may be in one's best interest."

Cross had expected a tough sell but was surprised that Stapleton was being so combative. He decided his angst was probably some combination of his request to look into the Fed's foreign accounts and fallout from a recent transgression in the banking industry. The Federal Reserve's failure to act on early information to expose the Libor rate scandal had put intense pressure on the central bank. Even the mainstream media had considered whether it could have something to do with a larger conspiracy among world finance leaders. There were endless profits that could be made by collectively manipulating global benchmark interest rates. The world was screaming cover-up, and Stapleton had put up a roadblock.

The president wasn't left with much choice, so he said, "I can assure you this isn't an excuse to poke around in the Fed's financial dealings. It's about making sure the bank remains stable."

"And there we have it," Stapleton said sharply. "No?"

Cross closed his eyes and shook his head. "No."

"It would be in the best interest of your presidency to end this conversation now," Stapleton added.

Cross maintained his cool, knowing this was bigger than him and his ego.

"Bart, we're still trying to crawl out of the economic crisis the previous administration put us in. America doesn't need another financial meltdown. We were lucky to pull out of this last one."

"We did what we had to do there," Stapleton said bitterly.

The tone of his comment reminded Cross that the central bank was still reeling from details uncovered about trillions of dollars in discount-window loans made by the central bank that had flowed out of the country. A major newspaper's Freedom of Information Act request to get said information had been upheld by a court order and given the Federal Reserve's reputation another hit. The maverick institution that answered to no one.

"I suppose this conversation is over then?"

"What conversation?" Stapleton said. "Like you said, this call never happened."

The chairman ended the call.

Cross knew there would be some political backlash for this, but if he were concerned, he didn't show it. He fixed his gaze to the opposite side of the Oval Office and admired the iconic painting of George Washington on the wall.

"Well, George," he said, "be thankful you didn't have to deal with these arrogant pricks when you were president."

He punched a button on his phone and placed a call to a building across the Potomac River.

"Hi, Cynthia. No, he wouldn't go for it. Go in and check things out anyway. Just do me a favor and don't get caught."

Chapter 55

TRENT TURNER GRABBED his newspaper off the seat and sat down at the packed gate. The old woman flashed him a friendly smile and settled herself contently, confirming she'd gone to battle to save his place. He returned the gesture and pulled out his vibrating XHD3. His jaw tightened as he read the message, and then he looked up to scan the area. It was an alert from Cannibal indicating Etzy Millar had been identified by a security camera.

The news meant the airport should have been crawling with agents by now, but he saw no signs of a takedown in the works. No one within eyeshot pinged his radar. He read further to see that the event had originated from an FBI system. It wasn't difficult for him to draw some conclusions. The bureau had left Millar out of the headlines, and keeping that morsel of information about his involvement from law enforcement only served to underscore the significance of what was going on. Boarding for his flight had begun, so Turner needed to stay vigilant and assume he'd be up against the bureau's elite.

Then he felt it. Even before looking up, he could sense the attention burning into him like the midday sun. She was leaning against the wall across the gate from him, a violin slung over her shoulder. He managed to avoid eye contact, but there was no doubt she noticed his recognition, and it pissed him off.

Her presence made the situation even more difficult. Now he'd need to work around that plane of view. He noted the monitor overhead was offering travel vouchers for those willing to take a later flight. He was wondering whether she might be a plant when his thoughts were interrupted by an announcement.

"Attention passengers traveling on United World Airlines flight three-six-three bound for Chicago's O'Hare Airport, the flight is full, and we are running out of space in the overhead compartments. Please check any carry-on bags with our attendant just before boarding the plane. We will make them available to you upon arrival in Chicago. Thank you for your cooperation, and have a safe flight."

The fact that he was carrying a small armory gave Turner plenty of cause for concern. He hadn't identified any threats, but under the circumstances, he wasn't crazy about separating himself from his weapons.

Millar had already boarded the flight by the time he reached the ticket scanner. The attendant processed his boarding pass, and he headed down the retractable tunnel toward the plane. None of the passengers in front of him had put up a fight about checking their carry-ons, which gave him some hope in finding space in an overhead compartment.

He smiled at the attendant gesturing to collect his carry-on bag and said, "No, thank you. I'll come back if I can't find a spot."

Turner couldn't help but notice the long, slender legs of Victoria Eden as she stepped across the plane's threshold a few meters in front of him.

He stepped into the plane, and as soon as he turned into the aisle, he knew what he had to do. He was pretty good at this game. The key was to take the first option that presented itself and not to worry about finding space in the overhead near his seat. If you started out being picky, you'd end up with a checked bag.

He spied a space on the right just in front of him and quickly pushed his way through the mass of passengers. He hoisted his bag up into the cavity, and it met resistance from a nylon case that was being shoved in from the opposite direction.

"There weren't any spots left in the back. Would you mind?" Victoria Eden smiled, her eyes hopeful.

"Uh, no..." Her striking green eyes sucked him in again, and it pissed him off. "I mean, yes. I do," he said flatly.

"Please?" she asked, clearly concerned. "I'd rather not put this in the cold and unknown below. I have an audition tomorrow and, well, if something happened to it, it would be a disaster." She bit her bottom lip and her expression pleaded.

He felt bad, and the feeling spread to his eyes, but he didn't have a choice.

"It'll be fine. Look at that case. This, on the other hand," he patted his bag, "won't offer much protection if it was to be stowed below." The words were truer than she could ever imagine.

She smiled and looked around the cabin. "You're a real charmer, Tony, aren't you?" She increased her volume and said, "I have an idea. Let's take a vote."

Eden was obviously amused with herself as she commanded the undivided attention of all passengers within earshot.

"Can we have a show of hands here?" She raised her right hand, scanned her audience and asked, "Who thinks my violin should stay in the cabin?"

Turner realized he needed to end this fast. He shoved his bag the rest of the way into the compartment and her violin shot out the other side.

"That'll about do it," he said with a wry smile.

He brushed past her to head for his seat, and when they touched he had to shake off the charge of electricity.

"It will, will it?" Eden said, as she reached for his bag. "Just what's so important here, Mr. Kalem?"

He looked over at Etzy Millar, and the hacker's eyes were full of worry as he watched the scene escalate. Turner shot her a nasty look when she began to pull open the zipper.

Chapter 56

ADDY SIMPSON READ the intel report on his tablet. He then looked to Jack Turner, who was driving his bright yellow RAM 1500 extended-cab pickup truck. "The place Matilde's daughter was taken from had an FBI agent present," he said.

"Yeah well, Culder is Soller's faithful puppet," Turner said, his eyes not leaving the road.

Simpson laughed. "Agreed. Imagine if this was all connected. Then you'd have to stop giving me a hard time."

"Whatever," Jack Turner said shaking his head.

"Poolesville's an easy location to sift through the cell tower signals. There aren't many people around. From the real-estate records, the house smells like a black site."

"I didn't realize the FBI ran locations like that. I'd figure this would be CIA."

"They shouldn't, and with the FBI presence you can rule out the CIA. The house is like a shadow. It's owned by the BR Corporation, and it looks like a shell company. Most of the other cell phones in the vicinity trace back to BR Corp as well. One of them has been turned off, but there are three that still have an active cell signal there. The phone tied to the FBI agent was also turned off at the location. Most of the other signals they picked up were from area residents."

Jack Turner turned to his friend and said, "This just keeps getting better, doesn't it?"

"Tell me about it." Simpson read the rest of the analysis and said, "There's a pay-as-you-go phone that stands out as well. It can't be traced to anyone, and it's also been turned off."

"The Russians she mentioned?"

Simpson nodded. "That's what I'm thinking. I'm sending a note to have the analysts at The Shop put all the numbers on alert and add them to our proximity zones."

Turner gave him a quizzical look. "Huh?"

"If one of the cell signals comes online, we'll know. If it's nearby, your phone will give you the heads up even quicker."

"Gotcha," Jack Turner said. "At least I think I do..."

"Are you ready to do this?" Simpson asked.

"You already know my opinion. Hitting this location is a bona fide bad idea. Especially now that it sounds like we'll have three for company."

Simpson couldn't disagree. His friend was absolutely right. There was a personal element in this, and he couldn't deny that it was affecting his judgment. He himself was even starting to question what they were doing when his cell phone rang.

"Hello?" he answered.

"Addy, sorry to call again," Matilde Soller said.

"It's okay, Bella, don't be." He nodded at Turner.

"There's something else, something I'd forgotten to tell you, and I think it's important. I can't believe I didn't mention it before. I don't know...I just wasn't thinking."

"You're under a lot of stress right now," Simpson said. "What is it?"

"Maria's boyfriend. He was with Max when he was killed," she said with great concern. "His name is Francis Millar. We call him Etzy. I can't believe he had anything to do with Max's death, I just can't. He's wonderful. I know it in my heart. People are after him, Addy. He's scared. Scared to death."

Simpson had his answer. She had just connected the dots. He looked over at Turner and asked her, "Have you told your husband?"

"Oh my God, yes. Maximillian flew off the handle when I told him I'd called you. He's lost it. I don't know what's happened to him, but please be careful." Her voice started to crack up. "He said he's coming after you. Well, in so many words. You know how he can be. I'm so sorry for bringing you into all of this."

Simpson ended the conversation with his best effort to comfort the grieving mother and then turned his attention back to Jack Turner.

"Well, my friend. We have our connection. You should be a fortune teller. Apparently the senator has already lost his mind, so this isn't going to make things any worse." Simpson flashed him a big grin and then explained the new developments. "This is part of the operation now, so we don't really have a choice."

Turner furrowed his brow. "Yeah, right. I can smell your epiphany," he joked, alluding to the bullshit. "So you're telling me if her daughter wasn't a part of the operation, you'd have backed off?"

His friend nodded emphatically and smiled.

"That explains why we're already here," Turner pointed out as he pulled the truck to the side of the road.

Simpson worked the display on his tablet, and a quiet whirring emitted from the back of the pickup truck. He worked the touch-screen controls, and the flying machine lifted into the sky and headed toward the target house a half a click down the road. In less than five minutes, the PMD II had canvased the location with its array of advanced surveillance technologies.

"There's nobody on the floors above ground, but the sensor isn't powerful enough to get all the way down to the basement," Simpson said.

"Always a catch with these gadgets, isn't there?" Turner smiled and motioned to Simpson's phone. "That reminds me. You might want to turn your ringer off so your old flame doesn't get you shot up when she calls back."

Both men burst out laughing. It had been a long time since either of them had carried out an operation in the field, and they were rusty. After a quick gear check, the men set off on their way.

By the time they reached the black site, the PMD II had already determined a clear route to the front door that would avoid setting off any alarms. Simpson touched the hood of the black SUV they passed in the driveway and confirmed the vehicle hadn't been driven recently. The PMD flying above disabled the motion sensors in front of the house as they moved silently to the front door.

They stood perfectly still and listened intently.

Chapter 57

Island Industries, Brooklyn, New York

THE LAST FEW weeks had been extremely stressful for Dr. Charles Reed. The avalanche of bad news had started with his daughter's arrest and the revelation that she was a drug addict. His level of anxiety had been freshly topped off knowing the man who had caused his unexpected resignation from Island Industries was calling on him. Reed sat at the desk in his sleek modern office, the damp smell of rain clinging to his clothes. He let the phone ring three more times and finally answered it, but chose not to speak. He'd never found himself in a compromised situation like this before, and his mind was reeling.

"I didn't realize Island Industries was in the business of assassinating US citizens," FBI Director Frank Culder said.

There was a long pause while Reed carefully considered his response. "I'll give you credit," he said. "You certainly have an active imagination."

"Tell me, Chuck, is Simpson that far gone? I mean really. Killing the son of a US senator isn't the most intelligent use of company resources, wouldn't you say?"

Reed's eyes narrowed. "I think you're the one who's fallen off the deep end."

"Careful, careful," FBI Director Frank Culder warned.

The doctor raised his hand to his forehead and said, "Look, I have no idea what you're talking about."

"Oh, I think you know more than you'd like to admit. I'm sure Shelly would appreciate it if you filled me in."

Reed took a deep breath and exhaled slowly to try to stay calm. His resignation was an attempt to protect Island Industries from the man on the other end of the line. He knew it would only be a matter of time before Culder would try to cash in on dropping his daughter's possession-with-intent-to-distribute charge. She was all he had left, and he was planning to leave his job for Chicago to straighten her life out in just over a week. He was so close to being off the hook, and now he wished he'd have quit without giving any notice.

"Speak," Culder insisted.

He didn't appreciate being spoken to like a dog, but he wasn't surprised, considering the source. The FBI director had it in for Island Industries. He had been trying to prove it was more than just a run-of-the-mill security firm since the day Addy Simpson opened its well-guarded doors.

"Soller's kid getting himself killed has nothing to do with us," Reed said impatiently.

"Interesting, Chuck. The information I have points straight to Island Industries," Culder said.

Reed hated when people called him Chuck. He clenched the phone and said evenly, "Your information is wrong."

"DARPA."

"What about DARPA?"

"They don't work with many people."

"Tell me something I don't know," Reed said dismissively.

"A young man named Francis Millar was with the senator's son when he was killed."

"And why should I care about that?"

"He's on a flight from Dulles to Chicago as we speak."

Reed closed his eyes and tried to maintain his composure. "Don't you try to bring my daughter into this. That's—"

He laughed. "Oh no, that's merely a coincidence." The FBI director cleared his throat obnoxiously and said, "What's not a coincidence is that the man a few places behind Francis Millar in the security line was in possession of a DARPA-made handheld device."

"Oh come on—"

"You know, Chuck. You've seen them, and I imagine you might even have one held up to your ear. They look like an everyday smartphone. You'd think nothing of it unless, of course, you've had the pleasure of visiting our friends in Arlington."

Reed could feel a bead of sweat trickle down his forehead.

"Fortunately for both of us, one of my analysts is, shall we say, in the know. Which brings me to you. How convenient, no?"

Reed's mind went straight to Trent Turner. Their operatives were some of the chosen few who had access to the DARPA-built devices. Turner recently went dark, and there was no other person who would be boarding a commercial flight with something from DARPA on his person. He needed to choose his words carefully.

"I can assure you there was no operation carried out to eliminate the senator's son," Reed said confidently.

"Your little girl—do you think she would survive in prison? That's one way to clean her up." Culder's smile came through in his voice. "A good friend of mine is looking out for her as we speak. I figured I'd let you know in case you were getting any crazy ideas that your good friend Addy can help you." He paused to let his words sink in. "It would be big of you to sacrifice a couple decades of her life to make sure she was safe. Well, from the drugs anyway."

Dr. Charles Reed didn't think it was possible to feel any lower than he had for the past couple of weeks, but his life had just sunk to an all-new low. He was being asked to choose between his daughter and Addy Simpson, a man—a friend—whom he had great admiration for and who had trusted him implicitly. His heavy heart didn't leave him a choice.

"A problem cropped up here recently," Reed said reluctantly.

"What kind of problem?"

"One of our operatives went dark." He cringed with betrayal as he said the words.

"Interesting. And this is recent?"

"The same day Soller's kid was shot, but I'm telling you," he said defensively, "there's no way he pulled the trigger."

Culder laughed. "And what makes you say that?"

"Let's just put it this way. He's not that sloppy."

"Everyone makes mistakes."

"Not him," he said frankly. "He would never make a careless move like that. Never."

"And what about him going dark?" Culder asked curiously. "Would you have said he would never go dark before it happened?"

"Look, Culder—"

"His name? I want his name."

"It depends on the day of the week. I'm telling you, he's not your man."

"You're so sure of yourself, aren't you?"

Reed knew he'd been backed into a corner and said, "Trent. You can take your pick of last names."

"Give me photos of him, anything you have," Culder demanded. "We didn't catch him on the security cameras like your friend Millar. Make young Shelly proud of Daddy for keeping her out of jail. I'll expect to hear from you soon," he said before ending the call.

Chapter 58

The Shop, Northern Virginia

THE MOOD AROUND The Shop had been somber from recent events, but a call from the President of the United States sent a wave of excitement through the CDWG division. Pronounced "Sea Dog" by those on the outside, the acronym stood for Cyber Defense and Warfare Group, but it was also referred to as The Shop by the operatives from the clandestine side of the house. The team was led by Dr. Cynthia Grayson, an MIT alumnus who was a pioneer in the field of information security. She had been personally recruited by the CEO to head the most critical division of one of the world's leading technology firms.

"That was fast," Grayson said standing over the desk of one of her top analysts. "You'd think the Federal Reserve would take at least thirty minutes to hack."

Thom Peterson smiled. He was leaned back in his chair wearing a Foo Fighters T-shirt and plaid shorts, which was a stark contrast to Grayson's gray business suit. "I don't think I'd be here if anything took me that long."

"Good point. Let me know what you find."

"Sure thing. I'm inside their DMZ at this point. I have at least one more layer before I'll be able to get to the workstations." He looked up at his boss with great concern. "I'll need at least ten more minutes," he said sarcastically.

She smiled and headed to The Bunker to check the progress on the bot software they had been reverse engineering. There were LCD monitors bolted to the walls of the futuristic hexagon-shaped room, with five developers at work around a six-sided table in the middle. The group of analysts looked up in unison as she entered.

"Almost there," the lead analyst said. "Etzy helped us get a new module deployed onto one of the bots he installed. We're almost ready to propagate it out to the rest of the botnet. It'll take some time to reach them all because of the way the botnet is set up to communicate."

"The sooner the better," Grayson said.

"I know. The more systems we have the module installed on, the faster we'll discover all of the nodes. Hopefully we'll have enough detail to figure out what they're up to before they pull the trigger."

"Good work," Grayson said. "We've never dealt with anything this complex before, so be extremely careful. Who knows what sort of traps they've set for us."

The analyst nodded in agreement. "We've been sifting through the code and didn't see anything that would report any changes back to a server. The footprint of this botnet will be limited, since each bot was installed manually. Fortunately it's not the same situation as a self-propagating worm, where it can spread all the way to Timbuktu in a few hours."

"Good, but just because you don't see some sort of tripwire, doesn't mean they haven't left us any presents."

"I know. We've got it under control. Whoever they are, they're too smart not to have some sort of early-warning system. We've tested the install on all of the systems we've built in-house with the bot software running, and adding a module didn't set anything off. I think we're ready to push the module out, but if you'd like to—"

"No, thanks," she said. "I'm afraid time is a luxury we don't have right now."

Grayson had always dreamed of having a job where the stakes were high, and her hard work and determination had paid off. Whenever the president was involved in an operation, she had to pinch herself to make sure she wasn't asleep.

"Have you found anything in Nations Bank since POTUS connected us with their CEO?" she asked.

"Not yet. We've got three people working on setting things up. Etzy is on his way to Chicago right now, and we're waiting for him to land before we start poking the bear."

"That's a good idea." Grayson knew Millar had the most experience with the malware, and proceeding without him wasn't a risk they could afford to take. "How long until he lands?"

"The flight is an hour, and I'm not sure if he's taken off yet."

Grayson clasped her hands together. "Damn." As if the sound had triggered the event, the top right corner of the room's central wall monitor lit up, and a series of beeps chirped from the overhead speakers. The alert meant another message had been sent to their s4feT account in the hacker forums.

"Incoming," an analyst said. "It looks like it's an IP address from Chicago. Whoever it is, they didn't bother to hide behind a proxy."

Grayson's eyes narrowed and she took a deep breath. "Let's hope we have another break."

Chapter 59

FBI black site, Poolesville, MD

BOTH MEN REGISTERED beeps coming in steady intervals from the alarm system as they entered the house. They had to assume someone would be monitoring the location, and if they had assets in the area, things could turn deadly. The PMD II hovering overhead confirmed there were no heat signatures in the rooms above grade, so they immediately worked their way down the stairs quickly and efficiently.

The three dead bodies they found sprawled out on the floor in the basement were good news. They meant Addy Simpson still had a chance to find the two young girls he was tracking alive. He entered the control room and pulled a wireless device from his tactical vest. He connected the device to corresponding ports on the security surveillance system. The piece of hardware gave The Shop's hackers direct access to a computer system via the mini drone patrolling overhead. They had nicknamed the connection device AirNet, and it allowed the operatives on the ground to concentrate on staying alive.

"Jack, how are you doing with the prints?" Simpson asked.

"I'm working on the last one. Whoever these guys are, they were taken out nice and tidy."

Simpson had also noted the execution-style head shots.

A voice came through their comms. "Command Central is in the system. Uploading the hard drives to AirNet now, how copy? Over."

Simpson looked through the doorway to Turner and said, "That was fast. I didn't even tell them I had it plugged in yet." He keyed the button on his comms and responded, "Copy good. We'll get out of this place before we have any visitors, over."

Jack nodded as Simpson entered the main room. "I'm done with the prints. Sounds like a plan."

They spent a little over five minutes inside before heading back to Jack Turner's pickup truck. Simpson couldn't remember the last time his heart rate had been this high. He laughed as his friend started the car and tried to catch his breath. Turner hit the gas and took a couple of turns before he parked the truck next to a cornfield.

Simpson sent their GPS location to the flying machine using his tablet and said, "Who says we're too old for this?"

Jack shook his head and cut off the engine. "You're a very sick man, Addy. Very sick."

Simpson turned and smiled at his friend. "I guess I should be worried, since it's coming from the resident expert on the subject."

Jack looked over at the tablet Simpson was entering commands into and said, "If we would have had that kind of gear back in the day, there wouldn't be any bad guys left."

Simpson laughed. "It's amazing. They're going to blow the device I hooked up to the computer as soon as they're finished uploading the data."

"That'll keep things nice and tidy. How long until it's back?"

"It shouldn't take long."

As if on cue, the whirring sound of rotors from the PMD II came to within earshot. They both turned to look through the back window so they could watch it land in the bed of the pickup.

"Crazy," Jack said.

"And expensive," Simpson added. "Let's head to the office. It'll take a while for them to go through the video, but hopefully they'll have enough downloaded by the time we get back. Once we're there, we can plug it in so they can pick up the rest over fiber."

"What do you think about all of this, Addy?"

"I'm still trying to get my head around what's happening."

"Me too, but I'm not talking about that."

"Matilde?"

"Yeah, Matilde. You're too close to this. What we did back there...we were lucky it went smoothly. It may have stroked our geriatric egos for five minutes, but it was dangerous. Really dangerous. If that place wasn't empty, it could have been another story."

Simpson shrugged. "I can't argue with that. We need to get Trent on this."

"We need to talk," Jack said.

Chapter 60

Exxon Station, Rockville, MD

JAKE SANDERS WAS on edge as he paid the cashier for the gas. He had been waiting anxiously with Agent Cathy Moynihan for further instructions. His cell phone rang at the same time he pushed open the glass door to exit. He answered and made his way around to the side of the building, out of view.

"What do you have for me?" he asked.

"I got a team in there, but someone had already broken in," FBI Director Frank Culder said. "They used some sort of device that trashed the security system."

"A team? You mean Pagano?"

"No," Culder said in an annoyed tone. "You're not my only card I have to play."

Sanders was pissed. He and Pagano were the only two left on the HVT Squad, and he wondered who else Culder could trust to pull into an operation like this. He began to pace back and forth.

"So, what? We don't have any images of the fuckers who took our men out?"

"That's right," Culder said. "I think it was Simpson. They had to be connected, based on the explosive used alone. It's not something you can pick up without some serious connections. They must have come back to finish the job by taking out the video."

Sanders and his team had been asked to investigate Island Industries in the past but had never been able to uncover anything untoward about the company. They were either on the level and providing security for high-profile clients, or simply too good to get caught.

"I don't know. Sure, they're advanced, but—"

"Listen, I had my doubts about it at first, but the pieces are falling in place."

Sanders checked around the corner of the building to make sure Moynihan was still in the car. "How so?"

"I spoke to Reed."

"The one with the crack-whore daughter?"

"Yes, the heroin addict I told you about," he corrected. "He said one of their operatives went dark. The timing of it makes him our prime suspect."

"Did Reed say it was him?"

"No, but he didn't have to. There's no doubt their operative was at the airport with Francis Millar. He all but confirmed it. You don't just buy DARPA-made devices at a shopping mall kiosk. He sounded nervous to me. Like he had something to hide."

"You're threatening his daughter. Of course he'll be nervous."

"Reed said this operative is too good to make a mistake. It matched up with the MO in Poolesville. It was professional."

"Yeah. No doubt, but he can't be in two places at once. He probably wouldn't have had the time to make it to Dulles."

Culder hadn't thought of the timing. "True, but Simpson has more than one operative. We'll have pictures of this one soon. Be ready to head to Chicago tomorrow. In the meantime, I need you to check out a place in Ashburn."

"Virginia?"

"Yes. The analysts picked up a cell signal from one of the phones that was near the black site. It looks like it was turned on to make a call. The signal was traced to Cochran Mill Road. A place called the Lucky Stone Quarry."

"How fitting."

"Is she still with you?" Culder asked.

"Yeah, she's in the car." He looked nervously around the corner again to confirm. "We're in Rockville, parked at a twenty-four-hour gas station."

"Good. This quarry, it might be a good place to take care of business once you have everything under control."

The hair on the back of Sanders's neck stood up. He had carried out his share of hits, but this was the first time that the director had ordered him to kill a woman. Not only that, but a fellow law enforcement officer. Someone who he knew didn't deserve to die. He'd had other jobs that didn't sit well with him for one reason or another, but this one opened up a whole new category of wrong. He believed in everything he did on the HVT Squad, but this time it would be difficult to separate the job from the person. This wouldn't be a memory that was easily wiped away. This hit would haunt him.

He headed back into the station and picked up some coffee before returning to the car. Moynihan reached across the front seat and opened his door with a push. He gave her an approving nod and followed it up with a smile.

"Thanks," he said as he passed her a cup.

"No problem. Thank you. Lord knows I need it after tonight. Was that Director Culder?"

He nodded. "About tonight," he said with a severity she hadn't seen before. "Culder doesn't want anything to get out about this operation. At least not yet. It's way too sensitive."

Her eyes narrowed. "Jake, three men are dead, and Melody Millar has disappeared. It's not something you can just sit on. A young girl's life is at stake."

Culder was right. She wasn't about to keep her mouth shut.

"Not permanently, Cathy," Sanders said in a "No shit, Sherlock" tone. "Culder is concerned. He thinks Poolesville might have been an inside job," he lied.

She looked at him in disbelief. "What?"

"Exactly. So, at least for now, we need to make sure we keep this under wraps. Our phones, the ones that were on at the house, need to stay off."

"Gotcha. Wow." She turned to look out the passenger window and quietly added, "I should really call someone about this. Damn cell phones."

"What was that?" Sanders asked.

Moynihan took a sip of her coffee. "Never mind," she said.

The FBI agent fixed her eyes to his, and he had no doubt that she could see right through him. Sanders shifted in his seat, increasingly uncomfortable with the situation.

"I'm not so sure I need this anymore," she said, placing her coffee into a cup holder in the center console. "That news pretty much woke me right up."

"Keep drinking," he said. He gave her an appraising look. "They were able to trace the location of one of the cell phones from the house. We need to go check it out."

Chapter 61

Dulles Airport, Northern Virginia

HIS SHOULDERS TIGHTENED, and he slouched down in his seat. Etzy Millar cringed as he watched the stunning beauty unzip the blue carry-on bag. His eyes widened as she pulled out a couple of small carbon parts for the device Trent Turner had referred to as the PMD. His heart pounded as she reached her hand into the bag once again. Her face wore a look of concern. She stopped short, leaving the item she had just grabbed inside his bag. Her face turned red, and she quickly put everything back and closed the overhead bin.

It was an awkward start to the flight, but everything had settled down for the rest of their trip. The woman had checked her instrument with the flight attendant and never spoke to Turner again. Before they landed, the operative handed Millar a cell phone and an earpiece. He planned to use them to guide him to their hotel from a distance.

The first several moves were preplanned to make sure no connection was made between the two of them. A couple of loops around the airport, a cab ride to a nightclub downtown, out the back door and into a waiting cab. And then things got interesting. Turner had given him a crash course on countersurveillance tactics at his townhouse, but Millar learned to appreciate the craft even more after putting it to use through the city of Chicago.

The two men entered the hotel room. It looked as if its last coat of white paint had been put on decades ago. There were two twin beds made up with well-worn blue bedding, a desk, and a small bathroom.

"That was nuts!" Millar said.

Turner immediately went to close the window shades and said, "It turns out you're a popular guy."

"Yeah, I saw him. This spy stuff is pretty cool."

Turner smiled. "You spotted one, did you?"

Millar gave him a quizzical look.

"Good thing I didn't give you a heads up about the others," Turner said. "We wouldn't want things to get too cool."

Millar raised an eyebrow in disbelief. "What?"

"Let's just say it was more than one guy."

"No way!"

"Way." Turner shook an angry finger at Millar and squinted one of his eyes. "You, my friend, are being watched by the FBI."

Millar's thoughts turned to the news program that showed the FBI processing the crime scene.

"It wasn't too hard to put it together," he said. "He's…" He looked down before continuing somberly. "Well, he was my best friend, so…"

"Sorry about your friend. That's tough." The operative met his eyes and said, "They didn't take you in because they were hoping you'd lead them to something or someone."

Millar smiled. "Well, I didn't."

Turner nodded and said, "No, you didn't."

"So what's the deal with that beauty on the plane? She had eyes on you, man. That was intense."

"That?" He shrugged his shoulders with a half smile. "Well, it's complicated."

"I take it that wasn't part of your being-anonymous script," Millar joked.

Turner shook his head and laughed. "You've got that right."

"I figured you two had hooked up before or something, you know?" Millar scratched his arm nervously as he remembered the scene. "When she started pulling stuff out of your bag… Man, that freaked me out. I thought we were busted."

Turner laughed and tossed the bag on the bed. "She wasn't going to get past this." He unzipped the bag and pulled out a book entitled *Coping with Loss—Honoring the Memory of a Loved One in Life*, written by Dr. Charles Reed.

"Holy crap."

"I'll pass it along to you when I'm finished," Turner said. "The author is a genius."

Millar nodded appreciatively in response. He was surprised that a man like him was affected by death.

"Besides," Turner continued, "she would have had a hell of a time getting past this."

He reached inside the back and began to pull. The sound of Velcro being torn apart filled the room. He tilted the bag toward Millar to show him a locked Kevlar compartment, where the weapons were stored.

"I should have guessed," Millar said.

"You'll figure out how things work soon enough. So where are we with the botnet?"

The hacker had connected his computer while they'd been talking and relayed the progress they had made with deploying a module, and what he had heard about the Federal Reserve.

Trent told Millar how the FBI had kept him out of the press, and then lightened the mood with his story about his first encounter with Victoria Eden.

"It looks like it's going to be a long night," Millar said.

"Indeed."

Millar looked at the operative, and fear crept into his eyes. "So, I haven't really thought about it until now," the hacker said, "but what do you think is going to happen to me?"

"I don't know, Etzy. What I can tell you is this: if you help figure this out"—he gestured to the laptop—"you'll make a lot of friends. Influential people who might be able to help you get your life back on track."

Millar appreciated the straight answer. "Then there's a chance...you know, that things will be okay?"

"Definitely. Don't give up hope, but we'll need a few miracles."

The hacker nodded and took a deep breath.

Turner changed the subject. "We could use some coffee." He smiled, thought of Victoria Eden, and knew what Millar was thinking. "Yeah, yeah. I'll stay away from Starbucks. I don't think they're open this late anyway."

Chapter 62

Lucky Stone Quarry, Ashburn, VA

EVENGI BARANOV WAS annoyed with having been left behind in such a dump. His comrades had taken off to their primary location in Virginia with the two girls they had snatched up. The Russian had no food, no women, and no Internet connection. His only entertainment was the stack of faded trade magazines in English fanned out on the table in front of him. He was chosen to wait for a delivery that was scheduled for later in the evening.

It took him a couple of tries to find a place that would deliver food at this hour. He made sure to turn off his cell phone once he'd finished making the calls. He had already caught considerable flak for leaving it on when they had picked up the girls. In fact, that was why he was the one stuck in the dingy trailer. He had managed to finish off an entire pizza and chased it down with most of the two-liter bottle of Coke he'd ordered.

It only took a few minutes for his stomach to grumble its dissatisfaction with his menu choice. The toilet situation at the quarry was questionable. The Johnny-on-the-spot just outside the trailer was filled with enough excrement to produce an eye-watering stench, and its throne had been splattered by the stories of past intestinal transgressions. He was a former Spetsnaz soldier, so he had no problems taking a dump in the woods, but the thing that pissed him off was the bare cardboard tube stripped of its toilet paper. His intestinal urgency increased as he went inside to grab his used dinner napkins. He made a beeline for a copse of trees and shrubs across the gravel driveway.

The sweat-inducing stomach cramps had almost gotten the best of him by the time he found a tree to lean against. He amused himself with thoughts of just how good it could feel to take a shit. He drew comparisons to his job, and the euphoric feeling he had after they had dispatched of the three FBI agents.

His tree-leaning contemplations were interrupted by the sound of tires crunching gravel from the main road. It was too early for the expected delivery, so he cleaned himself up and crept to the edge of his cover, where the bushes bordered the road.

He saw a car parked on the side of the road with a light tint to its windows. He was unable to make out any human silhouettes inside, but he could see the outline of the seats and the rearview mirror. He realized the driver must have gotten out while he was busy finishing up his business. He sensed the car wasn't parked there by chance. Adrenaline began to course through his veins and his mind sharpened.

His predatory drive took over as he silently weaved his way through the bushes to catch a view of the trailer. It was slight, but he saw it: a subtle shift in light in the shadows. He stared intently until his eyes fully adjusted to the darkness, and then he saw him. His weapon was drawn, and he was carefully working his way toward one of the windows in the trailer. His movements told the Russian his visitor was highly trained. He'd left his Makarov pistol inside the trailer, so he would have to take care of this the hard way.

A car passing on the main road momentarily broke his concentration. The thought of the takedown excited him. Only twenty feet separated the two men, and he would have the element of surprise. He got that feeling again, the heightened sense of power just before playing God. He needed to time his attack perfectly.

Chapter 63

TENSION BEGAN TO build as they took the exit for Shreve Mill Road and headed toward the quarry. This would mark the first time Agent Cathy Moynihan would knowingly go into a volatile situation with a relative stranger. Images of the dead men at the FBI black site unsettled her. Once Jake Sanders told her they were heading to Virginia to intercept the suspects, she went quiet for the first time since they'd met.

She had run through training exercises in her head on the way there in an effort to build her confidence. Her mind-set was shaken when Sanders broke the news that they would have to take care of this without any backup. He had explained that they didn't know who they could trust within the bureau. She didn't say it, but she didn't have to. His responses made it clear that he knew she wasn't buying the bullshit he was selling. She was far too smart to march forward with blinders on.

Moynihan gripped the steering wheel tight in order to stop her hands from shaking. They were only minutes away when she said, "I'm sorry."

"About what?" Sanders asked.

She glanced at him quickly and said, "Your friends. I know it must be tough to function right now, after what's happened…"

"That's why they pay us the big bucks," Sanders joked. He was trying to brush it off, but she knew better.

"Well, if you want to talk about it at some point…I'm here to listen. Okay?"

He looked over at her for a long moment and finally said, "Thanks."

"Don't mention it." She looked over and flashed him a nervous smile. "Almost there."

"Yep. Are you doing okay?"

"I'll be fine," she said. "You?"

"You don't need to be worried about me. I'll take the lead. You just watch your ass. It would be a shame if anything were to happen to it." He looked over at her with a sly smile.

They both laughed and it broke the tension.

"Gee, thanks. I guess?"

"I mean it," Sanders said.

"What? The comment about my ass, or worrying about you?"

He laughed again and this time shot her a wink. "Both."

From the satellite image they had brought up on Google, they knew the quarry had a thin border of trees that surrounded it and there was a trailer near the entrance. A gravel driveway ran from the road through the property and continued past the trailer to the back of the quarry, where it snaked through the mining areas. Tractors and heavy equipment were parked near the trailer at the time the image was taken, and there were several large buildings scattered around the site.

"Okay, are you clear on the plan?" Sanders asked.

"Definitely."

"Okay, run it by me again."

"Sure. I'll douse the lights early and park the car before we get to the driveway, so we have cover from the tree line. As we're rolling up, I'll check the woods for a good spot to cut through. You'll head around by way of the driveway and check the trailer while I backtrack to the cut-through spot and head toward the trailer from there. After that we'll just have to wing it."

"You've got it." He smiled and their eyes met. "Good luck."

She sensed he was distracted, that something other than losing his men had him deeply concerned, but she could also see that his words were sincere—it was in his eyes.

"Thanks, you too," she said.

Chapter 64

SANDERS WATCHED HER disappear into the trees and admired the view while he could. The order from Director Culder weighed heavily on his mind, but this was a business where you did what you were told or you didn't stay around for long. He realized it would be tough to make her death look like an accident, but he knew he'd figure something out—he always did.

He crept around the driveway and used the machinery lined up near the trailer for cover. The smell of oil was strong and his footfalls light and silent. His primary weapon, a standard-issue Glock 23, was already drawn as he made his way through the shadows. The weight of the weapon stowed in the small of his back was distracting. It was the gun he planned to use on Agent Moynihan, and feeling its weight prompted him to search for a sign of her across the gravel road.

A thin beam of light from a passing car sliced through the trees as he neared the trailer. He stood still and listened for movement, the dominant sound being his own heartbeat. Sanders emerged slowly from the shadows and worked his way toward one of the windows in the trailer. He moved to the door and heard the faint shuffling of feet on gravel grow louder just before his world went black.

Chapter 65

THE BRATVA BOSS gestured to one of the chairs in front of his desk, and his soldier sat down.

"What do you have for me?"

The soldier cleared his throat nervously and said, "It's Dennis Zander. He got away from me in a bar."

Kozlov's face twitched with anger, but he didn't speak.

"He was scared," the soldier continued, "so I think he is the one that you want. There was nothing else I could do in that situation."

Kozlov shook his head. "This is not good news." His anger began to boil, and he raised his voice. "We can't have any of these hackers running around telling the world what's been going on here, you idiot!"

The soldier lowered his head. "It will not happen again."

"I should think not," Kozlov yelled.

"I didn't realize he had so much information about our operation. Your orders were not to kill him on sight, or the job would have been done."

Kozlov balled his fists and took a deep breath. "He has enough to make things difficult, but not enough to take us down."

"I will go back out and find him."

"No. I need to send someone who can get the job done." He waved his hand dismissively. "Leave."

He watched the soldier leave his office and was tempted to put a bullet in his head, but decided against it only because of the mess it would make.

He picked up his phone and placed a call. Dimitri Sokov answered on the first ring.

"'Allo?" he said.

"It's Zander, one of the Americans," Kozlov said.

"I know. I just sent Mikhail to your office to inform you."

"How much damage can he do?"

"We're examining his code now. I want to make sure he hasn't left us with any surprises. We review the code changes weekly, so I should know within the hour."

"Good."

Kozlov considered his conversation with Khrushchev. This was a golden opportunity for the Union of Soviet Socialist Republics to rise up from the ashes. He visualized the hammer and sickle, a feared symbol of power, and it sent a wave of excitement through his body.

"We may need to move the operation up," Kozlov said. "It could be risky to put it off any longer."

Zander getting away had been the second dose of bad news this evening. Earlier, Bruce Campbell had informed the Russian that Francis Millar had escaped, and Kozlov was deeply concerned about the individual who had helped him to get away.

"They lost the hacker in Washington again," Kozlov explained. "It looks like he is working with our friend from Switzerland. The American."

Sokov was silent while he considered the connection. "I will run the selection algorithm on the most recent dataset so we can pull down a new set of targets."

"Do whatever you need to do to get it done," Kozlov demanded. This time his voice was markedly more intense.

"The most recent encryption keys were sent to Virginia and should be arriving soon, but we'll need to pull the recent information from the banks and then send an update of the targets. It might be possible to have things ready by Monday. I will try in case you decide to move forward."

Kozlov was angered by his response. Everything was riding on this operation. "Try?" he snapped, violence seeping into his voice.

"We will be ready if you need to launch the attack on Monday," Sokov confirmed.

Chapter 66

Lucky Stone Quarry, Ashburn, VA

SHE USED A metal chair in the trailer as an anchor for his restraints. Veins protruded unnaturally from his arms and demonstrated that the plastic tying him down wasn't there for comfort. Agent Cathy Moynihan had strapped the attacker securely when he was unconscious. The job was a difficult one, given the difference in size between the two of them. That didn't matter much to a woman with her qualities. She was tough and resourceful, and always found a way to get the job done.

The last fifteen minutes had been difficult. At first she thought Jake Sanders was dead, but it turned out he had been incredibly lucky. He owed his life to the FBI agent. She had the instincts and presence of mind to act under pressure and was able to stop the Russian from delivering a mortal blow.

Moynihan saw the Russian begin his charge when she was sixty feet away, and what she lacked in size, she more than made up for in speed. The years of passing batons on the track in college had served her well. She snatched up a stray metal pipe in mid-sprint and delivered a devastating blow to the back of the attacker's head. By that point he had hit Sanders hard but was knocked out cold before he could finish the job.

Jake started to regain consciousness again, so she filled up a cardboard cup from the water cooler and knelt beside him on the floor.

The neglected trailer was small, and it was getting hotter by the minute. "Jake?" She poured a little water on his face to help him come around. "Jake?"

She didn't know whether he could hear her. He finally managed to open his eyes. They were vacant. His mouth was the first thing to move, but he wasn't capable of forming words. Sanders tried to speak again, but he could only groan.

"Jake, wake up."

She shook him, and he groaned again.

"Come on!" she insisted. She dumped the rest of the water on his face, and his eyes snapped wide open.

He still wasn't moving, but he was regaining his ability to speak. "What...what the fuck? Uhhh, shit. My fuckin' head," he said. He closed his eyes and babbled incoherently.

"Thank God. I thought you were dead."

Sanders opened his eyes again and registered the look of concern on her face. It took him a few seconds to process who she was.

"Fuck," he said.

Moynihan wore half a smile and motioned to the man secured to the chair. "There's your buddy."

The Russian creased his eyebrows in response and barked a muted tirade through the duct tape covering his mouth. Sanders struggled to move his head so he could get a look at his attacker. He could see the man was angry and alert.

"He wouldn't stop bitching, so I taped his mouth shut," Moynihan said with a shoulder shrug. "I think he's Russian or something."

Sanders offered a brief smile that turned into a wince. "Holy shit, this sucks. The fuckin' pins and needles, man." His voice was slurred. "My arms and legs feel like lead."

She helped him sit up. He was still too disoriented to offer much help.

He rubbed the back of his head. "Jesus, I think he gave me a concussion. I feel like I'm gonna puke." Sanders finally processed what she'd told him. "Russian?"

A series of muted sounds erupted from the man secured to the chair, and Moynihan shot him an angry look.

"Shut up," she growled, still annoyed from his earlier taunting. She turned to Sanders and said, "Yeah. He was waiting for you in the trees."

The muffled babbling continued in the background, but this time it was more insistent.

"Just shut up," she said, without turning to him. "He's foul. It's like he learned English from a gangster."

Sanders was more coherent now. "I don't know what to say. Thanks. What did he hit me with? The lights just went out all of a sudden."

The Russian's mumbling started to die down in the background.

"He hit you hard at full speed. I didn't see anything on the ground, so I think he hit you with his hand. You fell back toward him, and he was wrapping his arm around your neck when I knocked him out with a metal pipe." She shrugged. "It was too risky to use my gun, since he was on top of you."

She smiled, and he smiled back.

"Good choice," he said.

"I think you hit your head on the metal step on your way down."

The trailer was ominously silent now, and they both turned to the prisoner.

"Oh shit!" they said in unison.

Chapter 67

Downtown hotel, Chicago, IL

THE LATE HOUR meant there weren't many options for picking up food, but Trent Turner managed to round up the essentials. He grabbed caffeine and sugar products that would help to keep them awake through the night. They needed to work as long and hard as they could to try to reverse engineer the code. In the thirty minutes Turner had been gone, there had already been some new developments with the botnet. It didn't take long for Etzy Millar to prove his worth to the team at The Shop, and he was beginning to feel like he was back in his element again.

Turner entered the hotel room with a bag in each hand and kicked the door shut behind him.

Millar turned around quickly and then relaxed when he saw it was the operative. "Something big is happening within the botnet."

Turner's eyes narrowed. "What's going on?"

"Data was pulled from surgeon bots inside at least some of the targets. It passed through a couple of the machines that Max and I had installed. We lost track once it left the bots we had our module installed on."

"You haven't installed your module on all the botnet machines yet?"

He shook his head and said, "Not enough machines to follow the path, but it did help us identify a few more we can propagate it to. Slowly but surely we're increasing the footprint and getting more coverage. They're deliberately zigzagging through the Internet. It makes it next to impossible to trace, and we can only increase our footprint one hop at a time."

"Understood." He tossed a bag of potato chips to Millar. "So what was it that they sent?"

"We don't know—the data was encrypted—but it looked like the bot modified the packets as they passed the data between themselves. I guess they just want to eliminate the possibility of finding the needle in a haystack altogether at the ISPs."

"They're trying to disguise the payload?"

"Yeah, I think so. Even if you had managed to capture all of the traffic, you still wouldn't be able to match anything up with known data packets."

"Smart, especially when they skip over a private wireless network."

"No kidding. They put a lot of effort into covering their tracks. The Shop analyzed packet captures from each of the bots we set up and correlated the timing to show when they were sent and received. It was like clockwork. The same stream of packets kept transforming itself. The farthest they could get was seven hops from bot to bot," Millar confirmed. Each hop represented another member machine of the botnet. "The bot transformed the data before it passed the data packet along so you'd never know it was all connected."

"Did you see anything initiate this?"

"Maybe…we think there was a command set transmitted from the C&C servers less than an hour ago. It was encrypted as well, so we have to assume the bots have some way to decrypt the commands we haven't found yet." Miller peeled open the bag of chips and tossed one in his mouth. "The Shop is working on decrypting the data it captured now. Apparently they have some serious supercomputers there."

Turner smiled to confirm his suspicions. "I guess the big news is that there's a lot of activity."

"Exactly. Judging by the amount of traffic, I'd say they're getting ready for something."

"How many more compromised systems have you been able to find with all of this traffic?"

"About a hundred machines that we didn't know about previously. Maybe more since the last time I spoke with someone at The Shop about it."

"Is it possible any of them had communication with a surgeon bot? We could use a solid lead."

"They're going through that now. Maybe. They just told me they're following up with another lead. It looks like someone contacted you guys the same way I did. Through the boards."

The operative raised an eyebrow and said, "Really? Do you know where?"

"They didn't say."

There was a loud crashing sound outside, and Turner peered through the window shade. "My bet is that all paths lead to the Windy City."

"They said they're going to have someone bring him in."

"Good. I imagine Heckler will reach out to me about it soon."

Millar's expression turned serious. "Thanks."

Turner looked at him questioningly.

"You know, for helping me out. This has been a lot to take in. I think I might have had a nervous breakdown if I wasn't so damn busy trying to help figure this out."

Trent smiled and said, "Don't mention it, Etzy. We've got a ways to go before we're out of the woods, so keep it up."

Chapter 68

Lucky Stone Quarry, Ashburn, VA

AGENT CATHY MOYNIHAN ran over to the slumped figure in the chair and ripped off the duct tape that covered his mouth. His head leaned lifelessly to the side as vomit spilled from his nostrils and mouth over his pallid skin. She grabbed his hair and pulled his head back, and then plunged her hand into his mouth so she could try to clear his airway.

"We're not going to find out much from him if he stays dead," she said in a stern but calm tone. "Since I saved your ass, you have mouth duty."

Sanders smiled. "I can't argue with that," he said. "It might be easier to get that shit out if his mouth if he was facing down."

She looked over at him and nodded, so he helped her lower the chair to the ground.

"Hold on a sec," she said.

Moynihan went to the water cooler and quickly filled two cups. The Russian's head was on its side as she poured the water into his mouth to wash out the vomit, and then she used his shirt to wipe off his mouth.

"Thanks," Sanders said with a wink.

She began counting out the compressions as she pumped the center of his chest. The rate was relatively fast—more than one per second.

"...twenty-eight, twenty-nine, thirty."

He pinched the Russian's nose and covered his mouth with his own. It looked as though his first breath was met with resistance, but she then heard the air push through and saw the man's chest begin to rise. Sanders blew another breath into his mouth; both were only for a second.

Moynihan quickly checked for a pulse and began counting out the compressions again. They continued to perform CPR on the Russian for several minutes. It was sweltering hot in the small trailer. Sweat poured from Moynihan's face when she checked his pulse one final time.

"Dammit," she said. "I can't believe he drowned in his own vomit." She looked at Sanders. "Do you think he was the new drummer for Spinal Tap?" She knew the joke was in poor taste, but she couldn't help herself.

She doubted he'd seen the movie, but then Sanders replied, "Well, it's pretty much an open-and-shut case here. Good thing because..."

"You can't really dust for vomit!" they said in unison.

Both of them laughed, and once the laughter subsided it turned uncomfortably silent. She looked down at the dead body and tried to take it all in.

"Your first?" he asked.

"Yeah. I guess so."

"Well, he wouldn't have extended the courtesy to either one of us, that's pretty obvious," Sanders said, referring to the CPR. "It was him or us."

She looked up at him. "Sure, but it doesn't make me feel any better about it."

"He had a concussion. That can make you nauseous. I nearly tossed my cookies too—he gave me a hard knock. Hell, I might puke my brains out yet."

He returned her look of guilt with a caring smile before putting his arm around her.

She pulled him closer. Moynihan pondered the possibilities, the chances of a relationship, until the vibration from Sanders's phone stole the moment. He pulled the phone out, and they both looked down at the display to see FBI Director Frank Culder was calling.

"I have to take this outside," Sanders said.

She could sense that there was something wrong. They both headed outside as Sanders answered the call. She stayed by the door to the trailer and watched him continue to walk until he was out of earshot.

"Yeah," she heard him answer.

Moynihan observed Sanders from a distance as he paced back and forth gesticulating, tugging up his pants at the small of his back on occasion. The electricity between the two of them had just been shorted out, and intuition was telling her it had nothing to do with the man she had just killed. He ended the call and stopped pacing before looking up to the sky. Sanders stayed that way for a long moment, looked down to the ground and then strode purposefully toward her. His eyes were somehow increasingly distant the closer he got, but they narrowed as he reached back to adjust his pants again.

Chapter 69

THE LIGHTS WERE off. Senator Soller had been steaming in silence at his desk since the call with his wife. His eyes were closed when he raised the tulip-shaped glass to his lips. The darkness enhanced the familiar smell that greeted his nose. It was the only sense that hadn't been overcome by anger. Scotch, Macallan, 1939. Its peaty taste and potency wiped away his thoughts once again.

There was a rhythm to his drinking. Pour, swill, close eyes, sip, and repeat. It was a sacred habit, a ritual he had developed over the years. Even in darkness, nothing changed. This was his escape, his paradise. He would take another drink when there wasn't enough taste for him to savor.

A ring destroyed his fleeting tranquility. He didn't recognize the number.

"Yes?" Soller answered.

"Max?" The voice sounded unsure.

"Who is this?" Soller barked impatiently.

"It's Bart."

There was a short pause while Soller connected the voice to Bart Stapleton. He had already spoken to the Federal Reserve chairman once today. As he tried to gather his thoughts, he realized the scotch was having its intended effect.

"Bart?"

"Did I wake you up?" Stapleton asked. "You sound distracted."

Soller rubbed the bridge of his nose and said, "No, no. What do you need?"

"It's that president of yours. He's trying to dig into our business."

The two men forever lamented the fact that Vincent Cross couldn't be bought, and referring to him in that manner had become commonplace.

"What? How do you mean?"

"He said he wants access to everything. He wants me to let some geek squad into the Fed's computer systems to"—his voice switched to a mocking tone—"check things out." The chairman let out an exaggerated sigh. "He says it has to do with national security. Convenient, wouldn't you say?"

Soller's brow creased. "You're kidding?"

"I would never joke about something like this. I'm not sure if he'll try to apply some pressure on you in the morning, so I wanted to give you a heads up."

"I see."

"Who knows what he's up to?" Stapleton said. "I don't like it. He could be trying to dig up some dirt."

Soller knew just what Stapleton meant. He was referring to the secret society to which they both belonged. The bankers and politicians who breathed the rarified air that had anointed them into its ranks simply referred to it as The Group. Death and the fall of communism had been the only events that had changed the faces of its membership, and they had begrudgingly agreed to involve the Russians.

The Group increased the wealth of its ranks in many ways, chief among them by manipulating interest rates and controlling the derivatives market. It was in the business of growing money and abusing the power that came with it. Recently, a crack had appeared in The Group's armor when a few of its members were implicated in a recent Libor rate scandal. Those involved were removed unceremoniously from The Group in an unprecedented action, and the subject still sparked flare ups between its members. The Group was still tying up loose ends from the incident, not the least of which was finding the leak, and they were still on edge after the recent shakedown. Soller was soon planning to take care of things on his own with his special arrangement.

Buzz about the possibility of The Group's existence had again found its way into the news, and any press was bad press. Soller was chairman of the Senate Committee on Finance, so the job to keep politicians in America in check fell squarely on him. President Cross wielded great media influence, and since he couldn't be bought, he was a difficult man to rein in.

"He won't get past me on this," Soller said.

"I know. I didn't want him to catch you by surprise, so I called."

"Maybe it's time we take care of Cross for good."

"I like the sound of that. We need to get someone who understands his place in the grand scheme of things back in office."

Not having the US presidency in their pocket had made things complicated.

Soller swilled his glass and snuffed another shot. "I think Culder might be able to help us out with this."

"Good. I'll be flying to Lisbon first thing in the morning for the meeting. I'll phone you from there to share the good news."

Chapter 70

Lucky Stone Quarry, Ashburn, VA

JAKE SANDERS WAS sitting next to Cathy Moynihan on the steps outside the trailer in silence. The mood had been tense since his conversation with FBI Director Frank Culder. He had cut the dead Russian from the chair and dragged him outside while they waited for his colleague to arrive. Their blank stares toward the road were occasionally interrupted by a shared uncomfortable glance.

Sanders felt the phone in his pocket vibrate. He pulled it out so he could read the message, and then responded. The pressure from the weapon he had tucked in the small of his back ripped away at his conscience. He waited anxiously for Moynihan to turn away so he could do the deed. She hadn't complied, and each time their eyes met, all he could do was force an awkward smile. This time her eyes held his gaze and penetrated his soul.

"What is it, Jake?" she asked.

Those four words and the sincerity behind them crushed his nerve. He found himself unable to answer. His eyes darted nervously when he heard the sound of crunching gravel, signaling the arrival of the SUV. It stopped in the driveway before it came into view.

Moynihan reached over and took his hand. "Jake, you can talk to me."

He looked away, so she leaned toward him and entered his field of view.

"I'm here for you. I just want you to know that."

He began to sweat and clenched his jaw and toes as he wrestled with his conflicting thoughts.

The noise of the vehicle's door opening and closing shattered the silence.

"We're going to be okay." Moynihan smiled confidently, her eyes reflecting her heart.

Sanders heard the back door of the truck open and stood up. It was followed by the sound of rustling material.

"I know," he said. He put his arm around her. "Come on. There's someone I want you to meet. Something's come up, and I need to head out, but I'll be in touch."

They walked around the trailer and rounded the back of the SUV. Rudy Pagano stood there with a confused look on his face.

"Hey, Rudy, this is Agent Moynihan."

Moynihan held her hand out and looked to the ground as he shook her hand. She froze when she saw the pair of body bags laid out next to the vehicle. Her face was ashen when she looked back up at Pagano. She turned to Sanders, and her body began to shake.

"Only one tonight," Sanders said to Pagano with a nod.

"Oh," he said, obviously confused. The two men exchanged an uncomfortable look. "Sorry about that. Where's the stiff?"

Sanders knew Moynihan had felt the tension between the two men.

"This way," he said.

He grabbed a body bag and led Pagano over to the trailer. The two shared severe glances as they stuffed the Russian into the bag, walked to the vehicle and heaved it into the back of the Chevy Tahoe. After a brief silence, Pagano grabbed the other body bag and threw it in the back before closing the hatch.

"We've got to head out. I'll be in touch," Sanders said, before the two men climbed into the SUV and drove off.

Chapter 71

SHE STOOD THERE in shock, afraid of what might happen next. The faint sound of gravel being crunched under the weight of a car's tires sent a cold shiver down Cathy Moynihan's spine. She wasn't sure how long she'd been standing there, but it had seemed like an eternity.

Her heart pounded from a combination of nervousness and fear as she scrambled into the bushes. A silver Honda Civic was slowly pulling into the quarry with its headlights turned off. A man got out and walked over to the trailer. He looked inside and then returned to the car.

The man placed a call on his cell phone. Moynihan couldn't understand Russian, but she could detect the urgency in his voice.

She stayed hidden and watched and waited, trying not to move a muscle. Within twenty minutes another car approached. The FBI agent recognized the black sedan and its tinted windows from earlier in the evening, and her pulse quickened. Her suspicions were confirmed when the driver's-side door opened and the dome light inside the car remained dark. She noted a man was in the passenger seat, before watching the driver get out and walk over to the Honda. He grabbed a package and headed back to his car.

Moynihan worked her way through the trees as quickly and silently as she could. There were no cars in sight, so she dashed to her Camry and carefully glided inside just before the black sedan pulled out of the driveway. Her heart thumped loudly as the car turned left. It was immediately followed by the silver Honda. She quickly ducked down into her seat and let the car pass. When she sat up, Moynihan realized she had been holding her breath and quickly filled her lungs with air before starting the engine.

She left her lights off and pulled out quickly in pursuit of the black sedan. A deer suddenly jumped out of the woods and forced her to slam on the brakes. She managed to avoid contact with the animal, before nervously continuing after the car.

The situation was overwhelming. Moynihan was almost certain that one of the two body bags Rudy Pagano had laid out was meant for her, but she had no proof. She decided the events of the past few hours were too far above her pay grade to sort out on her own. There was no doubt in her mind that the phone call she had been putting off needed to be made. Someone she could trust needed to know what was going on.

The FBI agent turned on her cell phone and punched in his number, but the answering machine picked up on the first ring. Things had already spun out of control, so her best bet was to leave a message.

"Uncle Ivor, sorry to bother you, but there's something going on that I think you should know about. Director Culder has pulled me into something he's claiming has to do with national security. I've been told not to let anyone at the bureau know about what's going on. The story I'm getting is that he thinks there's a mole at the bureau.

"I'm pretty sure he's full of shit, so I wanted to fill you in. People have died… We lost three agents at a house in Poolesville. They were taking a teenager in for questioning—off the record—which doesn't seem right. This poor girl's brother was connected to the death of Senator Soller's son.

"I'm worried about what's going on, so I need your help. At first I wasn't sure if you had something to do with my involvement in the case, but now I'm sure that couldn't be possible. I'm scared and don't want to make it four dead, if you know what I mean. Jake Sanders is one of the men involved. He's working with some other guy named Rudy… I can't remember his last name. I was a little distracted when I met him.

"Jake seemed to be okay at first, but I got the heebie-geebies just before this Rudy guy showed up. I don't think I'm in any immediate danger, but…I don't know, I just feel better knowing that you know, if that makes any sense.

"I love you. Call me soon."

The call to her uncle had helped settle her nerves. He wasn't her uncle by blood, but he was her father's best friend, and the very reason she had chosen law enforcement for her career path. Moynihan had been adamant about making it through the bureau on her own. Her uncle respected her decision, and together they had made sure nobody knew how significant their connection was. Right now she just wanted to find out where this car was heading, and then she would try to make sense of the rest of this in the morning.

Chapter 72

Route 267, Virginia

RUDY PAGANO SHOT a disgusted look at his friend and looked back to the road. "What was that all about?" he asked in his heavy New York accent.

"Don't worry about it, okay?" Jake Sanders said, clearly annoyed.

"Culder gave you the order to take her out. What the hell happened?"

"Look, man, she's FBI." Sanders stiffened. "There's no fucking way I'm going to kill someone who's just trying to do the right thing."

"Jesus. So that's it," Pagano said in an inquisitive tone. "You want to bang her." He laughed. "I should have put her out of your misery. I'd have been doing her a favor!"

"Yeah, right. Like you're some prize."

Pagano shot him a probing glance. "It ain't gonna happen. You realize that, don't you?" His tone had an uncomfortable finality. "She's as good as dead. She knows too much."

"That's my problem, all right?" Sanders poked Pagano in the arm with his index finger. "I don't need a fuckin' preacher. And if you hear anything about it going down, you tell me. Got that?"

They had been working on the HVT Squad together since its inception, and for two years prior to that on the FBI TacOps team. The two men had developed a strong bond over the years, and it ran deeper than their loyalty to the FBI director.

"She's really got you worked up. Did you already tap that shit? Man, you dog." Pagano couldn't help but laugh at the fact that he was half serious. "I didn't think you had it in you. A regular Prince Charming we've got here."

Sanders exhaled loudly and shot a disapproving look at his friend. "Do me a favor and shut the fuck up."

Pagano shook his head in disgust. "Look, Jake. We've been friends for a long time, so I'm going to give it to you straight. If it's not you, then he'll have someone else take care of it." He thumped Sanders on the chest with the back of his fist as if it would knock some sense into him. "You know that. You should've just saved yourself the shit storm this is going to cause."

"Whatever," Sanders snapped.

"I'm serious. Culder isn't bad if he likes you, but this is bound to piss him off. If you don't take care of it, it's going to come back and bite you in the ass."

"All right, all right, I get it. I fucking hear you. This conversation is over." Sanders fired an angry look at Pagano and said, "I'll deal with Culder, don't you fucking worry."

Pagano was starting to worry. "Man, did you hit your head on something?" He looked over at Sanders and could instantly tell the comment had struck a nerve.

"That's right," he spat.

"What?"

"Our buddy in the back there." He motioned with his thumb to the back of the truck. "He knocked the shit out of me." He turned to Pagano and said, "She saved my ass."

His friend could tell by the tone of his voice that he was serious.

"Un-fucking-real." Pagano shook his head and smiled. "Good to know Wonder Woman has stayed hot after all these years."

"Yeah, no shit." Sanders exhaled in relief after getting that off his chest. "I'd be in one of those bags if it wasn't for her."

"Got it." Pagano turned and shot him a grave look. "You're still trying to bang her. You can't bullshit me."

The two men burst out laughing.

"Prick," Sanders said. "Where are we heading?"

"The airport. We'll pick up Culder tomorrow when he's ready and head to Chicago." He glanced at his friend and then back to the road. "Oh, and make sure I have my phone ready when you tell him the news about your girlfriend."

"What?" Sanders asked, confused.

Pagano put on a big smile and said, "I want to take a picture of the look on his face."

"Fuck you."

Chapter 73

Khrushchev Residence, Moscow, Russia

THE SOUND OF the grandiose doorbell echoed through the mansion's cavernous hallways. Yuri Khrushchev had been expecting his guest. Normally the house staff would take care of tending to the door, but today was a special day, and he wasn't going to leave anything to chance. Everyone had been dismissed for the weekend so he could celebrate the occasion without distraction. For him, this marked the beginning of a new Soviet era. It was the culmination of decades of careful planning and preparation.

This was their time. A combination of technological breakthroughs and economic circumstance had presented the perfect opportunity to strike. In one crippling blow, they would destabilize the United States. The journey back to power was almost complete.

Khrushchev pulled the ornate wooden door open, and Andrei Tinkov stood before him. Tinkov's chauffeur was just beyond, waiting patiently next to a royal blue Rolls-Royce Phantom limousine. The exquisite yet beastly machine was less imposing on the cobblestones of the massive circular driveway than when driving through the streets of Moscow.

"Andrei," Khrushchev said in his booming voice. He vigorously shook his visitor's hand. "Come in, come in," he continued, leading his guest inside.

Tinkov smiled. "Thank you, Yuri. I apologize, but I cannot stay long."

"Yes, I know. You have a flight to Lisbon. That is what I wish to discuss."

Tinkov furrowed his brow in anticipation and followed his friend down a long hallway into a large study with wood-paneled walls.

"You have something you wish for me to bring up at the meeting?"

"It is time, my good friend," Khrushchev said with equal parts enthusiasm and concern.

"Oh?" Tinkov didn't look surprised. He looked up and admired the blue skies that were visible through the long line of rectangular skylights. He exhaled and said, "After all these years."

"Pavel almost has everything ready, but I wanted you to be the first to hear my decision to move forward. It is time to strike. Time for the motherland to rise once again, but we need your help."

"Of course," Tinkov said, nodding his head. "We've been waiting for this day to arrive for a long time."

"We know where everything is kept, but I need you to move forward with the plan at the meeting," Khrushchev explained. "That way, no suspicions will be raised. It will be too late by the time they realize what has happened."

The communists had always kept a working plan to take down America, and it was one that evolved with the times.

"Are you sure it is possible for us to succeed?" Tinkov questioned. "If the United States survives this, I fear we will not."

"Yes," he said emphatically. "By the end of the week, the country will be in complete and utter chaos." He smiled at his friend. "The devastation will send them back to the Stone Age. We will soon have our power and our revenge."

Khrushchev walked over to the bar and reached for two glasses before picking up a bottle. The drink he selected represented a time that was a distant memory for both of them. He chose a bottle of the Soviet Union's traditional Zelyonaya Marka vodka. Tinkov's chin inclined as his friend poured them each a measure.

Khrushchev creased his brow, and his eyes darkened. "I told the president to refuse to attend next week's G8 summit in Camp David," he said. "He can't be on American soil when this goes down. It would be too risky."

"Yes, I saw that the news wasn't taken lightly by the American president."

Khrushchev handed Tinkov his glass of vodka. "So be it." He raised his glass. "To Mother Russia."

Tinkov nodded and followed suit. "Yes, Yuri, to Mother Russia!"

They both swallowed their drinks and their wince gave way to smiles.
"Make this happen, Andrei."

"I will." Tinkov paused for a moment and corrected himself. "We will."

Chapter 74

Lucky Stone Quarry, Ashburn, VA

IT WAS THE brake lights that had tipped the Bratva courier off. The unexpected blast of red light this late at night in the middle of nowhere could only mean trouble. His job was to run packages from Chicago to Virginia for the organization several times a week. He didn't know anything about the dark blue Toyota Camry he had turned around to follow, but he remembered that it had been parked on the road outside the quarry. This was the sort of attention to detail for which he would be well rewarded.

The first call he made was to Chicago. Within a couple of minutes his cell phone rang.

"'Allo," he answered.

"We will be coming up behind you soon," the caller said in Russian.

"I will keep my distance. I do not have my lights on. There are no cars on the roads at this hour."

He buzzed with nervous excitement as the blacked-out car quickly overtook him. They were being led farther away from civilization by the driver at the front of the line. It was obvious that they didn't want any witnesses, and chose a game of Follow the Leader that would bring someone straight to hell.

His pulse began to quicken as the car in front of him dove onto a side road and increased its speed. He remained on the main road and maintained a safe distance to stay out of sight from the Camry. He noticed that the lead car had slowed its pace, before it turned abruptly onto a side road.

The action was over by the time he made it to the intersection. Four Bratva soldiers had surrounded the Toyota, and a woman was leaned up against the car with her hands on her head. They forced her into the lead car at gunpoint. One of the soldiers approached the courier's car and he rolled down his window.

"Nice work," the soldier said with a satisfied smile. "I will tell Pavel what you have done. She could have caused big problems for the operation."

"Is she from the police?"

"Something like that. You must head back immediately. It's possible you will need to make another run when you get back."

"So soon?"

"Yes, but it might be the last one."

He smiled and held up his thermos of coffee to show he was prepared. "I will head straight back."

"Perhaps you will be back home soon," the soldier said.

The courier watched the soldier jog to the woman's car and drive it into the woods. He liked the sound of home.

Chapter 75

Kozlov Bratva hideout, Leesburg, VA

THEY WERE LEFT alone in a basement room of the compound. The fluorescent lights buzzed rhythmically as they flickered. Maria Soller found it increasingly difficult to keep track of how much time had passed. She and Melody Millar had been handcuffed to steel railings that were bolted to the concrete wall. They were both seated in wooden chairs with metal frames that brought back memories from high school. The door to the yellow rectangular room was opposite a wall lined with government surplus desks. The musty smell of the basement was a vast improvement over the skanky hoods.

Soller had tucked her iPhone away and out of view at her first opportunity. Once their captors had left, she had tried to calm Millar down. The teenager was still in shock from the earlier killings, and focusing on someone else had proven to be a good way for Soller to deal with the situation.

"We'll be out of here before you know it, Melody. Just hang in there," she whispered.

"I'm really scared," she said.

She was no senator's daughter, which Soller realized might make her feel disposable. She leaned toward her, but the reassurance the gesture was meant to convey was quickly erased by an angry pull from her restraint.

"It's okay. We'll get out of here together," Soller insisted. "Soon. I promise."

Millar forced a smile, but it was quickly wiped away by commotion out in the hallway. They exchanged a fearful look as the men barked out commands in Russian. Seconds later the door flew open and three powerful men shoved a hooded, violently protesting figure toward the other side of the room. Soller recognized that it was a woman. The hood brought back unsettling memories. She felt a chill as she recalled the putrid smell of the canvas that was once fastened over her head.

"Fucking assholes!" the woman yelled.

She kicked one of the guards in the hip, clearly hoping to hit him in his groin. They immediately converged on her flailing body and secured her to the railing.

She must have known she had missed her target, but it did nothing to break her spirit.

"Touch me like that again, and I'll make sure I don't miss next time," she growled.

Two of the soldiers were forced to hold back the man she'd kicked. He struggled to get free from their hold and landed a blow to her head, which sent her to the ground.

"Bitch," he spat in Russian. "Next time you will be mine."

"Calm down, you idiot," the other soldier wearing a utility jacket said. "We need her to stay healthy. If you harm her, we won't have a chip to bargain with in case there is a problem. She's yours once we're in the clear."

The dazed woman dangled from the wrist that was secured to the steel railing. A soldier walked over and helped her into a chair. The soldiers argued bitterly in Russian for a few minutes before they exited the room. Soller listened to them bicker back and forth down the hall. She looked over at the woman, who was rising slowly out of her slumped posture. Her hood moved back and forth as if she was trying to scan the room, but she didn't make a sound.

Soller looked over at Millar, who again was on the brink of tears, and then back to the new arrival. "Are you okay?" she whispered across the room. There was no response, so she decided to try again. "Hey. Can you hear me? They left. It's okay." She wasn't sure what she should do to gain her trust. "Nod your head if you can hear me." Still the mysterious woman did nothing. "My name is Maria," she continued, "and my friend Melody is here too."

When the woman heard the name Melody, her head seemed to perk up.

"We were grabbed by these people from a house in Maryland," she explained quietly. "We're not sure what they're going to do to us..."

The sounds of footsteps were heard from the hall. It was more than one person, and the noise was growing louder. Maria stopped talking, closed her eyes and began to pray.

Chapter 76

Island Industries satellite office, Reston, VA

THE MORNING SUN punched its way through the blinds and slowly worked its way down the wall toward the couch. Jack Turner was in a deep sleep when it reached him. He opened an eye with a squint and instinctively jerked his head away from the beam. He sat up and put his hands on his knees.

"Shit." He tried to wipe away the morning grog with a head shake. "Addy? Hey, Addy?" He looked at his watch. "Motherfucker."

Turner walked into Addy Simpson's office, where Addy was slowly coming to life on the other couch.

"What? What is it?"

"It's already eight in the goddamn morning."

The two men looked at each other and shook their heads. Simpson took a deep breath and exhaled.

"I'm tellin' ya, we're too old for this shit, Addy," Turner said. "You know what the aching feeling you have is? I'll tell you what it is: it's the twenty-five-year-old inside beating on the walls that have him trapped. He's wondering what the fuck happened and how the hell he can get out."

"I can't remember the last time I slept past seven," Simpson said, indirectly agreeing with his friend. He pulled his cell phone out of his pocket and checked the display. "You've got to be kidding me." He read the text messages first and then punched in the code to listen to his voicemail. After listening to the message his expression turned to a grimace. "I turned the ringer off when we were in Poolesville and forgot to turn it back on."

"Shit. Did we miss something?"

"You could say that. The mystery cell phone from the FBI site came online last night."

Simpson shook his head in disbelief, and Turner mirrored his response.

"Yeah, tell me about it. They traced it to a place just down the road."

"You're kidding."

Simpson gave him a hard look. "We're like a couple of damn amateurs these days."

Addy Simpson sat in silence for a moment and then explained that just after Turner had fallen asleep last night, he had placed a call to Matilde Soller. The conversation had a painful but expected outcome, the sort of emotion that can only be conjured up when delivering bad news to a loved one. He explained that he had left out the details of what they had found at the house in Poolesville, telling his friend that he was afraid that would have been too much for her broken heart to take.

Turner and Simpson both had been up against worse odds through the years, and neither man was about to give up now. Jack Turner sensed a mixture of guilt, anger, and pain, and knew that being sloppy and missing the crucial communication had hit Simpson hard. It may well have been too late for young Maria Soller, but they needed to do what a good soldier did best: compartmentalize the emotion and focus on the job at hand.

"You know you're right," Simpson said.

Turner raised an eyebrow. "About what?"

"I'm too close to this…to the point where I'm making mistakes."

"Yeah, well, it happens—"

"Let's not sugarcoat it, Jack. I could very well have gotten you killed last night."

"But you didn't."

Simpson shook his head. "Now we've missed out on a lead that could have broken this wide open." He continued to shake his head, this time it was with guilt. "And maybe even led us to Maria," he said, the sadness evident in his voice.

"Look, we don't have many options right now," Jack Turner said as he sat down in one of the chairs. "We're doing the best that we can. Most of our guys are out of the country. It's not like we have an army of operatives. Feeling sorry for yourself isn't going to help matters," he said flatly.

"Have you spoken to Trent?" Simpson asked, and noted the surprise on Jack's face. "What I mean is, can you get in touch with him?"

Turner was clearly uncomfortable.

"Okay, look," Simpson said, "don't even answer that. If you can get in touch with him somehow, do it. We need him."

Turner furrowed his brow but remained silent.

"If I've learned anything since yesterday, it's how I would react to a situation similar to what happened with him and Ryan." Addy locked eyes with his friend and hid nothing behind them. "I get it. I could have handled things better. I could have been more supportive, understanding. I'm the one who signed up for the risk, despite the good doctor's recommendation not to bring a twin into the program. And you're right." His expression darkened. He bowed his head in thought for a moment before returning to his friend. "Feeling sorry for myself is stupid, I should know better than that."

They were the leaders of one of the most formidable paramilitary teams in the world. As much as the training served to prepare them for the horrors this world had to offer, at the end of the day they were all still human.

"I'll see what I can do about Trent," Turner said. "Now let's get over to that site and see if we can find anything."

Chapter 77

FRANK CULDER HAD slept very little. His eye was on the prize, and the thrill of a power grab provided enough of a buzz to top off his energy levels. Normally he wouldn't come into the office on a Sunday morning, but he had some loose ends to tie up before taking a trip to Chicago. His men had spent the night in the bureau's private hangar at Frederick Municipal Airport and were planning to pick up the director at Reagan National with the jet when he was ready.

His technology lab had delivered the expected news. The hard drive in the computer taken from Maximillian Soller II's car was useless; the techs weren't able to retrieve any data. The lab also confirmed that the other device the forensics team retrieved from the scene had been assembled by Francis Millar. His fingerprints were found on the inside of the system's chassis. They explained that the device was used to find wireless networks. The system would automatically connect to open wireless networks and scan for vulnerable computers. It was also programmed to exploit known hacks into any secure wireless networks it encountered.

Culder's patience was growing thin as he waited for a call. When his cell phone finally did come to life, he didn't recognize the caller.

"Culder," he answered.

"Director Culder, this is Bart Stapleton calling."

He recognized the name but couldn't connect a face or title. "Bart Stapleton?"

"Yes. That's right. Senator Soller said I should give you a call. He told me you might be able to help me out with a little problem."

Culder considered how much easier life would be once Soller stopped cashing favors in all the time. He still wasn't sure who the caller was, so he pulled a browser up on his computer and searched for the name. He was surprised.

"Sure, Mr. Chairman. What can I do to help?"

"Please, call me Bart."

"Okay. What can I do to help, Bart?"

"To be blunt, I want you to help me crucify someone."

The director was put off by the comment, until his eyes drifted to the requisite portrait of President Vincent Cross that was hung on his office wall. He smiled. "I see."

"Rumor has it there's a particular Island he enjoys. A place that makes the legendary Alcatraz look tame. If the public were to get wind that he's connected to a group of hoodlums, I think our friends in the media could do something with that."

There was history between Cross and Culder, and it wasn't pretty. The president had become aware of an attempt by the FBI director to pry into his private life. The action was done at Senator Soller's request and, in so many words, the president reminded Culder that J. Edgar Hoover was long dead, and that it wouldn't be wise to try to follow in his footsteps.

The director was amazed at the president's reach. He still hadn't figured out who the mole at the bureau was, but it was only a matter of time before he did. Cross was a man he would happily bring down, given the chance. His thoughts returned to the call he was expecting, and he decided he would take advantage of the opportunity.

"You know, I think there might be a little birdie on that Island that will sing for us."

"Splendid," Stapleton said. "I have an important meeting, but I will get back to you directly. If that birdie needs a little incentive to make its music, that is something that can be arranged."

Culder smiled. "I don't think that will be necessary."

Chapter 78

The Stradivari Society, Chicago, IL

THE HOPE THAT filled her eyes the previous evening had been extinguished. It all started when she connected with a kindred spirit. He had introduced himself as Tony Kalem. He was rugged, mysterious, and Victoria Eden sensed the danger, along with their mutual attraction. He was as suave as he was hard to get, and what began with turbulence on a personal level eventually escalated to something physical once the plane landed.

She had big aspirations for her first major audition, but things had gone horribly wrong. When the virtuoso violinist arrived at her hotel, she discovered her instrument had been damaged. The bombardment of emotions had been overwhelming. The tears came and went, but the emptiness remained. After her father had passed away, she discovered the violin was the only thing that could erase her feeling of being alone. It made her feel independent, like she didn't need anyone or anything else. Her beauty and attitude made relationships difficult. She was intimidating to most and couldn't be bothered by the rest.

Every blue moon she'd come across someone who was different—a man like Tony Kalem. Channeling despair into anger was easy for her. It was part of the survival instinct for someone who was alone, but the thought of being eternally lonely scared her. What happened to her mother scared her.

There was one person she could always count on to wipe away any despair that withstood the anger. She would never call him to discuss her problems with men, but he was someone who would always provide sound advice on life. This time she had desperately needed help, or her audition wouldn't happen. He was able to come through for her, the constant rock she could lean on. Nevin Perlman, her godfather, had a friend in Chicago who he was confident would lend her an instrument.

She approached the building on South Michigan Avenue on foot. The air was crisp, and she once again carried a hopeful attitude. The audition later that morning meant the world to her. She would be showcasing her talent with a heavy heart. This, she thought, would be the key that would unshackle her from the past. She knew it would make her mother and father proud, albeit in their absence.

The Stradivari Society occupied the entire fifth floor of the large building dedicated to the fine arts. The bell chimed, and she stepped out into the reception area with her violin slung over her shoulder. An aging woman with kind eyes returned her timid smile from the reception desk.

"Hello, dear. How may I help you?"

"I'm here to see Dr. Becker, please." Her voice was nervous, but hopeful.

"Dr. Becker?" The receptionist's tone didn't hide the fact that she was ready to play traffic cop.

"Yes. Dr. Nathan Becker, please. He's still here, isn't he?"

The receptionist laughed. "Of course he is. The Stradivari Society wouldn't be here without him."

She realized she needed to draw on her usual confidence to get past this one. "Nevin Perlman sent me."

The receptionist dropped her chin and fired a look of surprise over the top of her glasses. "Nevin Perlman?"

"Yes."

"My goodness. Isn't that a name from the past? Tragic what happened." She shook her head grievingly. "We've all wondered what had become of him."

Eden knew the woman was referring to the death of her father. Mentioning his name would be a mistake, but it was something she hoped she could do in time.

"He sent me here to see if I could borrow an instrument. Mine was damaged on the flight over, and I would greatly appreciate your help."

The receptionist held a warm smile. "A friend of Nevin's is a friend of ours. One second. I'll get him." She picked up the phone and pressed a button. "Honey, Nevin Perlman sent someone to speak with you. Can you come upfront? Wonderful." She looked up at Eden as she returned the phone to the cradle and said, "He'll be right here, dear."

Thirty seconds later a dapper elderly man in a brown tweed suit appeared from behind the reception area. He had short white hair and thick brown-rimmed glasses and was wearing a flashy orange bow tie. He lowered his chin to the side and approached with his hand extended.

"Nathan Becker. Pleased to meet you," he said.

She smiled. "Victoria Eden. Nice to meet you too."

He had a firm handshake that showed strength for his age.

"Rumor has it you've been sent by Nevin Perlman." Becker lowered his chin again as though he wanted a rumor confirmed.

"Yes. He said you might be able to help."

"Help?" He frowned. "Why I sure hope so. He's a very kind man. One of the best teachers the violin has ever known." His voice was soft, and his appraising look picked up the sadness in her eyes. It was as if he knew to leave the subject of her father alone. "Do send him my regards," he said with a curt nod. "And what can I do for you today? Are you here to request admission for this evening?"

The evening's annual black-tie performance commanded fifty thousand dollars a head to raise money for the society. They put the world's best classical instrumentalists on one stage in the same evening, and the gala event always sold out.

"Oh heavens no. I wouldn't want to trouble you with that," Victoria said. She slipped the case off her shoulder. "My violin was damaged on the flight over. I have an audition with the Chicago Symphony Orchestra later this morning." She shrugged sheepishly and showed her discomfort for the imposition. "I was here to see if I could borrow an instrument." She offered a hopeful smile.

Becker didn't answer immediately, so she added, "And possibly practice with it here for a little while first. So I can get used to how it plays."

She opened the case and showed him the damage from the flight over.

He let out a long exhale as he considered the question. "Hmm. Victoria Eden? I beg your pardon, but I don't recall hearing your name before. That's unusual considering for whom you will be auditioning." He raised his chin and pursed his lips curiously. "Is Nevin your teacher?"

"No, sorry. He worked with me for a couple years when I was a young girl, but it's been quite a long time. We're just old friends. He set up the audition for me."

"Then who, may I ask?"

She smiled weakly. "Nobody in your circles, I'm sure," she said, thinking of her father.

His expression softened when he met her eyes. "Interesting. Frankly, I'm surprised you're being given such an opportunity." He raised an index finger and said, "It mustn't be wasted. Nevin wouldn't send just anyone here." He smiled and gave a series of eager nods. "Let me see if I can get you set up with something to suit your needs."

She exhaled in relief. "Thank you. Thank you so much."

Chapter 79

Downtown hotel, Chicago, IL

TRENT TURNER AND Etzy Millar had worked through the night with The Shop's CDWG Division from their hotel room. The pair had shared the single desk available. Turner sat on the chair, while Millar used one of the two single beds for his seat. One of the largest financial institutions in the country, Nations Bank, had agreed to grant The Shop access to its computer systems.

Within a couple of hours they had managed to discover an infected computer in the wild. The team had quickly confirmed it was a surgeon bot, one of the systems that would carry out the most critical aspects of the operation. It represented an opportunity to uncover the attack vectors being used, but it was a job that would take time.

There was no way to know what the owners of the botnet were monitoring, so until they had more details about what they were dealing with, an intrusive large-scale search for the malware wasn't feasible. If the owners of the botnet found out they had been compromised, it could set off a destructive chain of events. Since they were now confident the operation was going to impact banks, and they had no idea to what extent, that risk wasn't one they were willing to take. All conversations between the bank's technology assets and The Shop were confined to private cell phones.

Etzy Millar exhaled in frustration and leaned back, supporting himself with his elbows on the bed. "We've got to narrow this down," he said. "An attack could start any second, and we don't even know what it's going to do."

"Any thoughts, Finger?" CDWG Director Cynthia Grayson asked, her voice coming through a connection over the computer.

Trent Turner had been deep in thought and was ready to chime in. "Okay, let's do it then," he said.

"Do what?" Millar asked.

"Narrow down the purpose of the botnet," she said. "We know that Nations Bank is a target, so let's start there. Let's talk out the likely targets inside the bank."

"They could be trying to bring all of the systems down," Millar said.

"Possibly," Grayson replied. "But if that was the purpose, they certainly didn't need something this elaborate to accomplish their goal."

"Sure," Millar agreed. "Why wait if that was the case? They designed it so you could plug in different modules, which wouldn't be necessary if that was their end game."

"I think there might be something more obvious than that, when you consider how the technology side of the banking systems works," Turner explained. "There are—what?—ten, maybe twenty banking systems that run the majority of the world's banks?"

"Probably. Go on," Grayson said.

"We know Nations runs its transactions through a banking software platform developed by Allegiance Financial Systems. It's called DataBank."

"Right," Grayson confirmed. "They know what they're doing, so let's assume they're targeting a specific banking platform."

"Exactly." Turner punched the keys on his laptop, and when he pressed Enter the search results displayed on the screen. He pulled up a sales presentation for the company and began reading. "DataBank is running in more than thirty percent of the world's banks. Eighty percent of the banks with assets over three hundred and fifty billion use it and—get this—ninety-five percent if you narrow it down to the United States."

"Nations is one of the largest banks out there," Grayson said. "If this is about transactions, we can split it down even further... Only look at banks big enough to move a significant amount of money without immediately raising eyebrows."

"The modules would come into play there," Millar added. "They might have a module that gets the money out somehow. Maybe they have another one set to wreak havoc on the systems to buy them some time afterward."

"That would be a solid plan," Turner said. "Cyndi, do we have anyone on the inside at one of the other major banks that uses DataBank?"

"Give me a sec," Grayson said. Mouse clicks and keyboard strokes could be heard in the background. "Here we go. Okay, say over fifty billion in assets. Here's one, Spartan Bank. They're almost one trillion. I'll have my analysts focus there and try to identify a pattern."

"What have you managed to dig up on the Federal Reserve?" Turner asked. "That's definitely going to be another common thread. All of these banks will be connected to the Federal Reserve system."

"We hacked into its network through a system that was downloading security updates," Grayson confirmed. "We hijacked the session and managed to look around and set up a couple more backdoors, but we haven't found anything yet. We're still in there poking around and wading through their traffic logs."

"There was a Federal Reserve branch that correlated with most of the dead hackers," Turner said.

"True. We can consider major locations for the big banks that correlate with Fed branches," Grayson suggested. "It's something else to narrow things down."

"Sounds good." Turner thought about the results from Cannibal. "What about the hackers that turned up dead on Interpol?"

"I've put a couple of analysts on that, and they haven't come up with anything," Grayson said. "We'll look for connections to big banks."

"The Federal Reserve is the central bank for the United States, so it's got more money than any other target," Turner pointed out. "We should assume they're going big, considering the level of sophistication."

"You know the Fed could well have its most significant assets abroad," Grayson replied. "The politicians have been fighting for visibility into its foreign dealings since the dawn of time."

"Good point. Try digging into its overseas accounts and see if anything lines up," Turner said. "Also see if there are ties to The Collective."

Grayson didn't respond immediately, and then said, "We'll focus on that angle for now and assume the US is the target."

Chapter 80

The Stradivari Society, Chicago, IL

PAVEL KOZLOV's EYES were cold, void of emotion. "I understand," he said in Russian.

The man on the other end of the phone didn't like to rush a plan, but recent events and a lifetime of experience had made the decision to put Operation Berlin on the fast track easy for him. Yuri Khrushchev was also smart enough to know that no good battle plan survived first contact with the enemy, so he wasn't alarmed. They needed to stay nimble.

"Are you on track with the operation?" Khrushchev asked, but the question was more of a command.

"Yes, we are. Tomorrow, correct?" Kozlov answered. There was too much at stake, so he wanted to make sure they were in sync.

"Tomorrow," Khrushchev confirmed. "Did your men take care of The American?"

Kozlov closed his eyes and bowed his head. He knew his delayed response had already given his mentor the answer.

"No. He has proven to be a very difficult man to kill."

There was an uncomfortable pause that could only mean the confidence in him from his comrades back in the Motherland had begun to wane.

"And the internal situation? The hacker that chose the senator's son?" Khrushchev pressed. When the response wasn't immediate he added, "No more mistakes, Pavel." His tone was reprimanding.

Kozlov raised his head and prepared to deliver new details he knew would strain their relationship further. "We had a problem with delivering the codes last night," he admitted. He could hear his mentor take in a deep breath.

"What kind of problem?"

"Our man was not there for the pickup. Other arrangements were made, and they made it safely to the backup site."

Khrushchev didn't respond for a long moment and finally said, "Continue."

"The men discovered an FBI agent was following them. They led her into a trap and were able to take her alive."

"What?" The hard line communist was irate.

"Yes. We will find out what she knows. Our men can be very persuasive."

Khrushchev was taken aback. The situation was much worse than he had thought. He knew Kozlov was loyal to their cause, but Yuri Khrushchev was now joining the ranks of those who doubted their comrade's effectiveness.

Kozlov heard a squeak from what he assumed was his comrade's chair as he sat down. Next he heard the rhythmic drumming of his fingers on the desk, like Khrushchev always did before he made a big decision.

"It is wise to keep the two operations completely separate," Khrushchev finally said.

Kozlov felt the loss of faith in his ability to execute physically. He rubbed the bridge of his nose and did what any good soldier would do.

"Yes, it is the best option," he said. "We'll remain prepared to handle things if the situation changes."

"Take care of this, Pavel," Khrushchev demanded, the importance of their operation evident.

This wouldn't be the first time Pavel Kozlov had his back against the wall, and his resolve to prove his doubters wrong was absolute.

"I will," he said.

"There is a meeting with The Group today," Khrushchev said. "Andrei will set everything into motion."

"We are receiving the latest data from the targets," Kozlov confirmed. "Dimitri said he will have everything completed to send the final commands in plenty of time."

"Good. And the FBI woman?"

"I have told the men to do whatever it takes to extract the information from her quickly," he answered in a dark tone. "Whatever it takes."

Chapter 81

Kozlov Bratva hideout, Leesburg, VA

SHE WAS FORCED to strip down to her underwear as soon as they entered the room. The sheer purple underwear she had once considered cute now made her feel vulnerable. They were intimidating. Hard men, definitely killers, and they enjoyed the show. At first it wasn't clear whether the two men were planning to rape her or just wanted to cause humiliation. They spoke in Russian, but lewd comments were a universal language, and she understood.

When they motioned her over to the bench, she reluctantly obeyed. She was paralyzed by the cold, deliberate eyes of her captors as they approached. Everything happened so fast. There was no time for her to react. They had strapped her to the bench and draped a damp cloth over her face before she could manage to take a breath. Her heart pounded as they fastened a restraint around her neck. She forced herself to breathe. She felt the bench rise up, which brought her feet above the rest of her body. Instinct told her to hold her legs together as the blood rushed to her head.

That was some minutes ago, she believed. She wasn't sure... Now she listened, her covered eyes wide with terror. The next assault was on its way. She could visualize what was making the sounds—a spigot shooting a stream of water into a metal bucket. The initial pitter-patter on the bottom, followed by a crescendo of water as it tinkled its way to the top. Then three steps toward her. At first they weren't sounds that tormented her. It was the third bucket that turned once-benign sounds into something she feared.

This was bucket number four, and the familiar noise had transformed yet again. Cathy Moynihan didn't know how to describe what she felt. It was beyond fear; she was much more than horrified. Whatever it was, it numbed her. It was what she imagined a claustrophobic person might experience when locked away in a small, dark place. She contemplated whether this was karma, after what had happened to the man in the trailer. Maybe this was his way of coming back to haunt her.

The Russian didn't bother to repeat the question this time, and he began to pour the water over her head. Panic set in.

"They took him!" she yelled through the water-soaked cloth.

The Russian poured the rest of the cold water over her bare skin as she coughed her airway clear. The last time they had emptied a full bucket over her head, she'd passed out and woke up with a Russian pressing on her stomach to drain the fluid through her mouth and nose.

Breathing was difficult. She gasped for air in between coughing the rest of the water out of her lungs. She didn't want to go there again. They had broken her. The violent shivering was a brutal combination of cold and fear.

"Who?" the Russian said.

"The FBI."

Moynihan began to cough violently again. She was afraid to tell them he was dead in case his life represented a way out of this.

"Where did they take him?" the Russian barked.

"I don't know. Maybe back to headquarters." She tried to control her breathing to suppress her panic.

There was silence for a moment, and then the two soldiers began to converse in Russian. She felt her muscles tense up as they turned on the water. Controlled breathing wasn't enough to keep her calm, the sounds triggering a frenzied hysteria to which her restraints answered back and held her down. The Russian had just taken the three steps toward her. Her eyes were covered by the cloth, but she still closed them tight, hoping doing so would somehow take her away from this nightmare.

The Russian dribbled some water onto the cloth, and her body jerked reflexively. The goose bumps on her body felt like they were growing with each shiver. She couldn't see the maniacal smile of satisfaction he shared with his accomplice, but she felt it.

"Why were you following us?" he demanded.

"You killed our people," she said, her voice desperate as she prepared for the inevitable.

"Tell me what you were looking for, or I will kill you." His voice was cold and calculating.

"The person who killed Senator Soller's son," Moynihan pleaded.

"What else do you know about us?"

Her fear turned to anger as she teetered on the edge of shock. The Russian poured the water over her head and stopped just before she was out of breath.

"Nothing!" she said coughing. "We thought you were Americans!"

This was good news for the Russians.

Chapter 82

The Stradivari Society, Chicago, IL

THEY HAD SPENT the last thirty minutes huddled in the hallway, listening to her warm up. It was an extraordinary moment for Dr. Nathan Becker and his wife. Their attention glided along every passage as they instinctively inched closer to the door. The hairs on his neck stood up when he took his first glimpse of Victoria Eden through the narrow, rectangular window in the door. The couple held hands, their cheeks pressed together, astonished by the sight.

He had stolen a glimpse of the sheet music stowed in her violin case and reasoned it would be impossible for a musician he'd never heard of to do that particular composition justice. By the time she was ready to perform the piece, it was clear that she was special. Her hands glided effortlessly up and down the neck of the violin.

He had left the door to the soundproof practice booth open a crack for two reasons: to let the musician know she was welcome to approach them if she needed anything further, and so he and his wife could listen in as she played. Seven and a half minutes went by, and he felt as if he hadn't taken a breath. Becker was considering an appropriate response, given the circumstances, when a deep voice startled him.

"Bravo! Bra-vo!" it said. His words carried the enthusiasm of a child waking to presents on Christmas morning. He clapped his hands triumphantly while he nodded his head in approval.

The couple joined in with smiles of adoration as Becker pushed the door open.

239

"Please. Excuse us. I'm at a loss for words," he admitted. There was a spark in Becker's voice that matched the fire in his eyes. "Absolutely enchanting."

"Yes, yes," the newcomer chimed in. "I don't believe there is an English word to describe something so beautiful. Please," he said with a raised index finger, "one minute. Come, Nathan. Come quickly."

The man gave a gentle tug to Becker's tweed suit and urged him toward the hallway. The proprietor hurried his pace when he remembered the provenance of an instrument he had locked in the vault down the hall.

"You're not thinking...?" Becker said, his eyes energized.

"Yes, I think it would be." The instrument's owner looked up as if he would find the appropriate word hanging in the air. "How do you say in English? Apropos?"

"Oh yes." Becker nodded emphatically. "Apropos is the word. Eugène will look down upon us with a smile!"

He unlocked the walk-in vault, and they both went straight to the place where the priceless treasure was stored. Its owner carefully removed the case and placed it on a mahogany table in the middle of the vault. He unlatched the case and handed the violin to Becker. They shared a knowing look.

Becker was blessed with perfect pitch and instantly responded. It took less than a minute for him to confirm that the instrument was in tune, and he handed it back to its owner, before they marched back to the practice space.

"Please." The man offered his violin to the musician with a slight bow. "Could you do this wonderful instrument the honor." He made a circle with his index finger as he smiled and said, "Your admiring trio here would also be most honored."

The old man could sense the butterflies that fluttered through his stomach were shared by the violinist. She handed him the violin she had been playing and accepted the mysterious instrument. She tilted the violin so she could peer into its f-hole.

Becker saw the sparkle in her eyes, and imagined her reading the maker's inscription. He knew exactly what it said: "Antonius Stradivarius Cremonensis Faciebat Anno 1732." He noticed her hands begin to tremble and her breathing quicken.

She cleared her throat. "It's beautiful."

The owner offered a broad smile. "Together you are a match made in heaven," he said.

Eden blushed, still unable to fully grasp the moment, the instrument, the stranger.

"Please, please. Get familiar with it. Become one with its song," the man insisted.

His enthusiasm managed to snap her out of the trance, and she began to play. First in short, quiet bursts, and then her fingers began to attack the instrument with confidence.

"It once belonged to Eugène Ysaÿe," the man said with an approving nod. "He no doubt performed, perhaps even composed, the ballade you just played on that very instrument."

She looked up in amazement, and he continued, "Herkules is his name, and it deserves to be played with the depth of expression and unbridled passion you command."

Victoria played scales up and down instrument for a minute. She then took a deep breath and began. The instrument sang the opening vocal-like passage that began the movement.

Becker, his wife, and the owner of the instrument were left hanging on every note. She swayed and shifted, sometimes violently, expressing the longing half steps and executing the composition's incredible leaps in pitch. She moved on to flawlessly play the rapid triplets and double-stops that climbed as she reached its conclusion.

There was absolute silence when she finished. She was exhausted from the emotion of it all, but after brief reflection, she came to life.

"That was better than sex," she proclaimed with a laugh. Her expression changed to embarrassment just as abruptly. She bit her bottom lip and winced.

There was an uncomfortable moment of silence.

"Yes it was," the man said with appreciative laughter and applause.

Becker remained speechless and slightly uncomfortable.

The stranger picked up the conversation to overcome the awkwardness. "And to what do we owe the privilege of your visit to the society?" he asked. Then, realizing they hadn't been formally introduced, he said, "I'm sorry, I don't know your name."

"Victoria. Victoria Eden. I have an audition with the Chicago Symphony Orchestra." She looked down at her watch. "In a couple of hours. A friend sent me here to get a loaner, since my violin was damaged on the plane."

"I'm sorry to hear that. Please do use this for your audition, if it's your pleasure," he said and smiled. "I will have them come here so you won't have to be bothered with the transport."

She was still in shock after what had just happened. "Thank you," Eden said. "That would be incredible, and that way I won't be in such a rush across town."

"There is one more thing." He looked to Becker and his wife with a raised eyebrow. "It would be a most delightful surprise, no?"

The couple looked at each other and smiled back at him.

"You mean?" Becker said, his eyes wide with excitement.

"Yes, I do." He motioned to Victoria. "This young lady's talent must be heard."

"It would be unprecedented, unexpected, and unbelievably well received," Becker admitted.

"Good. Victoria, have you any plans for this evening, say around six?" He reached into his coat pocket and handed her an envelope that held two tickets.

She looked down at the gift and then back up with surprise. "Tonight's performance? I couldn't. It's too much, but thank you for the generous offer." She smiled in appreciation. "You've already been far too kind."

"Victoria," the man said, understanding the need for clarification. "Those tickets are for your friends. Every performer, especially for an evening this special, deserves to have their friends present in the audience for support." He bowed his head respectfully. "You wouldn't mind doing us the honor, would you?" He could see she was stunned, so he added in a matter-of-fact tone, "It would certainly help fill the seats when you join the orchestra, and I have a friend who will be happy to set you up with the proper attire for such an occasion."

She shook her head as though she was unsure whether she would wake up from this fairytale. "Of course," she said nervously. "And you are?"

The silver-haired gentleman gave her a warm smile that spread to his eyes. The heavy lines on his face looked to have been chiseled from a hard life, but that looked to be behind him now.

"Forgive me. My name is Pavel," he said as he made his way out the door. "An absolute pleasure to make your acquaintance. I will see you in a few hours."

Chapter 83

The Artist's Café, Chicago, IL

TRENT TURNER WAS sitting outside underneath a green umbrella. The Artist's Café was a trendy spot that spilled out onto the sidewalk in front of the Romanesque building it called home. The Shop had made a last-minute discovery of Pavel Kozlov's Sunday routine, and the team collectively held its breath with the hope that the information was accurate.

The Fine Arts Building was only a ten-minute walk from the hotel where Turner and Etzy Millar were staying. Earlier this morning, Turner had quickly packed what he needed into his bag and headed to the park across the street from the building. Most Chicagoans had been engrossed in their morning run, so there was nobody paying him any attention when he assembled the PMD.

He initiated the quiet whirring sound from the touchscreen of his XHD3 and plugged a small attachment into the device to increase the range of its remote-control function. He selected its destination from a satellite map and sent the vehicle off ahead of him. The wind was a concern, but he didn't have a choice. There was no telling when they would have another opportunity to track their target.

By the time he reached the café, the PMD was already perched on top of the building. He had put the flying machine into what they called edge mode, so it would automatically select the optimal surveillance location to land. The PMD had been programmed to use image recognition to determine an approach that would minimize the risk of compromising its position.

He took a seat against the back wall next to the fence that separated him from one of the building's two main entrances. A few minutes had ticked away before Pavel Kozlov's limousine pulled up to the curb. It was surrounded by a pair of black Range Rovers.

The Russian traveled with a significant amount of firepower. His men operated with the precision of a presidential detail. Turner watched the mafia boss enter the building on his XHD3, courtesy of the video feed being taken from above. It was the safest way to preserve his cover. None of the men had spoken on the way inside, but he was able to mark each of them by touching their image on the screen. Modern technology would take care of the rest. The PMD had the capability to record every conversation, capture images and profile individuals, and catalog the signals from communication devices so they could be tracked.

The operative had had better luck when Kozlov was on his way out. Turner had just ordered another cup of coffee and was ready to go over the information he had collected. He was fluent in Russian, so he put in an earpiece and began the playback of Kozlov's conversation. A fire engine had passed by at the time, so some of what was said was unclear.

"...is short. Tell Dimitri we are moving forward quickly. After the performance, I will return to oversee things myself," Pavel Kozlov had said.

A familiar voice interrupted Turner's work. "Excuse me?"

He didn't look up until he realized it wasn't his waitress's voice. Their eyes locked as she pulled out the chair across from him and sat down. She tilted her head to one side and squinted as she spoke.

"Tony, isn't it?" she said, her voice betraying the questioning look she had feigned.

"That's right."

He felt the energy again. It was a strange combination of butterflies and excitement, but this time there was something else.

"I think you're full of shit, Tony."

He couldn't help but smile. There was definitely something else at play, and anger would be his first guess.

"I should be pissed off at you." She lowered her chin. "You know that, don't you?"

Turner wasn't in the mood to digest a plateful of drama. He took a sip of his coffee, stroked his five o'clock shadow and stayed engaged against his better judgment.

"Well, Victoria, I can assure you that wasn't my intention."

Her eyes softened. He could sense she was as uncomfortable as he was with the chemistry between them.

A smile followed and she said, "Thank you."

He smiled wryly without responding, so she elaborated.

"You made one of my dreams come true today." Victoria smiled when his expression showed even more confusion. "I just played Herkules," she said in a playful tone.

He smiled and took another sip of coffee. "Well, he's a lucky man." Her green eyes were even more captivating as they reflected the morning sun.

"It's a violin," she said. "A Stradivarius."

He laughed sarcastically. "Congratulations. I'm glad I was able to help you out with that."

She showed him the palms of her hands. "No, I'm serious. I won't bore you with the details, but trust me, it was amazing."

Eden was clearly excited from the experience, and it felt good to see her happy.

"What piece did you play?" he asked.

"Ah, that's not important," she said dismissively.

Turner took it as a polite way to say it wouldn't mean anything to him. "Try me," he said with an appraising eye.

She smiled at the challenge. "Okay. It was a piece by Eugène Ysaÿe."

Turner whistled. His mother loved classical music, and it was one of the few things left that could connect him to home. "The Belgian. Appropriate considering the instrument. You know that violin has an interesting history."

Eden's expression turned quizzical. She was obviously impressed that he was familiar with classical music.

"Oh yeah?" she said curiously.

"I believe it was stolen from a museum in Moscow."

"Russia?" She pursed her lips. "That explains it."

"Explains what?"

"The man who owns it. He's Russian."

"I see." The connection made him uncomfortable. He shifted in his chair knowing it wasn't a coincidence.

She reached into her bag and pulled out an envelope. "Here," she said. "I owe you this." She pushed it across the table to him.

He opened it and pulled out its contents. "Tickets?"

"Yep. Pavel gave them to me." She forced a smile and paused for a moment. "You can bring your girlfriend. I don't know anyone else in town, and it would be a shame if they went to waste." She shrugged and said, "I'll be performing."

Trent Turner could tell the stunning violinist was fishing for personal details. Heckler had called earlier and said he was sending someone to Chicago today, so this new development was convenient. It provided a safe place to meet, and he could keep tabs on Pavel Kozlov at the same time.

"Thank you," he said. "We'll try to make it."

Sadness clouded her eyes at the news that he would bring a companion. He diffused the moment with a smile, stood up and left money for the bill.

"Until then?" she said, trying to smile.

He nodded and shot her a playful wink.

Chapter 84

Island Industries satellite office, Reston, VA

"JACK SAID HE'LL bring him back online. Chicago, yeah. There's a performance at the Fine Arts Building later this evening. There will be a meeting there. Yes, send them straight to Chicago. We'll need them there as soon as possible in case we need more feet on the ground. Okay, thanks."

Addy Simpson leaned back in the chair at his desk, and felt a sense of relief after ending the call. A major source of the stress that had been occupying his mind was about to end. Trent Turner was coming back into the fold, and that development would help him relieve the other immediate stressors with the current operation. Trent had been in contact with his uncle Jack Turner, and while Simpson knew they would have a lot to discuss after the operation was over, he had no doubt that he could count on him.

He had just gotten off the phone with his second-in-command at The Island. His conversation with Dr. Charles Reed was brief. Simpson needed more resources on the current operation and had made the decision to bring someone new he'd been working with onto the team. He was an experienced individual who would need no training, and it was someone whom he knew his top operative would trust.

Simpson had been out of sorts since Matilde Soller had reached out to him. He still hadn't come to terms with missing the communication that was sent to him while he and Jack Turner had slept. They had searched Lucky Stone Quarry first thing in the morning and hoped something would turn up once the evidence was processed. It was time to call his good friend and give him an update on the status.

"Addy," President Vincent Cross answered the phone enthusiastically. "How are your people doing out there?"

"We're making progress, but things are moving slower than we'd like."

Cross couldn't help but laugh. "Isn't that always the case? You've always said the communists would try to make a comeback, I should know better than to doubt you. So is it as bad as you thought?"

"I think so," he said. "We still don't know much other than they have a lot of money behind them and it has something to do with the financial sector."

"Christ. Any idea when it will happen?"

"No, not yet. The CEO at Nations Bank has been extremely helpful. We've confirmed one of its computers has the bot software installed, and it's helped us make some headway." He sighed and reluctantly said, "It's going to take more time for The Shop to figure out what we're dealing with and how they plan on carrying out the attack."

"I spoke to Stapleton," the president said, his annoyed tone expected. "He was worthless as usual."

Simpson smiled. "Shocking," he said sarcastically. "You'd better watch your back with him."

"I expect some blowback, but I'm not worried about it. I had to try to do the right thing."

"Yeah, well, it's your nature," Simpson said, somewhat frustrated by his friend's willingness to give the snake a chance. "The Shop is poking around inside the Fed's systems. At this point, we're fairly certain they're a target."

"Have you been able to confirm the connection with Matilde's girl?"

"Yes. It's a bad situation. These are the sort of people that don't mess around."

"I'm sorry," Cross said. He tried to put himself in Matilde Soller's place. "Losing both of her children…" He realized it was the sort of pain one couldn't relate to. "I can't even begin to imagine."

Simpson didn't have any children, but seeing the woman he'd never stopped loving in pain had been eating away at him. "Me either."

"Let me know what you come up with and if there's anything I can do to help."

"Will do."

"And Addy…"

"Yeah?"

"You've made it through worse, so keep your chin up."

Chapter 85

MOUNTAINS AND MOUNTAINS of money. Andrei Tinkov knew that was the weapon of choice for the financial elite. The Group gained control of the world's political systems by manipulating financial markets, and increased its fortunes in the process. On the list of distinguished billionaires and powerful executives, were the chosen few who had been anointed into an organization that was so veiled in secrecy even its moniker was anonymous. The Group simply did not exist in any attributable form. Together, its members wielded enough power to ensure the secretive system of offshore havens used to move their money remained intact.

It was a nervous time for the secret organization, a time where its members were being held up to great scrutiny. Several among its ranks had been tied to a recent interest rate scandal. Their coconspirators had been careless and stupid. Those from their ranks who were embroiled in the mess had families that could be leveraged, so it opened up their options to include more than elimination. The consensus of The Group was leaning toward making them fend for themselves, whilst publicly condemning their actions and continuing business as usual behind the scenes.

Tinkov had been waiting for his chance. He was tasked to set the elaborate plan fashioned by his communist brethren into motion, but the banter about the recent Libor scandal had made the climate too intense for him to subtly introduce their scheme. Any abrupt change in the subject would attract unwanted attention. He continued to bide his time as he listened.

The Group's members were seated around a glistening mahogany conference table in the large rectangular room. All devices capable of recording or transmitting the meeting had been checked at the door.

"Cut off all ties, period," Sir Oliver Wright demanded. His plump face was still red from his long tirade. The Londoner had emphasized his complete and utter embarrassment by his countrymen who had been at the center of the scandal. His words had put him at odds with The Group's German contingent. He stared down the tall, slender Berliner in the gray suit who was seated across from him and declared, "Those imbeciles deserve nothing from us."

"No help whatsoever?" Herr Friedrich Ulrich asked in a snide tone. He stared the Briton down the length of his narrow nose. "They are, after all, your fellow countrymen."

Wright folded his arms tightly against his barrel chest, projecting the appearance of an immovable object. "No, absolutely none."

"I'm impressed," Ulrich said with a sarcastic look. "I suppose that now makes you the senior member when it comes to the United Kingdom's vote amongst this"—he motioned around the room—"distinguished company." It was a statement not a question.

Germany and the United Kingdom wielded significant influence over the European Union, since they represented two of its top economies. Ulrich, who had been the President of the European Central Bank since its inception, had made his displeasure with the situation known before an abrupt interruption served to conclude their heated exchange.

"Now that we have that settled," Bart Stapleton said taking command, "on to our next order of business." He searched the room for any objections. "The situation with our friends in Iraq."

The Federal Reserve chairman noted the rumblings around the table and cleared his throat to demand everyone's undivided attention.

"This is an investment that will start to pay off in just a couple of years." He smiled tightly as he scanned their faces. "Think of it as the sort of gift that will keep on giving."

Everyone knew he was referring to Iraq's oil reserves, and it wasn't the first time the subject had been raised by an American.

"I don't like it," a Belgian member said. "What will become of our investment if the situation with Iran escalates?"

"That is just what we're going to prevent," Stapleton said with a hint of condescension.

The Belgian's face soured. "At some point we have to say enough is enough. We've been at this for more than a decade, and the region is as unstable as it's ever been."

Andrei Tinkov sat back and watched the two men parry each other's comments. The semi-smile on his face had gone unnoticed. He had been nervously waiting for the right moment to make his move. The survival of the communist movement he had dedicated his life to, and the immediate resurgence of the Soviet Union, stood squarely on his shoulders. The fact that the situation had presented itself was a sign of things to come. He needed to manipulate the conversation perfectly, since it represented their only chance for an immediate and wide-sweeping success.

The irony wasn't lost on the Russian. The American was pushing for an action that would deliver the same outcome as the one he had planned. Now, though, Tinkov would be in the clear. There would be nothing to tie their master plan back to any action taken by The Group. He would laugh out loud if he could, and he was certainly bellowing inside. A Frenchman at the other side of the table attracted his attention and two words came to mind: *Carpe Diem*.

"They need an infusion of money to keep the government and basic services running," Stapleton insisted, "and if we don't act now you can kiss the world's largest oil reserves good-bye." His eyes darted around the room until he had made eye contact with every man. "You might as well put a big fat bow on Baghdad so the Supreme Leader can thoroughly enjoy his present."

Before the Belgian could jab back, Tinkov injected himself into the conversation.

"Russia will certainly honor the request from The Group's distinguished American member," he said.

Stapleton appeared surprised and nodded his appreciation.

Internal fireworks that would rival a Fourth of July display lit up the Russian's face. Iraq's secret dealings with the communists had spanned decades. Before the war broke out, they had helped the Iraqi government create an underground network similar to their own. The Americans were ill-equipped to understand the intricacies of the Iraqi power brokers, and had unwittingly empowered a regime that would be quick to turn and support their longtime ally.

"However," Tinkov probed, "I'm afraid I would take exception to Mr. Stapleton's proposed structure."

All eyes were now focused on the Russian.

"I think we can all agree that the actions of his bank are the reason we, for the second time, are having to discuss this point."

Stapleton's face turned red, as if he knew where this conversation was headed. Everyone remained silent, but the body language in the room was deafening.

Tinkov raised his eyebrows and surveyed the men who were present. "Had your Federal Reserve not shipped forty billion dollars in cash"—he emphasized the word "cash"—"to Baghdad so carelessly, the rest of us might not be in the position where we must, once again, fund its government."

Several uncomfortable glances were exchanged. Tinkov had never connected on a personal level with any of The Group's cliques, so his comments had been a collective surprise. His inclusion in The Group had been deemed necessary after the fall of communism. Russia and its vast resources represented a significant opportunity to increase the wealth they commanded. Tinkov took great pleasure in knowing Stapleton was on the verge of exploding.

"I suggest that our colleague either move to lower the total obligation by forty billion," he continued, "or increase their personal transfer by that amount."

Tinkov still had everyone's attention, so he decided it would be a good time for a dig. He knew ego trumped common sense in this crowd, and there was no way that a reduction by that amount would suffice.

"Perhaps if you decide the latter, your friends here will not have to make this decision to preserve their oil reserves again."

Stapleton's eyes were locked on the Russian. "Thank you for bringing that to our attention, Mr. Tinkov," he said bitterly.

It was clear the man wasn't used to being challenged, and being embarrassed appeared to infuriate him even more. The Russian had pulled his strings perfectly.

"Of course," Stapleton continued, "the Fed will happily increase our contribution."

"Will this be a wire transfer? Tomorrow? Is that your request?" Tinkov asked.

"Yes," he said, clearly annoyed. His tone turned to mocking. "The first business day following the meeting is tomorrow." He lowered his gaze. "Standard procedure, Mr. Tinkov."

The Russian smiled broadly and nodded his head in response. He couldn't believe everything had fallen into place so easily. The American's share of the aid to Iraq meant billions would be moved. The communists would soon throw enough chum in the water to start a feeding frenzy on the country's assets that even America's closest allies would be unable to resist. There would be an opportunity to climb the ladder of the New World Order. This day had been a long time coming for his motherland.

Chapter 86

Kozlov Bratva hideout, Leesburg, VA

CATHY MOYNIHAN WAS despondent when the men brought her back to the room and cuffed her to the railing. The other two women who were being held stared in disbelief. A tense fear thinned the air. Her clothes were soaking wet, and she shivered as she tried to warm herself in the cold, musty basement. It took her several long minutes to recover from the punishment she had just been dealt. Getting her bearings straight didn't come easy. The last time she'd been in the room, her head had been covered with a hood.

She immediately recognized Melody Millar from the house in Poolesville, but she had no idea who the person secured to the railing opposite her was. The waterboarding had affected her severely at first. She was disappointed that she had broken so quickly but was surprised by how well she had kept to her story. The nasty smell of the soiled canvas stayed with her. It was like the stench had crawled up her nose and camped, but as long as they didn't put the hood back on, she thought she'd be fine.

"Are you okay?" the girl she didn't recognize whispered from the other side of the room.

Moynihan looked up and gave her a slight nod and could see they were both afraid of being next.

"I remember you from the house," Millar said.

The other girl looked over at Melody Millar with surprise and asked, "Who are you?"

Moynihan was still slumped in the chair, weak from the abuse, but the fog in her head was slowly clearing.

"Don't worry," she said quietly. "You'll be fine. They're just not too crazy about cops."

She heard footsteps coming toward the room, and she drew in a deep breath. She flinched when the door opened and a heavyset man walked in. He avoided eye contact and headed to the other side of the room to sit down at a desk. He plugged his laptop into a jack in the wall and began to type. Moynihan watched the characters on his screen scroll by as he entered commands.

He stopped suddenly, pulled an iPod out of his pocket and began to fiddle with the cord that attached it to his earbuds. Unsatisfied, he fished around in his laptop bag until he found what he was looking for. He pulled out a familiar-looking white charger. She noticed movement on the opposite side of the room, and watched as the young woman slowly worked her way toward the desk where the man was sitting. Her movement came to a jarring stop when she met one of the brackets that secured the railing to the cement wall.

The man plugged the charger into a socket above the desk to recharge his iPod. Moynihan's glance darted between the man and the girl opposite her. She couldn't figure out what was going on. After what had seemed like an eternity, the man unplugged his laptop and headed out of the room. The girl started to pull on the railing as hard as she could, but it was sufficiently anchored to the wall, so it wouldn't budge. Before Moynihan could ask her what she was doing, the girl did something as unexpected as it was frightening.

"Hello?" she said. She projected her voice toward the door.

Moynihan's eyes widened at the volume. She was still coming to grips with what had just happened and wasn't sure she could handle more abuse.

"Hello?" she repeated. This time she was much louder and started messing with her chair.

Heavy footsteps approached.

Chapter 87

Hood Residence, Chevy Chase, MD

IVOR HOOD HAD just returned home from helping his neighbor put together a new shed. It started out as a simple request. He would hold the framing in place while his neighbor secured it to the foundation, but that would never do for the serial do-it-yourselfer. Within an hour he'd filled his neighbor's backyard with every tool the chore might require. He hadn't planned on the morning project, but this was the sort of activity that helped a man like Hood to relax.

He had put his tools back in order and cleaned himself up before he headed into the kitchen to get a drink. It was warm outside, so he grabbed a cold bottle of Gatorade from the refrigerator and began to chug it down. After his second swig, he decided to check his BlackBerry for messages. He noted nobody had called his cell, but there were several unread emails. He began reading in between sips and noticed one email was a notification from his office phone system. The communication informed him of a voice message that was marked as urgent on his work line. He had set the system up to send an email notification for new messages so he wouldn't have to waste the time calling into the phone system only to find out there was nothing new.

The time stamp on the email was late, so it piqued his interest further. When he opened the message, he recognized the number, but in the age of cell phones and autodial, he couldn't place the caller. He dialed into the office to retrieve the message. Within the first sentence, his beaming smile transformed to a look of concern.

"Uncle Ivor, sorry to bother you, but something is going on that I think you should know about…"

As he listened to his goddaughter explain the situation, his expression turned increasingly hard. He was no longer the helpful neighbor ready to lend a hand. He had transformed into the man who rose to the highest level one could achieve at the FBI without presidential appointment.

Ivor Hood earned his place as deputy director in what most would consider the hard way. He was ethical, honest, and forthright, qualities difficult to find in the upper echelons of Washington, DC's power structure. He found his way into the FBI after practicing law. His physical and mental attributes made him an excellent candidate for an agent, and he battled his way up the chain of command with an unrivaled determination.

On the job he was irascible. He had no patience for excuses; he only wanted facts and lessons learned. He was hard on his staff, but they respected him immensely for his leadership. His hardline approach was complemented by a remarkable sense of humor and genuine concern for his people. His attitude left him with few enemies at the bureau. Although he didn't always see eye to eye with Director Culder, his success as executive assistant director of the FBI National Security Branch made him an obvious candidate for the job when the position opened up. The fact that his sphere of influence didn't extend beyond the bureau was what sealed the deal, since that made him a man Culder felt he could control.

He called Cathy Moynihan's number as soon as the message finished. It rang a few times before he was sent to voicemail.

"I got your message. I see you're burning the midnight oil these days. Please call me back as soon as you get this. Your message has me concerned."

Hood looked out the window and thought about what she'd said. It was no secret he and Director Culder didn't get along, but they managed to get things done. He was certain very few at the FBI knew of his relationship with Moynihan, and Culder wasn't one of the handful who knew. Although not related by blood, Hood and Moynihan were very much alike. Like her godfather, Moynihan wanted to climb her way through the bureau on her own merits, and he respected her for it and kept his distance.

He decided he would take a quick shower. If he didn't hear back from her by the time he finished, he'd start to dig.

Chapter 88

THE FBI DIRECTOR couldn't help but smile when the display of his cell phone lit up. This was the call he had been anxiously awaiting. He saw it as the beginnings of a wave that he could ride all the way to the top of Washington's elite.

"Chuck, how good of you to call," Frank Culder said. He imagined the man on the other end of the line shrink in his chair. "Please don't keep me waiting. I always love it when people come bearing gifts."

Culder was relishing the fact that the man was about to go against everything he had stood for in his life. He was corrupting the incorruptible. What he was about to make him do wasn't simply crossing the line; he was erasing it.

Dr. Charles Reed drew in a deep breath and exhaled. "Tell me an email I can send the information to."

"No delays. I want the information now," Culder said. "I'm sure your little flower would appreciate that."

"Then give me a goddamn email address!"

Culder rattled off an email address that was a combination of numbers and letters. He leaned back in his chair with content, still amazed at the lengths a father would go to protect his daughter, and decided it was a good thing he never had children. This man was willing to destroy everything he'd worked for.

"Send it now," he demanded.

"I'm working on it."

Culder could hear the caller's fingers patting on a keyboard through his phone.

"It's on the way," Reed said.

Nothing was said as Culder retrieved the message. The only thing it contained was a link to a Facebook page, and it immediately set him off.

"Are you fucking kidding me?" He followed the link to the profile of an attractive woman named April Pearson. "What is this bullshit?" Culder barked.

"Scroll down the page." Reed's tone was full of anger.

"There's nothing to scroll, you idiot."

"Apparently, you haven't logged in. I didn't realize you were so socially inept," Reed said flatly.

He gave Culder a log-in so he could view her profile page on the social-networking website. Culder began to scroll down and saw that the web page was covered with loving condolences and expressions of sorrow from the woman's Facebook friends. Culder couldn't be bothered with that, but he made note that all of the images that had been recently posted included a young man. He stopped at one in particular and read the caption.

The smile that will stay with us for the rest of our lives. I love you both. Ryan, until we see each other again. Thanks for being the best friend I could ever have.

It wasn't only the smile that engaged Culder, it was the happiness that was punctuated by his eyes. He felt like a voyeur, secretly viewing something he would never have.

What the FBI director didn't know was that April Pearson's husband had always been extremely cautious about the way April used social-networking websites. The need for secrecy was something she never completely understood, but she loved and trusted him, so she didn't have a problem with his requests.

The first thing he asked was for her to sign up for accounts using her maiden name, April Pearson. He explained that using April Turner wasn't a good idea, due to the nature of his job. The next detail, and something that he had become increasingly adamant about over the last several years, was keeping his images from being linked to her account. When possible, he wanted her to ask her friends to remove his images from the websites altogether. At the very least, she needed to delete any image tagging that would link the two of them together.

That was then and this was now. It had been therapeutic for the grieving widow to browse through previously unseen images of her husband, Ryan, that her friends had posted. Now that he was gone, she didn't see any harm in leaving herself tagged. It made it easier for her to browse through them all.

After a long moment of scrolling through images, the director grunted his disapproval. "What is this?"

"It's your man."

"This man is dead," he said. "Listen, Chuck, don't test my patience."

"I suppose it's those masterful skills of deduction that landed you such an important job."

"Chuck, Chuck, Chuck." Culder cackled. "I thought you were smart enough to understand the position you're in, your daughter is in." His words turned scathing. "It would be wise to spare me the insults and get down to business."

"The man you are looking at on your screen is Ryan Turner," Reed said, his voice simmering with anger. "He's the identical twin brother of Trent Turner, the operative you're searching for." He hesitated for a moment and then said, "You'll find him at a performance at the Studebaker Theater in Chicago tonight at six."

A sinister smile crept its way onto Culder's face, and he began to laugh. "Reed, you've outdone yourself!" he said. "In fact," he continued with an air of humor in his voice, "I'm so impressed, I have another little job for you."

Reed remained silent for a moment as the tension increased. "Look, Culder, I've lived up to my side of the deal. You can't—"

"I can't what?" Culder barked.

Reed didn't speak.

"The last time I checked, your little girl was out blowing Chicago's lowlifes and trading crack for crack." Culder paused so the sickening image would burn into Reed's mind. "For now, anyway. Things can change rather quickly with one phone call."

"No more after this. No more!" Reed yelled. "My debt is paid."

Culder knew once he had the information he wanted he wouldn't need anything else.

"You've got a deal." The smile still hadn't left his face. "I want some dirt on Cross. I want you to connect the president to your little operation. I want details that will expose what really goes on at Addy Simpson's Island Industries. A monsoon of damning evidence, if you will. Then I'll be finished with you."

Chapter 89

Downtown hotel, Chicago, IL

SLEEP WAS A rare commodity for Trent Turner. He knew his effectiveness would be diminished if he didn't take the time to rest, so it was second nature to put his head down whenever the opportunity presented itself. Etzy Millar had continued working with The Shop while the operative went on his sortie to the Fine Arts Building. When Turner returned, he opted for a quick nap to help sharpen the edges of his mind. His body twitched every few seconds as he faded away into dream.

He relived walking up the ramp of the waiting Chinook helicopter, his mind and gear ready for the first training exercise with the big dogs. Simpson had pulled a last minute change on him to see how he would adapt.

"Welcome to DEVGRU, operative," the commander yelled over the noise. He patted Turner on his back and it calmed his nerves. "I guess this makes you PS 4."

The operative had already participated in progressively more difficult missions with Navy SEAL teams, and it was always assumed that he had been CIA. Before The Island would assign their operatives to work with DEVGRU, legendary SEAL Jack Turner would subject them to a gauntlet of training of his own that he'd dubbed Camp Looney.

The noise from the rotors was loud, and Turner was in his element. He looked at the commander inquisitively and spoke loud enough to be heard over the noise. "PS 4?"

The man answered with a slanted smile and a raised chin. "You know, we used to resent you crabs jumping into our business outside the selection process," he said. "Hell, some of the paramilitary boys the CIA sends over are downright unpredictable. Damn good but fuckin' crazy." The commander looked at Trent Turner appraisingly for a moment, and then said, "But you're in luck."

Turner furrowed his brow. "How so?"

"PS 1, 2, and 3 were so goddamn good we no longer doubt Addy and Jack's boys." He nodded toward a soldier seated on the canvas bench inside the aircraft. "And our other last-minute addition here vouched for you."

Turner lowered himself onto the bench opposite the soldier in question as the man raised his head. He looked past the layer of face paint and smiled with a nod. The soldier returned the gesture. The two men had become close during Hell Week, the most brutal segment of the Basic Underwater Demolition/SEAL training, or BUD/S for short. It was the point where a man's physical endurance and mental tenacity were pushed beyond the limits of what was thought humanly possible.

For the past several months, Trent Turner had experienced a recurring dream about the moment he had entered the helicopter. It was when he made the transition from Private Sector Number 4 to a hardened operative who would be unleashed into the world. Island Industries' boss and former admiral, John "Addy" Simpson, pulled the sacred strings that allowed his candidates to take part in the Navy SEAL selection process. If they made it through, they would then work alongside the various SEAL teams until they were deemed ready to take on Camp Looney.

While in the BUD/S program, prospective Islanders were advised to keep to themselves, but sometimes connections were a product of fate. Turner and Brendan Manion struck up what should have been a lifelong friendship during the grueling week-long ordeal known as Hell Week. The men were put in situations where life was stripped down to the basic primal need to survive, fostering an environment in which men forged strong connections. The extreme fight to stay alive as a viable candidate required the absolute trust of your fellow soldiers, and sometimes the will to help carry them along. Trent realized the effects of the BUD/S program in a way that most could not. It facilitated the same sort of bond he had had with his twin brother, Ryan.

It had been clear to everyone in their class that Manion and Turner were wired differently than the others. The suffering during BUD/S served as fuel for their motivation, and together they were able to share their advantage with the others to help pull them through. Brendan Manion was voted Honor Man of his class, the soldier the other candidates had looked up to the most. He had selflessly given then for his fellow candidates and continued to do so until making the ultimate sacrifice for his country.

The recurring dream of Turner's friend Brendan had been triggered by news that he had been killed in a Black Hawk helicopter crash in the southern-Afghanistan province of Zabul. He would dream about his final operation with the SEALs as a part of DEVGRU, also known as the famed SEAL Team 6, specifically the moment he reunited with Brendan. His friend had made it all the way to the top, as Turner suspected he would, and it made him proud. That was where the dream turned to a nightmare.

He would climb out of his sleep with thoughts of the first time Brendan had made the headlines. An investigative reporter had exposed Manion's identity when details were leaked about a mission he had taken part in where a top Al-Qaeda commander had been eliminated. It was an election year, and the White House had purposely leaked the details—a few too many—to gain reelection momentum needed to defeat Vincent Cross. The sensational exposé of an active covert operative proved to be a major ratings grabber and had thrown the top brass at the Pentagon into an uproar.

The reporter had been reckless and set off a chain of events that included death threats to the soldier's family, which culminated with the tragic and brutal murder of Manion's wife and unborn child by an Al-Qaeda cell based in the United States. A few months later, when the news broke that Manion had been killed in action, it set off a media frenzy that dwarfed the previous circus and ripped the scab off Trent Turner's wound. He and his friend had been fighting the same fight. He'd only wished they could have done it together, that he could have been alongside him and had a chance to change the outcome.

"Trent!" Millar's voice was desperate as he shook Turner back and forth.

The operative opened his eyes abruptly. "What's up?" he asked. He was alert, as if he'd never been asleep.

"That's freaky," Millar said with a disbelieving look.

"What?"

"That." He nodded to him. "One second you're sleeping like a baby, and the next you're wide awake. It's like you were faking it."

Turner laughed, but the concern in Millar's eyes stopped him short. "What's wrong?"

"Those fuckers grabbed Maria."

"Maria? Your girlfriend?"

Millar exhaled. "Well, she used to be my girlfriend. Kind of really doubtful now."

"Shit. How do you know?"

"I just found a message from the Russians on the boards. I've been monitoring for activity since all of this started. I just confirmed it with The Shop. They found out about it a little while ago from some guy named Addy. They didn't realize we knew each other."

Turner took a moment to consider the news. "Do you think they've made a connection and know who you are?"

"I don't know. They addressed the message to Max, which means they probably don't know my handle online, or they would have just sent something to me. They know I'm a hacker, sure, but deploying the bots didn't take a genius. I doubt they suspect I'm Slash ETC." He forced a smile. "We still have one over them, especially considering The Shop is on this too," he said confidently. His face turned grim again when he thought about Maria. "This is fucked."

Turner put his hands on Millar's shoulders. "I owe her one, remember? We'll stop this, and part of that will be getting her out." He locked eyes with Millar. "Okay?"

The hacker appeared unsure of what to say. Finally he said, "Yeah, sure."

"They had to be following you to get a line on her."

"Shit. I don't think I told you that she's Max's sister, did I?"

Turner blew out his breath and said, "No, you left that little detail out."

"Sorry, it's just we were so used to keeping things quiet. Max didn't know, and neither did his father. No one knew except for her mom." He closed his eyes and lowered his head. "Man, what a mess."

The operative thought about what this might mean. "What about your sister?"

Millar's eyes showed grave concern as he considered the question.

Chapter 90

Kozlov Bratva Compound, Chicago, Illinois

HE HAD JUST finished deploying the final version of the software to their servers in Europe. The head of the communists' operation, Yuri Khrushchev, had insisted the attacks be carried out separately after the complications in the United States. Nothing could be left to chance. Dimitri Sokov was proud of the work they had done. The testing was complete, and he was ready to put it to good use.

After he made his way to Pavel Kozlov's office, Sokov set his laptop down on the desk. His harsh voice broke the intricate rhythm of the classical music playing in the background.

"I have done as Yuri instructed. The operations are now separate," he confirmed.

"And the accounts? Have you determined the accounts that should be used?" Kozlov asked.

"Yes, the selection algorithm was run on the new dataset, and very little has changed. That is as expected. Soon the files we need to send to the bots will be complete, and we can send the changes to Virginia by courier this evening as planned."

Kozlov had a bemused look on his face and motioned to the laptop. "What is this?"

Sokov was hopeful to demo the voice-cloning software. "Would you like me to show you how it works?"

Kozlov waved his hand dismissively. "We haven't the time for that. We should call Yuri and provide him with an update." He held up his phone and smiled. "This is technology that a man like me can appreciate, Dimitri."

He punched a few buttons on the device, and a tinny ring sounded from its speaker.

"'Allo, Pavel?" Khrushchev answered.

"Yes, Yuri, it is Pavel." He looked to the hacker. "I have Dimitri with me."

"Has everything been taken care of on your end?"

"No, not everything," Kozlov admitted. He put on a confident voice. "But everything necessary to carry out the operation has been set in motion."

"The American?"

Kozlov closed his eyes. "No, Yuri," he said. "He is still out there, as are the hackers. The men are still working on tracking them down."

Sokov chimed in. "Yuri," he said, "we have everything in place. Everything has been tested in the labs, and the bots have reported back that there have been no software updates done on the target systems. There shouldn't be any problems with the bots functioning properly, so we are in very good shape."

"Yes, but these hackers—what do they know about the operation?" Khrushchev demanded.

"Not enough to cause problems," Sokov said with confidence. "We don't know much about the hacker in Washington, DC, but regardless, it would be impossible for one person to figure what we're doing in time to prevent this from happening."

"Will everything be ready for tomorrow?"

"Yes," Kozlov interrupted. "We have also taken the Washington, DC hacker's girlfriend."

"Good. What was his response?"

Kozlov's face hardened. "He has not responded yet, Yuri. When he does find out, we will bring him in."

Sokov decided to preempt Khrushchev's next question. "The other hacker was working on the algorithm we use to determine the accounts. He doesn't have the full picture of what we have going on. None of them do. He doesn't know anything about Europe. He had no involvement with that."

"Did everything go well with Andrei?" Kozlov asked, changing the subject. "As Dimitri said, the software is in place for the team."

Khrushchev began to laugh.

"What's so funny, Yuri?" Kozlov asked.

"Andrei told me he had very little to do at the meeting."

"Then what's so funny?" he pressed.

"It will be even bigger than we could have dreamed, Pavel. Much bigger."

Kozlov looked confused. "And Andrei did nothing?"

"Not quite. He put a cherry on the top. Fate is on our side. The Americans wanted to infuse cash into Iraq's central bank tomorrow." Khrushchev began to laugh again. "They wanted everyone else to help with the aid to preserve their oil grab. Andrei decided to bring up the forty billion those fools lost, and he challenged them to make up for their mistake."

Sokov wore an unsure smile on his face as Kozlov chuckled.

"Dimitri, the Americans lost forty billion dollars that they had sent to Iraq," Kozlov explained. "They stupidly sent cash and we were happy to help our friends there do the laundry." He smiled. "It sounds like they wanted The Group to agree to fund Iraq's government again. Is that right, Yuri?"

"Yes, yes," Khrushchev said.

"They keep shoveling us money," Kozlov added. "We must thank them when this is all over." He smiled before continuing. "Our comrade Andrei threw the previous catastrophe in their faces and insisted they make up for what happened by paying the forty billion again."

"No, Pavel," Khrushchev interrupted. "It's even better. They will be transferring forty billion on top of the original amount they had planned!"

Sokov now understood what this meant for the operation in Europe and joined in the laughter. Once they settled down, a serious look came over his face.

"Incredible. This means we'll be able do even more damage than we thought."

"Yes, comrade, we will," Kozlov said. "Indeed we will."

Chapter 91

"I'M SORRY, MR. President. I know you said not to disturb you, but he wouldn't take no for an answer," Press Secretary Stephanie Craig said nervously.

President Cross was annoyed. "Who is it?"

"It's Ivor Hood...from the FBI."

"Hood?" The president considered the caller and thought about the situation with his friend Addy Simpson. He knew Matilde Soller was indirectly connected to FBI Director Frank Culder through her husband and wondered if this might be a way for him to help.

He gave her a curt nod and said, "Go ahead and put him through."

Seconds later the phone on his desk rang.

"Deputy Director Hood, how can I help you?" he answered.

"Mr. President, I apologize for interrupting you on a Sunday, but I have a personal problem that I was hoping you could help me with."

Cross detected a measure of intensity in the man's voice. Nobody would try to cash in a favor from POTUS for something trivial.

"A personal problem?" he asked.

"Yes, sir. Please, let me explain."

The president leaned back in his chair. "Please do."

"Well, sir." He drew in a deep breath. "I hope this is something that can stay between the two of us."

"I can't promise that until I know what we're talking about."

269

"I understand. Suffice it to say that Director Culder is unaware of the inquiry I'm about to make."

"Okay." There was some hesitation in the president's voice.

"I received an alarming message from my goddaughter a short time ago," Hood said, choosing to be direct and to the point. "She also works for the FBI." There was a pause before he continued. "Sir, I'm very concerned that Director Culder has something going on off the books. I think her life might be in danger."

Cross leaned forward in his chair and stared intently at the grain of the wood along the edge of his desk. "Off the books?"

"She was working with two men, Jake Sanders and Rudy Pagano. Do those names ring a bell?"

The president searched his memory and couldn't place the names. "No. Should they?"

"Probably not. They both worked for the bureau until early 2003. They had both been involved in FBI black-bag operations in TacOps."

"I'm familiar with the program, but I'm not sure I follow."

"Several more FBI personnel went off the books the same day these two men did."

"Okay." Cross settled back in his chair expectantly.

Hood seemed to consider his words. "Do you remember anything taking place around that time that would give some of our best and most trusted agents, people that I'd see as FBI lifers, a reason to resign?"

The president remained silent, so Hood continued.

"Mr. President, with all due respect, I understand that there are certain"—there was a brief pause before he continued—"strategies that the government implements to deal with particularly troublesome issues. You were a member of the Senate Select Committee on Intelligence at the time, so if any unusual steps were taken to protect the country with the FBI, I thought you might recall."

The president was immediately engrossed by the conversation. He wondered if this could be connected with his indoctrination into the world of covert operations as a rookie on the committee.

"Sometimes, yes. We have to deal with problems that come up in creative ways," he said, obviously pondering something other than his answer. "The country was still reeling from the attacks on September 11, and Washington took many steps, some more extreme than others, to ensure the safety of our fellow Americans."

"Do you think Director Culder could have taken the liberty to develop a strategy of his own?" Hood asked.

The president considered the question and recalled a top-secret National Security Presidential Directive. It was an initiative for the FBI to eliminate terrorist threats inside the borders of the United States, and there were two things about the directive that immediately came to mind. The first was that it was rescinded by the president after only a few months, and the second was that the program had been one championed by Senator Maximillian Soller.

At the time several influential committee members had banded together and rallied around then-Senator Cross, who had finally won the reluctant ear of the president. Together, they created Island Industries. The security company would be a front for the committee's and executive branch's new weapon, and retired admiral John Simpson, who had just been forced out of the top spot at the CIA, would be the man in charge. Not only would the new setup provide an extra layer of insulation for deniability, it would also make the FBI hit squad they had reluctantly agreed to form redundant.

The behind-the-scenes move had been the beginning of the end of Senator Soller's time on the committee. He had managed to get his man into the FBI by cashing in a political IOU, but his sphere of influence would merely serve to keep Culder in place. The rift between the players involved was formed, and the committee would rally around its rising star, Senator Cross, and trust that he could control his longtime friend.

Cross had been at odds with Soller on the subject of Culder for years, unable to oust the man due to the senator's power. The recent two-year extension for the FBI director's ten-year term had been a tough pill to swallow, but he was now seeing the light at the end of the tunnel.

"Please, Mr. President," Hood said abruptly, interrupting his thoughts, "I wouldn't be coming to you if I didn't think my goddaughter's life was in danger."

Cross had to admit he appreciated the audacity of Hood to contact him. There was a level of desperation, but anyone with the guts to approach the President of the United States like this was okay in his book.

"We need to talk," Cross said. "How soon can you get to the White House?"

Chapter 92

CATHY MOYNIHAN WATCHED with curious shock as the young woman on the other side of the room repeatedly tipped her chair over in between shouts. It almost hit the ground once, and with each call out to the guards she made, the FBI agent's heart rate increased. She feared this would provoke a situation that none of them wanted. Cold, soaked, and afraid, she couldn't handle going back to that room for more.

"Hello? Hello!" the young woman shouted and then finally said, "Can someone please take me to the bathroom?"

The heavy footsteps had reached the door. Their power and urgency left no doubt that they belonged to the soldiers. Moynihan was increasingly nervous but kept her emotions in check. When the door swung open, two men entered the room, and both wore scowls on their weathered faces.

"Hi," the young woman across the room said. Her tone was apologetic. "I really need to go to the bathroom."

She was able to fashion an expression that satisfied one of the soldiers, and he walked over and began to reach for her handcuffs. The FBI agent noticed the young lady quickly move to face the keyhole of the cuff attached to the metal railing toward him. It was obvious that he had originally planned to unlock the cuff around her wrist. He paused for a second, as though he was confused, and then freed the cuff from the railing.

Once the restraint was removed, the soldier stood and motioned her to follow him. Moynihan watched the girl hook her leg around the chair, just like she'd done several times before. As she began to stand, she knocked her chair over and it fell over toward the computer desk. Moynihan's mind was reeling as she relived the punishment the soldiers had given her. She couldn't breathe. There was no doubt in her mind that they were capable of much worse. The girl managed a flustered look that also conveyed fear.

Both men laughed.

"I'm sorry," the young woman said apologetically. "I'll pick it up."

Moynihan studied the girl as she picked up the chair and placed it on the other side of the metal bracket securing the railing to the concrete, and headed out the door. The FBI agent would have smiled if she hadn't been starved for air. Before she could process what had just happened, a timid voice interrupted her thoughts.

"You're the woman from that house," Melody Millar whispered. "What did they do to you?"

Moynihan looked over at the teenager with a feeling of guilt. "Melody, I'm sorry they took you in like that."

Millar didn't respond.

"Believe me when I say I was completely against how this was handled." She still didn't answer.

"I don't know who these men are, but listen to me." Moynihan's eyes narrowed. "If they ask you a question, just tell them the answer. They'll manage to get it out of you anyway."

Millar returned her words with a look of concern. "Okay," she said softly.

Footsteps approached the room, and they stopped talking. The sound the footsteps made was quieter this time. She assumed it was the man with the computer coming back. A few seconds later he opened the door and went over to the desk. He picked up his iPod, put the headphones on and plugged the laptop into the wall jack.

His fingers stabbed at the keyboard for a couple minutes and then he closed the display. Footsteps could be heard outside, and by the time he had made it to the door, the girl had come into the room with the two Russians. The scent of cigarette smoke was overwhelming. The girl thanked the men for bringing her to the bathroom and cuffed herself to the metal railing. The soldiers left without speaking.

The young woman turned to the desk and looked upset. "Shit," she whispered. "Where did that guy's iPod go?"

Chapter 93

THE FLIGHT FROM Ronald Reagan National Airport to Chicago was short, but there was still plenty of time for FBI Director Frank Culder to piss off his men. Jack Sanders and Rudy Pagano had flown south from Frederick to pick up their boss in a Gulfstream V jet. The bureau had purchased the plane for use in counterterrorism work, and for the director, it had worked well for shuttling around his covert HVT squad. The three men then headed northwest to the Windy City.

A heated exchange between Culder and Sanders ignited shortly after takeoff. Sanders had told the director the hit on Agent Cathy Moynihan was out of the question. The director had always been careful about keeping FBI staff away from assignments that might rouse suspicion about his secret operation, what he and Senator Soller often called their 'special arrangement'. This had been a case where he needed to act quickly following the murder of Soller's son. Culder had been forced to pull in one of the local agents since the work involved interviews, and that meant the job would have be done in the public eye. There had to be a face to this covert operation—at least initially.

Sanders's anger rose to a boil as Culder continued to minimize his decision to take the agent's life. The back-and-forth banter had nearly seen Sanders clean the floor with the Brillo Pad-like hair on the director's head, before Pagano inserted himself between the two men. He sensed they knew there was something he wasn't telling them. They had kept it to themselves through silent gestures they thought went noticed.

Culder hadn't expected Moynihan to question his actions, and he had quickly determined she was the sort of loose end that could cause waves. He knew the only way to eliminate the risk of exposure was to stamp her out. Since his team leader wouldn't take care of it, he'd find someone else to do the deed.

"Are we finished?" Culder said with a dark stare.

Sanders didn't make eye contact. "For now."

"We can't have any distractions, Jake," the director reasoned. "You're no good to anyone if you've checked out mentally."

Sanders shifted his eyes to Pagano. "I said I'm done talking about it."

After an uncomfortable silence, Culder said, "You said for now."

Sanders shot the director a menacing look. "I'm not your bitch. I'm finished discussing this, for now," he responded with a seething finality. "It's not going to affect my ability to execute."

Culder knew pushing back right now wouldn't do any good.

Sanders looked to Pagano and then Culder. "You're smart enough to know that. If you have a problem beyond that, with the fact that I'm not gung ho about killing a fucking coworker, we can keep talking about it until I start swinging." He crossed his arms and locked eyes with the director, then offered a defiant shrug. "If that's what you'd like. You're the boss."

Culder was already regretting his reaction to the news about Moynihan. His anger had blinded him to the fact that his behavior and disregard for an FBI agent's life would be suspect to his men. It was a stupid mistake, the price for paying too much attention to the prize and ignoring the details. He needed to diffuse the situation quickly before it spun further out of control. His greatest achievement was so close he could almost taste it, and he needed Sanders on his side to pull it off. He decided it was time to swallow some pride in the name of his ultimate goal.

"I'm sorry, Jake," Culder said. He worked hard to sound sincere.

Both of his men shifted uncomfortably, and he realized it was probably because this was the first time he'd ever apologized.

"Look, I get it," Culder said. "We'll think of another way to deal with the situation."

Sanders raised his chin and said, "Okay?" It was more of a question. He wasn't convinced.

Culder realized it was high time to change the subject and motioned to the table in between them as the wheels touched down.

"Let's look at the blueprints for the Studebaker Theater and figure out the best way to approach this," he said. "Whoever this Trent is, let's hope he'll have Francis Millar with him, so we can kill two birds with one stone."

Sanders remained silent, visibly annoyed.

Pagano was the next to speak. "The place looks pretty big." His gaze shifted between the two men. "We'll need at least two more—four if we want to keep things zipped up tight outside."

The director didn't like the idea of any more agents getting involved. He had already ordered a surveillance team to keep tabs on Francis Millar, and it had managed to lose him after he had left the airport. Culder wasn't sure if it was due to incompetence or skill, and was concerned that with this Trent person, it could be the latter.

"Let's keep it to a minimum. You two take care of this on your own. Just be sure he doesn't make it out the door." Culder thought about the exponential increase in risk for each local agent they brought on board. "It's only one man," he continued, "two of them if Millar is there, but if he is there, the hacker will do him more harm than good when we move in."

He could tell by the expressions on their faces that Sanders and Pagano weren't happy. They had rarely worked with agents outside the team, but the previous night had seen the ranks of the HVT squad cut down to just the two of them. Culder knew they were currently motivated by revenge, and he would use that to his advantage.

He finally accepted the silent consensus that he would have to bring agents in from the local field office; otherwise, the risk of failure was too great. The trick would be making up a good story to go with the job. He was in a position of power, so he would exercise his option to keep the details fuzzy.

"I think we'll have an advantage if Millar's there. We'll do it your way," Culder agreed. "We'll keep it to a minimum." He nodded to Pagano. "Two locals, as you said. This will go down in a public place, and we can't afford mistakes from untested agents."

Culder had made a good point, and the three men nodded in agreement as the plane came to a stop in the hangar.

"All right," Pagano said.

"They won't get away with what they've done," Culder assured. "Just keep a level head. Time for payback will come soon enough."

Chapter 94

Kozlov Residence, Lake Forest, Illinois

PAVEL KOZLOV WHISTLED triumphantly along with the classical music thundering out of his Bang & Olufsen sound system. Music had always been therapeutic for the Russian and helped calm his nerves. This day would be one of the most important of his life. Not only was he a major player in the operation that would destroy the United States and see the Soviet Union rise once again, but he would also achieve something significant on a personal level. He knew Victoria Eden would become one of the most important violinists of his time, possibly of all time. This evening's performance would showcase him as the man who brought her talent to the world.

He stood in front of the full-length mirror in his master suite checking the fit of his Brioni tuxedo. He had a penchant for Italian fashion. The finer things in life were a satisfying reward for decades of sacrifice. He considered how his appearance had changed over the years. The gray hair and weathered face projected an air of sophistication. It was a façade that helped to mask his ruthless tendencies.

A sideways glance through the floor-to-ceiling windows was his gateway to the lake. His sprawling stone-crafted residence took advantage of the coveted views his neighborhood was famous for. A smile formed on his lips as he considered others who might also be taking in the view at this moment. His look of satisfaction had nothing to do with the beauty outside. The Russian knew many fortunes would change from his actions, and Tuesday morning would bring with it a catastrophic wake-up call for many who shared this view of the lake.

His smile disappeared as he placed a call. "You have been very disappointing to me lately," Kozlov said.

"I know," Bruce Campbell said.

The Russian fixed his eyes on a boat in the distance, and after a few moments decided he owed the man one more chance. His view would be that of a jail-cell wall if it wasn't for the man on the phone.

"We can't afford any more mistakes."

"What would you like me to do?" Campbell asked.

There was an air of surprise in his voice, and Kozlov realized he hadn't expected another chance.

"Two things."

"Sure. Whatever you need."

"I want you to get in touch with your friends," Kozlov said.

Campbell used to do contract work for a private security company before the Bratva had brought him on board. They were all ex-military who worked the protection circuit. They specialized in bodyguarding and perimeter security.

"I can do that," Campbell said.

"We need to secure the Chicago building for the next forty-eight hours," Kozlov explained. He straightened his bow tie in the mirror, with the phone pinched between his shoulder and ear. "They will be well paid."

"Should I have someone contact you?"

"No. Put them in touch with Dimitri. I want them in place as soon as possible."

"Will do. And me?"

"I want you to head to the Virginia operation," Kozlov said. "Nobody in or out. Seal the place up."

"Got it."

Chapter 95

Kozlov Bratva hideout, Leesburg, VA

MARIA SOLLER'S PANIC gave way to relief when Melody Millar told her the charger for the iPod had been tucked inside the bag the man had left on the desk. She made her way as far along the metal railing as she could, but when she stretched, the bag was just out of her reach. She exhaled in frustration and looked over at Melody and the woman she didn't know. She flashed them a quick look at her iPhone, and both women's expressions were lined with hope.

"The battery is dead," Soller whispered. She pointed to the wall socket. "If I can just get to that stupid bag, I can plug it in."

"I was wondering what you were doing with that chair," the woman said quietly, looking impressed. "Can you move the desk?"

Two quick nods from Soller acknowledged the good idea. She grabbed the corner of the desk with her free hand and tried to move it, but the desk was much heavier than it looked. She shored up her grip and put all her strength into pulling it toward her. A shrill screech erupted as the desk moved away from the wall, its metal legs protesting the effort. Soller's eyes showed fear, a pained grimace frozen on her face.

"Holy shit," she whispered.

The sudden sound of footsteps increased the tension.

"Get back to your chair," the woman insisted.

Maria scurried back down the railing to the sound of scraping metal and slumped down into the chair. She stole a quick glance at the desk and saw that it was noticeably crooked. Her heart pounded in desperation as she saw the door open in her peripheral vision. Her eyes darted to the visitor, and the panic began to erase her senses. She took in a deep breath, and was too scared to realize she was holding it.

The visitor didn't seem to notice the desk had moved, and just as he did the other times when he'd shown up, he avoided eye contact. He went through the same routine with his laptop. He plugged it into the jack and went to work punching commands into the keyboard. Soller strained to see what he was doing, but the text that scrolled on the screen didn't mean anything to her.

After a couple of minutes, he stood up and grabbed his bag. The three women watched with dread as he sifted through its contents. He pulled out a USB drive and set the bag down before leaving the room.

Maria Soller turned to the others. "Oh my God, that was close."

They nodded in agreement.

Soller waited for the footsteps to fade before she worked her way back to the desk. Her body formed a cross as she leaned toward the bag with the handcuff restraints supporting her weight. She was closer this time. Her fingernail made a scratching sound as it moved back and forth against the bag's material trying to find a hold. Maria quickly removed her shoe and assumed the same position. This time she used its rubber sole to push the bag down against the desk and then pull it toward her.

"Bingo," she said in victory. The word came out a little louder than she would have liked. A mixture of excitement and fear swirled through the air. "Sorry," she said, her voice much softer this time.

Soller sifted through the bag for the charger. She raised the white cord into the air with a smile and pushed the bag back across the desk to where it was. She stretched out as far as she could, and was barely able to push the charger into the wall socket. The woman confirmed the coast was clear with an eager nod, so Soller pulled out her iPhone and used its length to seat the charger's plug firmly into the socket. Her shoulders tensed up at the sound of the familiar beep that indicated power. They froze in the silence for a long moment, and then shared a celebratory look.

Maria Soller smiled and said, "Hot damn."

Chapter 96

WASHINGTON, DC SERVED as a breeding ground for political secrets. When it came to secrets, President Vincent Cross was no exception to the rule, and he had already carefully considered what he was about to do from every possible angle. He and FBI Deputy Director Ivor Hood barely knew each other, but Cross was a man who had risen to the highest office in the land with a keen instinct. Knowing whom he could trust and when to trust them was a skill that kept him several steps ahead of the game.

He had just finished getting everything he needed together when his guest arrived. He looked up as a secret service agent directed Hood into the Oval Office.

"Mr. President." Hood nodded respectfully. "Thank you for taking the time to meet with me."

The president stood up from his desk and approached him with his hand extended. "Assistant Director Hood," the president said as he waved off the secret service agent. "Not a problem. This isn't something that can wait." He offered a tight smile.

The politician was a big fan of the handshake. It was a simple gesture, but one that conveyed a lot of information. The initial acceptance of the gesture, the firmness of the grip, the amount of shake, and the duration of the action all told a story. He would measure eye contact, spoken and body language when he sized a person up. Hood managed to pass his test with flying colors, but Cross had expected as much.

Hood's face was full of concern.

"I appreciate your time," he repeated nervously. The deputy director instinctively looked around to make sure they were alone. "They found my goddaughter's car abandoned in Leesburg, Virginia. There wasn't any blood, but it was parked well off the road behind some bushes." Hood's eyes hardened. "It doesn't look good."

The president motioned for Hood to have a seat on one of the two couches that were separated by a coffee table in the middle of the room.

"I'm sorry to hear that."

When they were seated, the president pushed a white binder across the table between them. The binder was labeled *NSPD 26: Intelligence Priorities* and was dated February 26, 2003.

"Let's not waste any more time then," Cross said. "But before you open that…" the president leaned toward his visitor and locked eyes, "…I need to make something clear."

Hood glanced down at the binder, and Cross waited for his recognition that the circulation of its contents had been extremely limited.

Hood's eyes narrowed. "Of course."

"Your source for this information is even more confidential than the information itself," the president said in a tone that meant business.

"Yes, Mr. President. I understand."

Cross gave him an approving nod, and the deputy director picked up the binder.

Hood looked across the table and said, "Wherever this leads me, you can be sure that I will take our words today and this document to my grave."

"Good." The president leaned back, satisfied with the answer. "Maybe you could help me with something."

"Absolutely," Hood said.

The president gestured toward the binder and said, "Why don't you have a look at that first?"

Hood opened the binder and reviewed its table of contents. The president read the deputy director's facial expressions as he flipped to the first document. It was a National Security Presidential Directive from February 2003 titled *Intelligence Priorities: Eliminating Terrorist Risks on US Soil.* He noted the deputy director's brow crease as he read through the pages.

The document authorized and detailed the formation of a top-secret FBI team with the purpose of eliminating known terrorists operating within the United States' borders. The directive included a detailed decision tree, which provided the necessary criteria to authorize a hit. The definitions meant the team could act on its own, providing a layer of deniability to keep the politicians out of the loop.

Cross reflected on the irony of the situation. The impetus for the NSPD was the very incident that delivered Frank Culder to the bureau's top spot at the expense of his good friend. Now it had all come full circle, a sparkling example of the "what comes around goes around" theory.

Hood peeled his eyes away from the document and looked to the president. "Wow," he said, before continuing.

"It was rescinded soon thereafter. We found a more suitable arrangement," Cross said, referring to Island Industries. His tone grew angry as he considered what Culder had done. "It looks like our friend took dismantling the team as a suggestion rather than an order."

Hood nodded without commenting and continued to read. The next page held the personnel details.

"So they were part of the team." He shook his head in disbelief. "Jacob R. Sanders and Rudy M. Pagano. Unbelievable."

"It was funded by a shell corporation called BlackRock."

"Is that the redacted section?"

The president nodded slowly.

Hood exhaled. "He could have kept this going without anyone knowing? It's like J. Edgar Hoover all over again."

"I think so." Cross thought out loud. "With some help."

"Obviously, you weren't pushing for this. Can you tell me who was?"

The president looked at the FBI man. The wet team, Culder, everything about the situation had been a prime example of a political power play. The sort of move that in his mind screamed for the introduction of term limits in congress and the senate.

"Senator Soller," the president said flatly.

"So you think he's in on this?"

"Let's just say I think you're on the right track. The effort was needed, but the risk with doing it this way, with Culder being Soller's puppet, was too great."

"The Stagehand program," Hood said with contempt. "Culder makes sure everything that goes on there is well guarded. He keeps it a bit too close to his chest for comfort. I hear about some of what goes on secondhand, but only because everyone assumes I'm in the loop." He thought for a moment and said, "Nothing too outlandish, but I'd guess they only paint a partial picture under the circumstances."

Stagehand was the code name for the bureau's program to outfit the FBI's tactical operations teams. All of the individuals on the hit squad had once been a part of that team.

The president nodded. "Stagehand would be my guess too. Everything is hush-hush there anyway, so it's the perfect place to get things done off the radar."

Hood looked to the binder and then to the president as if something had occurred to him. "So the others involved—they might not even know the team had been ordered to shut down." He took a measured breath and exhaled. "They probably think their operations are legit."

The president nodded. "That's a distinct possibility."

Hood's eyes met the president's. "I need to find this Sanders guy," he said, looking to the document and then back to Cross. "And what is it that is it that I can do for you, Mr. President?"

"I want what you want," Cross said. "I want to know what Culder is up to, and I'll need your help to get this under control."

"That's it?"

"Almost," Cross said as he stood. "I want you to work with a close friend of mine on this. I'm certain you and your goddaughter will find the collaboration to be mutually beneficial."

Chapter 97

HE FOUND THE keys to the Chevy Impala under the visor. Traffic was light, so it took less than thirty minutes for Jake Sanders to drive the three of them to the hotel. He and Rudy Pagano had brought suits along and they had laid them out on the two beds. They were a requirement if they wanted to blend in with the attendees at the performance.

FBI Director Frank Culder was in rare form. His men had never seen him so anxious.

"We'll go in after the show has already started," Sanders said. "That way he'll be in his seat and preoccupied with the performance."

"Sounds good," Culder said. "We need to try to get him during an intermission. Keep it as low-key as possible. Only the elite can afford to attend this event, so going in there hard and fast isn't an option. Pissing off the wrong people could be problematic."

Sanders reached into one of his bags and pulled out a small black leather case. He shook it and smiled.

"M99," he said. "Pop him with this and he'll be out cold. We can make it look like he's sick and carry him out of there."

"Good." The FBI director clasped his hands together and said, "I'll put in a call to get the two men from the local office to help."

"We need four to cover the inside," Sanders reminded him. His tone was edgy and it was clear he wasn't on board with what they'd agreed to on the plane. "How will you cover the exits alone?"

"You four head inside," Culder said, and pointed to the blueprint that was spread out on the table. "There aren't too many exits, so if you make sure he doesn't get out the front door, I'll only have one exit to cover."

Sanders studied the blueprint for a long moment. "That works," he finally agreed. "We can squeeze him out the back if we miss him in his seat." He gave the director a probing look and asked, "What do we know about the target? Trent."

Culder's face was full of disdain. "He works for Island Industries."

Pagano rubbed his eyes and tried to remember where he'd heard the name. "Sounds familiar. Is that—?"

"It should." Culder's posture tightened. "It's the company Admiral John Simpson founded after he resigned from the CIA."

"Right," Pagano said. "I suppose we still haven't been able to get many details on their operation?"

"You suppose correctly," Sanders said, now remembering. The director had been trying to dig up dirt on Simpson since the day they'd met. "He'll be a pro," he continued. "You can count on that." He stood and began to pace as the details he had uncovered about their operation came back to him. "Don't underestimate him, or you'll find yourself pulling your head out of your ass. And that's only if he decides not to turn you into a ghost."

Pagano scrunched his nose. "Sounds awful," he said, referring to the former. "I don't know what I'd do if my head smelled like your breath."

Sanders stopped pacing and smiled for the first time since he and Culder had butted heads on the plane.

"Anything else we need to know?" Sanders asked.

"Yeah, wear a black suit. I assume that's what you have in those garment bags."

Both men nodded.

"Good." Culder slid a picture of the target out of a folder and placed it on the table. "Now burn this man into your memory. Losing him isn't an option."

Chapter 98

Downtown Hotel, Chicago, IL

BOTH MEN WERE focused. Trent Turner had been busy showing the hacker how to use the equipment he brought with him from his townhome. The operative was impressed with Etzy Millar's ability to operate the gear. He had picked it up much quicker than expected. Millar attributed his fast progress to playing too many video games, a guilty pleasure he likely thought would never give him an advantage in real life.

Turner had scouted around the area for a secluded place to launch the PMD so Millar could practice. Chicago was much busier now than it had been in the morning, but it wasn't long before he found a suitable location to launch the PMD and turn Millar loose. The hacker would be an extra set of eyes during Turner's planned meeting with Heckler at the performance.

He was awestruck by the capabilities of the toy-like flying machine, and Turner could tell he was looking forward to the opportunity to be a part of the action.

Millar commanded the PMD to return to their location and said, "This thing is insane."

"That's one way to put it." The operative laughed. "Tak is a genius. Wait until you meet him."

"So you never told me?" he asked curiously.

Turner fixed a questioning glance on the hacker. "Told you what?"

"What it stood for. You know, PMD."

Turner smiled. "That's right. You have to promise you won't lose respect for it if I tell you."

"Aw, come on," Millar implored.

"Promise." His tone was insistent.

Millar nodded his head in surrender. "Okay, fine. I promise."

Turner looked him square in the eye with a stone expression. "PMD stands for Poor Man's Drone." He sounded so serious it took Millar a couple seconds to process what he had said.

Millar burst into laughter. "Holy shit, that's funny," he blurted out as Turner cracked a smile.

"Chalk that one up to Tak," Turner said. "Without a sense of humor, this job can become dismal."

"I'll bet. I can't wait to meet him," Millar responded. Then he went ominously quiet as the drone landed in front of them.

Trent sensed Millar was feeling the gravity of the situation. "Are you okay?" he asked.

"Yeah," he said unconvincingly.

"We'll get through this, Etzy. You need to stay strong." He walked over and started to disassemble the PMD and then looked to the hacker. "It's the only way you'll make it out the other side."

"I know."

They walked back to the hotel room in silent contemplation. As soon as Millar sat down in front of the desk, his computer screen lit up. It was an audio call from The Shop. Millar clicked on the button to answer.

"Hello, Etzy, it's Cyndi."

"Any more news?" he asked.

"Yes. Both good and bad."

"Okay. Finger is here with me, so go ahead."

"Good. We've managed to find what we think are the remnants of a bot at the Federal Reserve locations in New York and in DC."

"Wow. What's wrong?" Turner said, reacting to the concern evident in her voice.

"Well, the bot doesn't appear to be on any of the systems. We got lucky in New York when we pulled traffic logs from an ISP they're using. We were able to trace communication activity by correlating information with one of the bots Etzy's module had propagated to."

He sat down next to Millar. "So they uninstalled the bot?"

"That's right, Finger," she confirmed. "It's no longer on the machine. Fortunately we were able to find backups of the systems in question close to the date indicated in the ISP's traffic log. We're trying to download the computer's image without the Fed picking up the traffic."

"How long until you'll have it downloaded?"

"An hour or two," she said. "We don't want to risk the Fed knowing we're there. It could bring with it a whole new set of problems."

"Better to be safe. There's a lot at stake here," Turner agreed. He considered the new information and realized they might have a problem. "Do you think they're onto us?"

"No, no. This happened well before we even knew the botnet existed. The backup image might not have anything on it, since it's a couple of days older than the time stamp for the traffic." She sighed in frustration. "It's a shot in the dark at this point, but we don't have much else to go on where the Fed is concerned."

"Have you been able to get Tak on this yet?" Turner asked, slightly annoyed.

"No," Grayson said. She fumbled her next words. "There is a personal issue. He can't be involved."

"Personal?" Turner asked with the tone of a skeptic.

"Finger," she said, obviously flustered, "I've probably said too much already. You know how it is. I'm not at liberty to say. I wish we could have him on this too."

Turner looked to Millar and shook his head. "I get it," he replied. "Thanks."

He knew the way it worked. He wasn't going to get any more information out of her. There was an awkward moment of silence before the operative turned to Millar.

"The bot modified another system then?" Turner asked. "Or maybe the Fed discovered their presence, and they bailed."

"It could be something destructive," Millar suggested. "Maybe there's some sort of code set to run on a certain date or trigger to wipe their systems out."

"You said it was sophisticated," Grayson said to Millar. "That's not a very sophisticated attack."

"Sure, but the Federal Reserve is the central bank. I'm a step ahead of you. If the plan is to target banks that are connected to it, maybe they're trying to bring the systems down after they do whatever they're going to do, so things can't be verified." He looked to Turner.

"Interesting thought," Turner agreed. "That's a good point."

"I'm not sure how the financial system works," Millar said, "but if you're going to take down something that massive, you'll need to coordinate and make sure you cut off all of its heads at once."

"I hadn't considered that," Grayson admitted. "You could be onto something, Etzy. We have two CEOs involved from large banks that use the DataBank software. They've been kind enough to direct their technology staff to work with us on this."

"That's good news," Turner said.

"Well, they've been a bit slow, unfortunately." Grayson was clearly frustrated. "I can understand their reluctance to break policy, but we can't give them as much information as we'd like to, since this is classified. It's also slower, since we're only using communication channels that aren't connected to the bank, just in case."

There was still an area that bothered Tuner. "What about the deaths overseas?"

"We're still working on that but have made some progress."

"Have you gotten into the Fed's accounting systems to see who they bank with internationally?"

"Yes," Grayson confirmed. "They have sizable balances at several institutions. Most correlate with the murdered hackers that belonged to The Collective. We have a team of analysts digging through all of the connections."

Turner's brow creased with concern. "What sort of balances are we talking about?"

"Trillions. They have vast amounts of money parked overseas. There's also continual movement. We're talking huge transfers, so we definitely can't rule that out."

Chapter 99

Kozlov Bratva hideout, Leesburg, VA

THE WAIT HAD been interminably long. Cathy Moynihan watched as the girl powered on her iPhone and began to wave it through the air. It was as if she were trying to wipe away the message on the display that indicated there was no signal. She waited on the edge of her seat, ready to recite the FBI deputy director's number, but the good news still hadn't been delivered. She glanced over at the teenager and could sense she was about to ask the same question again.

"Has it connected yet?" Melody Millar whispered.

The room was thick with anxiety, and the question grated like an impatient child on a long car trip.

"No, Melody," the girl said, clearly frustrated. "Don't worry. I'll let you know as soon as it does."

Moynihan decided to break the tension. "Just let it charge for a few more minutes, and then slide it over to Melody. She can pass it to me if it doesn't work for her. There might be a signal in our part of the room."

"Okay," the girl said nervously.

They heard heavy steps out in the hallway, and all three of them turned toward the door. Soller started to reach for the plug that fueled the charger, but the noise quickly faded into the background. They shared sighs of relief.

Moynihan noticed the girl with the phone was bothered by something, and she sensed she was about to find out what it was.

"So why did the FBI want to take Melody?" she asked.

The agent thought about how to answer the question. At this point she decided it couldn't hurt to tell them the basics of what she knew. It wasn't much anyway, and maybe she could learn something from the others.

She was careful to keep her voice down and said, "They wanted to question her about her brother." She noticed the girl sit up in her chair. "He was at the scene of a murder. The bureau wanted to find out the extent of his involvement. Right now he's a person of interest."

The girl lowered her gaze and stared down the FBI agent. "So, let me get this straight," she said, her voice growing louder with each word. "You think Etzy, other than being in the wrong place at the wrong time, had something to do with Max's murder?"

Moynihan pushed the palms of her hands toward the floor in an attempt to quiet her down, but it only served to wind the girl up.

"He didn't have anything to do with it. I can tell you that much," the girl insisted, this time a little quieter but with the same sentiment.

Moynihan shook her head. She didn't understand the girl's intended connection.

"Etzy?"

"Etzy is Francis Millar's nickname." She nodded to Melody. "Her brother. Nobody calls him Francis anymore," the girl said dismissively.

Moynihan inclined her head. "I see. And how can you be so sure about that?"

"For starters, Etzy is a good person." Tears began to well up in the girl's eyes. "He was taken by the man who killed Max." She turned to Melody and then back to the FBI agent. "They said they had taken her, and if he didn't do what they said, they were going to hurt her. He didn't have a choice."

Moynihan squinted in disbelief. "How do you know this?"

"He sent me a text just before they took him. He was scared to death."

Tears streamed down the girl's face while Moynihan tried to piece everything together.

"He did? How do you know Francis...I mean Etzy?"

"He's my boyfriend," the girl said.

Moynihan's eyebrows raised at the news. "What?" Still taken aback, she realized she needed to approach this delicately. "Is it possible...?" She paused to consider whether or not to edit what she was about to say. "Is it possible that you don't know him as well as you thought you did?"

The girl's teary visage hardened with anger.

Doing her best to sound compassionate, Moynihan said, "Love is a crazy thing. Sometimes it can affect the way you reason things."

"No!" the girl shouted, her voice echoing through the room. "He would never do anything to hurt my brother. I can promise you that!"

Melody cowered from the volume of Maria Soller's voice, and Moynihan was stunned by the revelation that the girl wasn't only Francis Millar's boyfriend, she was Senator Soller's daughter, Maria.

Moynihan shook her head. "What the…?"

Footsteps pounded their way down the hall toward the room. The FBI agent looked helplessly at Maria Soller. She had been overcome with emotion, and the men were almost to the door. Her heart pounded as she tried to motion for Soller to stash the iPhone away out of sight, but she wasn't responding to visual cues.

Chapter 100

Fillmore Hotel, Chicago, Illinois

HE WAS RUNNING late; it was atypical for the former operative. The Gulfstream G650 was a fast plane, but with the aviator's equivalent of a traffic jam at the small airport, they were forced to circle above the Illinois skies for more than thirty minutes. Time was short, so he dressed himself in the confines of the corporate jet.

It had been quite a while since Heckler had put on a tuxedo—so long, in fact, he was thankful the fashion had remained constant. He had been told it was a black-tie event, so wearing a regular suit would attract unwanted attention.

The plane was at the airport for less than fifteen minutes. Immediately after he climbed down the stairs, Heckler sealed the plane so the pilots could get their wheels up as soon as possible. Their next stop was New York to pick up more assets for the operation. There would be no time to spare, so every second saved had the potential to make a difference. Heckler had taken a cab into town and was in a rush to check in to his room so he could get to the theater to meet the Island Industries operative.

"Mr. Smith?" the clerk said as Heckler handed him his ID.

"Yeah, that's right," he replied. He liked the name: nice and forgettable. Heckler turned to size himself up in the hotel's floor-to-ceiling mirror and muttered an explicative to himself.

The clerk looked up at him, unable make out the words. "Excuse me?"

"Ah, sorry. It's nothing."

He frowned at the unsightly hanger crease that dominated the horizontal axis of his slacks. There was no time to iron, so he shrugged it off. The smell in the lobby had him wondering whether they had sprinkled baby powder on their cheesy plastic flowers.

"Do you have something for me here?" he asked.

The clerk disappeared below the counter and popped back up. "Why yes I do, Mr. Smith. Here you go."

The clerk wore an overly enthusiastic smile as he handed Heckler a sealed envelope.

He nodded and said, "Thanks."

Heckler quickly headed up to his room and unloaded the rest of his gear. He checked his watch to see how late he was. It was already well after six o'clock, so he proceeded down the stairs, headed out to the street and flagged down a cab.

"The Studebaker Theater," he told the cabdriver as he slid into the back seat.

The driver turned his head toward him and nodded without saying a word. Heckler noticed a vibration from his phone. He had felt it earlier, but when he checked the display, he didn't see anything out of the ordinary. The occasion had served as a reminder for him to turn the ringer off.

As the cab approached the venue, the vibration got stronger. Heckler pulled the device out of his pocket to see if he had pressed a button inadvertently. This time the display was dominated by a message: *Proximity Alert Warning, 34 meters to your east.* He touched the display, and the device provided more details. It indicated that a cell signal that had been flagged for alert had been detected. He handed the driver a ten dollar bill and told him to keep the change.

"Goddamn it," he said as he exited the cab. He took careful inventory of his surroundings, knowing things were about to get complicated.

Chapter 101

Studebaker Theater, Chicago, Illinois

FROM THE MOMENT Victoria Eden walked out onto the stage, everyone in attendance had been captivated. Her black evening gown, with its low-cut top and full-length slit down the side, showed just enough skin for her to exude the perfect combination of beauty and class. There was no doubt that the violinist was in her element. She had been showered by a standing ovation as she walked gracefully out of view from center stage, the sight nearly as stunning as the flawless execution of the sonata she had just played.

He was a big fan; he had to admit it. It wasn't just her playing, it was her performance. She drew you into her world and left no room for distraction. Trent Turner considered what he'd just witnessed and it felt good. It was better than good—it was intoxicating, as evidenced by the smile still plastered on his face. It was as if she were playing for him, and he knew making people feel that way was the mark of a great entertainer. But the operative felt something more. The eye contact they shared while she was performing served as his introduction to a whole new degree of uncomfortable. She was talented, smart, persistent, attractive, and witty. Everything you could hope for in a person.

But when he considered the danger she would put herself in by associating with a man in his line of work, he shook off any illusions that it would be a good idea for them to get involved romantically. Turner wasn't about to start a relationship with someone outside the business despite what he felt inside.

His resolute decision was interrupted by a gentle touch from a hand that now shook his arm. He sensed her presence and could feel every eye in the venue was now trained on the woman seated next to him. Turner dreaded the exposure the next few minutes might bring as he tried subtly to conceal his face. Whispers of intrigue circled the theater. He had a bad feeling about this place, and his instincts were rarely wrong. He needed to get rid of her quickly.

She smiled cautiously and asked, "Where's your date?"

"He's not here yet," Turner replied.

Victoria Eden sized him up playfully.

"He?" she said with a sense of relief. "Hopefully he won't give me too much competition in the dress-and-shoes department."

Turner couldn't help but laugh. "You never know."

As he smiled, he considered the chance that Heckler might be a woman.

Victoria Eden's smile now reflected that she already knew the answer to her next question. "So no girlfriend?" She sat up primly awaiting his response.

He shook his head, thinking this would be funny if it wasn't so dangerous. "No. I'm too complicated for relationships."

She rubbed his arm affectionately and said, "Hmm. A man of great mystery."

He pulled away slightly, but her touch stopped him.

"Like I said. I'm complicated." His tone turned serious. "Listen, thank you for the tickets. Your performance was…" He took in a deep breath, and the vanilla and rose-laden scent of her perfume had a calming effect. He smiled, knowing words wouldn't do her justice. "This has been one of the most enjoyable experiences I've had in a long, long time," he said, trying to maintain a smile that would disarm her. "Really, though, I'm no good for you. You'll just have to trust me on that one. Maybe in another life."

She stared him down and moved her hand to his knee. The blackness of her hair was highlighted by the lights from above. Her green eyes burned a path directly to his soul and his heartbeat quickened.

She toyed with the moment and motioned to the bathroom with her free hand. "Now look, Mr. Whoever-you-are, I need to go to the ladies' room." She lowered her chin and fixed a determined stare. "Let's start over when I get back. You can work on a new pickup line while I'm gone." She paused briefly and pursed her lips. "That 'I'm complicated' routine will get you nowhere with me." She wiped her brow with a melodramatic sigh and said, "I promise you, when I get back it'll be like you're talking to a whole new woman."

Victoria Eden flashed him a wink before she turned and headed to the bathroom.

Turner found himself both bemused and strangely satisfied.

Chapter 102

THERE WAS NO hiding the annoyed look on Pavel Kozlov's face.

"What is it?" he snapped.

The world of classical music was the Russian's escape. He had been in deep conversation with an old friend who had flown in from Japan for the performance.

"Sir, we must talk," his head of security insisted in Russian.

"Pardon me," Kozlov said in English to his friend. He looked over at his man and, changing back to Russian, said, "This had better be good."

His head of security led him over to one of the red curtains on the north side of the stage. He pulled the curtain back slightly and urged Kozlov to take a look with a flick of his head. The Russian peered through the slit and saw Victoria Eden seated and speaking to someone. Kozlov pulled his head away with a disgusted look.

"What is the meaning of this?" he demanded.

His man took another look for himself and realized the man's face couldn't be seen.

"Pavel," he said with grave concern, "she isn't speaking to just anyone. That is The American. I'm certain of it."

Kozlov's brow furrowed in disbelief. He looked through the curtains once again and saw Eden motion toward the bathroom and stand up. Every man within eyeshot had his sights trained on her beautiful form as she glided across the floor. That is, every man except for Pavel Kozlov. His eyes tightened as the operative turned slightly, just enough for Kozlov to recognize the face. The Russian's pulse quickened. There was no way he would let this man escape again. This time he knew exactly how to deal with the situation, should his elimination prove to be problematic.

"How many men do we have here?" Kozlov asked with urgency.

"Five. Most of them are at the compound to make sure there are no problems with the operation."

"Tell the driver to bring my car around to the front. Give me two men. Use the others to deal with The American." His obligation to the motherland now threatened his passion. He decided on a course of action. "No bloodshed in the theater. Do not make a mess of this event. Do you understand?"

His head of security nodded. "*Da.*"

Kozlov headed toward the women's bathroom he had seen Victoria Eden enter. He casually stood in the waiting area closest to the door. Within a minute, two of his men approached. He cautioned them to remain at a distance with a wave of his hand. The Russian pulled out his handheld device and pretended to read emails.

The sound of her voice produced a wry smile.

"Pavel!" she said enthusiastically.

He looked up and feigned surprise. "Victoria! Splendid performance. Absolutely splendid."

Her face beamed with excitement, which struck him as odd.

"I can't thank you enough," she said. "This was more than I could have ever dreamed."

She gave him an appreciative hug. The gesture threw him off.

"I'm so pleased that you enjoyed yourself. It is clear by the reception that the admiration was mutual." He searched her eyes for a flicker of deceit and saw nothing. He inclined his chin and asked, "Would you mind coming with me for a moment? I have another surprise for you." His smile was inviting.

"You've done too much already. I couldn't possibly—"

"Nonsense. Please. Humor me," he insisted.

"Of course," she said. "It's the least I could do."

"Wonderful. Come this way."

Chapter 103

THE FOUR FBI men had bullied their way into the establishment and were now working their way through the Studebaker Theater's three levels. Jake Sanders and Rudy Pagano each took a side. They both had a local agent with them to look after, not wanting to risk one of them trying a hero play to impress Director Culder. The locals were under strict orders to report a sighting before moving in. The seasoned veterans from HVT Squad knew all too well the kind of havoc an ill-timed shot of adrenaline could wreak.

No performers were on the stage when they arrived, so they assumed the show had reached an intermission. The men felt awkward in their suits. By the time they realized they should have been dressed for a formal black-tie event, it was too late. The break in attire meant they needed to work as quickly as possible. The men followed the plan and headed to their assigned locations so they could systematically scan the crowd.

"Top clear," one of the local agents said. He had checked the smallest section and headed downstairs to cover the stairwell and rear exits on the north side.

"Second floor clear," Sanders confirmed moments later. "I'm heading down the south stairwell."

Many of the patrons were mingling in the open spaces, which complicated the search.

"Continue down the south side and start at the curtain closest to the stage," Pagano told Sanders.

"Roger that."

Sanders reached his vantage point and peeled back the first of three sets of bright red curtains that ran along the side of the first-floor seating area. They stood out from the cream-colored walls and the golden art nouveau motifs that adorned them. His eyes darted around the massive room, its design causing him to follow the tall, arched windows up to the vaulted ceiling. He quickly scanned down to the second-floor balcony across from him before working his way through the crowd. It didn't take long for the former Delta Force operative to find who he was looking for.

"Got him," he said into the small microphone that protruded from his sleeve. "South side, third row back, six in."

The local agent who had cleared the top floor immediately came into view. Sanders's pulse quickened as the agent worked his way down the center aisle that separated the two main seating areas.

"Don't move in," Sanders commanded, the tension evident despite the whispered tone. "I repeat, do not move in."

The FBI agent froze midstride when Sanders barked out the order and instinctively looked away from the target's location. His brown suit and red tie stood out like a flashing siren against the sea of black. He scurried back to the lobby to join the other local.

"I was just made by Pavel Kozlov," the agent said.

"Who?" Sanders sounded annoyed this time.

"He's a local crime boss. He spotted me and took off toward the door with some babe," he said. "The guy is hard-core. He's the head of the Chicago Bratva."

"Bratva?" Sanders said with indifference.

"Yeah, it's what the Ruskkies call the mob. He—"

"We can't afford to blow this," Sanders interrupted. He wasn't interested in a lesson on the agent's local problems. "Move into position and report back when our man's boxed in."

Chapter 104

TRENT TURNER WAS trying to keep a low profile when the news came through his wireless earbud.

"Four guys just rolled in the front door a minute ago looking all the business," Etzy Millar said.

Turner's eyes narrowed. "What do you mean?"

"You know, the kind of guys who could use some of that classical music to relax."

He switched the throat mic concealed by his collar from push-to-talk to automatic VOX mode and said, "Gotcha. What else can you tell me about them?"

Millar searched for an adjective. "Uh, military looking, I guess. I was waiting to see if they could be identified by the system, but it hasn't come up with anything yet. One of them is wearing a brown suit and a red tie. The others are wearing dark blue or black suits. It's hard to tell in this light. Two of them had a tie, two didn't."

"Okay, good job," Turner said.

He was sure this marked the beginning of the problems he had expected. The operative began to scan the theater when Millar chimed in again.

"Looks like some guy is hanging around out back," he said nervously. "The PMD pointed him out. Be careful in there."

The mini drone had been set on autopilot, programmed to perform surveillance on the building. Millar had preset eight locations into the flying machine. He just needed to touch a point on a small map displayed on his screen and the PMD would break routine and head to the spot and process the area.

"Whoa, whoa, whoa," Millar said surprised. "I've got something for you."

"What is it?"

"You remember that hottie from the airplane?"

Turner had a bad feeling about this. "Sure, why?"

"That Russian guy, Pavel Kozlov. He's heading out the front door with her right now." Millar touched the screen, commanding the PMD to maintain its position at the front of the building so he could watch. "Wow, these cameras are great. Holy crap, she's got some legs."

The comment brought the hint of a smile to Turner's lips as he continued to scan the theater. He had already picked up on the man in the brown suit and saw him jerk his head away the instant Turner zeroed in. He made note of his location and continued his search for the others.

"She's in the car and they're driving off," Millar said. "I marked it with the PMD, like you showed me."

Turner was discreet with his reply. "Good," he said. He had an ominous feeling that he was being watched.

He thought about what Millar had just told him and grew concerned that the Bratva boss may have recognized him when he was with the violinist. His sixth sense told him he needed to worry about the present, but he expected to soon cross paths with the Russian again. There wasn't anything he could do about Victoria Eden right now, and if he wasn't careful, he knew he might not be around to help her later.

Trent Turner drew on his experience, and his eyes shifted to the red curtains to his left. He noted the narrow slit that appeared halfway up their length. He would want that covered if he were trying to corner someone in the theater, and knew that would be Goon Number 2.

"You said the back was covered. What about the sides?" Turner asked, now scanning the area intently. "It's not looking good in here. I'm going to have to bug out fast."

"Checking now."

The intermission was coming to a close, and the patrons had begun to return to their seats. He wasn't sure who he was dealing with, and it was possible that cross hairs might be trying to find their way to his head. Turner needed to use the foot traffic to his advantage, and Etzy Millar had yet to chime in with the status, so his options were limited.

"Try to pull up 3-D mode for the theater," he said impatiently as he searched for the remaining two men. "See if the PMD can identify their positions inside."

Etzy Millar had been a fast learner, and it was something the operative appreciated more by the minute. The drone's 3-D view of the theater used signals emitted from electronic devices to try to determine the position of the individuals who had been marked.

"Got it," Millar said. "Hey, hold on a second. The PMD traced the registration for the car those men came here in. It says the car belongs to the FBI. It also says one of the cell signals was marked in the system last night."

It was a mixture of good and bad news. Turner knew the likelihood of being shot in these crowds by an FBI agent was extremely low, but unless Heckler had sold him out, he wasn't sure how they might have found him. His only connection to the bureau was Millar. He didn't see any point in Addy Simpson sending the FBI after him, but this was no coincidence. These men knew he was here, and the list of people who had that information was suspiciously short.

"Okay, I'm making a move," he said casually. "Let me know what you find out. I need an exit."

Chapter 105

HECKLER FELT LIKE he had been running around in circles. The display on the operative's XHD3 had first led him up the stairs to the second floor, and now it was telling him he was standing directly on top of the cell signal that had been flagged for alert. He needed to see who the owner was before going ahead with the planned meeting.

There were no performers on the stage, so he weaved his way through the crowd while the patrons worked their way back to their seats. As he reached the bottom of the stairs, he noted two men who looked out of place. They were in suits standing in the large, open lobby area that led to the theater. He approximated the location where his target should be standing and slid the device into his pocket.

He quickly identified the empty seat that matched his ticket and noted his appointment was still there, waiting. He moved along the three sets of blood-red curtains until he saw a large man in a suit peering into the theater. He judged that the angle of the man's stare matched up with where his seat would be. His position also matched the location of the proximity signal.

The man suddenly flinched just before the curtains between them exploded to reveal a man in full sprint. Heckler pushed the material out of the way in time to see the suited man begin his pursuit. Heckler took two quick steps forward and threw a stiff shoulder that slowed his progress.

"Pardon me," he said under his breath.

The operative he had come there to meet had already disappeared up the stairs by the time he noticed two more suits had taken off after him. His eyes spied three more men sprinting off in the opposite direction.

Heckler headed toward the stairs and saw another man start up the flight at the other end of the theater.

"What the hell is going on here?" he muttered to himself.

Chapter 106

SHE WAS STILL on a high from her performance as the armored Bentley Mulsanne sped through the streets of Chicago. It didn't take long for Victoria Eden to realize there was a problem. A big problem. Excitement could only mask the dark intentions of her chaperone for so long. The car was eerily quiet as it whisked through the streets at an uncomfortable pace. She shared increasingly awkward glances with Pavel Kozlov. Her anxiety grew with the searing silence until she couldn't take it anymore.

"Pavel, where are you taking me?" she asked nervously.

"We'll be there soon," he said. His voice was void of emotion.

"What's going on?"

The mood in the car was tense. Her nervousness escalated to fear as they entered an industrial section of the city. Some of the buildings were run-down, and the streets were empty.

"Pavel?" she pleaded insistently.

He wore a mask of disdain when he turned to her. "One can never be too careful of the company we keep," he said.

"What's that supposed...?" She stopped herself midsentence. Her eyes filled with recognition as she conjured up the image of her mysterious acquaintance. He was attractive, confident, even kind, but she would never forget the words he spoke, and the tone with which he delivered them. "I'm no good for you," he had said so adamantly. "You'll just have to trust me on that. Maybe in another life." She bit her lower lip as she replayed their chance encounters in her head, the silent tension they had both felt.

Then she considered the man sitting next to her. Russian. Wealthy. A man who collected instruments worth millions and, judging by his hands, probably couldn't play a note.

Her body tensed up as she put the pieces together. Pavel was a powerful man—that much was clear. She now found herself tangled in the world the man she had begun to fall for had warned her about, and she desperately needed to find a way out.

Chapter 107

Studebaker Theater, Chicago, Illinois

JAKE SANDERS WINCED from the blow. He wasn't expecting the target to run up the stairs, but it didn't matter. Even though his forward motion had been slowed by one of the patrons, there was no way he would have been quick enough to cut him off. The two local agents were just ahead of him as he navigated the stone stairway two steps at a time. He was about to pass the slower of the two men and barked out an order for him to watch the stairwell as he passed. The FBI agent immediately hunched over and dropped his hands to his knees. Sanders knew it was the best way to keep all the assets he had in the game.

He continued to gain on the agent still in front of him. The man was in good shape but still no match for the HVT Squad leader. Both men reached the top of the stairs at the same time. The stairway spilled out into the front row of the third floor's amphitheater-styled seating. Each had an injection device loaded with M99 in his hand with enough of the substance to knock out Mike Tyson.

"I'll go after him alone," Sanders said as he tried to catch his breath. He didn't want the opportunity blown because a novice got in the way. "Stay here. Be ready for anything." He lifted his sleeve to his mouth and said, "Rudy, get to the lobby and keep your eyes peeled. Let me know when you're ready."

"Roger that," Pagano confirmed.

He went over the layout of the third floor in his head. He reasoned that the target was crouched behind the chest-high divider situated behind the final row of seats. He pushed the FBI agent back a couple of steps. Sanders wanted to keep him out of the line of fire in case things turned hot. He wished he had a way to deliver his payload without having to get up close and personal, but there wasn't anything he could do about that now.

"Ready when you are," Pagano said.

Sanders removed the plastic cap from his syringe and pushed the plunger just enough for a few drops of the liquid to drip out onto the floor. He had already recovered from the dash up the stairs and was mentally preparing himself for what needed to be done.

He lifted his sleeve to his mouth and said, "Preparing to engage."

He pulled his sidearm out of his shoulder holster and took a deep breath.

Chapter 108

TRENT TURNER HAD made it to the top floor first. He knew there were at least four men after him, but he also spotted three unknowns who fired him an unsettling glare as he headed toward the stairs.

"The top looks good from the plans," Millar confirmed. "You're right. The air return will take you out to the third-floor common area next to the theater. From there you can head down the fire escape on the south side of the building." There was a momentary pause before Millar continued. This time his excitement had turned to nervousness. "It looks like two of them are at the top of the stairs. One stayed behind on the second-floor landing. The PMD hasn't been able to mark number four yet."

Turner remained crouched in the back corner of the third-floor viewing area. He was low enough that nobody could see him. There was only one set of stairs that could bring them up.

"One of them is starting to close in," Millar said.

The operative pulled a tool out of his pocket and snapped off the screw heads securing the cover for the ventilation system's return duct. The theater had just been renovated, so he hoped the floor plans he had studied weren't out of date.

"He's really close," Millar said frantically.

Turner quickly ripped the cover off the wall and slid inside the dark tunnel. The aluminum popped and twisted as he snaked his way through the confined space and around a corner. It wasn't long before he recognized the same sound off in the distance. He knew someone else had made their way into the metal maze. He didn't have his light on, so when he bumped his head into what seemed to be the end of the ventilation system he was surprised.

"Etzy, it looks like I've reached a dead end. Can you confirm?"

"It shouldn't be," Millar said. Panic had crept into his voice. "The blueprints say it goes out to the third floor...a big common area."

The sound was getting closer. Turner didn't want a confrontation with an FBI agent, so he needed to get creative.

"What's below me?" he asked.

"Nothing that I can see. You're pretty much next to the stairwell."

The sound from his pursuer had stopped. Turner braced his hands on the sides of the metal ventilation shaft and began to rock it violently from side to side. At first there wasn't much noise or movement, but after a couple of hard shoves the sound increased until there was a massive thud.

Trent Turner shook his head and tried to get his bearings. It was still pitch black, and it felt like he had fallen quite a long way. He pulled out his XHD3 and shined its small LED light toward the immediate threat from above. He saw that he had snapped the vent shaft supports for the section he was in. He had fallen around fifteen feet, but his descent had been slowed initially when the metal had bent down toward the ground. The shaft had folded onto itself and now managed to obscure the view into the unclaimed space he currently occupied.

There were no doors leading out of the small room. It appeared to have been closed in for decades. He could see by the angle of the ceiling that one side faced the stairwell and the other the theater. Most of the wall was plastered, but he saw one section that had been repaired with drywall.

He knocked on the wall a couple of times to confirm and asked, "Etzy, what's in front of me?"

"It looks like the stairwell, but I'm not sure I trust these blueprints."

He laughed to himself. "I hear you."

The aluminum above him started to flex and rumble. It sounded like the man was testing the supports. Turner couldn't help but smile when he considered the advantage of being chased. You didn't have time to think about shit like that.

"Okay, I've got an update," Millar said. "There's one guy practically on top of you, one right next to you, one standing at the top of the stairs on the third floor, and I've picked up the other guy. He's down in the lobby, waiting."

Turner pulled a tool out of his pocket and used a knife-edge to slice into the drywall lengthwise along the vertical two-by-fours that held it in place.

He then punched a small hole into the drywall at eye level with a stabbing motion. He cleared away the debris with the tool and peeked through. It took him a second to realize he was staring at an eyeball on the other side of the hole. He heard pounding above as Millar chimed in once again.

"Man, you are standing right next to the guy in the stairwell," he said.

Turner was out of time. He brought his elbow back and delivered a devastating blow to the bridge of the man's nose through the drywall. The operative quickly kicked the rest of his way through producing a haze of white dust. He barely registered the people screaming as his now ghostly form popped through the wall. The FBI agent's face was bloody, and he had balled himself up on the floor as he groaned in pain.

"I need a little help," Turner said.

He knew Millar had been desperately searching for a way out.

"It's hard to see if the south side is clear," the hacker said, "and the PMD can't get a view into the covered alley between the theater's bathrooms and the school. The other options don't look good, if that's any help."

Turner heard a loud thump through the hole he had just emerged from, signaling the man had made it through. He quickly bolted down the stairs, and when he reached the bottom he could see the fourth agent charging toward him from across the lobby. Out of the corner of his eye he saw a sudden movement as he bolted to the bathroom. He hoped the window would be more cooperative this time around.

The operative shoved the bathroom door open and went straight to the window above the heat register. He had tried to pry it open in the morning when he had scoped the place out, but could only manage to crack it open part of the way. This time around he wasn't concerned about doing any damage. He needed to get outside—and fast.

Chapter 109

THE RUSSIANS HAD been waiting out back and were growing impatient. The FBI agents should have burst through the back door minutes ago, but they had yet to make their way outside. The three men had The American in their sights but had been caught off guard when he charged at them with the Feds they had recognized in tow. The leader of the Bratva soldiers lit his unfiltered cigarette in disgust, his other hand perched on his weapon of choice.

The directive from Pavel Kozlov had been no bloodshed inside the theater. He had been adamant about it. Their attempt to lure the agents out the back door and out of the public's view had failed. There were no more doubts; their plan didn't work. They had been eyeing the man in the car twenty meters away and had grown wary of his presence. They planned to pay him a visit after they finished with the FBI to make sure there were no witnesses.

"We need to check inside," the leader said to his squat comrade with the pockmarked face.

"*Da*. Let's make it quick in case they've called for more men."

The Russian followed his direction and tried to turn the knob on the door, but it was locked. He grabbed hold the doorknob again, this time with both hands, but it still wouldn't turn.

The leader took another drag off his smoke, and looked toward the car. His face wore a scowl. "Help me," he told the others.

The three men gathered around the door. The largest of the three grabbed a long piece of steel that was leaning against the wall and tried to pry the door open, while the other two men pulled on the handle. The door wouldn't budge.

"It's no use. Let's go around to the front," the Russian with the steel bar said.

The others nodded in agreement.

The Russian in charge flashed another look at the car and exhaled a stream of smoke from his nose before leading the men south to circle around the building. Chicago's Fine Arts Building was connected to Roosevelt University, so when they rounded the corner to head east toward Michigan Avenue, they faced a tunnel that ran beneath the second floor of the adjoining buildings.

"Pavel will be pissed if The American gets away again," he said before taking another pull on his cigarette.

"*Da, da.* we will be flipping hamburgers if he doesn't shoot us first," the pockmarked Russian agreed.

The leader shook his head. "I don't know what he was thinking when he asked us to take care of a man such as him with conditions."

"What do you think we should do about it?" the squat Russian asked.

"Fuck the conditions," he said in a dark tone. "If you see him, kill him. He should already be dead. It will be in our best interest to beg for forgiveness rather than to ask for permission."

The men nodded in agreement and increased their pace. They had made it halfway through the tunnel when a loud creaking sound caused them to freeze and take stock.

"What the hell is that?" the Russian said, flicking his cigarette to the ground.

The one with the pockmarked face pointed to a first-floor window. "There."

They watched curiously as the window rocked back and forth, its rusty metal hinges screaming out in protest.

Chapter 110

HE PUMPED THE window back and forth vigorously on its hinges.
Trent Turner heard a series of noises in the theater outside the bathroom as
he worked to force an opening large enough to fit through. First there was
a sliding sound, and then the sound of metal crashing, followed by gasps
from the crowd. Whatever it was that made the noise, he was thankful
knowing the FBI agents should have made it into the bathroom by now.
That was a confrontation he wanted to avoid if at all possible. He gave the
window one last heave, and it belted out its final wail in surrender.

He had made just enough room to squeeze through. He pushed himself
into a handstand from the top of the bathroom's heat register and thrust
himself legs first out the window. He slowed his fall using his elbows and
hands and landed softly on the concrete. The operative stood and spun 180
degrees from his crouched position. The three men standing in front of
him looked confused. He recognized one of them. He was part of Pavel
Kozlov's security detail.

The Russians looked stunned to see The American standing in front of
them. These men were well trained, so Turner's best option was to
introduce more confusion. He flicked his left thumb toward the window
behind him and waved his other hand in front of his nose.

"You do not want to go in there," he said in a deadpan tone. He forced
a smile. "It's absolutely brutal."

Two of the men looked at each other, and he reached for his pocket. It
was too late. The third man had already begun his charge. The operative
quickly moved forward and sidestepped, causing the linebacker-sized

Bratva man to miss. He threw an elbow into his spine to send him crashing into the brick wall.

Everything turned to slow motion as he addressed the others. They charged him simultaneously with crazed looks in their eyes. He waited until the last moment again and stepped forward. When they reached for his arms, he extended his fists and delivered a leopard punch to their throats. Instead of instinctively reaching toward the pain, both Russians tightened their grips on his arms.

That was exactly what Trent Turner had expected as he quickly stepped out of his tuxedo jacket. In a single motion he turned and channeled all of his energy into his feet with two perfectly timed blows. His initial strike landed on the back of the first man's neck, and the second connected with the other Bratva soldier's chin. Both men crumpled to the ground.

By the time his feet had gained solid footing, it was too late. The bull of a man he had dispatched with first was almost on top of him and was carrying incredible momentum. The Russian drove Turner the width of the alley and slammed him mercilessly into the brick wall on the other side. The wind had been knocked out of him, so his next actions were purely defensive.

The attacker delivered two more shots to his midsection as Turner struggled for air. He used his hands and elbows to fend off the blows. Every time the operative connected, it felt like he was assaulting a rock. He felt another angry blow to his midsection before he lost his balance and fell to the ground.

His vision was tunneled as he tried desperately to fill his lungs with air. He felt like a turtle that had been flipped onto its back. The Russian stood above him with steely eyes looking ready to deliver a finishing blow, but he suddenly turned away. Turner focused on breathing and tried desperately to regain his composure. He sat up and watched as the Bratva soldier brutalized the FBI agent who was stuck in the frame of the bathroom window. When the first shot was fired, he saw the big man drop to the ground.

Trent Turner slowly rose to his feet as the violence unfolded in front of him. Survival mode kicked in when the remaining Russians drew their weapons. They were still distracted by the assault from the window, so he sprinted down the alley toward Michigan Avenue. He decided the park would be as good a place as any to disappear. When he reached the street, he saw that the theater had already begun to clear out in a panic. Yellow cabs were already lined up along the curb.

He made a quick right to get out of the line of fire from the alley when someone called out to him.

"Hey, kiddo," a man shouted.

Turner recognized the voice, and it caught him by surprise. The cab drove alongside him as he ran down the street.

The man stuck his head out the window. "Hop on in," he said with a big smile.

Turner returned the smile and said, "Uncle Jack?"

The operative slowed to a stop alongside the cab and glanced behind him to make sure the men hadn't come after him. He looked down and brushed away some of the drywall dust from his black pants and then shook his head at his uncle.

"What the hell happened to you, kid? You look like shit."

"Long story," Trent said. "Good thing the tux is a rental." He smiled and hopped into the back of the cab. "What are you doing here?"

Jack Turner offered him a shit-eating grin. "Bailing your ass out. What else?"

"Shit, no way. What?" He was still a little dazed from the beating he had been given. What should have been obvious was now abundantly clear.

"You'd have had some company in the can if it wasn't for yours truly," he added matter-of-factly.

"Heckler?" The fact that his Uncle Jack was his handler threw him off. "I guess I should have known it was you with a call sign like that." He shook his head and feigned disappointment. "Safe to say you've watched *Top Gun* too many times."

"Cut me some slack. At my age it's hard to find good work." He shrugged. "Addy said he needed a babysitter for a problem child. How else am I supposed to afford my Viagra addiction and daily dose of Geritol?"

They shared a quick laugh, and Trent got down to business.

"Is he okay?" he asked, referring to Island Industries' boss, Addy Simpson. "You know, with what's happened?"

"I'm sorry about Ryan, Trent," Jack said in a solemn voice. "Addy understands. Let's just leave it at that." He looked out the window and then back to Trent. "He knows it was something you had to do, but don't pull that shit again." He shook his head. "It won't fly."

Trent nodded. "I know."

"Good."

"We need to get back to my hotel," Trent said. He tapped on the Plexiglas that separated them from the driver. "Please drop us off at the next block." He looked to his uncle. "I just ran into three of Kozlov's men in the alley. I planted a tracking device on one of them. Hopefully, the guy didn't get shot up too bad, and they'll head home soon."

Chapter 111

Kozlov Bratva hideout, Leesburg, VA

THE DOOR SWUNG open quickly and banged against the wall. The three women wore masks of fear as the former Spetsnaz soldiers stomped into the room. Maria Soller had barely managed to stash her iPhone away in time, but FBI agent Cathy Moynihan was still worried about the plug for the charger that was dangling precariously from the wall.

"What's going on in here?" the man with the utility jacket yelled.

No one answered. He looked to each of the prisoners deliberately, his gaze ending on Soller. Her eyes were still moist with tears, so she quickly wiped them away with her sleeve. His glare intensified.

"What's going on?" he growled.

She didn't respond. He was visibly angry at her refusal to speak. Moynihan tensed up as she watched him consider his next move.

Then one of the other men spoke. He motioned to Melody Millar. "She was together with this one," he barked in Russian. "We could teach her a lesson." He smiled in a way that suggested he was undressing her in his mind, which bared his crooked yellow teeth. "She is cute and young."

The FBI woman could see the lust in the man's eyes and decided he was bored and restless, having been stuck in this dump in the middle of nowhere. He walked over to Millar and flashed a repulsive wink before he reached out and touched her hair. She recoiled in disgust.

Moynihan's icy fear turned to a boiling anger, her forward lunge stopped by the restraint. Her anger mixed with horror as the soldier reached for the young girl again.

"Stop it!" Soller screamed at the top of her lungs. Her voice was shrill and had startled everyone in the room.

The Russian laughed and started to paw viciously at Millar's shirt. Cathy Moynihan stood in anger as the teenager strained to fend off her aggressor. She looked down at her chair, picked it up with her free hand and hurled it toward the Russian with every ounce of her being. One of its metal legs connected with the base of the soldier's skull, and he dropped to one knee.

He shook his head and raised his hand to the point of the impact. He turned and gave the FBI agent a deadly glare. She had been wearing a hood the last time she had tried to lash out at him, and now she'd evened up the score.

"You fucking bitch," he yelled in Russian, his teeth clenched. He picked up the chair and shook it. "I'm going to fuck you with this chair!"

Moynihan couldn't understand a word he said, but his intention for violence was clear.

The soldier wearing the utility jacket approached him and grabbed hold of the chair. "What the hell are you doing?" he barked.

The soldier had a crazed look in his eyes and said, "You want them to talk? I know how to get them to talk."

The man with the utility jacket yanked the chair from his grip and said, "We need them alive, Vladimir, you idiot."

The interruption had only managed to increase his anger. He nodded toward Moynihan. "I will only kill that bitch." His stained teeth were framed by a sickening smile. "Let the others watch, and once I'm finished with her they won't give us any more problems."

"She's FBI," he fired back. "What happens if they come for us and she's dead? Then what will we have to negotiate with?"

The Russian made a hissing sound, his face pulsed with anger. "Fine. I won't kill her. I'll just introduce her to the Pride of Mother Russia." He followed his comment with a laugh as he grabbed his crotch.

When his comrade nodded in agreement, he turned to the FBI woman with a lustful grin.

Moynihan couldn't understand what was said, but she stood there ready for a fight. She had noticed his uncomfortable attention since she had been forced to strip down to her underwear in front of him, and decided he was the type of man who would take great pleasure in torture.

Chapter 112

DUSK HAD BEGUN to settle along the Potomac River. Even with the Key Bridge looming above, the wooded areas surrounding the Capital Crescent Trail had an air of tranquility.

Ivor Hood looked curiously at the package sitting on his driver's seat and decided it would be best to lock it away in his briefcase. He had been flagged down as he left the Hoover Building to sign for the priority delivery. He was frustrated by the delay but had been the only person in the building with a pay grade high enough to accept the item.

Even with the interruption, it took Hood less than fifteen minutes to get to Jack's Boathouse. His mind was still racing through the sequence of events that had transpired. The deputy director found himself in uncharted territory. He was ready to risk everything for the little girl he had seen blossom into a formidable young woman. She had incredible potential, more than he could have imagined, and he wasn't about to sit back and let someone wipe it away.

His moment of contemplation was interrupted by the sound of an approaching vehicle. He was surprised to see a massive pickup truck pull over to the side of Water Street and park. The choice of transportation didn't quite fit with what he had expected from the man he had spoken to over the phone, but he wasn't one to judge.

Addy Simpson got out of the bright yellow truck and walked over to greet him.

"Deputy Director Hood, John Simpson." Simpson smiled as he gripped Hood's hand firmly. "Thanks for meeting last minute like this."

"Nice to meet you, Admiral Simpson," Hood said.

"Likewise. Please, call me Addy."

Hood nodded and said, "Call me Ivor."

Simpson returned his nod and surveyed the area before he continued. "Our mutual friend tells me the director might be running a black team."

Hood looked past him and said, "Looks that way." He smiled without any humor and returned his gaze to Simpson. "He really slipped up getting my goddaughter involved, or else he'd still be in business."

"The president told me. I'm sorry to hear that." His eyes showed genuine concern. "Suffice it to say this is now personal for both of us."

"Then I suppose we should get to the point."

"Indeed," Simpson agreed. "We traced Culder's men to a house in Poolesville. Three men had been killed there by professionals. We were able to match them up with the list our friend provided to confirm they left the bureau in February 2003. All but two of the men on that list are now dead."

Hood shook his head in disgust.

"There's more," Simpson said. "Agent Moynihan, your goddaughter, was also captured on video at the house."

The deputy director's eyes filled with dread.

"She arrived before and then appeared again shortly after the killings," Simpson continued. He shook his head. "We managed to trace the people who carried this out to a Russian named Pavel Kozlov."

Hood's expression bore recognition. "Chicago?"

"That's him. He's part of an underground network—"

"Of hardline communists," Hood said.

"You know our man then?"

"Sure. I used to work with the organized-crime task force, but I don't understand why he would be here, in the area." Hood's eyes narrowed as he tried to make sense of the information. "And Culder? What the hell is he involved with on the side that would have a connection to the Russian mob?"

Simpson went on to explain everything he knew. From the senator's involvement with Director Culder to what was turning out to be an imminent attack on the country's financial systems and its connection to the senator's son.

They compared notes and were able to determine that the BlackRock Corporation, which had been formed as part of the Presidential Directive, and the BR Corporation, which was tied to the Poolesville home and cellular phone records from devices in the area at the time of the killing, were one and the same. Hood confirmed that he had a number he thought belonged to Sanders. Simpson was able to match it to the cell records from Poolesville, and they developed a strategy to move forward.

"Do you need some men?" Hood asked.

"No, but thank you for the offer." The assistant director didn't look happy about being left out, so Simpson said, "You don't want a good cop getting mixed up in something as toxic as this. Their rules of engagement are different. Things won't end well, trust me."

Hood appreciated his candor and asked, "Then what can I do?"

"I need to know what Culder is up to. I'll make sure my men do whatever it takes to get Agent Moynihan back to you safe and sound, but you have to understand their primary objective will be to stop Kozlov."

"I understand. So is hers," Hood said.

Simpson was impressed with the man, and passed him an envelope. "I hope you'll find some of this information helpful."

"Thanks. I'll be in touch."

Chapter 113

The Shop, Arlington, Virginia

CDWG DIRECTOR CYNTHIA Grayson's team of white-hat hackers had been working like a well-oiled machine. They sifted through line after line of code as they unraveled the challenge their newest adversary had presented them. This was an extremely delicate operation, and everyone tasked with reverse engineering the code used extreme caution. Finding active surgeon bots installed on virtual desktops at one of the banks they were working closely with had been a huge breakthrough.

The virtual desktop computers were nearly identical to their physical counterparts but operated with a crucial difference. The operating system for the virtual machines ran on top of an abstraction layer, meaning the hardware for the computer was easily interchangeable. The virtualization software presented a logical view of computing resources rather than using actual physical components. Simplistically, the virtual machines were like a document that could be passed around and opened by a program that supported its format.

The abstraction layer made it easy for The Shop to make a copy of each computer and run it in an isolated environment using its virtualization software. The setup eliminated the risk of the bot communicating with the command-and-control servers. The innovation had been technology's version of pulling the rug out from under you. The team had made several copies of the surgeon bots so it could split into five teams of two. Now they were able to divide and conquer.

Grayson's strategy had rapidly begun to pay off. New information was flowing in at the speed of a Wall Street stock ticker. Etzy Millar had been off-line for nearly an hour, and the director was glad to have him back in the mix.

"There's an encrypted file that we haven't been able to crack," Grayson explained. "It was delivered about thirty minutes ago. We were able to make another clone of the machines and run a block-level comparison to isolate the file."

"Were you able to figure out when this is going to go down?" Millar asked.

"No, not yet," Grayson said with frustration. "It's the same file on all of the bots, so at least we have that going for us." If the files had been different from bot to bot, it could have meant that each individual bot had its own encryption key, which would have made things more complicated. "It does look like the bot has a trigger that's waiting for another communication from the C&C servers."

"How did you figure that out?" Millar asked after a brief pause.

She smiled and said, "We extended the version of the bot you developed with a module that lets us resend packets we've captured from other known C&C communications."

"When I went through the code, I thought it had been programmed to remove itself if it encountered anything unexpected." He stopped for a moment and then added, "If certain software was installed, or if—"

"You're right," she interrupted. "We've set up several virtual systems with the surgeon bots, and when the bot reacts to something it doesn't like and uninstalls itself, we can quickly restore it back to its original state and try again."

"Wow, you got that set up fast," Millar said.

"Our team is the best," Grayson said, pleased with herself. "The communication packets are encrypted, but we can see the bot react to them, and it's helped us isolate certain files and given us clues about what we might want to look for." Grayson reviewed her notes for a moment. "We think there's another set of C&C servers out there, and it looks like they need to be synced up to match the botnet's encryption key. From our analysis, it looks like the key changes on a regular basis, and without an updated key, the control servers are useless."

"Cyndi," Millar said tentatively, "can I have access to one of the virtual environments?"

"Of course. I would like to work with you on this personally, Etzy," she admitted. "There's a lot at stake here, and I want to do everything possible to make sure we undo everything these people have done."

Her concern for what he had on the line personally came through in her voice.

"Thanks," Millar replied with mixed emotions. "One of your analysts had called you Dr. Grayson. *The* Dr. Grayson?" he asked. The awkward silence answered his question. "Wow."

"That's classified," she said with a hint of concern in her voice.

"Sorry, I forgot this is sensitive kind of stuff. Besides," he continued with a reverent laugh, "I can't imagine the brilliant doctor I'm thinking of getting involved in this line of work."

She smiled to herself, appreciating his tact. The moment was interrupted by what sounded like the beep of a hotel room door unlocking and Etzy Millar's panicked reaction.

Chapter 114

Kozlov Bratva hideout, Leesburg, VA

SHE WAS HANDCUFFED to the railing, but FBI Agent Cathy Moynihan was too smart to dwell on the negatives at a time like this. Instead, she thought about how she could inflict the maximum amount of damage on the burly Russian with her three unshackled limbs. Her piercing eyes brought a lecherous look to the fast-approaching brute, and it all came down to one target. She turned and gripped the railing tightly with both hands while he prepared to pounce. She peered over her shoulder as he came into range, and used the metal bar for leverage. With one perfectly timed motion, she jumped and thrust her legs backwards, using her hands as an anchor to achieve maximum force.

He let out an animalistic groan that defied description. She had delivered a direct hit to his groin, and as his massive form collapsed to the floor in agony, she landed another crushing blow on his chin. Blood flowed from his mouth and began to pool on the floor. The other two soldiers looked at their comrade writhing in pain on the floor and then set their eyes on the FBI agent. She returned their glare with a look of defiance. There was no way in hell anyone was going rape her, or anyone else, if she had anything to say about it.

"You think this is good?" the Russian with the utility jacket asked, his face hard and cold.

She didn't respond.

"You think this is good?" This time he said it a little louder. When she refused to answer, he said, "I think this is good."

He smiled his approval and looked to the other soldier, who nodded an emphatic yes.

"*Da!*" the soldier confirmed.

They both began to laugh hysterically. Maria Soller and Melody Millar kept their eyes down to avoid eye contact, but Moynihan remained engaged as she tried to figure out what would come next. She wasn't convinced the laughter meant this was over. The surreal moment was broken by a loud voice.

"What the hell is going on in here?" it barked.

All three men looked over toward a man standing in the doorway. The injured soldier checked his stained teeth and spit a clump of blood onto the ground. The women were taken by surprise, since the newcomer had no accent. He was an American.

"Well?"

The man with the utility jacket grinned. "Vladimir likes to have rough sex." He motioned to the FBI agent.

Bruce Campbell laughed. "Good thing she was chained to the wall, or this could have gotten ugly."

The three men continued to laugh as Vladimir picked himself up off the ground. Moynihan's eyes followed the Russian while he slowly rose to his feet. He met her gaze with an angry stare.

"I'll be back for you later, bitch," he spat in Russian, before he hobbled out the door.

Campbell held his grin and looked over at the other two prisoners. Soller had kept her eyes down, but Melody Millar looked up curiously. His eyes flashed with recognition. The resemblance was uncanny. Millar shrunk in her chair, appearing to sense trouble.

Chapter 115

IF THE PAST two days had taught Etzy Millar anything, it was how to cope with fear. The hard-looking man who had just entered his hotel room caught him off guard, but the hacker had adapted to his new lifestyle quickly and immediately reached for the Beretta lying next to his computer. He leveled its sight at the intruder's head. The man gave him a sideways glance before casually looking back toward the hallway he had entered from.

"Jesus, Trent, didn't you show this kid how to turn off the safety?" Jack Turner asked.

"What?"

Millar quickly lowered the weapon when he heard Trent Turner's voice. His look of fear turned to confusion.

Trent walked through the door and sized up both men. "Did I miss something?" he asked.

"Finger, is that you?" a female voice came through the computer.

Millar's heart rate was returning to normal, and he said, "I'm working with Cyndi from The Shop." He looked up at the older man with great concern. "I'm really sorry about that."

Jack Turner smiled. "Not to worry, Etzy. You're doing great. You're handling yourself well. Just remember the safety next time."

The hacker was confused.

"Nice work you've been doing. I'm impressed." Jack offered a smile with a curt nod. "You know me as Heckler."

331

Millar thought about their previous conversations and returned the smile. Jack Turner didn't sound like the same person, but he was finding a lot of things weren't what they first seemed.

Trent chimed in to answer the earlier question. "Yes, I'm here," he said, directing his response to Millar's computer.

"Great, we could use your help on this," Grayson said. "Is that you, Jack?"

Etzy looked to Trent and was clearly concerned.

"Sure is, Cyn. I heard Chicago's a great place for a weekend getaway." He noticed Millar was uncomfortable and said, "Don't worry, Etzy, I've been around too long. Everyone at The Shop knows I'm Heckler." He pointed at Trent and added, "But they don't know who he is, so we'll have to keep that little secret between us."

Everyone laughed.

"Did you have any luck with the Federal Reserve?" Trent asked.

"We do have one development," Grayson replied. "After wading through the traffic logs, the team has managed to track communications from one of the known bots into the Fed. The strange thing is that the computer in question hasn't made any contact with any of its financial systems as far as we can tell. Aside from its normal processing, the only other significant communication has been with its corporate phone system." She paused so Trent could digest the information. "Quite a bit of traffic actually, and it didn't use the TCP and UDP ports we expect for the VoIP phone system they use." She sighed in frustration. "We're still pulling down information, but since they don't know we're in there, we've had to throttle the bandwidth down so we don't trip any alarms and risk being discovered. It will be a while yet before we're finished downloading everything."

"What about the accounts they have overseas?" Trent asked. "Have you been able to dig into that any deeper?"

"No luck so far. The banks we've examined look to be in good shape."

He thought of something else. "What kind of phone system does the Fed have?"

"GoldenGate Systems," she confirmed. "One of the best and most popular."

Trent Turner rubbed the back of his neck as he considered a new angle and said, "I suspect that they might be hedging their bets with a combination of attack vectors." The more he thought about it, the more it made sense. "We need to find out if any or all of the banks we're plugged into are using a GoldenGate phone system. These people are smart, and it's possible that they're exploiting the phone systems and the DataBank financial software."

"I think you might be onto something," Grayson agreed.

"Can you pass along all of the Fed's account numbers for the banks in Europe? I have a friend that I want to reach out to," Trent explained. "It's too early to call Europe right now, but he might be able to help us out with the intercept Tak had been working on. I think the program was called DEADPREZ."

"Absolutely, if it's ready it certainly couldn't hurt," Grayson said, reflecting on the possibility. They heard muted conversation in the background before she continued. "I just got word that the hacker who defected wants to come in as soon as possible."

All three of them perked up.

"I'll get him," Jack said. "I can't help with this computer geekery anyway. Cyn, just send the RV info to my phone and consider it done. Addy said we should have some help here soon."

"I'll send it directly," she confirmed.

Jack Turner started for the door and said, "I'll get changed, pick up some gear from my hotel room, grab the hacker and head back here."

In the background Trent had booted up his laptop and pulled up the GPS tracking software. The operation had gotten more complicated now that Victoria Eden had been taken. He already had enough innocent blood on his hands and was concerned about what horrors might meet the violinist if he didn't get to her soon. He navigated through a couple of screens and located the red dot.

"Let's see where our Russian friend made off to so we can figure out our next move," Trent said. "The heavies I had a run-in with were good. They might be holding her there."

Jack Turner stopped at the door and turned to his nephew. "Who?"

Trent shared a look with Millar and said, "I'll explain later. It's a long story."

Chapter 116

BRUCE CAMPBELL'S REVELATION was interrupted by his cell phone. He kept his stare trained on Melody Millar as he fished the device out of his pocket.

"Yeah?" he answered. He listened to the caller and nodded a few times in acknowledgment before responding. "Got it," he said. "Twenty?" He listened intently to the caller. "Sounds good. I'll let him know you'll be there."

Campbell smiled as he disconnected the call, his eyes never leaving the frightened teenager. The good news was welcome after his recent string of failures. He punched at the phone and lifted it to his ear.

The call was answered on the first ring.

"Tell me something I want to hear," Pavel Kozlov said.

Campbell jutted his jaw out confidently before answering. "They'll be at the gate soon, an hour tops."

"Good. You've come through," Kozlov said, sounding surprised. "We'll have the men keep an eye on the monitors so they can tend to the gate."

"There will be twenty of them," Campbell said.

"Splendid. How many have you worked with?"

"Most," he confirmed as he snuck a glance at the FBI agent. "There are some ex-Delta, Rangers, Marines. They've all worked the bodyguard circuit for Active Armor," he said, indicating the firm that had once employed him. "I'm sure the guys I don't know can handle themselves, or they wouldn't be there." Campbell needed to spell out the terms he'd agreed to for his boss. "They're expecting cash. Upfront," he explained.

"Of course. I'll take care of that directly."

"Jim Stratton will collect. He said he's going to bring some radios for your men so everyone can stay on the same page." He shifted nervously before adding, "It's in your best interest to let him run the show. His men trust him, and yours can too."

"I will take that under advisement," Kozlov said.

The corners of Campbell's lips formed a smile as he turned to the young girl. "There's something else I think you ought to know."

"Oh? And what's that?"

"The hacker that got away from me," Campbell said, this time speaking with a hint of amusement. "His sister landed here somehow. In Leesburg. Can you believe it?"

Melody Millar shuddered when he spoke the words.

"Really?"

"I'm positive," Campbell replied. "They're practically twins, only she's a bit younger."

"That might come in handy," the Russian said, a smile creeping into his voice. "Everything is falling into place."

Chapter 117

Kozlov Bratva compound, Chicago, Illinois

SHE WAS SITTING across the small metal table from him. He made her uncomfortable with his probing stare. She wasn't sure how long she'd been locked in the cold, drab room, but she was determined not to show her fear.

"Ms. Eden?" he said in a patronizing tone.

It sounded like a question, so she was confused. She decided it would be best not to answer.

"Or should I say Ms. D'Angelo?"

Victoria Eden's eyes widened, and her heart raced. It didn't take long for him to figure out who she was, and it felt like he had stripped away a layer of protection. Her fear increased as his icy stare penetrated her eyes.

"I knew him, your father," Pavel Kozlov said. "What a waste he was. Wouldn't you agree?"

His words hurt. She wasn't going to dignify them with an answer.

"Such an incredible talent down the drain." He lowered his chin and startled her with a sudden clap of his hands. "Or shall I be literal and say a drunk into a tree, as the case may be?"

The words stung, but the anger they provoked took the edge off her fear.

"And that mother of yours..." He brought his thumb and index finger to his lips and opened them as he spoke. "Mmmmwhah!" he said. "Now she was a loss. So beautiful."

His lustful smile disgusted her, and she pulled away sharply when he reached for her hand.

"Like her daughter."

He locked eyes with her and he looked pleased to see the fury in them.

That was his plan, and he had made significant progress. The Russian needed to uncover the extent of her involvement with The American, and to achieve that, he counted on her losing control.

"Tell me about your friend," Kozlov said.

She remained silent. Disgusted. Furious.

"I can tell you more details about your mother if you'd like," he said. "Everyone has their little secrets. Perhaps you'd be interested in some of Jaclyn's."

She shifted nervously in her seat at the mention of her mother's name. Her memories were sacred. He had already made it clear that he would say anything to get under her skin, and Victoria Eden didn't want the memory of her mother tainted with his lies. Even more frightening to the violinist were the truth's she might learn.

He smiled, although his eyes told a different story.

"I don't know who he is," Eden said.

"Please, Ms. D'Angelo, we haven't the time for lies. Would you like to hear why your father got started drinking?" Kozlov asked in a melancholy tone. He looked at her appraisingly, comparingly, and said, "It's hard to keep a beautiful woman like your mother all to yourself." He smiled a half smile, half sadly, and added, "Even when bound by holy matrimony."

"I told you, Pavel"—her eyes burned with rage, and he looked full of content—"I don't know who he is!"

Her mother's suicide had always been a mystery, and her greatest fear was that the impulse to take one's life was genetic. She tried to erase the obsessive thoughts from her mind. Who hadn't been in a dark place and felt alone? Who hadn't wished they could end the horrible circumstance they found themselves in? It was normal, she had told herself. Things would get better. Life would get better.

"He was on my flight to Chicago last night," Eden said. "We ran into each other at the coffee shop in the airport, and then the one at the Fine Arts Building this morning." She did her best to stay calm and decided the simple truth was the best way to end this. "I invited him to the show when I saw him there because, frankly, I don't know anyone in this fucked-up town. Now I'm beginning to think that's not such a bad thing." She tilted her head in annoyance and said, "He was cute, and I didn't want the tickets to go to waste. That's it. There. End of story. Can I leave now?"

Kozlov tilted his head to match hers and offered a patronizing smile. "I don't believe you," he said.

She exhaled in frustration.

"What is his name, Victoria?"

"Tony, okay. Tony Kalem. Check the flight. You'll see," she said sarcastically. "You seem to have access to everyone's information anyway. Can I go now?"

Kozlov stood up. The screech from his chair legs scraping the concrete floor caused her to jump. His tone turned threatening.

"Victoria, this is going to get ugly if you don't start telling me the truth. Your friend has killed a lot of my men."

She digested what he said, and her rage digressed to fear.

"Far too many have died for me to simply let this go and forget about it. Please forgive me for holding such a grudge. Typically, I'm..." He looked to the ceiling as he searched for the English saying. "How do you Americans say? Like a duck? Things normally just roll off me."

She shifted uncomfortably. Until now she hadn't considered that her life was in danger. The headstrong young woman had always blown off her borderline self-destructive behavior as being persistent or tenacious. Now she was contemplating whether the trait was an illness, like her mother's depression.

She had been determined to win over Tony Kalem. He was both dangerous and handsome, but for the first time she considered whether the former had been the bigger draw. Victoria D'Angelo began to wonder whether she, too, was destined to be the cause of her own demise, and it frightened her.

He slammed his fist on the table abruptly, ending her train of thought. "I will make him pay for what he's done." He raised his chin and shot her a menacing look. "And you're a good place to start."

Chapter 118

BOTH MEN TURNED in unison when the hotel door emitted a beep. Jack Turner entered the room with a pale, twitchy twentysomething who was obviously scared out of his mind.

"Have a seat," Jack said, motioning to one of the two beds.

The hacker nervously made his way over to take a seat. His eyes darted between the three men in the room as he sat down. He slowly peeled his backpack off and let it drop onto the bed.

Trent Turner stood up and walked over to the newcomer with his hand extended. "I'm Trent," he said.

Dennis Zander shook his hand with a cautious smile and replied, "Dennis."

The operative noticed his clammy hands. He needed to calm Zander down.

"Look, Dennis," Trent said, "you've gotten into a bad situation here, there's no doubt about it." He sat down on the bed across from Zander so he'd be at eye level, in a neutral position. "We're going to try to help you out. If you'll let us."

The hacker nodded.

"But you need to be straight with us," Trent said. "Understand?"

"Yeah," Zander said.

"So what's your story? How did you get mixed up with these people?"

Zander explained the strong-arm tactics the Bratva had used to bring him on board. He told them they had threatened to kill his mother, so he was left with no choice but to cooperate. The hacker told them that most of the other hackers were in a similar situation. His mood turned grim when he got to the part about his mother's unexpected death and how he had tried to expose the Bratva using Senator Soller's son.

Etzy Millar cringed when he realized this was the person who was indirectly responsible for the murder of his best friend and the nightmare that had ensued. Millar's face was red with anger when he blurted out, "I hope you're happy with what you've done."

Trent turned and gave Millar a sharp look that quickly diffused his temper.

"Listen, Etzy," Trent said, "we all do what we have to do to survive. Sometimes there's little choice." He thought of his twin brother, and his tone turned somber. "Unfortunately, sometimes the consequences aren't what you would have expected."

Zander's eyes were full of regret and sadness. "I'm sorry. I didn't know all of this would happen."

Trent hoped the hacker would come through for them with some more details about the Bratva. The tracking device he had placed on the man from Kozlov's security detail had ended up in the Mercy Hospital morgue, along with the dead Russian. His face hardened as he sized up Zander.

"Now you're in a position where you can help end this so more people don't get hurt," Trent said. "What can you tell us about their operation? Where are the other hackers being held?"

Zander explained where they were located and what he knew about the building's setup. He had Googled it once and found that the building was part of an old steel factory. He provided details around the manpower used to protect the building and explained how some of the men had been moved to another location a couple months ago, so there weren't as many guards present. He started to run through details about the software he had been working on when Turner stopped him short.

"Thank you. That's all very helpful," he said. He pointed to his uncle. "Jack and I are going to head to the compound to do a little recce while we wait for some friends to arrive. We'll need you to explain the details you have about the botnet to Etzy. You two can work with The Shop on this. Okay?" Turner gave Millar an appraising glance and was pleased that he had calmed down.

"Yeah, that sounds good," Millar said.

Zander looked confused. "What's The Shop?" he asked.

Trent smiled and said, "You'll find out soon enough." He addressed Millar. "We'll need you to run the PMD for us via the 4G connect."

"No problem." Millar answered Zander's look of confusion with a broad smile. "Just call me when you're set up and ready."

Chapter 119

FBI Headquarters, Washington, DC

HE SET HIS briefcase down on his desk, popped it open and picked up the envelope he'd taken for Director Culder and locked it into one of his desk drawers. He looked out his window onto the quiet streets of Washington, DC for a brief mental reprieve. How quickly fortunes could change, he thought, as he contemplated his next move. Ivor Hood's meeting with Addy Simpson had gone much as he'd expected. His only question now was whether information about the case involving his goddaughter would remain on a two-way street. He hoped it would. If anything happened to Cathy Moynihan, he would never forgive himself.

He shuffled through a stack of papers on his desk until he found what he was looking for. A red circle from a felt-tipped pen marked the call. Simpson had told Hood about the incident at the Studebaker Theater in Chicago, and that the evidence they had indicated Jake Sanders was involved. All of the details were provided in the envelope Simpson had given him. He zeroed in on the ten-digit number that called his goddaughter's cell phone last night.

Simpson had decided it would be best to put Sanders to the test by dropping the bomb about FBI Director Frank Culder. The degree to which the information would shock him would depend on how much he knew about what was going on. Hood dialed his number, and his voicemail picked up immediately.

"This is Jake. Leave a message after the beep and I'll get back to you."

Hood looked out the window as he waited for the sound. When the beep sounded he knew it was all on him now.

"Mr. Sanders," he started, "this is FBI Deputy Director Ivor Hood." He paused for effect. "One of our agents, Cathy Moynihan, who works out of the WFO, has gone missing, and, according to Ms. Moynihan's last report, you are the last person she was with." Hood decided to let Sanders think about what he'd said for a moment before he continued. "I see that you are a former employee of the bureau, Mr. Sanders, although Ms. Moynihan was under the impression that you were still employed at the FBI, based on her communication. Obviously she had been misinformed. Please give me a call as soon as you receive this message. We are very concerned about Ms. Moynihan. She was supposed to check in hours ago and has not yet made contact. Her car was found abandoned on the side of the road near Leesburg, VA, this afternoon. You can reach me at..." He provided the area code and number to dial

Hood disconnected the call and closed his eyes. He drew in a deep breath and exhaled slowly before opening his eyes again. He called Simpson.

"Addy here," he said.

"Addy, it's Ivor. I've taken care of it."

"Good. How did it go?"

"Voicemail as we expected."

"Right."

Hood shook his head. "He's in for a rude awakening if Culder's been playing him all of these years."

Chapter 120

Travelodge Hotel, Chicago, IL

FBI DIRECTOR FRANK Culder and his two men were silent during the short drive back to their hotel. They entered the main area of the hotel room, still coming down from the rush.

Jake Sanders sat down on the couch and shook his head. "That was too fucking close," he said.

Rudy Pagano looked over and nodded. He and the director were still standing. They had left the local FBI agents at the theater. Culder had made it abundantly clear that if the three of them were mentioned in any official reports, there would be hell to pay.

"So you think he's working with the Russians then?" Culder asked.

"Sure as shit looked that way to me," Sanders replied.

"The locals said those men were with the Kozlov Bratva," Pagano said. "No doubt in their minds."

Culder palmed both hands on his head. "This is insane. Even for Simpson," he said. "What could he possibly want with a commie turned mafia boss? It's just not making any sense."

"The hacker wasn't with him in the theater," Pagano said. "Maybe we stumbled onto some sort of drop."

"Look, here's how I see it." Sanders was getting animated. "One of the local guys went after that Trent character, and the Russian nearly took his head off when he chased him out through the bathroom. That's hard to explain away." He shrugged his shoulders. "Not only that, but one of the agents saw Kozlov take off before the shit hit the fan. It's pretty obvious he knew something was about to go down."

Culder's cell phone rang. He looked at the display and recognized the 312 area code.

"Yeah," he answered. He listened intently for a minute and worked his way over to the desk. "Hold on a sec. Okay, give it to me." He scribbled an address on a piece of paper and underlined it twice. "No, no. We'll take care of this." He listened for another few seconds. "Right, okay." He disconnected the call and looked at his men. "We've got them now," he said confidently.

Sanders answered the comment with a questioning look.

"We know where their operation is. You boys can go in and take them out."

Sanders and Pagano glanced at each other and then back to Culder.

"Do you have any intel on the place?" Sanders asked. "I don't want to go in there blind."

"I'll pull something together while you pick up what you need," Culder said.

His cell phone rang again. He handed a piece of paper with a number scribbled on it to Pagano before starting toward the door.

"I'll take this one outside. Give them a call and see what they have on the place." Once he was outside he answered the call. "Chuck?" he answered in a condescending tone.

"It's done."

"It is?" He was beginning to enjoy his little conversations with Dr. Charles Reed. The only thing that could make them better would be a video feed so he could watch him squirm.

"Yes," Reed said, his voice void of emotion.

"I'll be the judge of that," Culder said.

"Look, I have confirmation that the package was delivered by your guy from the New York office." Anger and desperation had started to seep into Reed's voice. "There's plenty of damning information in there that will connect President Cross to certain Island Industries' activities."

"I believe you," Culder said, knowing it was too late for the man to turn back. "This is something you can be proud of, Dr. Reed. You don't have the opportunity to bring down the most powerful man in the world every day."

Satisfied he had what he needed from the man, Culder decided to leave a lasting impression. "What do you think the press will call it? Islandgate?

Spygate? This has Hollywood written all over it." The director got no reaction, so he decided to up the ante. "Maybe you can go tell your story on the talk-show circuit? They can dub it crack-whore-gate." He paused to let his words fester. "I like that last one. How about you, Chuck?" He heard heavy breathing on the line and smiled. "Your little Shelly will be released once I have my confirmation, don't worry, Daddy." He disconnected the call and headed back into the hotel room.

Sanders looked up when Culder opened the door. The director wore a grin that showed his satisfaction.

"What happened to you? Did you get laid or something?" Sanders asked.

Culder laughed and replied, "It was better than sex."

Sanders looked over at Rudy Pagano, and they both shrugged.

"Are we ready to do this?" Culder asked, his grin replaced with intensity.

Sanders pulled out his cell phone and powered it on. "Not quite. Rudy just had a chat with the locals, and they said these Russians don't fuck around. Ex-military."

"He'll have some serious firepower," Pagano added.

"I have a local contact who can hook us up with some kit pronto," Sanders said. "I just need to give him a call."

"Nothing we can't handle," Pagano said. "The agent is putting a package together for us to pick up. We've been worse off."

Sanders nodded in agreement. "We should be good to go. On point within the hour."

His phone chimed after it finished powering up, signaling a new voicemail.

Chapter 121

Kozlov Bratva compound, Chicago, Illinois

A MIXTURE OF overgrown shrubs and run-down structures peppered the flat landscape of the former steel mill. It was like an abandoned set from a Western movie had been invaded by rusted post-apocalyptic props from *Mad Max*. The entire property was surrounded by a barbed-wire fence, with several locked gates that provided access for vehicles.

Jack and Trent Turner parked their rental car more than a kilometer away and sent the PMD off ahead of them to scan the area while they tabbed their way to the compound. Night was falling on the city of Chicago, and both men welcomed the extra cover the darkness would provide.

By the time they reached the outer perimeter of the fence, the PMD had processed the area and provided its preliminary analysis to the operatives. There were no telltale heat signatures that indicated recent vehicular activity, and its sensors were able to identify three sentries posted outside.

They had very little intel on the compound, so they were going to have to play it by ear. The PMD's flight time overhead had been limited, and both men understood the details it first supplied to their XHD3s might change. Dennis Zander had confirmed the concrete building that was situated closest to the northern end of the property as their objective.

Trent Turner scanned the area and turned to his Uncle Jack. "Good thing help is on the way," he whispered. He gestured toward his uncle's foot and said, "It looks like we'll need it."

Jack was obviously annoyed. "I'll be fine," he said.

"Didn't General Custer say that too?" Trent asked sarcastically. "You shouldn't be out here when you're gimpy like that."

Jack glared at his nephew, but the response acknowledged he was right.

"Do you know who they're bringing in?" Trent asked.

"No idea. Hopefully they're getting some sleep on the plane. All of our assets were in Europe. Addy said he had something in the works. He wanted to bring someone new on board if he could, but he wasn't sure whether it was going to work out. He didn't have time for details. Shit was hitting the fan all around us."

Trent flashed him a smile. "You do smell a little funny."

"Leave it to you, kiddo," Jack said with a laugh. "Busting balls, when here I thought you'd be glad to see me." He made a production of giving himself a sniff test.

"Ah, you know it's always great to see you, Unc, but would an occasional shower be asking too much?" He patted him on the shoulder and said, "What comes around goes around."

His uncle's verbal chops from his time as a SEAL instructor were legendary. Jack wanted to laugh but instead jabbed him in the ribs with his elbow.

"Let's save the beauty for last this time," he said, motioning Trent to head through the slit he'd just cut in the fence.

"Can you read us, Poor Man? Over." Trent asked. He'd given Millar the handle based on his reaction to what the PMD acronym stood for.

"Loud and clear. I'll let you know if I see anything, over."

"We're going in, over," Trent confirmed.

He then turned to hand signals as he directed their approach to the building. They leapfrogged positions and used what little cover was available to remain concealed. They quickly arrived at a small shed with a beat-up Ford F-150 parked alongside.

"You need to take a look at the monitor," Millar cut in nervously. "Lots of movement at the northeast gate, over."

Trent Turner positioned his head inside the tactical sleeve on his kit. The fabric was designed to stretch so that he could review the latest stream of information sent down from the PMD on the XHD3 mounted to his forearm. The purpose-built shroud concealed the light from the device so it wouldn't give away his position. His head was still buried in his sleeve when he said, "Not looking good, Unc."

"I know. It's getting pretty bad," he admitted. "I'm having a hard time keeping up."

Trent turned off the display and pulled his head out of the sleeve. "Not your foot. It looks like we've got company, and lots of it." He nodded down the driveway perpendicular to them as the approaching headlights came into view. Both men quickly improved their cover.

The perimeter security forces had gotten organized quicker than they would have expected, with some of the men hopping out at the gate. The PMD sent in a steady stream of information about their movements, and Millar was doing a good job of keeping them informed as the patrols closed in. The situation was getting progressively worse. Trent knew his uncle's foot injury was a major handicap to their mobility, and he wasn't about to let the Russians murder another member of his family.

"Look, Unc," Trent said, "half of them have swarmed the main compound and the others are working their way in fast from the perimeter."

They had just moved west from the shed into a small thicket of bushes thirty meters away.

"It's only a matter of time before they find us." Trent's voice was measured. "We're packing light, since we were just here for a quick recce."

Jack's eyes narrowed. "So, what are you trying to say?"

"I'll distract them while you make a break for it and bring back the cavalry." He turned toward a sharp noise off in the distance and back to his uncle. "I'm not leaving you to fend for yourself like this, and if we stay together, neither one of us will make it out. They're clearing this place too fast."

Millar's panicked voice increased the tension. "You guys probably know this already, but they're closing in fast. Really fast, over."

Trent quickly slid his head under his tactical sleeve and saw the heat signatures closing in on their position. The limited options for cover made an already bad situation worse.

"You're gonna get yourself killed, Trent," Jack said.

"Nah, you know me better than that." Trent mock punched Jack in the arm like his uncle used to do to him when he was a kid. "Besides, I've got a hot date waiting for me inside." His thoughts hadn't drifted far from Victoria Eden since the theater, and his concern had deepened by the minute. "I wouldn't want to miss that."

Jack shook his head. He wasn't sure if he was proud of his nephew or annoyed by him. He decided that maybe it was a little of both.

"What are you going to do?"

"Don't sweat it. I've got this covered," he said. "Poor Man, I'm sending Heckler home. Focus on getting him out of here and then come back to me, over."

"Copy that, Finger, over."

Trent checked his XHD again for an update and quickly worked through some menus. He pointed west. "Head that way. Keep it straight, and you should be okay." The two men pounded fists. "Be careful," Trent said, and then sprinted off to run interference.

"You too, kiddo," Jack replied under his breath.

Chapter 122

DIMITRI SOKOV HAD spent the last few hours sifting through tremendous amounts of data. He was finally at the point where he could see the light at the end of the tunnel. The Russian knew better than to relax, but everything was coming together, and a sense of pride lifted the spirits of the tired computer genius. He had expected to have everything completed by now, but had been forced to do the work himself. The American who was brought in to complete this part of the operation had betrayed them, and the Russian was thankful he had stayed intimately involved in every aspect of the operation. This was just a bump in the road, not a showstopper.

The hard work was now complete. Everything had been separated and verified. Each of the banks had a file that contained a list of account numbers. They weren't random account numbers. Most of the accounts that were flagged belonged to individuals who were targeted to get paid tomorrow through the Federal Reserve's Automated Clearing House (ACH) system. It was the system that nearly all American companies used to distribute their payrolls via Electronic Fund Transfers, more commonly known as EFTs.

There was one more attribute the list of account numbers could have that was equally as important as their payday. It marked the accounts that were active in the banking system but weren't monitored by their owners very often. The hackers knew this because they knew the DataBank financial software as well, if not better, than the software engineers at

Allegiance Financial Systems who created it. The Bratva's hackers knew the fields in the database that correlated to transactions that weren't automated, and on what dates they had occurred. Sokov knew most of the top banks in the United States relied on the DataBank program to store and process their customers' bank accounts, so it was the obvious choice.

He had taken a break to provide an update on his progress. His eyes were weary from staring at a computer monitor for so long.

The Russian looked up from his desk as the hacker entered his office. "Pavel, the work is nearly complete."

Pavel Kozlov did not look pleased. "You are behind schedule?"

"Yes." Sokov looked down to the floor and then back to the Bratva leader. "I needed to complete the work that was to be done by Dennis Zander. It took longer than I thought it would, but it is done. The files just need to be encrypted, and they will be ready to be deployed."

"You said you would be finished." Kozlov was edgy.

"The difficult part is behind us," Sokov assured him.

"How will the computers at the banks know what to do without these files?"

The question made Sokov uncomfortable, since Kozlov already knew the answer. "They will not," he said tentatively, "but you can be—"

"Enough," Kozlov barked. He took a deep breath in frustration. "Do not tell me you will be finished and then come back to me and say there is still work to be done."

Sokov managed a curt nod and headed back to the server room. The Russian knew they were cutting it too close for comfort, but if he could finish everything in the next twenty minutes, there would still be enough time to transport the files to their backup site in Virginia. Just in case.

Chapter 123

MOST PEOPLE WOULD think of it as a suicide mission, but most people weren't wired like Trent Turner. He had inserted himself in between the two approaching patrols and his Uncle Jack's escape route. Their guards were down, so it was fairly easy for the operative to maneuver into position. He heard them talking. They were American, and that explained the sudden increase in forces. Hired guns.

Based on the information the PMD had sent and his own observations, he knew the men had divided into pairs. He had secured some fishing line to a series of bushes and used the sound and motion to slow and redirect the soldier's progress.

"Clear, over," he heard Jack Turner broadcast over the comms.

Trent breathed a sigh of relief knowing his uncle had made it out. "Copy that. I'm going to dump my gear and cause a big ruckus. Looks like our new guests are locals for hire." He slowed his pace. "Do me a favor and get that rescue party in here before their boss tries some of that crazy Cold War shit on me." He was only half joking. "I don't want to get my twig and berries electrocuted off, if you know what I mean." Trent imagined both men laughing and added, "I mean it. I'm giving you up before I'll let myself go through that sort of cruel and unusual punishment, over."

"I'll get you out of there, kiddo. Don't you worry, over." Jack's voice conveyed lightheartedness, but it was laced with concern.

Millar was nervous and sensed the danger. "Poor Man's got your back too, Finger, over."

Distracting the enemy with the bushes had taken care of Trent Turner's immediate problem, and he'd just sent a message abroad from his XHD3 in case things didn't work out as expected. Executing the next part of his plan would be where things got tricky. This was something that could easily get him killed. He no longer had a visual on the soldiers, so he needed some help.

"Poor Man, I'm flying solo now. I ditched my kit. I've just got the comms. I'll switch from throat to open mic and ditch them just before I make my move, over."

"Copy that, over," Millar confirmed.

"Keep the PMD right on top of me, twenty meters max, and tell me where the Tangos are. When I give you the signal, give them a haircut with the PMD on the side farthest from me, over."

"Copy that, over," Millar confirmed. His voice was shaky, showing the effects of knowing that someone's life was hanging in the balance.

Turner knew this would be risky but considered it his best move, since they knew so little about the Bratva's operation. He knew he could evade the security details for a while and possibly make it out, but there were no guarantees. There was another reason he wanted to make it inside sooner rather than later, and it came in the form of two words: Victoria Eden. This represented his only chance of pulling the violinist out of there before her nightmare became unforgettable.

If he didn't make any mistakes, his plan would put him in control of the situation, and that's the way he liked it.

Millar helped Trent navigate to a location he had made note of earlier. The operative considered his bold play as he wiped the sweat from his forehead.

"Two men approaching fast from the east, over," he said nervously as the men closed in.

"I've got visual, over," Trent confirmed.

There was a tense pause.

"Poor Man, go, go, go," Turner ordered as he stashed his comms under a fallen metal sign and switched the line to open mic in one motion. The operative charged the two soldiers, reaching them just as the PMD hit the apex of its dive.

Chapter 124

Downtown hotel, Chicago, IL

ETZY MILLAR AND Dennis Zander were stunned, mouths wide open, staring at the display. The last thing they saw before the video feed had frozen was Trent Turner's aggressive approach toward the two men. They had followed the rest of the action with the sound transmitted by the operative's microphone. First they heard a bunch of shouting, and then they sunk down in their chairs at the sound of gunshots. The scene had escalated, and muted conversations were heard in between commands that were barked out.

By the time the video feed had been restored, there were three bodies on the ground. Millar was scared. None of the men were moving. He thought Trent was the body sprawled out in the middle, but he couldn't be sure.

The hackers were jolted from their immediate shock when the door opened and a dark figure entered the room.

"Nice work, Etzy," Jack Turner said.

Millar started to breathe again when he recognized the voice. "Thanks, but Trent went down," he said with grave concern.

Zander was speechless, his gaze darting between the two men and the computer screen.

Turner tightened his lips before he spoke. "Don't worry. Trent knows what he's doing."

"But." Millar gestured to the laptop's display.

The three of them watched the video feed showing the three men being taken into the main building.

"It's all going according to plan," Jack said.

He looked like he believed what he said, but Zander wore a sour look of disbelief. "That's crazy," he said.

Turner smiled. "Trent would call it ballsy, so let's humor him, okay?" He tossed his gear onto one of the beds. "Now we've got someone on the inside," he said confidently.

The words did little to calm Millar down. "He wasn't moving."

"Over the years I've learned not to doubt that kid," Turner said flatly. "He knows what he's doing, there's no doubt about it."

"You're not even the least bit concerned?" Millar asked.

"I didn't say that." Turner's tone was measured. "He's family—of course I'm concerned." He sat on the bed and took off his boot to check his injury. "But I'm not worried."

"I'm going to pick up some reinforcements," Turner said. "I got a call on my way here and they'll be at the airport within the hour. How much fly time does the saucer have left?" he asked as he slid his boot back on.

Millar looked at the readout from the PMD and said, "Not long. Twenty minutes."

"Land it with some juice left, just in case," Turner said as he grabbed a fresh battery from Trent's bag. He pushed the button on its side to verify it had a full charge. He figured it should last a couple hours. "I'll call you in a couple minutes so we can do a quick swap before I pick up the cavalry. We need to keep tabs on that compound."

The hacker's brain was still frazzled as he watched Jack Turner stand up with a pained grimace, grab one the bags at the foot of the bed and limp out the door.

Chapter 125

Kozlov Bratva compound, Chicago, Illinois

ABSOLUTE PERFECTION. SHE possessed the beauty of a goddess, but the cold metal chair she was perched upon told a less glamorous story. It had been a long time since Victoria Eden had felt so alone. The Russian had left her locked in the room, and she imagined the walls slowly closing in around her. She was a creative individual, so it wasn't unusual for her to find herself lost in thought, but the fact that she had been unable to imagine anything other than her imminent demise had been disconcerting.

"Have you made up your mind?"

The sudden sound of his voice caused her to jump, but she didn't turn around. She knew he had frightened her on purpose, and she wouldn't give him the pleasure of seeing the fear in her eyes.

"Well, Victoria?" Pavel Kozlov pressed. There was a sudden sharpness in his voice.

She didn't respond immediately, sensing the Russian was struggling with the situation. Her beauty had been an asset in life for the most part, but she was convinced his conflicted reaction was more than skin deep. He was one of those men who had decisiveness and brutality in their DNA. She decided it must have been the way she played the violin that had put indecision in play. She turned her head to him. Her eyes met his, and in a twisted moment, his gaze invaded her, and it was as if he were pondering the idea of somehow keeping her for his pet.

"Listen, thanks for letting me play in the show," she said, her tone marked with frustration. "I really appreciate it, but I really should be going." She turned away.

Kozlov laughed the sort of laugh that wasn't intended to convey humor. Eden twitched when she felt something touch her hair. It must have been his hand, but she was too scared and repulsed to turn and look.

"Perhaps you need a little encouragement," he said. His voice was cold and hostile.

The loud pounding of a fist on the door caused her to jump again. There was a sudden flurry of activity out in the hallway. Kozlov opened the door, and he spoke in Russian to someone. The tone was urgent, and he left without saying another word.

Chapter 126

TRENT TURNER BEGAN to regain consciousness as they strung him
up. He wasn't sure if they were securing him to a wall or some sort of
torture device. He knew better than to open his eyes and try to assess the
situation. Wherever he was, it was cold, and he could tell by the musty
smell that it was damp. His body ached in several places, but physical abuse
came with the territory, and he didn't notice anything alarming.

He had taken two of their men out, so he had expected to be roughed
up. He chose the route of incapacitation rather than elimination. Keeping
them alive was something he thought might play in his favor. The Russians
were just getting started with him, though, and his thoughts turned to how
evil an interrogation by a man like Kozlov could be. Turner knew he would
need to keep his head on straight, so he wiped the thought of extreme
torture from his mind.

"He was alone," a voice said.

"How can you be so sure?"

Turner recognized the second man. It was Pavel Kozlov.

"You know the layout. It doesn't take long to clear this place with
twenty men—"

"Eighteen," Kozlov interrupted.

Turner could sense the tension build between the two men. Now he
knew the amount of firepower they would be dealing with.

"Right," the man said. "Before we get too comfortable, forty grand. In
cash."

Trent Turner knew Russians were critical by nature and smiled inside as
he listened to the Bratva leader size up the American. Treating him like shit

wouldn't do him any favors, so he was enjoying the radio show. He heard a rustling sound before Kozlov said, "Here's your money, plus a twenty-thousand-dollar bonus."

He felt a slap on his face he assumed was a stack of bills, before Kozlov said, "For him."

Turner knew the money would smooth over the previous conversation, so a rift between them when the shit hit the fan would now be unlikely.

"Works for me," the man said. "He didn't have a radio or ID on him, so it looks like he was flying solo."

Turner had to fight back a smile. He knew what the man had said would match any MO that Kozlov would have assumed for him. Based on the timing of events, the operative suspected it was his recent job in Europe that had exposed him. He had been there alone.

"I trust your people are in place to deal with any other unwanted visitors?" Kozlov said.

"That they are. I've given your men some radios so we can stay in touch."

"Good, and the men he took down? They'll be okay?"

"They're unconscious but alive. They'll live."

"I'm impressed," Kozlov admitted. "Most people who have had a run-in with him don't survive."

Turner could sense the Russian's glare on him.

"We'll be sure to tie up this loose end quickly," Kozlov added. "We wouldn't want any more surprises."

Chapter 127

THINGS HAD FINALLY settled down enough for Etzy Millar to connect with The Shop using his computer. Dennis Zander was able to lay out what he knew about the underlying software that made up the Russian's botnet. He had only been working on one aspect of the operation, information acquisition, but he made it a point to learn as much as he could from his roommate and the other hackers he had gotten to know. Zander was able to confirm much of the information they already knew but shared some new details with the analysts that he hoped would prove useful.

"It's in Northern Virginia somewhere," Zander said, referring to the Bratva's backup location. "Near the airport. It's off a main road close to one of the big data centers."

"So you've been there?" Cynthia Grayson asked.

"Once," Zander said dismissively. "It was at night. I rode in the car with the courier to set a server up with my stuff. I wasn't familiar with the area, and he took a lot of back roads. The only thing I really remember was seeing signs for the airport."

"Did you ever connect to the servers there to remotely transfer files?" she questioned.

"No. No way," Zander said. "Dmitri, the Russian hacker guy who ran the operation, wouldn't allow it. They were pretty paranoid about stuff like that. The funny part is that I was supposed to be blindfolded when we got close to the place, but the courier forgot to put it on, and by the time he realized what he'd done it was too late." Zander thought about what else he

361

knew that might be helpful. "I overheard a lot of their conversations. The backup location was to stay off-line, and they would only bring it up if something happened to the place in Chicago. I would encrypt the account files I was responsible for and put them on a USB drive for delivery. Same with the others."

"You mentioned a courier?"

"Yeah. The courier drove back and forth with the files and the encryption key updates. He didn't say much. I'm not really sure if he could speak English. I had to hit the bathroom on the way there, and it took me a minute to get him to understand."

"Were they the encryption keys for the files?" Grayson asked.

Zander thought about it for a moment, knowing any details would help to narrow things down. "That and the botnet, I think. My Russian isn't that great, so I'm not one hundred percent sure."

"The keys were different? One for the files and one to control the bots?"

"I'm pretty sure. I overheard conversations to that effect. At least I think that's what they said."

"Did all of you use the same keys to encrypt the various files?" she pressed.

"Yeah, Dimitri wrote the encryption algorithm," Zander said. "He's really smart, arrogant too, but he knew his stuff." He looked at Millar and shrugged. "There was an internal server that we'd browse to, similar to uploading a photo to Facebook or whatever. You'd select the files you wanted to encrypt and then click on a button to encrypt them. The server would do its thing and encrypt the files and then copy them onto the USB drive for you. It was pretty simple really. I couldn't tell you if anyone else created files, though."

"Were your files always the same name?"

"Yeah. The same name and listed by bank, by its ABA number, only it was backwards. Nothing complicated, just a way to hide them in plain sight in case someone happened onto the files somehow." He thought some more and laughed. "In fact, the files I created were always the same."

"What do you mean?" Grayson asked.

"Like I said before, I was trying to figure out how I could screw their operation up without getting caught, so I'd messed with my code in ways I thought I could get away with."

"I'm not sure I follow."

"Dimitri didn't trust anyone. The obvious place to hose up the account file was in the query I wrote that selected the accounts—you know, the accounts that were active—but the owners didn't bother to check their balances very often." He started to get animated. "I made sure that part was right, since I knew how critical it was to the operation. Instead of messing with the obvious, I tweaked the code that outputs the results to the file instead. It was supposed to use the data retrieved by the query to create the new file, but I coded it to load the accounts from the old file instead of the updated list of accounts from the query." He smiled smugly at Millar. "That way the file would always have stale information. I don't know. I was hoping it would trip them up somehow."

They continued to pepper the hacker with questions about the various aspects of the operation. He named several target banks in the US that the team was unaware of and explained that the vector of the attack was centered on the browser. They had found an exploit and were able to manipulate the HTML and CSS so that what the user was presented with on the screen was different than the actual transactions that were being processed and sent to the server. The premise was simple. They used legitimate user credentials to post fraudulent transactions.

One other crucial detail Zander was able to confirm was that there was another operation going on in Europe. He didn't have much detail other than it existed, but was able to provide the name for one of the foreign banks. The news raised more questions than answers, since the bank in question had already come up clean as part of their investigation, but now they knew they needed to dig deeper.

"So how soon do you think they could execute the operation?" Grayson asked.

"It would take some time for sure," Zander said.

"Good," Grayson said, her sense of relief evident.

The hacker realized his mistake—time was relative after all—and clarified. "My guess is if they started today, they wouldn't be ready until tomorrow morning sometime. They couldn't do it today. That's what I meant."

Grayson let out an audible sigh and said, "That's what I was afraid of."

Chapter 128

Kozlov Bratva compound, Chicago, Illinois

THEY LED HER down the hallway into another room. Her stomach knotted up when she peered through the one-way mirror. The stage was set for something evil, and Victoria Eden realized she would be an unwilling participant. She didn't want to know what a man like Pavel Kozlov was capable of, but it became immediately apparent that she wouldn't have a choice.

She recognized the man strung up in a crucifixion-like pose. He was the man from the airport whom she knew as Tony.

She never would have thought the connection they shared would lead to this. Until now Eden had enjoyed their meetings and thought of them as a challenge. Her fun-loving personality and persistence had their good points—and bad. She drew in a deep breath in contemplation. He was the reason she had gotten into this mess, but that didn't matter. What mattered now was that she paid attention and looked for an opportunity. One of her many qualities was resourcefulness, and she knew, now more than ever, she would have to depend on it.

She turned to the door when it opened and Kozlov walked in. He looked more relaxed this time. He had changed into an Adidas tracksuit and moved with the same swagger as when they'd first met.

"You have a visitor," he said. His voice was calm but cold.

She watched the Russian set Trent Turner's clothes down on the table, and then she glanced at the operative on the other side of the two-way mirror. He was in perfect physical condition, and she was sure the series of marks that punctuated his chest would tell a story that, despite everything that had happened, she wanted to hear.

"I guess he was playing hard to get," she said sarcastically.

She feared that he was about to get the life sucked out of him. His story, she thought to herself. Making sure she could hear his story was her motivation now. That would give her the determination she needed to make it through this. She closed her eyes, said a silent prayer, and resolved to herself that she would soon know who this man was.

"Ah, Victoria." Kozlov clasped his hands in mock prayer. "It's nice to see you haven't lost your sense of humor in all of this."

She held her breath for a moment before speaking. "You don't get it, do you?" The remark wasn't a question. "I don't know this man, and whatever you and your Neanderthal cohorts are up to makes no difference to me." She exhaled in frustration. "Well, correction. I only care about what you're up to because you decided to kidnap me and lock me up in this shithole of a building."

The Russian smiled unkindly. "Have you ever watched a man being tortured?"

Eden gave the Russian a dirty look. She decided to answer his stupid question in kind by flicking her middle finger up and leveling it at his face. Kozlov's stare hardened, and she noticed a change in his demeanor. Her resolve to do something was strengthening by the second. She could see the rage burning in his eyes and her fear began to melt away.

A smile formed on her face as she realized the extent of her insult. The heated exchange reminded her of her teenage years. When she'd sparred with the big boys on the mat and had proven the utility of the martial arts. She didn't lose often then, and she wasn't planning to now. She kicked off her shoes as she sensed the big Russian losing control.

Chapter 129

THE TWO MEN had just picked up some weapons from one of Jake Sanders's contacts in Chicago. They chose Heckler & Koch MP5s with tactical torches, some ballistic-level IIIa SafeGuard vests, and retained their personal sidearms for the operation. There would be no communication devices. They had decided they would stick together. They had no complaints about the quality of the kit, especially on such short notice.

"We're gonna light those fuckers up," Rudy Pagano said, his thick New York drawl reflecting his anger. "I still can't believe what happened in Poolesville."

Sanders had been thinking about the same thing trying to psych himself up. "Un-fuckin'-believable," he agreed.

"You okay?"

"Yeah, I'm all right. It's just fucked."

Pagano took his eyes off the road and looked over at his friend. "I hear ya."

The team was a close-knit crew, and their loss was starting to sink in, especially since they were the only two left.

Sanders shook his head. "And that bullshit with Culder…"

Pagano started laughing. "She must've really gotten to you, tough guy."

"Yeah, fuck off already," Sanders spat. "This job is getting crazier every year. The shit we do…I don't know, man." He realized this was a bad subject to discuss just before the operation. Doubt could get them killed.

Pagano kept his eyes on the road as they neared the Bratva compound and as if reading his mind, changed the subject. "Too bad the locals didn't have more details about this place," he said.

"Fuck it," Sanders barked as he stared out the side window. "We've got what we need to do some damage. How long until we're there?"

"A couple minutes."

"Cool."

Sanders smiled. He had just enough time to check his voicemail. Secretly he hoped it had been Cathy Moynihan trying to call him, but he'd never hear the end of it if Pagano knew that. Hearing from her would give him some much-needed motivation. He navigated to his voicemail and put the phone to his ear.

"*Mr. Sanders,*" the message began. "*This is FBI Deputy Director Ivor Hood. One of our agents, Cathy Moynihan, who works out of the WFO, has gone missing, and, according to Ms. Moynihan's last report, you are the last person she was with.*" Sanders's eyes glazed over. "*I see that you are a former employee of the bureau, Mr. Sanders, although Ms. Moynihan was under the impression that you were still employed here, based on her communication. Obviously she had been misinformed.*" His adrenaline began to flow as he processed the deputy director's last sentence. "*Please give me a call as soon as you receive this message. We are very concerned about Ms. Moynihan. She was supposed to check in hours ago and has not yet made contact. Her car was found abandoned on the side of the road near Leesburg, VA, this afternoon. You can reach me at...*" He provided the area code and number for him to dial.

When the message ended, Sanders was left frozen, the phone still held to his ear. His head spun as he processed what he'd just heard, and everything around him faded out. He was in denial. He pressed the button to replay the message. His eyes were still glazed, and he hoped somehow that the words would be different this time. When it finished playing for the second time, he slowly turned toward Pagano and took a deep breath.

"You're not going to believe this," Sanders said. He passed the phone to Pagano so he could hear the message.

Now everything had changed. Their world had been turned upside down.

Pagano parked the car out of sight from the Bratva compound and turned to Sanders.

"Man, I don't know," Pagano said, the confusion evident. "I mean, I guess it's possible that Hood wouldn't know about us, but shit, it's not like I'm feelin' all warm and fuzzy about it, if you know what I mean."

Sanders squirmed in his seat before breaking the uncomfortable silence. "He's prick-arrogant enough to think he's above it all. I mean, shit, if you're on his good side it's a happy day, but we both know what happens when Culder's got a serious beef."

Pagano's thoughts turned to the incident on the plane. "Damn."

"What?"

"Good thing you didn't waste her."

Sanders's eyes narrowed, and Pagano thought better of the comment.

"Sorry, man. I know you dug that bird." He saw his friend's reaction to his use of past tense and quickly said, "She's probably fine. Culder couldn't have brought someone else in to do the deed that fast."

Sanders felt like shit. "What if she's not? I'll have a hard time explaining that I had nothing to do with it, based on the circumstances." He shook his head. "What the fuck do we do now?"

"We do what we're paid to do," Pagano said. "We won't let Culder know Hood called us, and we'll sort that shit out tomorrow." He looked down at the picture of Trent Turner on the seat between them. "That fucker took out family," he reminded him. "That's what matters right now."

"Yeah, I guess you're right. He deserves a little payback, and so do the assholes he works for, that's for damn sure."

They had checked their gear and were headed toward the compound when gunfire erupted.

Chapter 130

Kozlov Bratva compound, Chicago, Illinois

A LOUD GROAN signaled the air leaving his lungs. The blow was as devastating as it was unexpected. Victoria Eden had put Pavel Kozlov in an unfamiliar situation—a situation where he wasn't in control. She had delivered a direct hit to the Russian's solar plexus from her seated position and followed it up with an elbow to the temple as he doubled over in pain. Kozlov was unconscious by the time his head smacked the ground. He lay motionless on the concrete floor. The surreal moment of silence and indecision was broken by the cracking sounds of gunfire. It was distant, but the soundtrack heightened her adrenaline rush.

Eden ran to the door and latched the deadbolt. She stepped to the side, her palms and back to the cold cinder-block wall, and tried to think. The only person who could possibly help her was restrained on the other side of the glass. She took inventory of the room, her eyes darting between the motionless Kozlov, a metal chair, and the one-way mirror. Victoria picked the chair up and threw it against the glass. It bounced back and made a loud clatter as it slid across the concrete floor.

Frustrated, she picked it up again. When her eye caught the industrial metal table it was positioned in front of, she decided to change her strategy. The table was extremely heavy, but determination gave her the strength to lift it. The clothes slid off its surface to the floor as she backed herself up to the wall, her bare feet unsure under the unevenly distributed weight.

Using the wall to leverage the weight, she bent her legs so the table could rest on the top of her thighs. She nervously looked down at Kozlov as her limbs began to shake from the strain. She took in a deep breath, focused on the mirror, and ran the table toward the glass like a linebacker with a quarterback in her sights. The glass shattered into a crystalline shower that exploded into the other room.

Their eyes locked. Trent Turner smiled, obviously impressed with her effort.

"What the hell are you doing here?" she asked.

"Getting you out of here," he said. "Amongst other things."

Trent Turner was hopelessly shackled to the wall in his boxers.

"And how's that going for you?" she asked, using her sense of humor to cope with the fear.

The smile still hadn't left his face. "I'm working on it," he said. His confidence was off-putting.

"You're just too much, Tony, aren't you?" Eden shook her head. "I guess it's nice to know chivalry isn't dead after all." She gave him an appraising look, and all she could do was laugh. "Not bad," she said with a playful smile. "This could have been fun if we didn't have so much company."

Turner returned her laugh and said, "A rain check, perhaps?"

She carefully headed back into the viewing room to check on Kozlov. She had been lucky that they hadn't selected the glass separating the rooms with security in mind, and that most of the debris had landed in the other room. The Russian was still unconscious, so she began to pull off his shoes.

Eden was both startled and confused by Turner's sudden presence.

"Weren't you just locked up in there?"

"Yeah, well, they don't make restraints like they used to," Turner joked. "What happened to him?"

Eden smiled, more with her eyes than lips.

He picked his clothes up off the floor and began to get dressed. "The name's Trent, by the way," he said.

"Trent?" She pursed her lips. "I liked Tony better."

He laughed. "Then call me Tony." His tone turned serious as the sound of automatic weapons spat out in the background. "Listen, Victoria, I'm sorry to have gotten you involved in this mess. Believe me, that wasn't my intention. Now I need you to listen to what I say. No questions."

The fun-loving banter was over. She was scared, and the situation gave her plenty of reason to listen.

"I mean it," Turner said, his eyes willing her to comply. "I'll get you out of here, but you need to do exactly what I tell you." He motioned to the unconscious Russian. "These people play for keeps."

She gave him a consenting nod as he picked the glass out of his bloody feet and slipped on his boots. She noticed that Turner hadn't so much as flinched from the pain, which was strangely reassuring. He motioned for her to stand against the concrete wall, and then he dragged Kozlov over to the door.

A flurry of gunfire erupted out in the hallway as Turner searched the Bratva leader for a weapon. He was unarmed. Turner slowly worked his way to the small window in the door so he could survey the hallway before deciding on their next move. He whisked his head away from the window and appeared completely stunned by what he'd seen. Eden moved carefully, so she could see outside. The penetrating eyes that stared back at her through the window were the eyes of a killer.

Chapter 131

THE ENEMY OF your enemy is your friend. It wasn't the same as having reinforcements, but Jake Sanders and Rudy Pagano were masters of improvisation. They had been working together for so long they knew what the other man was thinking. The operation had evolved into hunting down an operative they knew as Trent, and his hacker accomplice Francis Millar, who was directly involved in the death of Senator Soller's son. The senator was a man their boss wanted to keep happy. The FBI director had specified that the hacker should be taken alive, and that was the extent of the detail they had. On a personal level, they both wanted to exact revenge for the deaths of their HVT squad members. Revenge was the single motivation for staying the course considering the circumstances.

Following the incident at the theater, they knew the Russian crime family was involved. There were a lot of loose ends, and some things didn't add up, and while that had been commonplace for the men of the HVT squad over the past decade, the message from FBI Assistant Director Ivor Hood had brought with it questions and given them cause for concern.

"What do you think?" Pagano asked Sanders as the two huddled behind overgrown bushes.

"Looks like the action's moved inside. Let's find a way in and check it out."

Pagano nodded, and they carefully worked their way toward the building. The New Yorker examined the first door they came to and decided it was safe to open. He signaled to Sanders as he counted down to action. He threw open the door, and his heart rate spiked when he saw the armed soldier standing guard inside.

The sentry's back was turned to them, so Sanders quickly moved in to snap his neck before helping him fall quietly to the ground. This clearly wasn't his first time around the block.

"One down," he whispered to Pagano.

The pair headed inside and quietly descended a flight of stairs that led toward the commotion. The stairwell spilled out into the middle of a long, dimly lit hallway. More shots rang out as they continued moving toward the chaos, with Sanders in the lead.

Pagano had only taken a few steps when a familiar rat-tat-tat erupted from behind. The weapon carved out a swath of chips in the cement floor and cinder blocks around them. The burst appeared to have been squeezed off as a reaction rather than a concerted action. Pagano slid into the recess of a doorway, and Sanders turned to loose off some defensive rounds as he dove behind a cement column.

The New Yorker was pinned down, and things weren't looking good, his only consolation being the fact that they should already be dead. He had an angle to see Sanders's position. They shared a look that acknowledged their dire straits. He watched as Sanders crouched down to sneak a quick look at the gunmen. His glance was immediately returned with a burst of automatic gunfire.

Pagano motioned for him to keep going, but the stubborn ex-soldier fired a fuck-you glance as he wiped the sweat and debris from his eyes. Then Sanders's eyes told him something different, something much more sobering. Nothing short of divine intervention could get him out of his current situation alive.

Chapter 132

HE WAS LOOKING at a dead man. He had to check himself to make sure he was awake, to make sure this wasn't some crazy dream. America had been duly informed that Lieutenant Brendan Manion, US Navy SEAL, had been killed in action in Afghanistan. The fact that he was on the other side of the window was impossible, but Turner couldn't be happier knowing that they had all been wrong. He unlatched the deadbolt and opened the door.

"Holy shit," Turner said. The two men clasped hands and exchanged a shoulder-check hug.

He stepped aside as Manion passed him a pack loaded with gear.

"Tell me about it," Manion replied. He motioned toward the hallway with his thumb. "Twenty-five, maybe thirty Tangos. I just took a couple out down the other hallway, so let's move fast before they get bold and come for us. They're slinging lead like they're taking a Scantron test."

There was a groan as the Russian began to regain consciousness. Turner ejected the magazine from the Sig Sauer pistol Manion had handed him, racked the slide and familiarized himself with the weapon.

He then motioned to the groaning Kozlov and said, "I think he can help us with our exit strategy."

Manion nodded his recognition of the Bratva leader. "Nice catch," he said, and he noticed Turner's smile spread to his eyes.

"No doubt." He pointed out Victoria Eden, who had hidden off to the side behind the door and said, "She took care of him for us. Victoria meet Brendan."

"Impressive," he said. "Pleasure to meet you."

The stunning beauty forced a nervous smile and shook his hand stiffly.

Turner addressed Manion. "Apparently you're a tough man to kill," he said, still shocked. "Good thing. It's hard to find good help these days."

Turner was still smiling. "Who did you bring with you?" he asked.

"It's me, Heckler, and Throaty," Manion confirmed.

Throaty's real name was Chris Livingstone, a former British soldier in the Special Air Service, better known as the SAS. His mother had been a diplomat who worked at the United States embassy in London when she met his father. The highly decorated soldier had been brought into Island Industries by Addy Simpson after he retired from the service.

The SAS sergeant had worked closely with the American military on sensitive joint operations in the Middle East. His gruff voice lent itself to his nickname, Throaty, and Turner knew from experience that he was the kind of man you wanted on your team.

"There are three of you?" Eden said nervously. "That's it?"

Turner gave her a sideways glance with his piercing blue eyes and then moved his thumb and pinky back and forth between the two of them. "Five," he said confidently. "And we've also got a Poor Man watching over us."

She returned a quizzical look mixed with annoyance.

Turner smiled. "Let's roll."

Chapter 133

NERVOUS EYES DARTED around the dimly lit room as the sound of gunfire erupted outside. The captive team of Bratva hackers flinched with the deadly chorus as it grew louder.

Dimitri Sokov had locked himself in the server room. For the past several minutes, he had been working frantically to encrypt the remaining files for transit to Northern Virginia. He encountered a program error each time he had tried to run the process to secure the files, and had been unable to figure out and correct the problem.

He was used to working under pressure, but not this sort of pressure. The muted staccato of violence rose over the sound of computer fans and air-conditioning units. Something had gone horribly wrong. From the soundtrack outside, he knew he'd be lucky if he made it out of the server room, so he no longer considered giving the files to the courier for transport. He decided to change his tactic to the option of last resort when the sound of pressurized air interrupted his thoughts.

"Dimitri, we are being attacked," a soldier barked in Russian. "Kozlov said to make sure you have everything ready."

Sokov nodded, his eyes still glued to the computer screen. "*Da*," he responded. It was a single word, but the panic was evident in his voice. "I am very close. Do not let anyone come through that door!"

His command was followed by the sucking sound of air as the soldier sealed the door shut behind him.

Sokov had to improvise. He connected to a server he had hacked into and created a user account for his counterpart in Virginia to use. He created a directory where he could copy the files necessary to carry out the

US-based operation. He had contacted the men in Virginia, and they were on standby, waiting to hear from him.

The gunfire was getting louder as he typed in the command to securely copy the files over the Internet. He hadn't had the time to encrypt all of them, but at least the transmission itself would be secure. As soon as the transfer finished, he pulled out his phone and made the call.

"They're waiting for you. Get them fast, and have him delete them from the server immediately. Let me know when he's finished."

He rattled off the user name, password, and location of the files before ending the call. Sokov turned to a metal box that was bolted to the server-room wall. He pulled open the small metal door and flipped on the power switch inside. It was one of several like it that had been affixed to the walls. Within a minute the hacker had activated all of the triggers to blow the Semtex that was housed inside.

Sokov and Pavel Kozlov were the only two people who knew the phone number that could be called to detonate the explosives. He rushed to the door. They needed to get out fast so the deed could be done.

Chapter 134

IT HAPPENED IN an instant. It was a potent mix of speed and aggression. The Bratva men who had them pinned down were so fixated on their positions that they didn't even see the deadly blast of fire that spat out from behind them.

Rudy Pagano made a quick check amidst the moans of their attackers.

"Cover," he yelled, and followed up with a dash to reach the relative safety of Jake Sanders's location.

Sanders did a good job with peppering the already-crippled men with rounds.

"Holy shit, that was close," Pagano said, sounding somewhat relieved, somewhat annoyed.

The two men pounded fists, and Sanders shook his head.

"Lucky bastard," he said. It wasn't the first time he'd seen the New Yorker walk away from what seemed to be certain death. "Just how many lives do you have?"

Pagano almost smiled. "Where the fuck did that come from?"

"Looks like you've got a guardian angel," Sanders said sarcastically.

Pagano exhaled. "I didn't think angels used automatic weapons."

Sanders laughed a silent laugh. "You're too fuckin' much, Pagano."

It got quiet. They exchanged a look that acknowledged it was the quiet before the storm. Footsteps were heard converging on the enemy's location.

"Incoming," Pagano said in a hushed voice.

The two men met eyes before retreating in the direction from which Pagano's saving grace had emerged.

Chapter 135

"HALLWAY IS SECURE, over," Throaty confirmed.

"Moving out now, over," Trent Turner said as the four of them rushed down the hallway to his location. Brendan Manion took the lead, brandishing his Heckler & Koch MP7A1 submachine gun, a weapon that, having a low recoil with its suppressor attached to keep the barrel steady, was more deadly than it was quiet. Turner held up the rear with Pavel Kozlov in tow, the P226 he had been given pressed firmly into the Russian's side. They didn't know who might come at them from behind, so it was the obvious location for their human shield considering Turner's weapon.

Turner listened intently as Manion shared what they knew about the compound. There had been no blueprints available for the building, so the only intel they had was from the hacker Dennis Zander. They knew how to get to the server room, which was all that mattered at this point in the operation. They had sketched together a plan and would stick to it as much as possible.

The four of them quickly made it to Throaty's position and immediately pressed on. The three operatives knew the drill: keep your cool and concentrate on actions that bring you closer to your objective. A reactive force, no matter how large or small, usually ended up dead. They had taken what advantage they could from the element of surprise. Now speed and aggression would have to carry them through.

They approached a corner, and the Russian barked, "You won't make it out of here."

Turner answered the comment with a painful blow from the butt of his weapon.

"Another sound, and I'll use it to turn you into an eunuch," Turner said, knowing the Russian's intention had been to give away their position.

Kozlov's eyes were spiteful, but held no doubt about the operative's intention to follow through on his promise.

The group continued to navigate through the maze that made up the old steel plant's subterranean level. Dennis Zander was in the hotel watching the live video feed from the helmet cams on Throaty and Manion and providing direction. The place was littered with rusted-out machinery in disrepair. A mildew smell hung in the air, which had mixed with the sulfurous remnants of gunfire.

It wasn't long before they encountered heavy resistance from the Bratva's former Spetsnaz contingent. It happened as they reached a large central area that appeared to be the hub of the compound. Two hallways shot out from the vaulted room in front of them like the top half of a lowercase Y.

"Either one of those two hallways in front of Throaty will take you there," Zander said nervously to the sounds of another barrage of fire.

The shots had come from the hallway to the left and had forced them to take cover low.

"Heckler, you still have the exit covered, over?" Throaty asked.

"Roger that. Nobody's going in or out the front door without paying for it, over."

Jack Turner was down but not out. He had been given a quick shot to numb his foot that sent him back into the action, albeit from a distance. Putting down for-hire contractors wasn't a part of the plan unless absolutely needed, but the Russians inside were definitely on the menu. The problem would be trying to tell them apart.

Jack had taken position on top of a building across the street with an MK 11 Mod 0 sniper rifle fitted with Leupold scope, a swivel-base bipod, and a QD sound suppressor that hushed its deadly 7.62 x 51 mm NATO rounds. He had enough preloaded magazines to take down the small army.

He had been given a lowlight tablet display that received real-time information about combatant locations from the PMD scouting above. It worked in tandem with the custom scope fitted to his weapon and fed vital information to the small LCD display housed inside. The details it provided were used to locate the enemy and make the weapon deadly accurate for a lone operative. Used in conjunction with the PMD, it was modern technology's answer to a spotter.

Trent Turner motioned toward the shots that had just echoed through the hallway behind them. "Looks like we've got more company," he said. The situation was getting tense. He could hear enemy reinforcements getting closer.

"Who the hell are they shooting at?" Manion asked.

Turner turned to Throaty and Manion and said, "That's a damn good question."

Chapter 136

Kozlov Bratva hideout, Leesburg, VA

HE WAS BACK, and he was pissed. FBI agent Cathy Moynihan knew the yellow-toothed Russian would return. It was an eventuality she'd been contemplating over and over in her head. After the blow she'd dealt to his groin, she was sure he'd want a little payback. He had come alone, as she suspected he would. A vicious combination of hatred and anger projected from his eyes as he stared her down. That was something she'd planned to use against him.

She broke the silence. "Well, well," she said. "How's the you know?" Moynihan pointed her index finger downward, waist high, and wiggled it back and forth with a mocking whistle. "Oh, excuse me." She flashed a cheeky smile and wiggled her pinky instead.

The Russian looked like a volcano ready to blow. Melody Millar and Maria Soller both were on the edge of their seats, watching intently. This was something they'd all discussed, but the situation was completely unpredictable. They didn't have a choice. The cell signal for Soller's service provider wasn't strong enough to reach her iPhone.

Soller and Millar exchanged nods, and both of them began to scream at the top of their lungs. It caused the Russian to jump, and Moynihan started to laugh. She rather enjoyed pushing the Russian's buttons.

Within seconds, footsteps were stomping toward the room. Soller and Millar wore masks of fear despite knowing Moynihan had planned to taunt the man into action before the others arrived. Moynihan was still laughing, and when she pointed her finger at the Russian, he erupted with an uncontrolled fury. He charged at her hard and fast, and this time he was ready. Soller and Millar screamed louder as they watched the man unload on the FBI agent.

The door swung open, and the American entered the room, followed by the Russian who wore the utility jacket. Moynihan was losing to her attacker but still managed to frustrate him with speed and determination. The American took a few hits as he worked to separate the fight. This was the opportunity the FBI agent had been waiting for.

She struggled to turn around so she could grab hold of the railing with both hands, but the yellow-toothed bastard proved too strong. Fortunately, the hand that was cuffed didn't break in the scuffle. Moynihan continued to strain for the railing with her right hand, but it remained just out of reach. All would be lost unless she could pull off her part of the plan.

The Russian continued to maul her, until they finally shifted toward the wall, where she was finally able to lock her fingers around the railing. She suddenly thrust out her powerful legs, kicking the Russian into the other two men. They slammed into the soldier with the utility jacket, and he fell backward toward Soller. She quickly stuffed her iPhone into one of the pockets on his utility jacket. Maria Soller had pointed out that there was no lingering smoke during her trip to the bathroom, so she reasoned the soldier had been going outside to smoke his cigarettes.

Moynihan slumped into her chair and watched the three men face off. She was breathing heavily and had been hurt, but not too badly. Soller nodded, and a sense of relief came over her. Now they just needed a little luck for the phone to find a signal.

"What the hell are you doing?" The American soldier yelled at the Russian. "Stay out of this room. Do you hear me?"

The Russian spat at the FBI woman and stomped out the door. The others followed.

Seconds later the heavyset man entered the room with his laptop and spoke with urgency to the man in the utility jacket. He was speaking in Russian, so Moynihan couldn't understand what he was saying.

Chapter 137

Kozlov Bratva compound, Chicago, Illinois

THE CONSTANT EXCHANGE of cover fire had helped them work their way through the building. They had no way of knowing how many men they were up against, but Jake Sanders understood he and Rudy Pagano were in serious trouble. The distinct streams of gunfire provided them all of the information needed to come to that conclusion. The force they were up against was much bigger than they had expected.

As they approached the end of a long hallway, gunfire erupted from the large room they were about to enter.

"Shit, this is getting messy," Sanders said.

Pagano nodded as both men slapped fresh magazines into their weapons. The exchange of fire in front of them had died down. They heard Russians yelling on the other side of the room.

"What the hell is going on in there?" Sanders asked.

He watched Pagano crane his head around a piece of machinery to get a better look. The operative headed inside, and he quickly followed.

"It's hard to see anything in here," Pagano said. "It looks like a group of guys are in the middle of the room, and there are some on the other side dug in near that hallway on the left." He had a puzzled look. "It sounds like the other guys are Russians too."

Sanders turned toward the hallway they had just come from. He could hear the footfalls of men behind them as they got closer and said, "Great. This is gonna be messy." He knew they wouldn't last long if they were taking fire from two sides.

Pagano tapped him on the shoulder and said, "I'll try to move in and get a closer look."

Sanders nodded and shored up his position so he could keep their chasers at bay. His eyes darted from the hallway to Pagano as he inched forward using the industrial machinery for cover. He contemplated their situation and wasn't sure if it was worse than being surrounded by the enemy. An unknown force had entered into the equation, and he knew they would soon be overrun from behind. The shouting between the Russians grew louder and more heated. It sounded like something was about to go down.

Chapter 138

WHEN CWDG DIRECTOR Cynthia Grayson spoke to the most powerful man in the free world, it typically meant there was some sort of crisis—and this was no exception. In fact, it had the potential to be the most significant cyber threat to the United States she had ever seen. She cleared her throat before pressing the button to place the call, and was immediately connected to the White House Situation Room.

"Yes, Cyndi," President Vincent Cross answered.

"Mr. President," Grayson started, "we've been able to confirm the presence of the bots in several financial institutions. The attack is widespread, but we don't have all of the targets at this point in time. We're also aware of something involving the Federal Reserve, but we have reason to believe it to be a different attack vector."

"Addy and I are still waiting for news on the Chicago operation. What are our options at this point?" the president asked.

"We have two, maybe three that I can see," she said. "The first would be to continue our investigation and wait until we've learned enough to take the necessary action to prevent whatever they're planning from happening."

"The risks? And please, you know I respect your candor."

She smiled a half smile. "We don't know how long it will take for us to be in a position to prevent the attack. It could be twenty minutes, twenty-four hours, or even six months from now."

"I see," he replied.

She knew he wasn't happy, but she wasn't there as a pastry chef meant to sugarcoat things.

"Sir, I wish I could give you a better answer, but it's just not possible. We've made a significant amount of progress, but it's like any major investigation. We have no shortage of skill, but we'll need a bit of luck to uncover the clues that will help us to make sense of their operation."

"Understood. What's option two?"

Grayson took a deep breath. "Shut down all major US financial institutions until we get a better handle on what we're dealing with." She could sense the president cringe on the other end of the line.

He took a moment to consider the option. "For how long?"

"It could be a couple of days, maybe more while they rebuild infected systems, unless we get lucky."

Closing down the country's financial sector for any period of time would bring forth disastrous results in the current economic climate. The economy had slowly begun its recovery from the combined effects of the real-estate-market crash, Ponzi schemes, and interest rate scandals, but times were still tough for much of the country. Despite the progress that had been made in terms of the economy, it was still a patient that needed to be handled in intensive care. Any problem in the financial sector significant enough to raise a red flag would breed irreparable distrust, and turn the economy into a terminal patient.

"That would have to be our last resort," Cross finally said. "If the people lose confidence in the banking system again…we'll be in for a long, destructive ride. Maybe if we had more details, but as it stands, we don't even know what the risk is."

"Agreed," Simpson said. "Shutting everything down without pointing to a concrete reason wouldn't be pretty."

There was an uncomfortable silence before the president spoke. "Ms. Grayson, how much damage do you think they could do?"

"Significant damage, sir," she said bluntly. "Which brings me to the third option."

"I'm listening."

"It's the same as option one, only we inform the banks of the possible threat. At least that way they'll know to keep a close eye on things. They can do more system backups and keep them for a longer period of time just in case." Grayson looked down at her desk and took another deep breath, trying to keep her disappointment with their progress at bay.

The president finally asked, "If it got out that we knew something was up, couldn't it jeopardize your work?"

"Yes, sir, it could. One cowboy techie bragging on the Internet could blow it and give it all away."

President Cross took a moment before he replied. "Ms. Grayson, can you pull this off? You know, figure this all out in time to stop it?"

She sat up and nervously rubbed her forehead. The gravity of the president's question weighed on her. His words meant that he believed in her, and that was enough.

"I don't know for sure, sir, but yes, it's possible. My team is working extremely hard."

"Then do it. Make it happen. I'll take option number four. You're our best option. We're"—he corrected himself—"the nation is counting on you and your team over there, and there isn't much time."

Chapter 139

Kozlov Bratva compound, Chicago, Illinois

THERE WAS NO shortage of cover, but the Island Industries operatives were outnumbered and wouldn't last long if they didn't keep moving. The smell of oil from the dilapidated machinery was thick enough to taste, and their ammunition was limited, so they made sure each round was delivered with purpose. Brendan Manion signaled that he would check into the approaching chaos from the rear. Trent Turner and Throaty were charged to neutralize the aggressors in front.

"Damn gadgets!" Heckler said gruffly over the comms. "Looks like our FBI friends are in the neighborhood as well. Damned proximity alert fired off and I didn't even notice, over."

Turner cracked a brief smile at his uncle's technology woes, and decided their best option would be to use the Bratva leader, Pavel Kozlov, to help them advance to the server room. He could see that Victoria Eden was on edge, and paid special attention to make sure she remained safe. The operative was surprised by how tough the woman was. Her ability to cope with, and even contribute to the situation by taking down Kozlov, had been a pleasant surprise.

"We have Pavel Kozlov!" Turner yelled in Russian.

The gunfire died down to an eerie silence. Whispers echoed from the hallway where the soldiers were stationed. The hushed sounds of the enemy ratcheted up the tension.

After the hushed words faded, one of the Russians responded. "Surrender, and we will let you live!"

Turner looked at Throaty and shook his head, before shouting in Russian again. "Hold your fire. I repeat, hold your fire. I will let you see him." The Russian tried to resist as the operative pushed his head above the rusty hunk of steel they'd taken refuge behind. Kozlov tried to shout, but Turner delivered a silencing blow before he finished his first word.

"Caretaker, we're going to light it up here, over," Turner said into his mic.

"Copy that, Finger," Manion responded. "About to make contact with the approaching Tangos, over."

"Roger that. On five," Turner said. He motioned to the hallway on the right and looked deep into Victoria Eden's eyes. "Run like you've never run before and stay close," he said in a hushed tone.

She looked down at the loose-fitting shoes she'd taken from Kozlov and took a deep breath to calm her nerves.

Seconds later Turner tossed the Russian out into the open. Kozlov began to run toward his men as the operative sighted his kneecap and squeezed the trigger. The Russian screamed out in pain, his momentum taking him forward. He flopped face-first onto the concrete floor. Throaty quickly heaved a flashbang toward the enemy's location, before advancing rapidly with the violinist in tow. The operatives would have preferred to have grenades, but the choice of gear was based on hostage extraction rather than enemy elimination. They were able to pick off two of the blinded soldiers like targets at a carnival shooting range.

Bursts of automatic gunfire rang out from Manion's location as the three of them reached the safety of the hallway. Turner surveyed their position, and the path to their destination provided few options for cover. If their fellow operative was overrun, their chances for survival would all but disappear.

Trent exchanged an uncomfortable look with Throaty and activated his comms.

"On my way, Caretaker. Standby, over."

He backed up into the hallway far enough for him to reach full speed by the time he emerged from cover, and sprinted off toward Brendan's location.

Chapter 140

SHOTS FROM THE Russians peppered his path as Trent Turner made his way to the other end of the massive room. Most of the enemy's surviving force had been busy trying to bring their leader to safety.

"Caretaker, I'm on point, over?" Turner said softly into his mic. There was no response. "Repeat, Caretaker, I'm on point. Go ahead, over."

Turner didn't like this one bit. Radio silence could mean a lot of things, and most of them were bad. His first thoughts were that Brendan Manion's radio had stopped working or he was hiding somewhere with the Tangos nearby. He could be down or have been caught, but that wasn't what he sensed. He sensed something major was about to go down.

Everything happened in a split second. Turner slowly peered around a machine and found himself looking down the barrel of an MP5. Before he could blink, Manion had swooped in from behind and neutralized the Tango, his Sig Sauer TacOps 1911 pistol pressed firmly into the man's chin. Turner's attention immediately went to a second man, who had taken dead aim at Manion.

"Whoa, whoa, whoa," Manion said calmly, before shots were exchanged.

Turner noted a flicker in the eyes of the man he had lined up in his sights. His aggression had turned to confusion.

"Hold on a second there, buddy," Manion continued as he nodded toward Turner.

The man turned his head to see the operative and slowly, deliberately lowered his weapon. His eyes darted back and forth between the two men while he tried to assess the situation.

"Fuck, man. Brendan?" one of the men said. "I thought you were dead."

"Chill out, Jake," Manion said calmly. The two men had known each other for practically a lifetime. "I'm going to let your boy go, okay?"

"Yeah," Sanders responded. "Rudy, it's cool. Don't shoot."

Shots flew in from behind as the four men scrambled for cover.

"What the hell are you doing here?" Manion whispered to Sanders.

He nodded toward Turner. "We're after him," he said flatly.

"What?"

"He's with the fuckin' Russians," Sanders said. "He had something to do with the death of Senator Soller's kid."

Manion shook his head slowly and said, "No, Jake, you've got it all wrong. We'll sort this out later." He took a quick look behind as a few shots ricocheted around the equipment. "No time to explain now. We're as good as dead if we don't pull together."

"Right," Sanders agreed with a wry smile. "After you."

Chapter 141

"IT'S DONE, LET'S go!" he yelled to the soldiers in Russian.

Four of the Bratva's heavies had been guarding the server room and its contingent of hackers. The men gave Dimitri Sokov a questioning look.

"Do it," Sokov said with the coldness and ease of a Caesar ordering the death of a failed gladiator.

The men turned to the defenseless hackers huddled to one side of the room and unloaded their weapons. The salvo gave way to Sokov's ringing ears as the mass of bloodied bodies collapsed to the floor.

The five of them headed for the exit, leaving the carnage behind.

"We're coming," one of the men barked into his radio.

They carefully worked their way down the hall. It wasn't long before they reached Pavel Kozlov and the three soldiers who were protecting him.

"Pavel, it is done," Sokov confirmed, his cell phone clutched in his hand. "We need to take the tunnel out and blow the room." His expression turned to panic when he noticed the Bratva boss had been shot. "Are you okay?"

Kozlov's eyes reflected extreme pain. He was a tough bastard and managed keep his composure.

"Good, I'm fine," he said. "I was lucky. He missed my knee."

"You four stay behind and kill The American," Kozlov ordered. He turned to Sokov and said, "Let's go."

Two of the men pulled him up and stood him on his good leg before they headed down the hallway past the server room. They shuffled through the series of doors that led to Kozlov's office, quickly locking them behind.

"Open it," Kozlov said harshly as he gestured to one of the bookshelves. He hobbled over to his desk and pulled a first-aid kit out of one of the drawers.

Sokov watched the two soldiers pull a section of the bookshelves out on its hinge to uncover a thick metal door. They unlatched the door and swung it open revealing a dark passageway. The smell of dirt filled the air.

Kozlov finished tightening a tourniquet around his leg and grabbed an LED torch from his desk.

"Move, now."

Chapter 142

THE FOUR MEN began to make their way through the massive room toward the others. They were taking fire from two directions, but the aggressors behind were clearly a much stronger force. Their forward progress had come to a stop. In order to cross the gap to Throaty and Victoria Eden, they needed to deal with the four motivated Russians in the hallway adjacent to their destination.

Trust was an issue amongst them, but each man understood friends of convenience could prove to be just as helpful as those of choice. It was a sticky situation, but there was enough experience between them to honor their truce.

"Throaty, we're four strong now, over," Brendan Manion confirmed.

"Roger that, over," Throaty responded, a question mark formed by his tone.

The soldiers behind were getting closer by the second. Jake Sanders looked in the direction of the incoming onslaught and back to Manion.

"Where's your boy, Brendan?" he asked, pointing out that they were now a trio.

Manion shot him an annoyed look.

Rudy Pagano jumped in and said, "He took off that way." He motioned to the other side of the room. "I hope he's got something in mind. Otherwise, we're screwed."

"Shit," Sanders said, shaking his head, "we need to get the fuck out of here pronto. I'm low on ammo."

Manion surveyed the room and quickly looked toward the pool of red where the pair of dead Russians lay, and just beyond them, saw signs of the other four ready to pounce.

"Throaty, we've got Tangos breathing down our back, and if we don't do something to move forward, soon they'll be up our ass. Any way you can part the Red Sea, over?"

"Negative, Caretaker," Throaty answered. "I can't get a shot on them, and there's no more ka-pow to toss out there, over."

A violent screeching erupted from behind. Manion looked back and saw a massive piece of equipment being pushed toward them. It didn't take a rocket scientist to understand there were several combatants tucked in safely behind. Each effort caused it to screech in protest as the steel object moved several inches closer. The makeshift shield was effective, and before long they would be sandwiched in. The situation for the three operatives had reached the critical point. The looming confrontation was about to turn bloody.

"Finger, we're in the shit," Manion said. "Whatever you've got cookin' out there, we need you to serve it up, or you'll be eating supper alone, over."

Chapter 143

TRENT TURNER HAD just made it to his precarious perch high above the action. Time was short, so he worked quickly.

"Copy that, Caretaker." He could see the enemy closing in on the three operatives, "I'm at your eight high and have eyes on you. Head to Throaty on three, over."

Brendan Manion gave the signal to the others and started counting down with his fingers at three, two, one... Four shots spat out from Turner's position when the three men began their sprint. Two men dropped to the floor, while Throaty provided cover fire so they wouldn't get hit from behind.

Turner worked his way down the massive piece of machinery he had climbed. His position had been compromised. Sparks marked the heavy fire that followed his shadowed form. When he reached the bottom, he quickly dropped down to the prone position. He crawled toward the men he'd just eliminated, careful to stay out of the line of fire.

"I'll need some cover fire, folks," he said, "I'll be making tracks toward the stiffs. Light it up whenever you're ready, over."

"Copy that, Finger. The two hallways meet up near the server room. We'll meet you there. Go on three, over."

Like clockwork, Turner launched his move toward the hallway. He armed himself with a stray AK-74 and scored a spare magazine before he headed off to meet the others. It didn't take long to reach the intersection.

Throaty motioned him to stop and examined a door before kicking it open. Curiously, the door wasn't completely shut. Had it been, it would have been sturdy enough to have given them a problem. Manion and

Turner headed inside the room, while Throaty guided the others back to the position he had come from to hold off the men advancing on them.

The metallic smell of blood led Turner's eyes to the gruesome mass of corpses. They were riddled with gunshot wounds, and the overuse of force resembled the final scene of the movie *Bonnie and Clyde*.

"Jesus," Turner said in a grim tone. "They didn't want anybody talking, that's for sure."

"The server room is through that door in the back," Manion said, apparently receiving word from Zander through the comms.

They were headed toward the server room when a flicker of movement stopped Manion in his tracks. One of the men had crawled his way over to a desk and struggled to scribble something on a piece of paper. Turner continued toward the server room, while Manion headed to check out the lone survivor.

"Ghhe...t."

The man struggled to speak as he coughed up blood. Hatred and betrayal were in his eyes. This was a man who had given everything for his motherland and had been left for dead. Pavel Kozlov's promises had been empty.

"That's Mikhail," Zander said nervously as he saw the image from Manion's helmet cam. "He's the Russian guy who worked with us. He was one of them."

Mikhail's eyes showed grave concern, and his voice was more desperate. "Ghhe...t!" He coughed as he made one final effort and offered Manion the piece of paper clutched in his hand. "Ghhe...t!"

Manion pried the piece of paper from his hand and turned the cryptic message toward him. His eyes focused on the writing, he understood, and his heart began to pound. It was a four-letter word. One that could kill.

"Shit, Trent. Get the hell out of here. There's a bomb!"

Chapter 144

Roadside, Herndon, VA

HE PULLED OUT another cigarette and held it between his thick, nicotine-stained fingers. The hacker squirmed in the passenger seat, noting it was the man's second since they had left the compound in Leesburg, Virginia. Through the corner of his eye he watched the Bratva soldier flick his lighter open, fire it up and take a slow drag as he lit the tobacco. The thick cloud of smoke he exhaled was annoying, but he knew better than to complain.

"Is this far enough?" he questioned in Russian. It was the third time he had asked the question.

The passenger turned to the driver and nodded quickly, just wanting to get this over with. "*Da*, I think so."

The driver clenched the cigarette between his teeth and pulled the car off to the side of the road. He wiped the ashes that had fallen onto his utility jacket toward his passenger and flashed him an intimidating glance, prompting him to get on with things.

The hacker looked nervously out the windows of the car as he plugged the USB stick into his computer and initiated a connection to the Internet. He pulled out a slip of paper and used the information written on it to log in to the compromised system somewhere out in the ether. He punched in the commands to transfer the files Dimitri Sokov had copied to the server onto his computer. The hacker fidgeted in his seat as the files trickled in slowly over the connection, his eyes darting from the screen to the car windows and then to the soldier next to him.

Normally, the hacker wouldn't have been permitted to connect to the Internet, but Sokov had been forced to improvise by transferring the files over the wire, since driving them via courier this time hadn't been an option. Another thick waft of cigarette smoke interrupted his concentration, and this time it caused his eyes to water. He blinked several times in frustration from the smoke building up in the car, and could sense his discomfort was a form of amusement for his companion. All he wanted was for the files to finish copying so he could get the hell out of there.

Chapter 145

Kozlov Bratva compound, Chicago, Illinois

THE FIVE BRATVA men emerged from the small shed and piled into a Ford pickup truck parked outside. The vehicle wasn't in line with Pavel Kozlov's usual tastes, but that was the point. A battered old truck wouldn't draw attention and would be a discreet getaway option if he ever needed one. The truck was kept in good working order, so the engine fired up immediately. He was in excruciating pain but still managed to remain stoic.

"Pavel, we need to blow the server room," Sokov said nervously in Russian.

Kozlov turned to him and winced with a nod. He pulled his phone out and began to thumb through the display. "You are certain we have everything we need at the other location?" The Russian wanted absolute confirmation before they blew away nearly two years of work.

Sokov's voice was confident. "Yes, the necessary files have been copied to another location. Everything will be ready, and there will be no time for the Americans to react."

"You're sure of this?" Kozlov questioned further. The pain from his wound reflected in his voice. "The hackers that got away, they cannot stop this?"

"No, the hackers do not know enough to stop us. The operation will go as planned. They are collecting the necessary files as we speak."

Kozlov closed his eyes and exhaled. "As we speak?"

Sokov shrunk in the seat. "Yes, I am awaiting confirmation."

Kozlov remained silent, with a scornful look on his face. Earlier, Sokov had overstated what had been done, and it was frustrating for the Bratva leader that to him, any work in progress was considered to be as good as done. Minor details were what led to failure.

"But we will wait to hear from Virginia first," Sokov said, interrupting Kozlov's thoughts. "Before we blow the place."

Sokov pulled up the video-camera feed for the server room on his phone. Kozlov felt the hacker prodding his arm with his elbow before turning the display so the Bratva leader could see it.

Kozlov shifted his eyes to the screen, first with lack of interest and annoyance, but it quickly turned to hatred as The American and another operative came into view.

"That's the server room?" he asked abruptly.

"Yes," Sokov said. "We can take care of two things at once." The pickup truck began to ease forward, and he was startled when his phone rang.

Kozlov looked over at Sokov and nodded his approval to answer, hopeful it would be good news.

"'Allo?" Sokov answered. He listened for a moment and flashed Kozlov a smile. "Very good." He breathed a sigh of relief. "Make sure you shred the files on the server," he insisted.

It wasn't good enough for the hacker to simply delete the files. They needed to make sure that the sectors on the hard disk wouldn't have remnants from which a forensic specialist could recreate them. Sokov needed him to be thorough, and execute a hacker's version of wiping away fingerprints.

Sokov gave Pavel Kozlov an approving nod, and the Bratva leader punched at the display on his phone. Seconds later they saw a flash from the massive explosion just before they heard it.

Kozlov closed his eyes, tilted his head back and took a deep breath. His small victory brought a cautious smile.

Chapter 146

Kozlov Bratva compound, Chicago, Illinois

THE RINGING SOUND dominated his ears. Throaty shook his head, trying to wipe the cobwebs from the massive concussion. He pulled his shirt over his nose and buried his eyes into his sleeve trying to blink out the darkness. The ringing eventually gave way to a muted voice in the background.

"What the hell was that, over?" Heckler repeated.

Throaty listened intently, still trying to regain his senses.

"The compound has men charging out of the exits like rats from a sinking ship," Heckler continued, his concern evident. "Poor Man, do you see anything on the cameras, over?"

"Uh, nothing on the feed here, Heckler, over," he responded. There was a measure of fear in his voice from seeing that the helmet cams were now ominously blank.

"Throaty, Caretaker, do you read, over?" Jack Turner repeated. "I see a Ford pickup headed for the exit. Throaty, Caretaker, do you read, over?"

Throaty coughed and was slowly starting to come around. He heard the voices but still couldn't process the words.

There was a long, nervous silence over the radio.

"Heckler, this is Poor Man. We're still not getting a feed from the helmet cams, over," Millar chimed in anxiously.

"Copy that, Poor Man. I just sent two rounds into the vehicle, but it managed to crash out through the gate, over," Heckler said, a hint of annoyance in his voice.

"Heckler," Throaty finally coughed, his voice even harsher than normal. "I can't see a damn thing down here." He continued to cough violently as he brought his sleeve up to filter the dust and smoke from his nose. The ringing in his ears had just started to settle down. He had cranked up the volume on his radio but was still having difficulty understanding what was being said. "It's tough to breathe. I'm trying to make my way to the blast so I can check on the others, over." The dust had settled enough for him to see the outline of Victoria Eden sitting on the floor. "Stay here," he said.

"Okay," she responded before launching into an uncontrollable cough.

The violinist had already pulled her shirt up over her nose, but now she closed her eyes and wrapped her arms tightly around her knees.

"Do you know how to use this?" Throaty asked as he held out his pistol, inching closer to see her face more clearly. When she opened her eyes and nodded, he handed it to her and said, "The safety is off. All you need to do is squeeze the trigger." He looked to Jake Sanders and Rudy Pagano. "Can you keep an eye on her?"

"Rudy can stay with her," Sanders said. "I'll give you a hand. There's two of them."

Throaty's mind digested Sanders's comment, and it conveyed a sobering fact. He would indeed need help with carrying the bodies. His hearing was still unreliable with the ringing, so his head was on a swivel as he and Sanders crept forward, their weapons ready to fire.

"What's going on down there, over?" Heckler asked impatiently.

"Something big blew. I think it was the server room," Throaty said. His tone turned grim. "Finger and Caretaker were in there. I don't think they could have made it out."

"Don't use the front door," he said, the gravity of the loss weighing on his words. "The Tangos have RVed there, over."

"Roger that," Throaty replied. "I'll check with you on an exit and head straight to the ERV once we're sorted." His sight was improving as more dust settled. The operative stumbled over a body and quickly caught his balance on the wall. "It's not looking good down here, over."

Chapter 147

SENATOR MAXIMILLIAN SOLLER'S mood continued to swing between foul, angry, and grim as he relived recent events. He had continued to drink, which was having an effect on his concentration and ability to reason. The lights in his office were now turned on as he watched nothing in particular on the flat-screen television bolted to the wall. He had closed his eyes to take another swig of scotch when the sudden ring of his cell phone unsteadied his hand.

The senator grumbled incoherently as he reached for the device. "What?" he snarled.

"We've got a problem," FBI Director Culder said.

Soller shook his head; in his state unable to comprehend how things could get any worse. "And what might that be?" he said, his tone bordering sarcasm.

"I sent our guys to meet with your friend," Culder said, referring to Jake Sanders and Rudy Pagano.

Soller didn't have the mental capacity to put clues together; there was too much alcohol swirling around in his blood. Culder's reference to their two operatives going after the man from Island Industries had been completely lost on him.

"My friend?" he said, his slurred words punctuating his confusion.

Culder allowed himself a pause in frustration. "Yes." His voice conveyed his annoyance. "Your friend. The one you want to question about your son."

Soller's eyes snapped open, the mention of his son having a sobering effect. "I see, and how is that going?"

"It doesn't seem to be going very well at the moment. I haven't heard from them since they left for the meeting. Apparently somebody crashed the party, literally."

Soller's mind struggled to understand the somewhat cryptic message.

"From what I can see on the local news footage," Culder explained, referring to the massive explosion at the Bratva compound, "it's possible that we're looking at a forced early retirement."

Soller's face turned to a nasty frown. "You mean like our friends at the house last night?"

"That's right," Culder said.

The senator had mixed feelings about the news. Now his illicit gang of operatives no longer carried the threat of exposure. Dead men couldn't be dragged in front of a hearing to testify against him. He decided the loss might not be such a bad thing, and before he could consider whom he might contact to finish the job, his thoughts were interrupted.

"I also got a call from your old friend," Culder said. The senator didn't respond, so he added, "John Simpson."

Soller remained silent.

"He said to pull back. He told me that we're 'in over our heads' with this one," Culder added.

The senator was fuming. Telling him what he could or couldn't do was a surefire way to meet resistance. "It sounds like he's taken care of our pulling back, wouldn't you say?" Soller quipped. He raised his glass and took another swig as he contemplated the news. "How the hell did he find out about what we were up to?"

"I have no idea," Culder said.

Soller's thoughts turned to the FBI director. Before long, it would be time for him to find a new job. He had managed to get his ten-year tenure extended by another two, but not without cashing in some favors. He drained his glass and decided that since the HVT squad was now out of commission, it was time to cut Culder loose.

"It's not as bad as it could be," the director said flatly.

"Oh?" the senator slurred, curious of the man who had seemingly read his mind. He reached for the bottle, bemused, and refilled his glass.

"I have what we need to crucify your friend."

Soller smiled—truly smiled—for the first time since his son had been killed. Even in his state, he understood the allusion to President Cross.

"Brilliant," he said. "I'll make it worth your while."

He abruptly ended the call and began to raise his glass.

A ring interrupted the motion again. "Goddamn it," he growled as he snatched the phone off his desk.

He looked at the display and savored a taste of his scotch before answering. "I hope you have good news for me," he said.

"That I do," Federal Reserve Chairman Bart Stapleton said. "The meeting was a success. Everything is set for the morning. All of the transfers will be made. I have a good feeling about this. We're in the oil business again."

Soller took a deep breath in content. It was getting late, and he needed some sleep.

"Excellent news," he said. "Excellent."

Chapter 148

Route 66 near Arlington, VA

THE SOUND OF an incoming text message interrupted his train of thought. Etzy Millar was still out of sorts from the message he had received from his girlfriend, Maria Soller, last night. The Shop was able to trace the signal to a location in Virginia, and his only option was to trust the operatives there could pull off a miracle and save the two women he loved. Part of him didn't want to know what this new message said. He feared for his sister and girlfriend after all the senseless killing of the past two days. He knew the message was something he couldn't ignore, so he slid his finger across the screen and began to read.

Call this number now or we will kill them both.

His heart skipped a beat before it pounded like a sledgehammer trying to break through his chest. His breath had become short, and he started to feel ill. He took a couple of deep breaths before he was able to speak.

"Take this exit please," Millar told the cabbie, his voice sickly.

Dennis Zander looked over at his new friend.

"What's wrong, Etzy?" he asked quietly.

Millar glanced at Zander. Sweat beaded on his forehead as he closed his eyes and tried to stop his hands from shaking. His breathing was concentrated while he tried to regain control. The cabdriver had reached the end of the exit ramp by the time he opened his eyes.

"Here. Pull over here," he said urgently, pointing at a hotel.

The cabdriver quickly turned into the driveway, and Millar opened the door. He looked to Zander and said, "Look, you need to take care of things with The Shop. Something's come up, and I can't help you guys out right now."

He slammed the door shut before Zander could speak.

Millar's mind raced. He would be damned if he was going to let someone else die. He'd figure something out on his own. By now whoever had his sister and girlfriend realized they couldn't trace the number he was using to send the text messages. Once he placed the call, things would be different. They would be able to find him, but he didn't care. He planned on taking that option away.

He dialed Maria Soller's cell phone number and took in another deep breath.

"Today is your lucky day," the man answered.

Millar was confused. He stuttered and finally asked, "Who is this?"

"This is the person who will kill your sister and your girlfriend if you don't do what you're told. Do you understand?"

"Yeah, sure," Millar said nervously. The man didn't have a Russian accent, and his voice sounded vaguely familiar.

"Please don't hurt them. We can make a trade."

"A trade?"

"Me for them. How does that sound?"

"It sounds like you're on the right track," he said, sounding amused, almost baiting. "How do you suggest we handle this?"

"I'll come to you."

"You will?"

Millar sensed angst in the man's voice and decided it had something to do with him figuring out where they were.

"Yes," Millar said confidently. He looked over at a cab waiting for a fare in front of the hotel and said, "I'll be there in thirty minutes."

"We'll be expecting you."

The familiarity of the man's voice bothered Millar.

"I want to see them outside when I get there. When I get out of the cab, you send them over to me and I'll take their place. Got it?"

"Okay, sure," the man said, his tone bordering playful.

Millar knew The Shop would be monitoring Maria Soller's cell phone—probably his as well—so he didn't have much doubt that their analysts would discover what he was doing. Maybe they would even figure out a way to save him once he got the girls out of there.

Chapter 149

Eden Household, Great Falls, VA

SHE WAS TRYING to come to terms with everything that had happened over the past two nights. Victoria Eden's emotions had been on a roller-coaster ride, and she was left with a sadness that she hadn't felt for quite some time. Her fierce independence had been predetermined from the moment her mother died, and now more than ever it left her feeling alone, wondering if she would ever find someone to share her life with.

That was the crux of her immediate problem. A man she knew only as Trent had managed to connect with her in a way she'd never before experienced. The feelings she knew they both felt were as powerful as they were brief. Now he was gone. Forever.

She thought of the missed connections ads she and her friends used to read for entertainment in the *City Paper* as teenagers. The people who placed the ads were almost always crazed and delusional, but every once in a while they would find the genuine sadness and desperation of a love lost. If she were to place an ad, she wondered whether she would come off as one of the crazies, or was this really a love lost? It didn't matter; that wouldn't be an option. Nothing could bring him back. Whoever he was— Tony, Trent—he was now a ghost who would haunt her memory; he was now a what-if punctuated with a regretful question mark.

A part of her realized that she should be thankful for making it out of that place alive, but to what end? Life had dished out its share of cruelty to Victoria Eden. There was enough troubled history for her to consider whether or not she somehow deserved what she got. She wondered if it was karma as she reflected on a path littered with broken hearts she'd left behind. Most of those hearts belonged to good people, some even amazing, but none able to make that magical connection Trent had sparked off with a simple smile and alluring eyes. Maybe she was crazy.

The cab ride home from Dulles Airport was a solemn one. Her house was empty, although hanging in the back of her mind was the possibility of unwanted company. Pavel Kozlov knew everything there was to know about her, she was sure of it, and the scariest part was that she didn't care. She would be damned if that bastard would take her alive again. This time she would fight from the onset, and it would feel good. She would deliver some kind of payback. She realized her state of mind had been altered, and the jury was still out on whether that was a good thing.

She had changed into her blue Under Armour running clothes and pulled her hair back into a ponytail by the time she decided there was something else she needed to do. This would make the third time she had cycled through her things, and she still couldn't find it. Purse, carry-on, violin case, pockets. Repeat. She let out an exasperated sigh.

"Shit," she said. "Nice job, Vic. At least you know the first three digits, two-oh-two…uhhhhh!"

It had been years since she had actually memorized a phone number. She walked over to her landline and pressed the redial button, but the memory held some random number she wasn't familiar with. She never really used a landline anyway, and she wasn't even sure why she kept it. Eden was tempted to drive to her godfather's place in Georgetown unannounced, but she wasn't convinced it was a good idea to have this conversation in person. Then it hit her, and she walked over to her computer.

"Maybe I'm just tired," she said to the empty house. "Maybe I should get a cat."

She began to pull up an online phone book to look up Nevin Perlman's number when she thought of something. A smile transformed her mood. Within seconds she had the website pulled up and was logging in to her account. When she saw how close her iPhone was to her and where she'd left it, a chill shot down her spine. It wouldn't take long to get there. She stared at the screen and contemplated what she should do, and in that moment she realized something. Victoria D'Angelo realized she wasn't going to suffer the same fate as her mother. Time was the key—it just took time for things to get better—and you needed to respect yourself enough to take that time. Fear diminished with time. Everything changed with time.

She had sent the address that was displayed on her screen to the printer when a loud clatter broke the silence. She stood up slowly from the chair, and her heart began to race. She grabbed the piece of paper and crept to the front of the house, where the sound had originated from. There were several windows, and she chose the one with the blinds drawn from which to make her observation. She slowly began to lift a single slat up and jumped when she heard the noise again. This time it was louder.

Fear crept into her eyes as she carefully lifted the blind high enough to peer through. When she saw a deer rummaging through her trash, she breathed a sigh of relief. She noticed she had crumpled the piece of paper with the address and laughed. She now regretted her decision to ignore the advice she was given about the Russian. Another loud crack sounded, and she decided she needed to get the hell out of there.

"Screw it," she said, feeling empowered once again. "You only live once."

Chapter 150

PAVEL KOZLOV STARED at the bank of monitors in front of him. He had a grimace on his face from the pain in his leg, but aside from the injury, things had been looking up for the Russian. He was about to take care of the hacker who had thus far managed to elude his men. They just needed to buy a little more time and it would all be over.

His men couldn't simply put a bullet in his head. First they needed to find out what Francis Millar knew and what he might have done. But with him under their control, the biggest threat to their operation would be neutralized. The pain in Kozlov's leg had been tempered by the fact that he had gotten the upper hand on The American this time. Too many of his communist brethren had died at his hands, and as he reflected on the accomplishment his lips nearly morphed into a smile.

"What did he say?" Kozlov asked.

Bruce Campbell shrugged his shoulders. "He wants us out front with the girls. He's taking a cab."

The Bratva leader didn't like the situation but knew they didn't have much of a choice in the matter.

"What are you thinking?"

"I'll give him hope that this will work out until we've got him where we want him," Campbell said. "We'll keep the guns put away so he doesn't get skittish." He knew the look he saw in his boss's eyes all too well. "Don't worry. I won't fuck this up. We don't want to spook him and have to chase him down again. A couple of your former Spetsnaz boys will be here with the girls directly."

Kozlov felt a little more at ease knowing the best the motherland had to offer would be involved.

"We just need a little more time and it will be too late," the Russian said. "Nobody will be able to stop the attack once it's in motion. There's no room for mistakes this time around."

They were interrupted by a knock on the door.

"Enter," Kozlov said.

The door opened to show the three prisoners in the hallway guarded by two of his men.

"We just needed the two younger girls," Campbell scoffed.

The Russians gave him a confused look. These men were old school, fresh from Russia, so their English was limited.

Campbell waved his arm dismissively and said, "Never mind. Let's get this over with."

Kozlov watched them leave the room and then turned to the bank of monitors in front of him. He looked down at the bandage on his leg and noted that his injury continued to bleed. It wasn't the worst gunshot wound he'd had, but he'd need to see a doctor soon to get it stitched up and some better drugs to avoid infection. He reached for a bottle of pills and popped another antibiotic and a painkiller to take the edge off. He had enough time to see this through first. The Russian would stay off-line to avoid risk, and then he could celebrate his success in Europe with his comrade Yuri Khrushchev and the president.

His men emerged from a dead spot in the camera's view at the front of the compound. He reached over and turned up the volume on the camera's microphone so he could follow things more closely. The three prisoners still had canvas hoods over their heads as the yellow cab came into view. He heard a cell phone ring, and his man answered.

"Get out. Take ten steps toward us, and we'll send the girls to the cab," Campbell said.

The cab came to a stop, and its back door opened. The driver looked around nervously. Millar got out and walked toward Kozlov's men cautiously. There was a loud cracking sound, and the cab lurched forward before it coasted into a tree.

The hacker turned around quickly and then back to the men. He pulled a gun from the small of his back and yelled, "Don't move, or I'll just start shooting."

Kozlov's heart rate increased as he watched the scene unfold. His men had been caught off guard by the hacker, and their weapons were still tucked away. A standoff with an amateur was always unpredictable. It would be easy if they didn't need to take him alive, but the operation was too important to risk the unknown.

"Take off their hoods," Millar shouted. "Do it now!"

The Russians looked at one another and started to remove the canvas hoods one by one.

"Don't worry, Melody, Maria. I'll figure this out, I promise," Millar said in a panicked voice.

His eyes burned with anger when he saw the black eye on Maria Soller's face, and then his gaze went to his sister and his demeanor changed. His shoulders dropped and Pavel Kozlov knew for certain he was a beaten man.

There was a sound coming through the microphone that he couldn't quite place. He squinted at the monitor as an object came into view in the background. He got an uneasy feeling when he noticed the car was approaching a little faster than it should have been.

It was the blur at the bottom of the monitor that caught his attention next. One of the prisoners had body checked his men to the side and began to sprint toward the hacker. She was on a direct path for them to intercept the convertible Audi S5 that was now in plain view. He realized it was the FBI agent by the time she lowered her shoulder on the hacker and launched them both into the backseat of the moving car.

The Russian instantly recognized Victoria Eden, before she ducked down low in the driver's seat and headed down the fire road connected to the back of the compound.

Chapter 151

THE STAKES HAD just been raised, and they were now working against the clock. It had been a long night, but at least the men had gotten some much-needed shut-eye on the plane.

The Island Industries Gulfstream G650 had some unplanned guests on the flight from Chicago to Dulles Airport. The passengers included two rogue FBI operatives, a pair of hackers, and a strikingly beautiful violinist. A mechanical problem caused the pilots to delay their takeoff for several hours, but the plane still managed to make it to their destination before six in the morning.

Once they arrived at the hangar, the plane's occupants split up. The hackers and violinist were driven to the airport's cab stand by Jack Turner, with Etzy Millar and Dennis Zander headed to The Shop's secure location in Arlington, Virginia. The musician insisted on going home, still in a daze after what had happened during her Chicago visit. The remaining operatives headed to the Island Industries satellite location in Reston, Virginia to kit up and devise a plan.

That was nearly an hour ago, and things had progressed rapidly over the past twenty minutes.

The team of operatives had reviewed the satellite images of the Bratva compound and noted the two entrances. One was a gravel driveway directly off the main road, and the other a fire road that wound its way to the back of the building from a neighboring property. The latter provided the best opportunity to preserve the element of surprise when they made their move.

The team had stopped half a kilometer from the compound and started to assemble and check their gear. The road was flanked by heavily wooded areas that offered good cover.

Trent Turner and Brendan Manion were working their way back from a quick recce of the compound. It was the first time the close friends had a chance to talk without anyone else present since Chicago.

"What happened over there?" Trent asked, curious about how the headlines had reported his death in the Middle East.

"I lost my edge," Manion said. "It's hard to explain."

Trent shared a knowing look with him and said, "You don't have to. I know what you mean. Did you hear about Ryan?"

"I did. I'm sorry. I know you had hoped to one day…" He stopped short.

Turner shrugged, acknowledging what was left unsaid. "That's what got me into this business. When I realized he took a bullet for me, I started to lose myself. All I could think about was never having the opportunity to make things right between us. Never is a long fucking time." He looked down, in deep thought, and then back to his friend, feeling for his loss. "Sorry about Katie," he said, his tone softening. Manion hadn't responded to anyone after his wife and unborn child had been murdered.

The silence was thick as both men fought back emotion.

"Yeah, me too…me too," Manion said.

Their situations were frighteningly similar. Each had lost someone they cared deeply for because of his job, and both men believed strongly in what they were doing.

"Hey, man, I'm just happy to see you again," Turner said with a smile. "How did Addy end up pulling you into The Island?"

"When that reporter leaked my name and Katie was murdered, I was lost."

Turner could tell through his friend's tentative voice that he wasn't yet ready to open that wound.

"First," Brendan continued, "I wanted to hunt the bastards down and slit their throats, but the guys on the team talked me down." Manion took a deep breath. "When that happened, my commander gave me some time, but I started drinking. I wasn't doing what I was trained to do. In my state, it was too dangerous for the team to have me out there on operations." He shook his head. "At first I didn't see it that way. I just wanted to get out there and try to work through it, but this time it was different."

"The guilt?"

"Yeah," Manion said. "I mean it's one thing when you lose a SEAL on the team, a fellow soldier, a friend. The scars are something we all have to live with." He took another deep breath. "But when something you do on an operation bleeds into your life outside of your work. It reaches your loved ones, people who didn't sign up for this shit." He took a moment to reflect. "It messes you up pretty bad, man. Pretty damn bad."

Trent turned to his friend and understood perfectly. "Ryan's death—I don't know, I'm still not sure how I'm going to file that one away. I almost got myself killed a couple of times going after the guy who did it," Turner admitted. "My head wasn't there. It's just a good thing I wasn't on an operation working with anyone else, or I could have gotten someone killed."

"And that was my problem. I was worried about my family at home. We're so close, and it had me scared." He shook his head. "Was some other terror cell going to come out of the woodwork and take out my family? Her family? Someone I cared about? It was a distraction that was weighing me down. I couldn't function, and I was on my way to becoming an alcoholic."

Turner thought about his own situation and could easily see himself in Brendan's shoes.

"You can't expect to eliminate a fanatic and not have his lemmings come for you," Turner said. "The fucking press, they can be so ignorant."

Manion laughed, but there was no humor. "Some of them could stand for some common sense and decency," he agreed. "My commander reached out to Addy before he approached me with the idea. You know, kill me off so I wouldn't have to worry about my family anymore, so I wouldn't have that hanging over my head." He looked to Turner. "So that's what we did. Addy's got some serious pull and made it happen. I was listed as a casualty on a bird that went down." He looked to the sky. "A lot of good soldiers lost their life on that Apache," he said bitterly. "It's ironic that they gave me mine back."

"Now you have all the more reason to make a difference," Turner said.

Manion nodded. "I'd been getting my feet wet doing some work in Afghanistan, and when your brother was killed Addy decided it was time to let the cat out of the bag and officially bring me on board."

"He's a smart man. Jesus, it's great to see you, Brendan," Trent said as the two pounded fists.

They had just made it back to the others when they heard the loud report of a weapon.

Chapter 152

"WE'VE GOT IT," CDWG Director Cynthia Grayson said with a smile. "Nice work everyone, incredible job."

Her team had been working feverishly to break the encryption on the files they had intercepted from the Bratva just before their Chicago compound was destroyed. Hacker Dennis Zander had provided them with the crucial piece of information that led to their breakthrough. He had told them that the bank account numbers in the files the Russians were using for their operation never changed, and that detail ended up being the key to breaking the encryption relatively fast.

The transmission they had intercepted had been done in haste just before the explosion at the Bratva's compound in Chicago. The Shop had identified the communication from a USB modem when it connected to the same cell tower that Maria Soller's phone had used. Once the team of analysts utilized an NSA back door to decrypt the secure copy between the computers, they quickly realized that some of the files had been sent unencrypted. From there, it was a matter of comparing an unencrypted file with an encrypted file that Zander had helped them identify from the financial institution data that had been archived in the NSA's Top Secret Stellar Wind data collection program.

Now it was time for Grayson to collect her thoughts and report on the progress. She headed into her office and went straight for the special phone on her desk. She pressed the button labeled "Situation Room" and eagerly awaited an answer.

"Cyndi, good morning," President Cross said.

"Good morning, Mr. President. Do you have Addy with you?"

"He's here, and also Assistant Director Hood from the FBI."

"Gentlemen," she said.

"Good morning, Cyndi," Addy Simpson chimed in. "I sure hope you have some good news for us."

She tried to quietly clear her throat. "I do, both good and bad. My team has broken the encryption on the files."

"Great news," the president said before she continued.

"We've also confirmed that they're using the surgeon bots to modify the Automated Clearing House files from the Federal Reserve. You may know them as ACH files."

"ACH files?" Simpson said, and then paused as if the wheels were turning in his head. "Is that the system the Fed uses to distribute electronic transfers for payroll and payments?"

"That's right," she confirmed. "The hacker we brought in from Chicago has been a big help. Between what he's told us and the code the team here has reverse engineered, we've confirmed that the Russians plan to modify each of the target bank's incoming ACH files. It looks like their plan is to change the amount of the transfers within each ACH file so it will take funds from and aggregate those funds into accounts that are seldom used."

"Wouldn't that be easy to spot?" President Cross asked.

"You would think so, but from what we've been able to determine, the way they're going about this will maintain the correct amounts for total debits and credits for each ACH file, and that's how the banks verify everything once the payment file is finished processing."

"You're saying their overall numbers won't be off, so it won't immediately be brought to their attention?" Simpson said, pausing for a moment. "So, let's say I'm supposed to get a thousand dollars," he continued, "but instead they send it to another account that's in the same file and zero out mine? They just swap the amounts out?"

"That's right, they'd send you something like twenty dollars and change, and the rest would go into some other account where they're building up a large balance. These files can total tens of millions of dollars in transactions, and they typically process several per day, so it's impossible to verify the amount for each individual account was correct."

"That sounds too easy," the president said.

"It's not as hard as it should be," Grayson agreed. "There should be more protective measures in place. Since they're targeting accounts with low activity, it could be a week, maybe more, before the magnitude of what's going on will be discovered."

The president took a long moment to respond. "Do you know how they plan to move the money around?"

"I was just getting to that. Let me try to keep it simple," she said. "The DataBank software application is accessed with a web browser. What they're doing is injecting hidden transactions into the browser of a user who is legitimately authorized to do wire transfers."

"So they're piggybacking off of a real transaction?" Simpson asked.

"That, and not to get too technical, but they've cleverly manipulated the browsers to display what they want the user to see. In other words, at least initially, those extra transactions will be invisible on the screen."

"Got it," Cross said. "They don't need that much time."

"Correct. They just need the bank to process an ACH file, and typically you're two people with the proper authorizations and a couple of clicks away from funneling out millions."

The president grunted his understanding. "Once the money is wired out into a money-laundering haven—take your pick, Lichtenburg, Switzerland, the Caribbean—it will be too late to pull it back." Cross drew in a deep breath and exhaled. "Now for the most important question. Can you stop them?"

"Well, sir, I believe they've already started with some financial institutions. My team is working on it, but it's touch and go. I suppose the good news is that we'll be able to figure out who was affected by this, but as far as stopping it without shutting down the banking system goes, we're still working hard to figure that out. We won't stop until we do."

Shutting down the banks posed many of the same risks as the attack itself did. The president drummed his fingers on the table as he considered the options.

"Can you stop them from doing any more damage? Maybe block the ACH files from leaving the Fed in the first place."

"It's going to be close," Grayson said. "Most banks on the East Coast will start processing the files from the Fed soon. Once that starts, if they've got things ready to go and they've initiated the attack, we'll need a miracle to stop them."

"Please figure this out fast," the president said flatly. "We're counting on you and your team. Do you have any details on the other matter?"

"Yes, I do. Senator Soller was intoxicated when he was killed in the automobile accident," Grayson explained. "Toxicology tests confirmed that he had no business being behind the wheel of a car."

"Were you able to pull the call?" Simpson asked.

"Yes," Grayson confirmed. "His voice was slurred, and as he apologized to his wife, his tone seemed to turn increasingly dark. The analyst identified the sound of an engine accelerating in the background before he ended the call. We're trying to confirm whether it was from his vehicle, but at this point we believe that to be the case." She knew what they were thinking, and she had come to the same conclusion. "The call disconnected at almost the same time the phone's signal disappeared. The police found the device smashed inside the car. It was ugly. All indications point to the senator taking his own life by driving off the bridge on MacArthur Drive. Otherwise, he wouldn't have been driving that fast. It's a fair plunge all the way down to Cabin John Parkway, so that would be a good place to make sure you did the job. The police are going to speculate that it was an animal on the road."

"And the Federal Reserve?" the president asked.

Grayson had been unnerved by what she'd found, knowing the impact this single attack would have on the United States.

"They're in a complete panic. Bart Stapleton tried to call Soller several times this morning. He'll quickly find out about his death. It sounds like they've lost nearly two trillion dollars from their foreign accounts so far."

"Jesus," Simpson said.

The president remained silent.

Grayson could sense the tension and added, "Chairman Stapleton has mentioned a call with you, Mr. President, in some of the communications we've intercepted. He stopped short of saying you were involved, but the death of the senator has him paranoid."

"Mr. President," Ivor Hood chimed in, "I'm not sure if this would help, but we did finally find Stapleton. He came in late last night from Portugal."

"We'll check with our sources over there," President Cross said. "Let's see if our friendly neighborhood cabal had a meeting. If they did, maybe that will help us figure out what's happened to the money. It looks like our long forgotten communist pals have figured out how to hit us where it hurts. Shit, if they pull this off…"

"Mr. President," Grayson said, "we've been monitoring the Fed very closely, considering the circumstances, and we do have some limited information."

"Go ahead."

"Someone from the Fed did initiate a transfer of sixty-seven billion dollars from Banque Suisse to Iraq's central bank. It happened at six fourteen this morning, and almost immediately after that transaction every substantial bank account of theirs we know of also made a transfer of the same amount. A couple of them fired it off twice." She paused for a moment to collect her thoughts. "We've just seen that one of the banks with a duplicate transfer tried to call for verification of the wire, and it was redirected to a number in Europe. We hope to have the conversation pulled from Red Hook to see what was said. We suspect they've hacked the phone system to pull this off and we'll come to find the same situation with the other transfers."

"How do you know the first transfer was legit?" When she didn't immediately respond, Cross said, "Never mind, Cyndi, I don't need to know. I'm sure you have your ways. Can we get the money back somehow?"

"I highly doubt it. I suspect they've moved the money several times by now, but the team is looking into it as we speak," she said, and then her voice saddened. "Unfortunately, the one man who might have been able to help was killed recently."

"Talk about timing," the president lamented. "You're probably right, they would have moved it too quickly. If this second attack goes through"—he paused and then blew out a deep breath—"I'm afraid it will make the Great Depression look like a night at the Four Seasons in Paris. Let's hope Karl Marx wasn't right about history repeating itself, and we don't have the reincarnation of the Bolsheviks."

Chapter 153

Kozlov Bratva hideout, Leesburg, VA

TRENT TURNER'S HEAD swung back toward the sound of the gunshot. He was thankful not to hear the familiar sound of a bullet cutting through the air.

"Shit, who are they shooting at?" he asked.

They had just come to within earshot of the others when Manion said, "I don't know, but that was a large-caliber rifle for sure. Lucky we didn't run into him when we were down there." He turned to Throaty, Jake Sanders, and Rudy Pagano. "We need to be more careful. Those Spetsnaz boys are deadly accurate behind the scope."

"Does that increase the pucker factor?" Turner joked.

Rudy Pagano shook his head and laughed. "The only pucker I've seen in this crew was from that little beauty queen who had eyes for you." His accent was Bronx to the core. "I'll tell ya, Trent, I thought she was gonna cry when you didn't return that little peck on the cheek."

Turner shook his head in embarrassment. He hoped nobody had noticed, but all of these men had been trained to pick up the kind of details an average person would miss.

"Tough crowd here," he said, amused with the banter. "You don't waste any time busting balls, do you?"

Pagano smiled. He headed toward Jack Turner's pickup truck and said, "Hey, you're a friend of a friend of a friend. It's like I've known you for years. We're practically family." He wore an infectious grin. "It only gets worse."

Everyone burst out in hushed laughter.

Turner was beginning to enjoy having Pagano and Sanders around. A sense of humor was good for the tense moments before going into battle.

"I'm sure it does. I'll be looking forward to that," Turner said with a laugh.

Pagano gave him a sideways glance.

Turner smiled. "Seriously, I mean it. As far as the other subject goes"—he circled his index finger in the air to indicate the motley group of operatives—"the last thing she needs is to get mixed up in all of this."

Turner was certain they had chewed through their fair share of relationships and had all come to the conclusion the job wasn't conducive to romance.

"A little help?" Pagano said as he reached into the back of the pickup for the PMD II. "We need to get this thing up in the air so we can figure out if there are any other surprises waiting for us."

The overhanging trees made it impossible to launch this larger version of the flying machine from the back of the vehicle.

Jack Turner was closest, so he went over to help.

"There's a clearing we can launch it from over there," he said as they pulled the portable drone out of the truck.

"I've got it now, Jack," Pagano said with a wink after it had cleared the bed. The gesture obviously referred to his foot injury. "We wouldn't want you to throw out your back too."

Jack Turner shook his head with a smile and looked over to Sanders. "Is he always like this? We should charge admission."

"Afraid so," Sanders said. "Pretty soon you'll want to pay him to shut the fuck up."

The sudden rev of an engine commanded their attention. It was coming from the direction of the compound. The operatives quickly took cover and drew their weapons as the sound approached.

Trent Turner was closest to the vehicle when it careened around a curve in the fire road practically out of control. The driver's head was ducked down so far, he could only make out the whirling jet-black ponytail and see a woman's head from the eyes up. The Audi whisked by his location, and the driver slammed on its brakes just after it passed his uncle's pickup truck.

They heard a female's voice and then three pairs of hands slowly raised up from inside the convertible. Sanders and Pagano approached cautiously with their suppressed Heckler & Koch MP7A1s trained on the vehicle. As

Sanders crept toward the car, his eyes filled with surprise, and he lowered his weapon.

"Holy shit. Cathy?" he said, recognizing the FBI agent.

"Don't forget to mention Etzy and Victoria, lover boy," Pagano joked.

"Hey guys," Victoria Eden said. "I saw that beast of a truck"—she motioned to Jack Turner's Hemi—"and I figured it might be a good idea to stop in case those assholes came after us. They've still got Melody and Maria in there." Her voice conveyed fear and desperation. "Those poor girls need your help."

She scanned around the area expectantly with a look of disappointment on her face, until Trent Turner emerged from a thicket of bushes. She cocked her head to the side and produced a smile that could thaw a glacier. After what she'd seen last night, she knew the girls would need him for the best chance to survive.

Trent looked to the sky with a shake of his head and said, "I'll give it to you, you sure know how to make a guy feel stalked." He couldn't help but laugh at the improbability of seeing her again. "How in the hell did you end up here?"

"My phone," she said. "It must have fallen out in your uncle's truck when he gave us a ride to catch a cab. I looked it up online, and it led me to that building back there." She motioned toward the compound. "I guess that's the closest house to this yellow beast," she said with a shrug of her shoulders.

The operatives listened to see if they could hear anything coming, when the silence was broken by the ring of a cell phone.

Chapter 154

PAVEL KOZLOV GRABBED the iPad that displayed the video streams throughout the compound and quickly limped to the basement room where they held the prisoners. Inside, Dimitri Sokov sat at a metal desk, and two laptops were plugged into a switch connecting them to the Ethernet jack on the wall. The Russian's fingers pecked away at the keyboard in a constant rhythm. He was a picture of focus as he prepared the backup command-and-control server to send out its final instruction to the botnet. He had only been able to get the commands out for a handful of banks thus far. This time, with a single keystroke, the Russian would set a chain of events in motion that would turn the United States of America into a third-world country.

"Dimitri, how much longer until you're finished?" Kozlov asked in Russian.

"Very soon, very soon," he responded, completely engrossed in what he was doing.

Kozlov's brow creased. This time his voice carried a hint of anger. "How long, Dimitri? I need to know how long."

The hacker snapped out of his rhythm and turned to his boss. His eyes expressed shock, and Kozlov understood it was due to his pale, sweaty appearance. The effects of his wound had been worsening.

"It will be just a couple of minutes," he said. "I'm almost finished. Then there will be no way to stop the attack from happening."

"Good. Hurry," Kozlov said. "We don't have much time."

Bruce Campbell entered the room with the remaining two prisoners who were flanked by the two Russians.

Kozlov's expression turned angry. The American looked too content for his liking.

"Why have you not gone after them?" he spat, his eyes seething with rage.

Campbell reached into his pocket and pulled out a cell phone. "Why waste the energy when we can get him to come back voluntarily?" He motioned to the hacker's sister and girlfriend. "We're only a phone call away. Shall we?"

Kozlov almost smiled. Sometimes the solution to a problem was so obvious, you failed to see it. He observed Campbell curiously as he worked the phone's display.

"No signal," Campbell said. "Looks like we'll have to go upstairs."

Kozlov followed him out of the room, up the stairs and to the control room on the first floor.

"We've got a signal here," Campbell confirmed. He worked the touch screen to return Etzy Millar's call and put the phone on speaker. "You can do the honors, boss."

The phone rang five times before Etzy Millar answered.

"Hello," he said.

"It would be a shame if something unspeakable happened to these two young ladies with me here, now wouldn't it?" Kozlov said.

His plan was to put the hacker off-balance.

"Please—"

Kozlov's tone turned sadistic. "Did you know there are several men here with me, very large and strong men, who haven't had the pleasure of a woman in months? I suspect they would appreciate some fresh meat to entertain themselves with."

There was a short pause before the hacker spoke, his voice shaky. "I'll do whatever you want. Just don't hurt them."

A smile formed a slash across the Russian's pale face. "Come back here now, and bring the two women with you, or the next time you see your sister and girlfriend will be on the Internet. I doubt either one of them has made a sex video. Maybe they're exhibitionists at heart—what do you think? It could be an enjoyable final salvo, something dramatic and titillating for the world to remember them by." He waited to see if the hacker would respond, but he didn't. "If that's not how you want them to live out their last few moments, I suggest you turn the car around. You have five minutes. We start with your girlfriend. She could use a couple of men to warm her up before the finale."

He didn't wait for an answer before he ended the call.

"Do you think the police are on their way?" Campbell asked.

"I have no idea, but we should proceed as if they are," Kozlov said. "Make sure the men are ready for anything."

Campbell nodded to Kozlov. They heard a single shot come from outside.

"Do you think the cops could be here already?" Campbell asked.

The Russian looked down at the display on his iPad and flipped through the screen. He didn't see anyone on the cameras trained outside.

"Nothing here. Come, let's check on Dimitri's progress. You can take a couple of men and find out what he was shooting at."

The two men headed back downstairs, Kozlov enduring the excruciating pain from his leg. Once they made it to the room with the laptops, Dimitri Sokov turned around with a smile.

"Dimitri, have you done it?" Kozlov asked with an air of satisfaction in his voice.

"Yes, Pavel. It's done."

"Is there anyone who can stop this now?"

"No. We are in the clear. Nobody can stop us."

Kozlov stared at his comrade in deep thought and said, "Can you stop this from happening?"

Sokov looked at him with a nervous smile that faded quickly. His mouth transformed into a thin slit of tension, and sweat formed on his brow.

"Thank you for your service to Mother Russia," Kozlov said.

Sokov exhaled in relief and began to breathe again. Just as he turned back to his laptop, the Bratva boss leveled a Makarov pistol at his head and squeezed the trigger. He immediately turned the weapon on the remaining hacker and hammered a round into his head. He shot a quick glance toward the corner of the room and saw Millar and Soller huddled together. Scared—just how he wanted them.

"Get outside and bring some men," he told Campbell. "I'll keep the prisoners here with me."

Chapter 155

NO ONE COULD have predicted this. Just seconds after they had hung up the phone with Pavel Kozlov, they heard the whizzing sound of a bullet, followed by the report of a rifle. They all turned to the groan in the clearing and were horrified by the sight. Trent Turner and Brendan Manion instinctively clasped onto the shoulders of Jake Sanders and Cathy Moynihan as they tried to surge forward toward the blood-soaked mass of Rudy Pagano. It was the sniper again. The operatives realized he must have nestled himself in a tree stand high enough to have a vantage point to the small clearing.

The sniper had been trained well. Pagano had been shot in the stomach, sentenced to an agonizing death that would last several minutes. The gunman now sat in waiting, hoping the injured man would draw someone out, someone only concerned with helping him. Someone who would make an easy next victim.

Jack Turner quickly launched the PMD on its predetermined path to scout out the Russian's compound. At least the New Yorker's effort wouldn't have been in vain.

"He needs help," Moynihan demanded. "Let me go!"

Sanders shook his head with a grave finality. "Cathy, he's a dead man now, and thanks to them we haven't joined him," he said.

She didn't understand why that would be the case but realized he was serious. The FBI agent had already gone over what she knew about the Russian's compound and manpower, so she and Sanders headed quickly to the edge of the trees. He had to put out his arm to stop her from going too far.

"Rudy, buddy," Sanders said, "come this way. You can make it. Come on, man."

Pagano looked to his friend, his eyes already resigned to his fate. "Sorry, Jake."

"Come on, you can do it," Sanders insisted. "Just get close enough for me to grab your hand, and we'll get you help. You'll be fine. Don't worry." He forced a smile. "Assholes don't die young."

Rudy took his hand off his shredded gut and tried to drag himself across the ground. With each passing second, his groans of pain grew weaker.

"Hold on there, buddy," Sanders said. "I'll be right back. Just hold on. I'll grab some rope." He turned to her and put up his palms. "That sniper left him alive to lure us out there. Trust me. He's bait in a cruel reality."

Moynihan watched Sanders run back toward the others. She was horrified by the tactic. The call they had just received had been a telling prelude of what might come, and she knew she'd need to get back to the car soon. She looked to her side and saw a long branch on the ground. She picked it up and offered it to Pagano, stretching as far as she could.

"Here. Grab hold of this, and I'll pull you to me," she said.

Pagano's eyes were desperate. He reached out and clamped his hands onto his only hope. Adrenaline fueled Moynihan as she reeled in the wounded man. With each heave he came inches closer, until he was close enough that she could grab his hands to pull him in.

"Thanks," he strained.

She held his head tenderly and then noticed his eyes change. This would be Rudy Pagano's last moment of clarity.

"Tell that asshole I love him like a brother," he said.

She nodded, and the tears began to well up in her eyes. "I will, I promise," she said.

He coughed when he tried to speak again and finally said, "He may be an asshole, but he means well. Take care of him for me." Pagano began to cough again. This time he was much weaker, and blood trickled out of his mouth. "I've never seen him in love with a woman until now. He loves you..."

Moynihan heard footsteps shuffle through the leaves behind her as she considered his last words. Then she felt Sanders's presence over her shoulder.

Sanders bent down and realized he was too late to say good-bye. Moynihan gently laid Pagano's head down and stood.

He ran his hand over Pagano's eyes to close them and said, "Rest in peace, buddy. I love you."

He kissed his friend on the forehead, and looked up at Moynihan.

She began to cry and reflexively threw her arms around him. "I'm so sorry, Jake."

He uncomfortably returned the embrace as he stood to meet her. A voice shattered their moment of loss.

"Look, we've got to get going, or we'll lose two more," Jack Turner said. "Sorry, Jake. You should stay here with me. I could use your help," he lied.

Sanders shot him an angry look.

"I'm going to level with you," Jack said. "You just lost a good friend, and none of us know you well enough to send you into battle under the circumstances." He motioned to Moynihan and said, "She has to go, or they'll kill those two kids."

Sanders nodded his understanding.

"I'll see you soon," Moynihan said.

She started toward the car and turned back to Sanders. She gave him a tear-filled smile and knew his friend would have wanted him to hear what he had said. It could be now or never, and that fact wasn't lost on the FBI agent.

"He said you're an asshole." She nodded toward his fallen friend with a tearful laugh. "But that he loves you like a brother anyway."

Sanders smiled as she turned away and ran to the car. When she got there, Victoria and Etzy were ready to go, and no one else was in sight.

"Where is everyone?" Moynihan asked.

Etzy Millar handed her a pistol. "Mostly down there waiting for us. They put a plan together and took off. They wanted to get there before us." She checked the weapon and tucked it away. "What's the plan?"

Victoria Eden started the car and laughed. "Don't get yourself killed," she said.

Chapter 156

THE AUDI APPROACHED the front of the Bratva compound slowly over the sparsely graveled road. Bruce Campbell was feeling confident, although he didn't like the communication barrier between him and some of the Russians. Pavel Kozlov always put the men fresh from the motherland in Virginia for that very reason. The lack of radios to keep them in constant contact was also a concern, but he knew these men were experienced. Otherwise, they wouldn't have been here. There was a sense that they would soon have company, if not originating from a call for help from the individuals in the car in front of them, then certainly from the dead cabbie's dispatcher. Like any good soldiers, they would rely on their training and instincts.

Three of the soldiers had come with the Bratva leader from Chicago, and Campbell knew them well. That made a difference. Including him, there were seven capable men— more than enough to keep things in order and quickly dispatch any uniforms that happened by. Campbell's driver had already proven himself to be useless. Kozlov was injured, which compromised his effectiveness, and the two hackers, having finished their jobs, had already been snuffed out.

Campbell was standing at the front edge of the covered entrance flanked by columns. He was trying to put his finger on the strange feeling he had when he noticed a flash of movement. He shifted his eyes upward to get a better look. From what he could tell, something was casing the place from above—some sort of eye in the sky.

Campbell looked at the Russian standing next to him and said, "There's something up there." He motioned to the sky. "Make sure your men are on point. I don't think it's a teenager playing with a new toy."

The Russian looked up, acknowledged the flying machine and then turned his attention back to the Audi.

"It's too soon for the FBI or police to have something that small in place. Perhaps it is nothing," the Russian reasoned.

"Good point," Campbell agreed, still feeling uneasy. "I don't know what it is, but it can't be good. We don't need any surprises. Just make sure the men are ready."

The Bratva soldier rattled something off to the man next to him in Russian and gave Campbell a nod. The American looked down at their AK-74 assault rifles and smiled to himself. He couldn't blame them for sticking with a weapon that felt like home, but as he gripped his HK416 with its compact eleven-inch barrel, there was no doubt he preferred the precision of the German-made weapon.

"Hands where we can see them," Campbell yelled as the car came to a stop.

The occupants complied, carefully raising their hands into view.

"Driver," Campbell continued, "slowly reach down and turn off the car. Take the keys out of the ignition, and throw them over here to me."

Victoria Eden moved with deliberation—slower than Campbell would have liked—but not slow enough for him to bark his frustration.

"Now reach down to the door handle on the outside of the car and slowly open the door." Campbell waved his Heckler & Koch for emphasis and said, "I want all of you to exit the car from this door. And I need to see your hands. Do you understand?"

All three of the passengers nodded, then crept out of the vehicle one by one.

"I want you to lock your hands behind your heads, turn around, and back up slowly until I say stop." Nothing happened. "Now!" Campbell barked.

His impatience turned into doubt as he studied the faces of the three people lined up in front of him. The muted crack of a gun confirmed what he had sensed, and he instinctively dove for cover behind a column at the entrance to the building. Shards of brick lashed out at his face. He eyed the pockmarks they left in their wake.

The burst of gunfire had been effective. He noted the pool of blood welling where he once stood and looked to the lifeless body of the sniper hanging precariously from the tree stand. Whoever it was, they knew what they were doing. Two of the four men outside were now dead, and it appeared the would-be prisoners had made a break for the woods. One of the Russians, the one with the stained teeth, had made it to the car amidst the flurry of gunfire. He signaled that he had one of the attackers pinned and was clearly waiting for the target to present itself again, this time for the kill.

Bruce Campbell knew by their weapons and controlled bursts that this couldn't be the police, and he doubted the FBI could have gotten a SWAT team there so quickly. They had used the advantage of surprise well, and the only way to regain control of the situation was to be aggressive. He was contemplating his next move when the door to the compound flew open. The Bratva soldier was cut down before he could take two full steps. That left four men he thought he could count on in a fight. At this point he had only heard two distinct enemy weapons fire.

Chapter 157

IT WAS PITCH black, and they had stopped moving. Trent Turner listened intently to the man's voice and tried to make out what was being said. He was rocked side to side slowly several times and sensed things would begin to unfold as the first cracks of gunfire broke the silence. He remained still, waiting for his cue. He shifted to improve his position, knowing they needed to move quickly in order to have a chance at stopping the Russians. Another short burst of gunfire was followed by a familiar voice in his earpiece.

"Somewhere a village is missing an idiot," Brendan Manion said quietly into the comms. "Three Tangos down. Throaty nailed the birdcage, and I've installed two door mats on the front porch, over."

Turner wouldn't have known his friend had just chopped down the Russian who had mindlessly sprinted out the front door, but his imagination elaborated on the radio commentary and brought a sly smile. With the information the FBI agent had provided on their numbers, they still had plenty of work left to do.

"One of their guys has me pinned down," Throaty grumbled. "Finger, he's at your twelve last I saw. I'm at seven o'clock, and Caretaker is at your five. Caretaker, let Finger know when to pop the weasel, or I'll be a clump of Swiss cheese the next time you see me. I'm behind a tree stump, over."

"Caretaker copies that, Throaty. I don't have a shot, repeat, do not have a shot on the Tango by the car. The Tango by the front door has me cut off, over," Manion explained.

Trent could now sense the Russian crouched down in front of the Audi preparing to make his move on Throaty. He heard him yell in accented English, "Cover me."

"You'll have to work fast, Finger," Manion said. "He only has a few steps before he's on top of our man."

Turner could hear the tension in his voice, and the truth of the matter was sinking in. Missing the Russian at the front of the car now looked to have been a fatal mistake. He knew the only thing going in Throaty's favor was the morning sun burning brightly in the sky just behind him.

"Wait for my mark," Manion added. "I'll cover the porch, over."

"Roger that, over," Turner said quietly.

There was an anxious silence.

"Go, go, go," Manion shot into the comms.

Trent Turner pushed up on the trunk of the Audi—and it wouldn't open. He tried again amidst the sounds of automatic gunfire—and still no luck. He worked quickly on the release, knowing Throaty's life was in the balance.

"Finger, go!" he heard Manion yell again when the first cracks of daylight pierced the trunk. His eyes adjusted to the bright light as he leveled his weapon to the eight-o'clock position he had anticipated for his target. It took him a split second to process the scene. He looked down at a scowl-faced Russian fumbling to turn his weapon toward the source of his fall, his yellow teeth looking more like fangs.

Turner recognized the long legs and torso extending from underneath the car. They belonged to Victoria Eden. He reflexively hammered two rounds into the Russian just before the violinist had slid into the soldier's sights. He helped her from beneath the car and into a crouched position.

"We've got to stop meeting like this," she said with a mix of amusement and fear.

"You owe me dinner," Turner said.

She shook her head and motioned toward Throaty's position. "No, he owes us both dinner."

Turner smiled and relayed the news. "Throaty, it looks like you've got an angel. Tango down, over."

She snuck him a quick kiss on the lips and Turner smiled, surprised.

He saw Throaty's head peek around the stump and then heard him say, "Roger that. Let's move in before they get too comfy inside, over."

"Looks like the Tango by the front door headed inside," Turner said into the comms as Throaty sprinted across to their position behind the car.

"I'll take the lead," Trent continued, "Keep your eyes on. After Chicago, who knows what sort of tunnels and passages they have here to circle back around on us, over."

Chapter 158

BRUCE CAMPBELL SHOT down the stairway in search of the Bratva leader. He reached the room where they held the prisoners and saw that only the bodies of the dead hackers and their two laptops were left inside, so he continued farther down the hallway. At the end, in an open-area rectangular room near the underground exit, he was greeted by the two remaining soldiers, his driver, Pavel Kozlov, and the two prisoners. The space had several small tables around the walls, and once he had taken a couple of steps into the room, he could see the recessed hallway that led to the exit.

"They're coming in fast, Pavel," Campbell said.

The Russian looked down at the device that displayed the video-camera feeds and back to his man. "How the hell did The American make it out of Chicago?"

Campbell could sense the hatred in his voice, and could see his condition was worsening from the gunshot wound.

The Russian looked each of his men in the eye and said, "We were successful with the cyber-attack. That is what was most important, but there is one thing more I ask of you. I want that American dead before you leave this building. No exceptions."

Kozlov looked at the remaining pair of Russians and commanded what Campbell thought might be the same thing in his native tongue to make sure they understood. They both responded with a curt nod.

"I want to take one of the girls with us," Campbell said.

Kozlov nodded his approval, so Campbell looked at Maria Soller and said, "You. You're coming with us."

Her skin went from flush to pale as Campbell approached, grabbed her by the shoulder and pulled her toward him. He grabbed a roll of duct tape from the small table next to him and tore off a piece before forcing it over her mouth. He looked to Kozlov.

"Where are they?" he said.

The Russian looked down at the display and back to Campbell. "Three of them have just come in the door and are clearing the first floor. They will soon make their way down the stairs."

Campbell nodded and signaled for the soldiers and his driver to follow him.

"Wait," Kozlov said.

Campbell turned to him.

"The FBI woman has just come in the front door as well," Kozlov confirmed. "She is armed."

As they worked their way down the hallway, Campbell grew concerned with how his human shield might slow his response time. With a man like The American on the prowl, every fraction of a second would be crucial. He wasn't ready to become another statistic.

"Here," he said to his driver. "Keep her in front of you and do what I say."

The driver nodded and grabbed hold of the girl with his lanky arm.

The men carefully worked their way down the hall at Campbell's direction, using recessed doorways for cover when it was possible and Soller as a human shield when it wasn't. Campbell quickly jumped to the front and stopped them fifteen feet short of the only stairwell that led upstairs. The men listened for any sign of the operatives approaching. He was leery of the loud noises coming from the level above. The men they were up against were professionals, and he knew he couldn't lose sight of that. Every second that ticked by served to whittle away their advantage, so he motioned for one of the Russians to advance.

As the Bratva soldier moved forward, he grabbed Campbell's driver by the shoulder with his massive hand. The soldier had been around long enough to know that the operatives hunting them down would need to consider whom they were shooting before squeezing the trigger. That gave them a significant advantage that he planned to exploit with the girl.

His AK-74 remained trained on the opening to the stairwell as they began to close in. The former Spetsnaz soldier moved like a great cat stalking its prey, which was in stark contrast with the nervous pair he directed beside him.

He stopped and held up his hand. It was clear that he had heard something—or it was one of those times when an experienced operative knew something was about to happen.

Chapter 159

EVERY STEP HE took was as deliberate as it was silent. He timed his movement with the noises from above, sounds that were designed to seem random unless you knew the count. Trent Turner found himself in a position a covert operative tried to avoid at all cost. Getting in a fight was always a last resort. In his line of work, it was something that only happened when you couldn't take the enemy out in one fell swoop. They had taken all the advantage they could with the element of surprise, and now they were left to rely on their experience, and no Island Industries operative would bet against another.

He descended the staircase, and the musty smell from the basement grew stronger. His eyes were trained like a laser on the entrance to the stairwell, the sight of his Heckler & Koch MP7A1 framed and ready to inflict damage. When he neared the bottom, he keyed a button on his comms to silently acknowledge he had arrived at his position to Brendan Manion and Throaty. He waited a few seconds and checked that Manion had started down the first flight of stairs.

His next move would be suicide without cover fire. Turner gave his friend a hand signal to let him know he was ready and grabbed a flashbang from his tactical jacket. He stole a quick glance at Manion, who returned it with a nod.

Turner crept closer to the opening. The FBI agent had said that it led to a long hallway where they could access the area she had been held. He pulled the pin and quickly tossed the cylindrical container through the opening, making sure it landed at the angle that would provide him with the most protection. He heard shuffling sounds just before the device erupted into a concussive thud and blinding flash.

The operative turned the corner with the determination of a moth headed into the flame, while Manion quickly closed in from behind. Turner spotted five individuals along the hallway when he turned the corner. All but two were in motion. He lined up his sight with the forehead of the lanky, disoriented Tango he recognized from the park in Washington, DC as he squeezed the trigger. The others had moved too quickly for him to take a shot, so he sprinted toward the dead man as he fell, hoping to snatch up Maria Soller before the remaining men went on the offensive. Their keen reflexes told him this wasn't the first time they'd seen action.

He latched onto her shoulder and started to pull. She began to panic, and he decided it was because the blast had taken both her hearing and sight away.

"I'm with Etzy," Turner yelled in her ear.

Soller stopped struggling and began to move in the direction he was pulling her. The familiar rat-tat-tat of AK-74s erupted from behind and burrowed pockmarks on the walls and floor around him. He shoved Soller into the stairwell before turning with his weapon to help Manion silence the deadly barrage of fire.

Turner turned to his friend and said, "Keep them pinned down. I'm going to get her out of here. I'll be back before you can say blueberry pie."

Manion couldn't help but laugh at the *Pulp Fiction* reference. "Don't wake the gimp up," he replied with a sideways glance.

Turner ushered Soller up the stairs and met Throaty and Cathy Moynihan at the top. He motioned for them to follow him to the exit. He planted his palms firmly on her shoulders and gave her a reassuring look.

"Maria, I need your help. Can I ask you a few questions?"

She nodded and began to cry. "They've got Melody," she said. "You have to get her out of there."

"That's the plan, but I need you to think—I mean really think hard about what I'm about to ask you. Okay?"

"Okay."

"How many of them are down there?" He met her eyes as she tried to remember.

"The guy that was holding me, is he...?"

"Don't count him," Turner said.

"The older man killed two of them. I think there are four of them down there now."

"Are you sure?"

"Pretty sure."

"Okay, good. What can you tell me about them? Let's start with the older man."

"His leg is hurt. He wasn't looking very good. He's got an accent. I'm not sure, but I think he might be Russian."

Turner nodded in confirmation. "And the others? Anything in particular about them?"

"They're all pretty big and mean looking. One of them is an American, and the other two have an accent."

"The same kind of accent that the old man has?"

She nodded.

"Okay, you've done really well. Really well considering everything you've been through. Thank you." Turner looked to Throaty and said, "Keep her, Etzy, and Victoria safe. Brendan and I can handle the rest of them. Make sure they don't surprise us like they did in Chicago."

Turner noticed Etzy Millar running toward them, and motioned for Maria to turn around.

Millar put his arms around her, and she hugged him tight. "I'm so sorry, Maria," he said.

"Melody is down there," she said, her voice shaking from fear. She turned to Turner. "Oh my God, please get her out of there."

Turner looked to Millar and said, "I'm going in for her now. See you soon."

"I'm coming," Moynihan said. "I know the inside better than any of you guys. I might be able to help."

Turner nodded, and they headed back down the stairs.

Chapter 160

HIS EARS WERE ringing like mad, but he and the two Russians had managed to avoid being blinded by the flashbang that had just been tossed into the hallway.

Bruce Campbell quickly snuck a look at the hallway around the recessed doorway again. This time he wasn't forced back by an onslaught of automatic weapons fire. He saw his driver's lifeless body sprawled out on the floor in a growing pool of blood, but no sign of the prisoner. His face soured with the thought that they had lost her.

He made eye contact with the closer of the two Russians and signaled that he was going to retreat and look after Pavel Kozlov. The soldier acknowledged and counted down from three, before whipping his weapon around the recess and opening fire toward the stairwell. Campbell quickly sprinted down the hall and turned the corner just as the magazine had emptied its final round.

Kozlov was leaning against one of the small tables with the barrel of his Makarov pistol pressed firmly into Melody Millar's skin. The teenager had a distant look in her eyes, and Campbell shook off the inclination to feel sorry for her. "We just have her now," he said.

More shots rang out from the hallway. The bursts were controlled, and the lack of return fire was alarming.

"You'd better head out now. I'll hold them off with the girl," Campbell said.

"I don't know that I can make it out this time. They've surely learned from Chicago."

Kozlov took his tablet from the desk and reviewed the camera that displayed the hallway leading to their location. "It's not looking good, my friend. I can die proud knowing we've accomplished what we've set out to do."

Campbell was beside himself. He'd never seen the bastard give up on anything, and now when things had gone belly-up he was ready to throw in the towel? He was seething with anger until he realized the problem. The man in front of him was fading. The gunshot wound had been sucking the life out of him and bled his resolve.

"Go. I've got this," Campbell said. "You can make it out of here, and I'll be right behind you, if I can help it."

Kozlov smiled. "Okay. I will go. Take her and make sure you make it out behind me. Driving with my leg like this will be a bitch."

Campbell nodded and grabbed Melody Millar. They both watched the Russian limp away and Campbell grabbed his Sig Sauer P226R from its holster and assumed the position Kozlov had left. He looked to the hallway, and did a double take when his gaze was met by The American. His heart pounded as he stared down the silencer fitted to the man's MP7A1 and wondered whether this would be how it all ended.

"What's the cliché? So we meet again… Is that how it goes?" Campbell said.

The American didn't answer, and his silence brought with it the realization that Campbell had been transformed from the hunter into the hunted. He felt beads of sweat forming on his forehead which were in direct contrast to the coldness of the man's eyes. He considered his options, subconsciously pushing his gun deeper into the flesh of the frightened teenager.

"What now?" Campbell asked as his thoughts spiraled out of control. He firmed his finger's grip on the trigger, desperately grasping for a position of strength.

Chapter 161

TRENT TURNER REALIZED that he had just cornered a wild animal. Experience told him that the man in front of him holding the gun to Melody Millar's head was smart enough to know he was out of options. He could see the man's confidence drip away with the sweat down his forehead. His voice had lacked confidence, but more than anything else, it was the desperation in his eyes.

"It's over. Put the gun down and let the girl go," Turner said, emotionless.

The words only further agitated the man.

"What, so you can kill me?" he said sarcastically. "Sure. I'll just hand over my gun, maybe bend over and grab my ankles, if that suits you. How does that sound?" He shook his head in disgust. "How about this…?" he said, stabbing the barrel of his gun into Millar's skin with each syllable. "You can keep your gun. Just turn the fuck around and leave. Then this will be over."

Turner remained silent. He recognized him as the man from the park in DC and knew the gunman's ego would also be in play.

He tightened his grip on the girl. "No?" he spat. He motioned his head in the direction his gun was pointing. "Then how about we make that wall our canvas and try a little Jackson Pollock experiment?"

Turner's eyes narrowed.

"Blood and brain matter make a unique medium for a work of art," the gunman said. "We can take art to the next level." He smiled with a crazed expression on his face. "You only have one chance to get it right. Perhaps we'll get lucky and some clumps of hair will make it to the wall too. I've always been a fan of modern art. How about you?"

It was painful for Turner to see the teenager having to deal with this stress. The operative knew his limits. His expertise was in killing people and vanishing. They were things for which he had an incredible talent. Trying to negotiate a hostage situation wasn't part of his playbook, and the man in front of him was coming unraveled.

"You know it's too late, don't you?" the Bratva soldier said in desperation. "One of the dead guys in the other room," he continued, "he's the only one who could've stopped whatever shit they're up to from happening."

Those were words Turner didn't want to hear. Unless The Shop could work some kind of miracle, he'd failed. The only upside was that he was now left with only one concern: saving the young woman in front of him.

The lack of response continued to unnerve the gunman. "So if I were to let her go, where would that leave me?" he asked.

The stone-cold face of The American gave nothing away.

"You'll make it out of here alive," Trent Turner finally said.

He could tell his answer didn't sit well. This was a man who would do anything to avoid prison, and with every passing second he could see the man's eyes processing the fact that life as he knew it was over.

At fifteen feet, Turner had no doubt that he could quickly sink several of the DM11 Penetrator rounds into the man's head without harming the girl. He just needed an opportunity to do it before the bastard could squeeze the trigger. It was clear that his target had a short fuse—and it was burning fast. Turner remained a picture of focus, detached from any emotion Melody Millar's despondent eyes might bring to the surface.

He first sensed it, and then he saw someone in his peripheral vision approaching from the left. He took a step back so he could have a clearer view without taking his eye off the Bratva soldier. The person's frame was much smaller than Manion's or Throaty's, so he knew it had to be FBI agent Cathy Moynihan. He began to breathe slowly to reduce his heart rate, knowing there was no margin for error with Melody Millar's life in the balance.

Turner was confident Moynihan would walk into the target's view, based on the aggressive position he'd taken with his weapon and stance. He just needed a little luck for her to provide the distraction he needed before it was too late. He waited patiently for a flicker of movement in the killer's crazed eyes, the momentary blip that represented the infinitesimal window of opportunity.

In a flash it was over. Turner squeezed the trigger and hammered a burst of rounds into the Bratva man. He collapsed to the ground like a stretched-out accordion that had played its final tune. Melody Millar's face went from horror to relief as Turner took a deep breath and exhaled his stress away. The teenager locked eyes with him, and just as they had begun to soften, three sudden shots were fired.

Millar's expression turned to shock as blood pumped from the side of her neck. Her legs started to give as Trent Turner sprinted forward to break her fall. He swung his gun in the direction the gunshots had come from when the long passageway came into view. He recognized the form of Pavel Kozlov and he squeezed the trigger, but he didn't break stride. His focus was on Etzy Millar's sister. Trent made a final lunge to catch her before she hit the ground.

He wasn't sure if he'd hit Kozlov at first, but that wasn't his main concern. He trusted the FBI agent could handle the Russian. Turner looked down at the young girl in his arms and knew her wounds would be fatal. She didn't deserve any of this. He knew he couldn't live with himself if he let her die scared and alone. The fear was something he couldn't do much about, but at least he could be there for her.

He looked into her eyes and said, "Stay with me, Melody. Your brother is on his way. Hang on. You're going to be okay."

She coughed up blood when she tried to speak, tears welling up in her eyes. Turner looked down and realized she had also been shot in the chest, and her lung had probably been damaged. He felt useless and was full of rage. As he looked back into her eyes, he heard the expected report of several gunshots. They came from two guns. He looked into the fading eyes of Melody Millar, willing away the pain from the lead that had just ripped through his chest. He needed to stay with her. Until the end.

"Just hang in there, Melody. Etzy loves you. He'll be here soon," he said. His voice wasn't as steady this time; bitter sadness was now mixed with pain.

He knew all too well what it was like to look into the eyes of someone who was dying, but this time it was different. She didn't sign up for a life of violence—she was an innocent. He watched helplessly as the person behind the frightened eyes faded away to nothing. She didn't die alone, but that didn't change the fact that she was dead. He had failed to save her.

He surrendered to the pain.

"I got him," he heard Moynihan say as the world swam around him and slowly faded to black.

Chapter 162

THE RATCHETING SOUND of a roller coaster being towed uphill was overpowering, and then he had the sensation that he was falling. Suddenly the brakes came on, and Trent Turner's eyes abruptly opened as he gasped for air.

"Goddamn it, wake up. Wake up, kiddo," he heard echoing over and over. He could see the blurry outline of Jack Turner kneeling over him, but his voice was still muffled and distant, like a radio station that he couldn't quite tune in. Trent closed his eyes again, and his thoughts turned to Melody Millar, and he felt an overwhelming sense of regret.

"Open your eyes, Trent." His voice boomed like a drill sergeant's. "We need you, so don't go dying on me, you little shit!"

Jack Turner's words worked like a primal call to wake a beast from hibernation. Trent's survival instincts overrode his pain, and he tried to sit up. He opened his eyes. Maria Soller and Etzy Millar were in tears, looking down on him. The last few minutes played back in his head all at once. His eyes fell to the floor next to him. Someone had covered Melody Millar up the best they could, but he felt his spirits deflate the moment he saw the pool of blood surrounding her body.

"That's what I'm talking about, kiddo," Jack said. "We need you, buddy. There might be a chance to stop this thing from going down after all."

"What?" Trent said, still confused. "It's too late, Uncle Jack. They've already sent the commands."

"I know, buddy, but we've gotta try. Etzy's a mess. We've gotta get you to the laptop in the other room. The shit on the screen's some kinda

Russian-commie-Chinese or something, and nobody can read what the hell it says but you."

Russian was one of the languages the operative was fluent in. He tried to stand, but he immediately dropped back down to the ground. He felt weak, like he was going to lose consciousness again.

"Easy, kiddo, easy. You're a tough bastard, but you're not Superman. Etzy did good. He remembered something about the piece of paper the Russian handed Brendan that saved your lives. It told you a bomb was about to go off."

Trent remained silent and still didn't understand why that mattered.

"Etzy remembered that there was something else written on the paper. The Shop pulled the video feed from Brendan's helmet cam, and he was right. There was a sixteen-digit code they think might be the missing encryption key. They want to see if there's some way to send a command that will stop this, but nobody can read the screen on the computers."

He felt himself fading again, and then he saw Victoria Eden. Their eyes met for a brief moment. The concern in her eyes helped to melt away some of his pain. She was what his mom would call a keeper. He thought about the impossibility of a relationship, and with that thought he closed his eyes and sunk back to the ground.

"Your brother would be proud of you, Trent," Jack said. His eyes opened, and his uncle's tone had changed. There was a combination of tenderness and regret. "He wanted to let you know that he'd figured out who you were. That you were Finger."

Trent perked up, not quite comprehending what his uncle was saying. "What?" he said.

"You two had become best friends again and didn't even know it." Jack Turner smiled warmly. "Ryan was Tak, your handler."

The words swirled around in his head like a merry-go-round. It was like the animals had come to life and were sprinting around the platform.

"Tak?" he said, still trying to process what was said.

"Yeah, Tak," Jack said, his eyes now betraying his smile.

Trent sat up on his own at the revelation. Conversations the two had had over the years started to flash through his mind. He connected the dots, and now it was all painfully obvious. He smiled at the thought of his brother as Tak and the times they had shared.

"When did he find out?"

"Recently. Addy didn't even know yet. Only me."

Chapter 163

THE WORLD WAS still spinning around him. Trent Turner looked up at Etzy Millar and shared a silent moment of sadness.

"I'm sorry, Etzy," he said.

The hacker gave him a solemn nod.

Trent looked to his uncle. "Help me up," he said. "Let's get this shit done quick. I need a doctor."

"The ambulance is on its way," Jack said as he and Brendan picked Trent up. "Cyn, are you online?"

They had been working to patch her through their comms.

"Yes, Jack, I'm here. Can you hear me?"

"Roger that," he confirmed. "Finger won't say much, but he's listening."

"Okay," she said. "Finger, we think we have the encryption code. There were some files sent earlier, we know that, but we don't think we can monitor the entire botnet yet, so we're not in a position to know whether they're sending the attack in waves or not. It could be that they haven't sent files and commands to all of the banks."

Trent could hear the hopeful desperation in her voice.

"We need to see if there's any way to send a command to abort the process," she continued. "They have a C&C server there, and we think they've dug out a small bunker near the property line by the highway and somehow tapped into one of the fiber lines leading to the area data centers. Jack said it's too risky to try to get in there. It might be rigged to blow like the other place."

"So that's it?" Trent asked in disbelief. "We're just going in there on blind luck, hoping you actually have the encryption key and there's a way to stop this from the console?"

The two men had carefully guided him to the room with the laptops.

"That about sums it up," she said flatly.

"Fuck," Trent said.

"Fuck is right," Cyndi Grayson said uncharacteristically.

They all shared a quick laugh. This was the first time she'd ever cursed, and it underscored the dire situation they were in.

"The entire US economy is riding on one of us having a golden horseshoe up our ass," she added.

"Well it could be our lucky day, because it sure as hell feels like I've had something stuffed inside me," Turner joked as he sat down tenderly in front of one of the laptops.

He could feel himself fading, but thoughts of his brother and Melody Millar kept him motivated. He needed to pull this off for them.

"Jack, I sent you the image," Grayson said.

Jack Turner pulled out his device and held it so his nephew could see what they hoped was the encryption key.

Trent Turner moved back and forth through several screens trying to find somewhere that would let him send a command to the bots. After a minute he found what he was looking for and said, "Here goes nothing."

He typed in the encryption key and pressed Enter.

"Damn, I must have typed it in wrong," he said.

His vision was getting blurry. He deliberately worked the keyboard and punched in the encryption key again.

"Uncle Jack, do they match up?" he asked.

His uncle went back and forth from the image to the screen. "Yeah, it looks good to me."

Trent hit Enter again, and a message popped up in Russian.

"Shit. It says we have one more chance. If we don't get it right, the program will kick us out." He could feel the stress building as he struggled to punch the code into the keyboard one final time. "Unc, make sure that's right," he said. His voice was weaker but still managed to convey the importance.

Jack Turner wiped the sweat from his brow and checked it twice. "Brendan, you have a look too, will ya?" he said, concern evident in his voice.

"Sure thing," Manion said.

He went over each character one by one and said, "Winner winner," and he and Trent blurted out, "Chicken dinner," before Trent pressed the Enter key.

"Dammit!" Trent shoved the laptop and closed his eyes as the medics entered the room.

"No luck?" Grayson asked.

"No, Cyn, we're screwed," Jack Turner said.

There was a long moment of silence as the medics worked to cut off Trent Turner's gear.

"Talk to Hector about the operation in Europe," Trent told his uncle.

That was the call sign for a contact they had made in Switzerland. He handed Jack Turner his XHD3.

"He's in my contacts. Hopefully he's had better luck than us."

"Okay, we've got to move you, buddy," one of the medics said as he motioned to a stretcher by the door.

Trent could feel his body shutting down. The deflation from failure had sucked away all of his adrenaline. He placed his hands on the desk to help the men lift his weight and listened as they counted to three. They heaved him upright, and he felt his head drop forward before he peeled his eyes open one final time.

"Whoa. Hold on," he snapped.

"Sorry, pal," the medic said as he helped him toward the stretcher. "This is going to be painful. There's nothing we can do about that."

"No, no. Get me back to that other laptop."

"Can't do that, buddy. You've lost a lot of blood. We need to get you to the hospital."

"Take me to that gaddamn laptop!" he yelled, and attempted to break free.

Jack Turner could see the intensity on his nephew's face and said, "Boys, it's okay. Take him over there." He knew Trent wouldn't bet on his life without a good reason.

"But sir, he might—"

"Do it," Manion demanded as he helped the men turn Trent around.

They nursed Trent back over to the second laptop, and he started laughing.

"Shit, he's delusional," Manion said. "Sorry about that, fellas."

Trent kept laughing and said, "Hold on a second."

The text on the screen was in Russian, so nobody else would understand. It said, "Press Enter to distribute the commands to the botnet;

press Escape to cancel." It took just about everything he had left to reach his hand out and press the Escape key. He struggled to stay conscious and looked over to his uncle and said, "Sometimes it's better to be lucky than good."

Jack and Brendan shared a confused look.

Trent struggled to speak again, and instead of using his last moment of consciousness to let them in on what had happened, he said, "Look after Etzy. You'll need him now that Ryan's gone."

His eyes slid shut.

"What the hell was that about?" Manion asked.

"I have no idea," Jack said. "No fucking idea."

"I hope he makes it," Manion said, shaking his head.

"Me too, Brendan. Me too."

Chapter 164

THE THREE MEN sat around the long table and listened intently to the anger seething from the voice coming through the phone's speaker. President Vincent Cross was growing impatient with the caller. It had been a long weekend for everyone involved, and Addy Simpson had filled him in on the details about Trent Turner's contact, who went by the name Hector.

Federal Reserve Chairman Bart Stapleton barked into the phone again and said, "Are you incapable of understanding the magnitude of what's happened here? The entire country is at risk. It's not about saving my ass."

Cross blinked slowly as he composed his answer. "Let's run through this again, Mr. Chairman, just to make sure I'm following you correctly. I seem to recall speaking with you on the phone, asking for your help with an investigation into something I referred to as a matter of national security, did I not?"

They could hear Stapleton take a deep breath before he spoke. "Listen—"

"No, you listen!" the president demanded. "You had your chance to do something about this, and you let politics, personality, ego—whatever the hell it was—burn the olive branch I extended to you. Then for good measure you returned my goodwill with a pointed threat." He pounded his fist on the table. "Now you're telling me you want my help? No, wait. You demand my help, and you shouldn't be held accountable for what's happened?" He laughed, but it was crystal clear that he wasn't the least bit amused. "You're too much," he said dismissively.

"I'm not resigning my post," Stapleton spat defiantly.

The president knew more than Stapleton would have liked. The Shop had been listening to the chairman's conversations all day. The team of analysts had been able to determine that the Russians had hacked into the Federal Reserve's phone system and redirected calls intended for the individuals who were responsible for approving a series of large wire transfers. From what they could tell, over a period of several months the communists had figured out the central bank's approval processes. The Russian's had been able to stand in for Federal Reserve employees with advanced voice-emulation software that leveraged voice samples from previously recorded conversations.

The cherry on top was having a legitimate transfer in the amount of more than seventy billion dollars to Iraq to piggyback the fraudulent transfers onto. It was a failsafe in case a call was made outside their phone system hack. Using the amount of a legitimate transfer for the fraudulent ones was a ruse they hoped would buy them at least a day before the transactions were noticed.

Cross had Bart Stapleton right where he wanted him.

"You actually think you have a choice in the matter? You don't have a leg to stand on after the disaster you've just presided over. Even if we can recover some of the money, you've put your personal ambitions ahead of your responsibilities as the chairman of the Federal Reserve, and the economy of the United States of America is now at grave risk."

"I won't do it," Stapleton said, his tone lacking confidence. "And a recovery fee? In the billions of dollars?"

The president glanced up at the two men sitting at the table with him and smiled. They were all having a hard time keeping a straight face.

"There is one other option, Mr. Chairman," he said, baiting him.

Stapleton didn't respond for a moment, and finally asked, "And what's that?"

"You can stay in the Fed with my full support, but I'll want you to work very closely with me." He paused for effect. "Especially when it comes to those meetings that we're not supposed to know about."

With Senator Soller dead, the only person with enough power to help him navigate his way through this was gone and the president knew that. After an uncomfortable pause, Stapleton cleared his throat.

"I don't know what you're talking about," he said unconvincingly.

"Well, when you finally figure it out, why don't you give me a call and see about possibly keeping your job? I've heard Lisbon is a great place to visit this time of year, so maybe having some free time wouldn't be such a bad thing," Cross said before abruptly ending the call.

"Nice closer," Simpson said.

The president smiled. "You're sure your man in Europe was able to put out the safety net for the accounts?"

Simpson nodded. "Both Ryan and Trent Turner had helped to put a new system together to flag at-risk accounts and defined a protocol to follow when a restricted account was accessed. Trent passed along the accounts first thing in the morning GMT, before they left Chicago, and they were able to redirect everything leaving Federal Reserve accounts to the predetermined holding account. We were lucky that all of the banks they held money in had already implemented the new initiative."

Cross shook his head. "This was too close for comfort. They almost pulled it off." His eyes met each of them. "We take a lot for granted." He exhaled. "We can't afford any more close calls like this. How many US consumer accounts slipped through?"

"We lost around thirty million, but the good news is that we know which accounts were affected, and they were used sparingly, so we can put Humpty Dumpty back together again by midweek and nobody will be the wiser."

The president leaned back in his chair, not wanting to think about the consequences if the hack into the banks had gone public, or even worse, been fully carried out.

"And your operative? Will he be okay?" Cross asked.

Simpson knocked a knuckle on the wooden table. "He's already had a couple of operations," he said solemnly. "It's been touch and go. I hope so...I really hope so." He managed a laugh and said, "Before he went under, he told Jack they never pressed Enter to send the final command to the bots for the remaining banks." He shook his head in disbelief. "Unreal."

The president nodded. "Dumb luck, but I'll take it." He looked at the other man who was sitting at the table and asked, "What about our other problem?"

Ivor Hood twisted his wrist, looked down at his watch and then back to the president. "We should know something any time now."

Chapter 165

Alexandria, Virginia

JAKE SANDERS REMINDED himself that he needed to keep cool. He had to check his emotions at the door so he wouldn't make a mistake. There was no margin for error. This represented a new beginning for him, a way to wipe the slate clean and try to move on from the past—a past that he had once been proud of.

The drive to Pennsylvania and back had been therapeutic. He ran through all the operations HVT squad had done over the years, and it was the events of this past Saturday that grated on him the most. A thirty-second exchange with a mysterious contact in a parking lot interrupted his thoughts, and then he turned the car around and headed back to Virginia. He'd picked up a box and a black bag. Their contents held the key to his future, and he knew better than to break the seal. There would be no remorse for what he was about to do. None whatsoever. In fact, he knew this was the only way to set things straight.

He had never before dared visit his residence. It was located in a quiet upper-middle-class neighborhood with more luxury cars than minivans and SUVs. He parked the rental car at a shopping center less than a mile away from the house and nonchalantly made his way there and to the sliding glass door off the backyard deck. This needed to be done with the utmost care and discretion. He could see the alarm panel through the glass and confirmed that it wasn't armed. Gaining entry would be a piece of cake, but that didn't stop his heart from pounding rapidly inside his chest.

This was new territory for the operative, so he tried to convince himself that the nerves were normal. He made easy work of unlocking the door and began to slowly slide it open. He froze when it began to protest with a loud screech. He held his breath and tried to listen, but the heartbeat throbbing in his ears made it impossible to trust what he heard. Instead, he looked for shadows, any sign of movement in the home. He saw nothing.

He began to slide the door open again, this time pushing inward and upward to take the weight off of the rail. The door was silent. He stopped when the opening was large enough for him to squeeze through and slid inside the home.

Within a minute he found himself at the top of the stairs. He had memorized the layout of the house, and he knew the upstairs room where the light was on was his study. After taking a few deep breaths to control his breathing, he was ready. His heart rate was still high, but his face was a picture of control. He was like a duck—calm on the surface, with the manic kicking below, hidden from view. He took one more deep breath and strode silently into the room.

The man looked up from his desk in surprise. "Oh my God, I thought you were dead."

"Nice to see you too," Jake Sanders said.

FBI Director Frank Culder was visibly uncomfortable.

"What's wrong, boss?"

"Nothing, nothing." He wasn't particularly convincing. "It's just good to see you," Culder lied.

"So, it's just you and me now." He jutted his chin out. "With BlackRock, that is. Rudy's dead. We lost a lot of guys over the weekend."

Culder had started to sweat. "I know."

"It's funny," Sanders said, "but if I didn't know any better, I'd think that you weren't happy to see me."

The director remained silent but shifted his weight ever so slightly in his chair.

Sanders tossed a package onto his desk and said, "Here." He knew the director would have a gun hidden somewhere, so he needed to get to the point fast. He doubted Culder had ever shot anyone, but he had no intention of becoming victim number one. Their business together was unfinished; he would soon figure that out.

"What's this?"

"Open it."

Culder grabbed a letter opener and began to slice open the manila envelope. He pulled out the documents inside and started to read. His eyes lit up, and his lips formed a smile.

"Where did you get this?"

They were the documents sent from Dr. Charles Reed to implicate the president in dealings with Island Industries.

Sanders laughed. "Come on now. It's poor form to reveal your sources. It should come in handy while we're putting the team back together," he said flatly. "Do you think that will be enough dirt on Cross, or should I try to find another pile?"

Sanders could tell the gears were turning in Culder's head. His demeanor had changed significantly. He was looking more like his bastard self by the second.

"I'll have to go over this to be sure," Culder said, and gave Sanders a proud look. "Do you think you can get more information?" he asked enthusiastically.

Sanders nodded. Now he knew the director didn't have anything on the president.

"I think so," he said. "I'll need some cash. There is something else."

"There is?" Culder asked expectantly.

Sanders showed him the black bag he was holding. He tossed it up in the air a couple of times before throwing it onto the director's desk.

"What is this?"

Sanders plastered a smile on his face. His heart rate spiked as he watched the FBI director break the seal and dig his hand into the bag.

The elastic material closed around his wrist as he reached inside.

"Shit!" he yelled. "What the fuck is in here?"

He quickly pulled his hand out of the bag and shot an angry look at Sanders.

"What do you mean?" Sanders asked with contemptuous look.

Culder began to look ill. "What have you done?"

"How could you be so stupid?" Sanders spat. "Did you think we'd never find out what was going on?"

The director fumbled around his desk, his condition was getting worse by the second. He reached desperately for a desk drawer, but Sanders stepped forward and held it closed with his knee.

"Were you hoping we would all get killed eventually so you could just move on, all the fun and games over?" Sanders asked.

He could see the Culder's eyes begin to glaze over as his skin turned flush. "Shake it to piss them off." That was the only thing the man had said when he handed him the bag. Apparently it worked.

"At least one of those stupid childhood stories you told me wasn't useless," he said, referring to Culder's tale about a near-fatal bee sting.

It had been less than a minute, but Culder's breathing was already labored.

"What the hell have you done?" he spat in anger.

"I'm no doctor, but the technical term is 'anaphylactic shock,'" Sanders said. "Those wasps aren't half as pissed as I am."

He collected the incriminating information on President Cross and stared at the man's pitiful form. "You won't be needing these anymore. I'll tell Agent Moynihan you said hello, you useless prick."

Epilogue

SHE STOOD JUST outside the room and listened. Her mother-in-law's back was turned to her, and the three occupants were too engrossed in their conversation to notice her. She didn't know who the younger woman with the jet-black hair was, but she guessed she might be his girlfriend. Her clothes were expensive and refined, and she was incredibly beautiful.

"It's touch and go right now," the doctor said in a solemn voice. "He's extremely fit, so at least he has that going for him, but he lost a lot of blood. The team did an excellent job, but when he arrived at the hospital he was in oligemic shock."

"Oligemic what?" Cathy Turner said.

"Pardon me," the doctor said. "It's shock from an extreme decrease in blood volume. From the gunshot wounds."

She nodded, and he continued.

"There is great risk of organ failure and disseminated intravascular coagulation. Basically he's at high risk for blood clots."

"Do you know the extent of the damage?" she asked.

"Not at this time. I can tell you that his brain scan checked out, but we won't know for sure what the real damage is until he wakes up." He furrowed his brow and switched the clipboard to his other hand. "The men he was with had phoned the hospital ahead of his arrival, so the restoration of blood volume to maintain tissue perfusion and oxygenation was done as quickly as it could have been. They were ready and waiting for him when he came through the emergency room door. It seems your son has some friends in high places."

The doctor smiled. He wasn't only referring to the operative's unlikely survival, he also meant the two doctors who were helicoptered in to operate.

"So we're not out of the woods yet?"

"Oh heavens no, but I have to tell you, it's not every day you have the best in the world looking after a single patient. Let's just say the deck's been stacked in his favor. We just need to hope he's up to playing the hand."

April Turner's thoughts were conflicted as she listened to the doctor brief the women. She clutched the envelope in her hand, and tears welled up in her eyes. The envelope had "Trent" handwritten on the front, and the seal her husband had secured it with was still intact. Opening it to see what her husband Ryan had written to his twin brother had never even crossed her mind. His intention was to send it to Trent to initiate the healing process for their relationship, but mending the bridges would be impossible now.

The conversation she had with Jack Turner two hours ago had given her a lot to think about. She hadn't known many of the details about her husband's life, and now things had started to come together. She was proud of what her husband had been doing, but she wished with all of her heart there would have been a different outcome. Now that she knew the details, she wasn't sure that passing the message in the envelope along to Trent was the right thing to do. The envelope wasn't something she could leave in his room. She knew its contents would be too toxic for the family to happen upon right now, and the doctors still weren't convinced that he would survive.

She had just lost the father of one of her children in this very hospital. Ryan Turner had been the love of her life, and mentally she wasn't sure if she'd ever recover. Based on her conversation with Jack, she wasn't sure it would ever be safe to let the father of her oldest child know the truth.

Tears streamed down her face as she was overcome with guilt. April contemplated whether it might be better if Trent Turner didn't make it through, and quickly tried to erase the selfish thought from her mind. She was ashamed. The secret she held, the very reason her relationship with Ryan survived, was something that would become exponentially more difficult to explain to her astute young child as time passed by.

She wiped the tears from her face, turned and walked away. She had two children at home who missed their father dearly, and that's where she needed to be right now. This was something that would have to wait. She just wasn't sure if the wait would take a lifetime.

A Note to Readers

Thank you for reading my debut novel THE CODE WITHIN. If you've enjoyed the book, be sure to leave a brief review on Amazon or Goodreads, and then share the book with your friends through the social media outlets that you frequent. I believe that word of mouth from readers is the most powerful endorsement an author can have.

You can contact S L Jones using the following:

Email: contact@sljones.co
Website: http://sljones.co

You can sign up for my mailing list to be notified of new releases and contests.

S L Jones
PO Box 7626
Silver Spring, MD 20907

Acknowledgements

I'd like to send out a heartfelt thank you to family and friends who have encouraged me to follow through with my writing. For those of you who provided insight into three letter agencies, the military and the police, your perspectives and insight have made this novel better than I could have ever imagined, and I appreciate your willingness to help - rest assured the next round is on me. To my copyeditor Marcus Trower: thanks for taking the time and having enough patience to guide me through the early stages of learning to write fiction. I've still got a long way to go, but you're valuable advice has helped me to write a novel that I can be proud of. To Carol and Craig Jones, Ed Quackenbush, Karen Caroscio, Malina Fowler, Nick Selby, Peyton Jones and Teresa Hargett: thanks for helping me to beat down doubt and get back to the task at hand - writing. To Hristo Kovatliev: Awesome work on the cover, you have given the novel a face that will surely get noticed. To my son, Tyler, who will soon turn four: you are a bolt of positive energy and hope that lights up my world with love and gratitude – you're the perfect little soundtrack to my life and you keep me going. Last and far from least, to my wife, Carey: yes, I am crazy, and thank you for putting up with me and for your love and patience - I love you.

The Seeds of Inspiration

This book would have never been written if it wasn't for a ridiculously long layover at Heathrow airport in London, England around 2004. I was so incredibly bored that I picked up a book called The Increment written by Chris Ryan. Sadly enough, that was the first time I had read fiction for pleasure as an adult. After I finished that novel, I kept reading and reading and reading – perhaps I've been trying to make up for lost time. I would like to thank Chris for waking the reading beast inside me, and I hope to thank him in person one day.

At some point, I'd say around 2008 or so, I had figured out enough books before I had finished them to where I decided it might be fun to take a shot at writing one myself. I was a decent musician at one point in my life, after all, and I simply looked at writing as another creative outlet, so it was easy to carry over my confidence from writing music. Initially, I only gave writing a half-hearted effort. I had a sliver of an idea that continued to grow in my head, but only a few poorly written chapters (that had I thought were great at the time) to show for it. Then I told my sister what I had been up to and she introduced me to Vince Flynn and his Mitch Rapp series of books, and for that I owe her big time. Vince's writing struck a chord with me. I devoured his novels at what most (aside from my wife) would consider an unhealthy pace. If Chris Ryan was the spark for my interest in reading, Vince Flynn represented the fuel thrown on the fire to take writing seriously. Unfortunately, Vince Flynn passed away last year, so I'll never have the opportunity to thank him in person for his inspiration. I'd like to think he would have enjoyed my first effort.

Aside from Vince Flynn and Chris Ryan, my influences include the great Robert Ludlum, a few local guys who go by the names Tom Clancy, David Baldacci and Daniel Silva, as well as Dan Brown as the inspiration for my pacing and James Patterson for teaching me to keep my prose simple enough to stay out of the way of the story.

Made in the USA
Lexington, KY
11 September 2014